"They think I have something to do with it," Felicity said, her voice so quiet Gage almost couldn't make out the words. "I can tell."

"No. You've been through this before. You know how it goes." He found a loaf of bread and dropped a slice in the toaster. "They have questions they have to ask just to make sure, but—"

"It's the second time." She lifted her gaze to meet his, and there was nothing timid or uncertain about her like there had been in the past. No, she was in complete control, even lost and scared. "The questions were different. And they're right. It does. It has something to do with me. I know it does."

BADLANDS PURSUIT

NICOLE HELM

Previously published as *Backcountry Escape*
and *Badlands Beware*

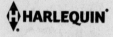

ISBN-13: 978-1-335-42722-9

Badlands Pursuit

Copyright © 2022 by Harlequin Books S.A.

Backcountry Escape
First published in 2020. This edition published in 2022.
Copyright © 2020 by Nicole Helm

Badlands Beware
First published in 2020. This edition published in 2022.
Copyright © 2020 by Nicole Helm

Recycling programs
for this product may
not exist in your area.

This edition published by arrangement with Harlequin Books S.A.

For questions and comments about the quality of this book,
please contact us at CustomerService@Harlequin.com.

Harlequin Enterprises ULC
22 Adelaide St. West, 41st Floor
Toronto, Ontario M5H 4E3, Canada
www.Harlequin.com

Printed in U.S.A.

CONTENTS

Nicole Helm grew up with her nose in a book and the dream of one day becoming a writer. Luckily, after a few failed career choices, she gets to follow that dream—writing down-to-earth contemporary romance and romantic suspense. From farmers to cowboys, Midwest to *the* West, Nicole writes stories about people finding themselves and finding love in the process. She lives in Missouri with her husband and two sons and dreams of someday owning a barn.

BACKCOUNTRY ESCAPE

For the helpers.

Chapter One

Felicity Harrison had learned two things since coming to live with Duke and Eva Knight when she'd been just four years old, with a broken arm and black eye courtesy of her father.

First, she loved the outdoors. She could hike for days and sleep under the stars every night given the chance. Didn't matter the season or the weather. In her mind the winds of the South Dakota Badlands had made her, and she was part of that stark, awe-inspiring landscape.

The second thing had taken her a little longer to figure out, but once she'd hit puberty she'd been sure.

She was desperately, irrevocably in love with Brady Wyatt.

Despite the fact she was nearing thirty and he'd never shown any interest in her that he didn't show all of her foster sisters, Felicity hadn't fully given up on the prospect that Brady might notice her at some point.

It was possible. She had made changes in her life the past few years. Between her epic shyness and intermittent stutter, high school and college had been a bit of a disaster but she'd found her passion in parks and recreation—as much as people would laugh at her zeal for nature.

In finding her passion at an early age, and making it her career, parks and rec had ended up being the thing that gave her some confidence. The drive to succeed had helped—or maybe forced—her to overcome some of her issues and bumps in the road.

After years of seasonal work in the national park system, she'd finally landed her dream job as a park ranger at Badlands National Park, her home. The job had been hard and challenging, and it had *changed her*.

She wasn't the same Felicity she'd been.

Brady hadn't noticed yet because he was so busy. Being a police officer and EMT in Valiant County took up a lot of his time. Plus, he lived a good hour away and spent free time at his grandmother's ranch even farther out.

She just needed the opportunity to show him who she'd become, and *surely* he'd fall for her the way she'd fallen for him all those years ago.

She daydreamed about that opportunity while she took her normal morning hike. Summer was inching its way into the mornings so she didn't need her park jacket over her sweatshirt. It was her favorite time of year, and that put a smile on her face and pep in her step.

The sky was a moody gray. Likely they'd have storms by afternoon, but she imagined the sky was a bright summer blue and Brady was hiking with her. He'd hold her hand and they'd talk about what birds they were hearing.

Her fantasies about Brady were always just like that. Soft, sweet, relaxing. Brady was steady. Calm. His five brothers were wilder or edgier, even Jamison. As the oldest, Jamison was serious, and seriously noble, but there was a sharpness to him that had taken Felicity time to grow accustomed to.

But Brady? He was even-keeled. He didn't shout or swear. He believed in right and wrong, and he appreciated the importance of his duties as an EMT. He took care of people. *Healed* people.

Calm and good and healing were definitely things she wanted in her life.

She was so caught up in her fantasy she almost tripped over the boot in the middle of the path.

She regained her footing and looked down at the brown boot. It was unlaced, and the soles were caked with dirt.

Felicity stared at it as the slow roll of cold shock spread out through her body. For a second her vision blurred and sound disappeared. She couldn't suck in a breath. She could only stand and look at the boot.

She'd seen this before, done this before. It was happening again.

No.

Her mind rejected the possibility and she managed to breathe in, let it slowly out. It was just a boot. People lost weird things on the trail all the time. Maybe it had gotten too heavy. Maybe it was broken.

There were a million reasons. A million. Besides, it wasn't even the same kind of boot as…the last time. This one was clearly a woman's, if the bright pink laces were anything to go by. It was an accident. A coincidence.

You have to check.

She nodded to herself as if that would make her move. Make this okay. As if she could will away all the similarities to last year.

There wouldn't be a body this time. Couldn't be.

Just keep walking.

You can't just keep walking!

Her mind turned over and over, reminding herself of a Felicity she didn't like very much. She stepped purposefully away from the boot. It wouldn't be like last year. She would turn to the right and look off the path. She would see nothing but rocks and the stray scrubby flora.

First she looked left. Because…because she had to work up to it. There was nothing but mixed grass prairie that existed on that side of the trail. It was fine.

The right side was where the last body had been. There wouldn't be one. There *couldn't* be one. She forced herself to turn, to take the few steps to the very edge of the trail.

This side was rock, geological deposits that brought people to the Badlands in droves every summer. There wouldn't be a body. Couldn't be.

But there was.

She stared at the mess of limbs all at wrong angles. She stared, frozen, willing the image to disappear. The canyon to the side of the trail was narrow and deep, but you'd have to be sincerely not paying attention to fall down it, or…

Or.

She finally managed to squeeze her eyes shut, last year's memories rushing back like a movie in her head.

Unseeing eyes and a black beard then. Now, a woman facedown in the rock, hair moving in the wind.

Nausea rolled through her, but she swallowed it down and tried to think. Tried to remember where and what she was.

Don't touch anything. Don't touch. Don't touch.

She took a few stumbling steps back on the trail.

Last time, she'd checked the body with a thought to help. Last time, she'd compromised the crime scene trying to identify the person while waiting for the cops. Last time, she'd made so many mistakes.

Not this time.

She nodded to herself again. This time she'd do it right. Not mess with anything. Not ruin anything.

How could it be *happening again*?

"One step at a time, Felicity. One step at a time."

She was calmed by the sound of her own voice, even if there was no one around she was talking to. She pulled out her phone, called the local police department and radioed her boss so he could get someone out to seal off the area.

Then she called Brady. She couldn't help it. When she was in trouble—when she or any of her foster sisters were in trouble—they always turned to the Wyatt boys.

They always came, and they always helped. Because they were good men, and Brady was the best of them, in her estimation.

When he answered, she managed to tell him what had happened, though she felt detached and as if she was speaking through dense fog. He promised she wouldn't have to be alone.

She tried to allow that reassurance to soothe her, but mostly she settled in to wait, hoping she wouldn't throw up.

"SHE CALLED YOU," Gage Wyatt grumbled at his brother through the phone receiver tucked between his ear and shoulder as he navigated the highway in front of him.

Summer had turned the hills green, and the tall grass waved in the wind. Gage had always gotten a kick out of the fact that's exactly what his ancestors would have seen when they'd arrived here by cart and horse.

He couldn't find amusement today as his twin brother tasked him with something he most especially did not want to do.

"I can't make it," Brady lectured. "I called Tuck, but he didn't answer. He's likely on a case. You're closer than Jamison, Cody and Dev—not that I'd send Dev. She needs someone there ASAP, Gage."

Gage swore inwardly, not sure how out of the six Wyatt brothers he was the *only* one available. He kept his voice light and offhanded, the Gage Wyatt special. "She's moon-eyed over you. That's why she called *you*."

There was only the briefest of pauses in return. "She found a body." Brady's tone was flat, the kind of flat his voice got when no amount of coaxing, arguing or nonchalance was going to irritate him into caving. "Another body."

"All right, all right," Gage muttered. "I'm not too far off." At least in the grand scheme of things in South Dakota. An hour, tops. "Same place?"

"No." Brady related where exactly in the park Felicity had stumbled across a body. Not too far from her park ranger cabin.

She'd found *another* body. The same thing had happened to Felicity last year, and it was horrible, to say the least, that she was dealing with that again. Gage listened as Brady explained where he'd need to go to get to Felicity. He turned his truck around and started heading for the park while Brady spoke.

"Be gentle with her," Brady said. "You know Felicity."

"Yeah." He did, he thought grimly as he hung up and tossed his cell phone onto the passenger seat. He knew her better than his brother did apparently.

Felicity wasn't the same shy wallflower she'd been growing up. Ever since she'd gotten that job at Badlands and moved home—well, closer to home—she'd been more sure of herself, more…something. He didn't like to dwell on that considering she was so hung up on Brady.

Who apparently didn't even notice she'd grown up, no matter how long it had taken her.

She'd held up really well last year when she'd found the body. It had seemed like a freak accident, and she had seemed able to handle it, especially admirable since she wasn't used to dealing with dead bodies. As a police officer, he had dealt with quite a few, not always violent or tragic. Sometimes as simple as someone going to sleep and not waking up.

It was part of the job, and even if it wasn't, he'd grown up in a biker gang until his oldest brother had gotten him and Brady out when they'd been eleven. He'd seen worse there living among the Sons of the Badlands those eleven years, especially considering his father ran the group. Ace Wyatt didn't deal in mercy—he dealt in his own warped version of justice.

Thanks to his oldest brother, Jamison, Gage had never believed in his father's justice. But he'd had to survive it, and the body count, before he'd had the maturity or the badge to cope with it.

Now he had both, but no matter how much Felicity had come into her own lately, she wasn't supposed to have to deal with dead bodies.

Plural. The pattern here made him uneasy. It was rare park rangers found bodies when not part of a search for missing people. Rarer still to have it happen to the same ranger twice.

She did need someone, but Gage didn't know why Brady hadn't called one of her foster sisters. Most of them would do better with the whole soothing and reassuring task ahead of him.

Likely Brady had called him because he knew some of the police officers with Pennington County, and none of the Knight fosters would. They might soothe, but Gage would be able to get some answers.

Gage would get those answers for Felicity. It was the soothing and reassuring part he wasn't so keen on. He tended to keep a hands-off policy as much as possible when it came to her.

"Grown woman," Gage muttered to himself, tapping his agitated fingers against the wheel as he drove. "Did this before. She'll do it again."

He pressed the gas pedal a little hard.

"Didn't she just help save Cody and Nina's butts?" he demanded in an imaginary argument with Brady. "She's capable. More than." Wasn't that half the reason he kept his distance? Capable Felicity in love with his twin brother was dangerous to his well-being.

He muttered to himself on the long, empty drive to the Badlands. Usually he'd marvel at the scenery. Even living here his whole life, he didn't take for granted the rolling grassland that turned into buttes and the grand rock formations that made up the park and its surrounding areas. But he was working up a good irritated steam—mostly as a defense mechanism against Felicity in particular.

She *was* moon-eyed over Brady. So it made sense that since she'd grown a spine and begun showing it off, Gage had started having a little more than friendly thoughts about her. What didn't make sense was harboring those more-than-friendly feelings knowing full well she worshipped the ground Brady walked on.

Who could blame her? His brothers were saints as far as he was concerned. Oh, Cody and Dev had a bit of an edge to them, but at the heart of it they were all good men.

Then there was Brady, something better than a good man. Smartest of all of them, honorable without being hard about it. By the book and serious, yet affable enough that everyone *loved* Brady. He never said the wrong thing, never offered an inappropriate joke to ease the tension. If all his brothers were saints, Brady was the king saint.

On the other hand Gage was the one who said the wrong thing for a laugh. Who didn't take anything as earnestly as his brothers took their breakfast choices.

Of *course* Felicity had a thing for Brady, and it

seemed inevitable that Gage had the bad luck to be hung up on someone in love with his perfect twin.

He rolled his shoulders as he pulled into the parking lot for the trail Felicity had been hiking. This wasn't about him, his issues or even his stupid feelings.

This was about Felicity. Helping her with a sad coincidence. Coming across her second dead body in as many years.

He ignored a tingly *this is all wrong* feeling between his shoulder blades and flashed a broad grin to the cop stationed at the blocked-off trailhead.

He pulled out his badge, did some sweet-talking and was heading toward Felicity in a few minutes.

Once he reached the area where the cops and park rangers were huddled, he stopped short and took a minute to observe Felicity. She sat on a rock away from the circle of people. She was deathly pale, her fingers twisted together, and she stared hard at them.

His heart ached, very much against his will. As a sheriff's deputy for Valiant County, he'd dealt with his share of victims and innocent bystanders of awful things. He knew how to deal with the walking wounded.

But he actually *knew* Felicity, and had since he'd escaped to Grandma's ranch. He'd been eleven to her nine. He'd witnessed her nearly mute elementary years, an awkward-at-best adolescence and then eventually this change in her. Now, in front of him sat a woman who was not falling apart though she had every right to.

That twisting feeling dug deeper so he pushed himself forward. "Hey."

She looked up slowly, her eyebrows drawing together in dawning confusion. "I called Brady."

The twist grew teeth, and he might have grinned negligently in a different situation. But she'd just found a body, so Gage shrugged instead and didn't let the burn of her disappointment settle inside of him. "He sent me. I was closest."

She stared at him for a few seconds before she finally jerked her chin in some approximation of a nod. "They already—" she swallowed, a slight tremor going through her body "—moved the body out."

"Any ID?"

Felicity shook her head. "Nothing on her."

"Her. So, this is different than…" He winced at how insensitive he sounded. Sure, it worked when you were a cop. Not so much when you were here as a friend.

She paused. "Yes," she said finally, in a way that was not convincing at all. "Different."

"Let's get you back to your place, huh?"

She gestured helplessly at the team of cops and park officials. "I have to…"

"They know where to find you if they need more information. Come on. You probably haven't eaten since breakfast." He pulled her to her feet and easily slid his arm around her shoulders since he knew she'd balk at moving if he didn't give her a physical push.

She smelled like flowers and summer. Quite the opposite of the situation they were dealing with.

She pressed a hand to her stomach, her heels all but digging in where she stood. "I couldn't eat. I can't."

"We'll see. You want to walk back?"

She looked around, dismay clear as day on her face. "No, but I need to."

He understood that. If she didn't walk back the way

she'd come, she'd be afraid of returning this way even when her job necessitated it.

Still, he had to give her a push, and he tried not to feel a bit sick over the fact he was forcing her to do something she didn't want to do. Even if she needed to. He followed the trail back toward her cabin, keeping a tight grip on her shoulders as they walked.

A cold drizzle began to fall, but neither of them commented on it or hurried their pace. It felt like a slow trudge through chilled molasses, and Gage didn't have the heart to speed her up even as she began to shiver.

When they got to the authorized-user-only trail, Gage took it without qualm. It would lead to her park housing, and he'd get some food in her. Encourage her to rest.

Then, when she wasn't so pale, he'd head back to the ranch. Felicity wouldn't want him to stay anyway. She'd either handle it on her own, or he'd call one of her sisters for her.

Her little cabin was situated in a small grove of trees. It was old, but she'd infused it with a kind of hominess, though he couldn't identify how. Just that it looked like a nice place.

He reached the door and waited for her to pull out her keys. She unlocked the door and stepped inside.

He'd hoped the walk would have helped put some color back in her cheeks, but she still looked pale as death and like a stray wind might knock her over. Her red hair was damp, and the tendrils that had escaped her braid stuck to her ashen skin.

"Go change into something dry."

She looked up at him, her green eyes lost and sad. She didn't say anything, just stood there looking at him.

"Go on. I'll fix you something to eat while you change."

She shook her head. "I'll just throw it up."

"We'll see. Go on now." He shooed her toward where he figured her bedroom was, down a short, narrow hallway.

He went to the cramped kitchen and poked around for something to make that would go down easy. He found an unreasonable amount of tea and picked one that looked particularly soothing. He followed the instructions, trying not to feel claustrophobic in her closet of a kitchen.

When she returned she didn't look any less lost, but she was in dry sweatpants and a long-sleeved T-shirt for Mammoth Cave National Park. She stood at the entrance to the kitchen taking in her surroundings like it was somewhere she'd never been before.

"Sit," he ordered, uncomfortable with how fragile she seemed.

She nodded after a time and then took a seat at her tiny table. He set the mug of tea in front of her. "You'll drink all of that," he said, trying to sound as commanding as his grandmother did when she was forcing food on someone.

She didn't drink, just stared at the mug. "They think I have something to do with it," she said, her voice so quiet he almost couldn't make out the words. "I can tell."

"No. You've been through this before. You know how it goes." He found a loaf of bread and dropped a slice in the toaster. "They have questions they have to ask just to make sure, but—"

"It's the second time." She lifted her gaze to meet his, and there was nothing timid or uncertain about her, as there had been in the past. No, she was in complete control, even lost and scared. "The questions were different. And they're right. It does. It has something to do with me. I know it does."

Chapter Two

Something about Gage's large form taking up almost the entire space in her tiny kitchen made Felicity want to blurt out everything that was going on in her brain.

He was making her tea and toast. She wanted to lay down her head and cry. She expected her sisters to take care of her. She even expected Duke to take care of her—he'd had to step in as mother along with father when Eva had died. He'd done his best.

Her foster family had always done their best, just like their friends the Wyatts.

But this was Gage. Gage always made her feel edgy. Like she was on uneven ground. You never knew what Gage was going to do or say, and she preferred knowing exactly what was going to happen.

Sometimes she blamed his size for the discomfort she felt. He was so tall and broad and, Lord, he packed on the muscle. But Brady was the exact same size, just as strong and broad, and Brady only ever made her feel safe. Comfortable.

Gage set down a plate with a piece of buttered toast

in front of her. Her cheap, cute floral dishes looked all wrong in his hands.

Today was all, *all* wrong.

"Why do you think it has something to do with you?" he asked as he took a seat across from her.

"You made me tea and toast." She could only stare at the wisps of steam drifting up from the mug. Gage Wyatt…had made her tea and toast?

"You're lucky. If Grandma Pauline was here, she would have made a five-course meal and insisted you eat every bite."

It was true. His grandmother soothed with food— whether you wanted food as soothing or not. Tea and toast was a lighter option, and her stomach might actually be able to handle it. So she sipped the tea, took a bite of toast and avoided the topic of conversation at hand.

"Felicity."

She winced at the gentleness in his tone. "Why did Brady send you?" She squeezed her eyes shut. "I'm sorry. That sounds ungrateful."

He shrugged again, just as he had outside when she'd made a point of telling him he wasn't who she'd been expecting. There was something in his gaze when he gave those careless shrugs that made her heart feel weighted. Like she'd said something all wrong and hurt his feelings.

Which was ludicrous. Gage did not get hurt feelings, especially at her hands.

"Like I said outside, I was closest." He tapped his fingers on the table, the only sign of agitation.

"You've been very…nice," she said, not even sure

why she wanted to try to make him feel better when any hurt or agitation had to be her imagination.

"I'm always nice."

"No. That is not true. Not that you're mean, but I'm not sure anyone would describe you as nice." Gage was challenging. He was irreverent. He made her jumpy. Even when he was doing something nice.

"Felicity. Why do you think this crime connects to you?"

The toast turned to lead in her throat and she had to work to swallow it down. She didn't want to talk about it, but she needed to. She needed help. From someone in law enforcement who would listen to her. "It was the same."

"A woman this time," he noted. "So, not exactly the same."

"Maybe not the *who*, but it was my morning hike. My routine. I've changed it a little since last year, but I always have a routine." Routine steadied her. Made her feel strong and in control, and now she wasn't sure she'd be able to have one or feel that ever again. "The last time, it was my routine hike. My personal routine hike—not work related. Just like this time."

He nodded and waited patiently for her to work up to say the rest of it.

"The boot in the trail. Unlaced. That happened last time, too. I stumbled over the boot last time. This time I saw it in the nick of time—probably the pink laces." Those laces would haunt her forever.

"Okay. So you saw the boot, and then what?"

She'd already told the Pennington County deputies and her boss the answer to that question. Over and over in a circle. But she hadn't explained to them what she was about to explain to Gage. "I told them I looked on the sides of the trail to see if anyone had had an accident."

"You told them…"

"I knew where the body would be. I looked on the left side first because that wasn't where the body was last time. I looked to the left and there was no one there, but I had to check. It would be on the right side of the trail. I didn't want there to be, but I just… I just knew the body would be where it had been last time. Only a few feet off the trail." She shoved away the tea and the toast and got to her feet. "I can't…"

There was nowhere to go in her tiny cabin. Stomp off to her room like a child? Tempting.

But Gage walked right over to her, putting his big hands on her shoulders and squeezing them enough to center her in the moment.

He was so dang tall, and it was unreasonable how broad-shouldered he was. When he was clean-shaven, he looked so much like Brady it got hard to tell them apart. But their eyes were different. Brady's hazel edged toward brown, and Gage's green. Gage's nose was crooked, and he had a scar through his eyebrow.

Brady's face was perfect. Gage's was…

"You know, Brady told me I needed to be gentle with you."

Those words felt like cold water being splashed in her face. "I'm not a shy little girl anymore," she snapped, trying to shrug off his hands. When would they all see that? It wasn't enough she'd helped save Cody and Nina from one of the Sons last month? Honestly.

"That's what I told him," Gage said, which had her looking up in confusion.

"You…"

"Anyone who's paying attention can see you've changed, Felicity. You're an adult. You've found yourself or whatever you want to call it."

Did that mean *Gage* was paying attention? Impossible.

"Now. You've done this before. So, don't say you can't when we both know you can and you will."

She sucked in a breath. He was right. It didn't quite steady her, though. Why was Gage of all people right? And why were his big hands on her narrow shoulders?

As if he'd read her thoughts, his hands slid away and he stepped back, shoving his hands into his pockets.

"Why couldn't it be random? I mean, it looks like the killings connect. It's not accidental and it's not suicide. It's murder—even I could see that no matter how much they tried to BS me. But just because it's murder, doesn't mean you're the key. Maybe Badlands is the common denominator. Maybe you're just…"

"Unlucky?"

"Sure. Why not? The bodies aren't showing up on your doorstep."

"Just on trails I walk as a matter of course," she returned, wishing she could believe his coincidence theory. "That boot wasn't an accident, and it wasn't placed there yesterday when anyone could have come across it. It was put there so *I* would come across it."

"Okay." He nodded, taking a few more steps away from her.

It seemed odd, the forced distance, but she could

hardly think about anything going on with Gage when she had a dead body to worry about.

"If you're being targeted…why?"

"I don't know." She didn't have a clue. Maybe she'd believe it was her connection to the Wyatts. She'd shot one of the Sons of the Badlands men to help Nina and Cody escape Ace Wyatt's machinations. Except she'd never had a personal interaction with Ace Wyatt, the president of the gang and Gage's father, who was now in jail.

But jail hadn't stopped Ace from making things happen on the outside last month. Why would she think he couldn't reach her now?

The problem was that last month was the first time she'd ever interfered with Sons business, which didn't explain the first body from a year ago.

Unless that *had* been an accident and this was a copy-cat?

"You think it's Ace."

Felicity looked up at Gage because his voice was so flat. Even when Gage got angry he usually hid it under that natural irreverence. It was why she preferred Brady. Brady was rather stoic, but when he showed an emotion you knew what emotion you were getting. Gage was unpredictable.

Even now. She didn't know what that cold, flat voice meant. She only knew it was possible this connected to his crime boss of a father, even if Ace was in jail and the Sons of the Badlands seemed to be getting weaker.

"I don't know. I don't know, but I interfered last month."

"It wouldn't connect all the way back to last year."

He kept talking before she could offer her theory. "But it wouldn't have to—it would just have to look like it. Sounds like Ace."

She nodded. "I need you to help me figure out if it is, Gage. I can't trust the local police to do it. I'm sure they're fine at their jobs, but they don't know Ace, and they're afraid of the Sons. You aren't."

"Everyone is afraid of the Sons, Felicity. It's stupid not to be." He sighed, presumably at the horrified look on her face. "We'll figure it out. Okay?"

SHE WAS STANDING still as a statue, looking at him like he'd slapped her across the face when he'd simply told her the truth.

Even if the Sons were weaker than they'd been, they were still dangerous. Too dangerous, and anyone with a connection to Ace Wyatt was definitely in the most danger.

They were working on getting more charges leveled against Ace, thanks to three of the men who had been arrested after trying to hurt Cody and Nina and their daughter last month. But it still wouldn't add up to a life sentence, even if he was found guilty at his upcoming trial for the first round of charges.

Unfortunately, no matter how sure Jamison and Cody were that the law would keep Ace powerless— when Ace had already proved jail couldn't—Gage had doubts.

Major doubts.

Felicity *had* been integral in the arrest of one of those men who was potentially going to take the stand against Ace. It made sense she'd be targeted.

Gage's phone chimed and he looked down at the text from Brady.

I can relieve you if you want.

Felicity would want Brady. She deserved the Wyatt brother she preferred even if her crush was hopeless. Brady didn't have a clue who Felicity really was. Gage wasn't convinced his twin could ever look at the Knight fosters and not see a *sister*. Or at the least think, *Hands off.*

Brady would always toe the unofficial line. Gage never did.

No worries, he typed and hit Send before he could talk himself into doing the right thing.

Maybe Felicity wanted Brady, but Gage would be the better helper in this situation. He was willing to bend a few more rules than Brady. Besides, she'd said she needed *his* help. Maybe it was only because he was here, but hell, he was here.

"Once they ID her, we'll want to see how she connects to the first victim."

Felicity shook her head and took a seat. "I don't think the victims matter. I mean, they matter. To their families. To me. But they're not the point to whoever is doing this."

"Maybe not, but we'll research it all the same. We'll go over things. Maybe you should stay at the ranch until this blows over."

She was shaking her head. "I have a job to do. If I run away from that—"

"They're going to put you on leave. They did last time, didn't they?"

"They can't. It's summer this time. It's busy season. I'm scheduled for programs and…" She trailed off as her phone buzzed. She swallowed and looked at the screen. "It's my boss."

Gage didn't say *I told you so.* He didn't need to. Didn't want to after having to stand and listen to her desperate attempts to change her boss's mind.

When she finally hung up, she stared at her phone. "I can't work for at least a week."

"That's not such a bad thing."

Her head whipped up, fury in her green eyes. "It's a terrible thing. On every level. I can't *be* here. It will haunt me—her body. Every night. You can't get rid of something you never face. It puts my job, my *dream* job, in jeopardy. Do you have any idea how hard I've worked to get this position?"

The color had come back to her face, the faintest blush rising in her cheeks. She was breathing a little heavier after that tirade, and she had her fingers curled into fists.

She was possibly the most beautiful woman he'd ever seen, and he knew that made him a jerk. "Yeah," he finally managed. "You worked your butt off."

His simple affirmative had her slumping in her seat. "I don't want to go to the ranch. Duke will worry. Sarah and Rachel will worry and fuss. Your grandmother will make a feast for seventy and expect a handful of us to eat it all. Worst of all, you Wyatt boys will push me out of this when it is my fight."

"It's our fight."

"And yet I'm the one with blood on my hands." She held them up as if she'd been the one to do any kind of killing.

He knelt in front of her and, though he knew it would be a mistake, took both her raised hands in his. "There's no blood here."

"There might as well be," she returned, her voice breaking on the last word. She blinked back tears. "I can't sit idly by. If you take me back there, you'll push me out. All of you."

Brady would lead that charge, but Gage didn't tell her that. He held her hands in his, irritated that both were so cold. She should have drunk the tea. He should have made her.

"No, you can't sit idly by," he agreed, if irritably. "But that doesn't mean we can't go to the ranches and work through it. Let the police do their jobs here. Let your boss do his job for the park. Back home, we'll work together to figure out what this really is. Together. I promise. No one will push you out."

She stared at him, eyebrows drawn together, frown digging lines around her mouth. Her eyes were suspicious, but she sat there and let him hold her hands. She sat there and stared at him. Thinking.

While she was *thinking*, he was *feeling* quite a bit too much.

She tugged her hands out of his grasp and stood abruptly. She stalked away from him, though it ended up being only a few steps because the cabin was so small. She whirled and pointed at him. "You promise?"

"I promise," he replied solemnly.

Because Gage Wyatt would break rules and didn't mind lying when it suited, but he wouldn't break a promise to Felicity. Not even if it killed him.

Chapter Three

Felicity sat in the passenger seat of Gage's truck, brooding over the lack of her own vehicle. The lack of her job for at least a week. The lack of her little cabin that wasn't her home exactly. It wasn't *hers* to own—it was the park's.

But neither were the ranches hers, though they made up the tapestry of her childhood and adolescence. The Wyatt boys and the foster girls of Duke and Eva Knight had run wild over both ranches. They were a piece of her, yes, but she didn't own them.

She'd gotten into the wrong business if she was worried about owning things, though. Apparently, the wrong business if she didn't want to find dead bodies.

She closed her eyes, but that only made said bodies pop up in her head, so she opened them and leaned her forehead against the window. She watched the scenery pass, from the stark browns, tans and whites of the Badlands to the verdant green and rolling hills with only the occasional ridge of rock formations that would lead them to the ranches they'd grown up on.

"Brady said for us to meet at my grandma's."

Felicity sighed. "I don't want a fuss." She didn't want all the attention or the attempts at soothing. Right now she wanted to be alone.

Except then her company would be the images of the dead bodies she'd found, and that didn't exactly appeal, either.

"Maybe it'd be a good time to tell them about our Ace connection theory," Gage offered as if he was trying to make her feel better. Which was odd coming from Gage, who was known more for making a joke out of serious things. Still, if she really thought about it, he often did that in a way that made people feel better, even if only momentarily.

"So it's *our* theory now?"

Gage lifted a negligent shoulder. "We can call it yours, but I agree with it."

"Will they?"

"Not sure. Don't see why they wouldn't. It makes sense. We'll look into it one way or another."

"*We* or you guys?"

He spared her a look as he pulled through the gate to the Reaves Ranch. Pauline Reaves had run this ranch since she'd been younger than Felicity, and though she'd married, she'd kept the ranch in her name and never let anyone believe her husband ran things.

As the story went, her late husband had been in love with her enough not to care. Felicity had never met the Wyatt boys' grandfather, who had died before Felicity had come to live with the Knights.

Felicity loved Grandma Pauline like her own. Not such a strange thing for a girl who'd grown up with the care and love of foster parents to love nonfamily like family. Pauline had always represented a strong, independent feminine ideal to Felicity. One she'd thought she'd never live up to.

But the older she got, the more Felicity felt that if she worked hard enough at it, she could be as strong and determined as Grandma Pauline. She could forge her own path.

Thoughts of Pauline's strength disappeared as the line of cars in front of Pauline's old ranch house came into view. Despite its sprawling size, piecemeal additions and modernizations over the years, and the fact only two people lived full-time in it, the house was well cared for. The boys always made sure repairs were done quickly, and Grandma kept it spick-and-span.

Still, it showed its age and wear. There was something comforting in that—or there would be if there wasn't this line of cars in front of it.

"*Everyone's* here."

"I mean, not…everyone," Gage said, trying for what she assumed was a cheerful tone.

He'd failed. Miserably. Everyone or almost everyone's vehicle being here meant something…something big at that. It was more than her stumbling across a dead body.

Felicity frowned as Gage parked in line. Based on the vehicles she recognized, Tucker and Brady were here, as was Duke and potentially Rachel and Sarah if they'd driven over with him. Dev and Grandma Pauline lived on the property, but it was Cody's truck that really bothered her. Why would he come all the way out from Bonesteel? The only vehicle missing was one belonging to Jamison and Liza. Hopefully they were at home in Bonesteel, safe and sound, taking care of Gigi, Liza's young half sister. "What is all this? Why is everyone here?"

"I don't know," he replied, sounding confused enough that she believed him. He got out of the truck and she followed. Dev's ranch dogs pranced at their feet, whimpering excitedly as they'd been trained not to bark at Wyatts or Knights.

Felicity wanted to dawdle or trudge, spend some time playing with the dogs, or maybe make a run for it to the Knight Ranch, where she knew she still had a bed waiting for her.

But that was cowardly, and it wouldn't change whatever this was. It would only avoid it for a while.

She followed Gage's brisk pace to the back door, which led to a mudroom. The dogs wouldn't follow inside at this entrance since you had to go through the kitchen to get to the rest of the house—and Grandma Pauline did *not* allow dogs in her kitchen.

Felicity stepped into the kitchen behind Gage. A very full room.

Duke and Rachel were there, sitting at the table. When Felicity had been younger, she'd been jealous of Rachel. She was Duke and Eva's only biological child, and she looked like she belonged in the Knight family. Even though with the fosters they'd been a conglomeration of black, Lakota and white—no one looking too much like anyone else—Felicity had always felt the odd man out with her particularly pale skin and bright red hair.

But she was older now, and today she was glad to see the people who were her family.

It was a little harder to be grateful for the presence of the Wyatt brothers. All of them being here in this moment only meant trouble. They brought it with them, and though they fought it as much as they could, it was always there.

Tucker stood next to Cody *and* Jamison—so they must have driven together from Bonesteel. Dev and Brady sat at the table while Grandma Pauline bustled around the kitchen.

They all looked at Felicity with smiles that were in turn sad, sympathetic or pitying. Felicity's chest got tight and panic beat through her, its own insistent drum of a heartbeat. "What's going on?"

Grandma Pauline all but pushed her into a chair and set a plate with a brownie on it in front of her. Duke took her hand and patted it.

All the eyes in the room except Gage's turned to Tucker.

His smile was the most pitying and apologetic of all. "When Brady told me what happened I asked a buddy over in Pennington County to let me know if they found anything out."

Felicity had to pause before she spoke. Getting upset often made her stutter return, but if she kept herself from rushing, she could handle it. "And they did?"

"The victim's name is Melody Harrison."

Everyone was quiet. So quiet and this was usually a noisy group.

"It's a common enough last name," Felicity forced herself to say slowly and calmly. "It might be a coincidence." She didn't know anyone named Melody, even if they shared a last name. Of course she'd been taken away from her abusive father at four. She hardly knew her biological family.

"It is common. Unfortunately, the next of kin who identified her..." If it was possible, the pitying expression grew worse. "He was her father. Michael Harrison."

"M-my father. B-but that's common, too, and—"

Tucker nodded grimly. "I confirmed it, Felicity. Your father. Melody was twenty-two, so she was born after you were placed with the Knights."

"Y-you're s-saying that..." She winced at how badly the stutter sounded in the quiet room. She made sure to take breaths between each word as she spoke. "The dead body I found is my sister."

"At least by half. Which means..." Tucker scraped a hand over his jaw.

She didn't let him say it. She might have before last year. Let him say it. Let the Wyatt boys take care of it. But no one could really take care of what was going on in her head. Even when she was weary enough to wish someone else could.

"The cops will try to connect me to it even more now."

Gage swore and felt a stab of guilt when Felicity flinched as if she'd received some kind of blow.

This was ludicrous. "How? When she didn't even know the sister existed?" Gage demanded.

His brothers gave him *that* look. The *you should know better, Gage* look. Because he was a cop. He knew how to investigate a suspicious death, and Felicity tripping over her alleged half sister was certainly suspicious.

He looked at Felicity. She'd made him promise that she wouldn't get elbowed out of dealing with this herself, so he waited for her to bring it up.

Though mostly he wanted Grandma Pauline to shove her full of brownies while he took care of everything.

However, he had enough women in his life to know they didn't particularly appreciate that method. Besides, he'd promised. So… He all but bit his tongue.

He gave Felicity a go-ahead nod, and then gestured when she simply stared at him. She blew out a slow breath.

"It could be Ace," Felicity finally said. She looked down at the plate and the brownie on it, but her voice was clear and steady no matter how little eye contact she made.

"How?" Jamison returned.

She looked up and met Jamison's gaze. "I interfered. I helped Nina and Cody. I don't know *how* it's Ace, but I know why it could be. It makes sense." Her gaze shifted to Gage, looking for some kind of support or backup. *Me not Brady.* Which was very much not the point. "Obviously, the timing of the first one doesn't work, but it could be a copycat type thing. It could be a way to make it look like she's involved—and I think the family connection only makes that more plausible."

His brothers mulled that over.

"Possibly a setup. To get Felicity in trouble. A punishment for interfering," Jamison said, clearly trying to work out the logistics. "I buy that. It's Ace's MO. But how would he have orchestrated it? Since the attempt on Nina's life, we've been keeping tabs on everyone Ace talks to."

Gage had thought about that on the long, silent drive over to Grandma Pauline's. "We keep tabs on everyone who visits him in jail. Not who he talks to inside. He could be paying off a guard or threatening another inmate. Problem is, until Ace is sentenced and sent to a more secure facility, he has ample ways to outwit the system *and* us."

"His lawyer keeps getting the trial pushed back," Tucker said, disgust lacing his tone. "They're going to drag it out as long as they can."

"Don't you have any informants on the inside, Detective?" Gage asked, infusing the word *detective* with only a little sarcasm.

Tucker rolled his eyes. "Not anyone I'd trust enough to tangle with Ace."

"What do we do?" Duke asked. Demanded.

"The park forced me to take a week's leave of absence, and then they'll *reevaluate*," Felicity said miserably.

"So, you'll be home." Duke didn't have to say *where you belong* for it to be heard echoing in the silence.

Felicity smiled at Duke, but surely everyone saw how sad that smile was.

"There's not much we can do right now," Jamison said, always the de facto leader, no matter the situation. "Tucker will keep his ear to the ground when it comes to the investigation. Cody and I can look into getting some more information about who Ace talks to in the jail."

"What about…" Gage hesitated at the word *father*, considering he barely liked to call his own one. "Michael Harrison. Where did this guy come from?"

"He was the victim's father."

Gage shook his head. "That's an awful big coincidence. There was a reason Felicity was removed from his care. Was this girl?"

"Okay, point taken. We'll look into both of them."

"And what will I do?" Felicity asked, and though Gage thought she tried to turn it into a demand like Duke had done, it didn't quite hit the mark.

"Come home and rest, girl," Duke instructed.

Gage opened his mouth to come to her defense because he'd *promised*, but she shook her head.

She smiled at her foster father. "That's a good idea, Duke."

They both stood up from the table, and since she hadn't taken even a single bite of the brownie Grandma had put in front of her, Grandma immediately shoved a plastic container full of brownies into her hands.

Felicity smiled and gave Grandma a one-armed hug. "Thank you, Grandma Pauline."

"You eat, you hear me?"

"Yes, ma'am." Felicity glanced back at Gage. "Keep me up-to-date?"

He ignored the fact he got a little something out of her asking *him* and not Brady. He was very good at ignoring things he didn't particularly care for.

He gave her a nod, and Duke, Rachel and Felicity left Grandma's kitchen. Leaving Gage with his brothers and Grandma.

Dev stood first. "I've got work."

"I'll help," Gage offered. "I was supposed to anyway." He paused and looked at Jamison, Cody and Tucker. They had the best ways to get information. Gage had a few buddies over at Pennington, but Tucker knew the detectives. Jamison and Cody had been integral in getting Ace arrested in the first place, so they had a lot of ways to find information on the Ace side of things.

Gage rode the road. He had a bit too much of a mouth on him to receive the promotions Tucker and Brady seemed to rack up without even trying.

It didn't bother him. He preferred the in-the-trenches view from the bottom, but right now the lack of resources to get information made him superfluous.

So why not sweat away some frustration on ranch work? He'd spend the night, check in on Felicity tomorrow morning, then head back to his apartment to pick up his take-home car for his evening shift.

If that itch between his shoulder blades stayed there all through the afternoon and night, well, he'd deal.

WHEN HE WOKE up the next morning and trudged down to breakfast, Brady was waiting at the breakfast table. Gage rubbed bleary eyes and knew the news was bad without even a word passing between them.

"They searched Felicity's cabin," Brady said without preamble.

"And?"

"They found evidence of clothing being burned in the fire grate outside the cabin. They've collected some hair they found—clearly not Felicity's."

"Doesn't mean it's that woman's hair. That doesn't mean anything. Good Lord, she's not a suspect."

"They've sent the hair and what was left of the burnt clothes in for DNA testing," Brady said, his calm poking at Gage's agitation.

Brady sighed and shook his head, showing his first sign of emotion. "I've got a bad feeling about this."

"So do I." It smelled of a setup. But not enough of one to tip off cops who didn't know Felicity. Or Ace, for that matter.

"We've got to get her a lawyer," Brady said. With a straight face and everything.

"A lawyer? Are you insane? We have to get her out of here."

Brady's expression went carefully blank. "You can't run from the police, Gage. You *are* the police."

"Yeah, and I know this is garbage. *You* know it. Felicity wouldn't hurt a fly, and I'm not going to let her be arrested and God knows what else. Can you imagine her stuck in a cell somewhere? It's not happening."

Brady didn't move even as Gage paced the room. Cody often called them two sides of the same coin. The way they reacted, or acted in general, was often in big sweeping opposites, but when it came to it—twin junk or just the way life worked—they were the same deep down.

They might not *react* the same, but they understood.

"Where would you go?" Brady asked, without Gage even having to say he'd be the one to hide her.

"I don't know yet, but I'll figure it out."

He had to.

Chapter Four

Felicity woke up in her childhood bed. There was a deep, soothing relief in that familiarity, that cocoon of safety...for about five seconds before the anxiety started to creep in.

Luckily, there was plenty to do to keep a mind occupied when you woke up on a ranch. Though Duke and Sarah ran the cattle operation with their seasonal workers, Felicity knew a chore or two could always be picked up.

It wouldn't keep her mind from running in circles, but it might help exhaust her enough she could manage a decent night's sleep tonight instead of tossing and turning as she'd done last night.

She rolled out of bed and looked around the empty room. She'd once shared it with Sarah, but when Liza, Nina and Cecilia had all moved out, each of the remaining girls had gotten their own room instead of sharing with one other sister.

Felicity had learned how to be alone, but she did it best and most comfortably when she could be outdoors. When she could listen to birdsong and watch the stars move across the sky. When the fresh air and unique landscape made her feel *awe* at her place in the world.

Indoors, alone was just alone. Too quiet and too claustrophobic.

The thought had her walking into the hallway, determined to find someone to eat breakfast with and then find chores.

She ran into Rachel in the hallway and raised an eyebrow at her notoriously bad-at-mornings sister. "Aren't you up early."

"That class I'm teaching at the rez this summer started last week." Rachel yawned. "It might kill me."

"I thought you were going to stay with Cecilia while you did that." As a tribal police officer, Cecilia lived on the rez. Though she wasn't Duke's biological daughter, she was Eva's niece. Neither Cecilia nor Rachel would have ever said it aloud, but they had more of a connection with each other than with her, Sarah, Liza and Nina. Blood mattered, even in a foster family.

"I've been spending weeknights with Cee, and weekends here. But Daddy was grumbling last night so I stayed an extra night. I'm staying there the rest of the week after class today." Rachel yawned again, then her eyes brightened. "Hey, drive me over instead of Sarah? You can spend a few nights with us at Cecilia's, take your mind off everything. We'll have a sleepover. Sarah won't stay because of the ranch, and Liza and Nina have their girls to worry about, but the three of us could have fun."

"I don't—"

"I won't take no for an answer."

Felicity smiled. It wasn't such a bad idea. She could clear her head, enjoy her sisters. Maybe Rachel and Cecilia had a deeper connection, but Felicity only seemed to feel that when she was alone and overthinking things. When they were all together, they were sisters.

Maybe all those thoughts about deeper connections were more her own issues than the truth.

"Well, then I guess… Damn, I don't have a car."

"We'll take Duke's. He can use Sarah's truck for the weekend. You drop me off at the school, then you can do whatever. I'm sure the park will let you go back to work next week once the police have figured this out."

Felicity smiled, though she was not at all sure. Nothing about what was going on felt like last time. Last time had been a shock. It had been scary and a little traumatic, but she'd been able to convince herself it was a one-time thing. She'd just had the bad luck to be the one to find him. Bad luck was life.

Twice in two years felt a lot less like random bad luck.

"Come on," Rachel said, slipping her arm around Felicity's taller shoulders. "I'll make you breakfast. Pancakes."

"You don't have to go to all that trouble."

Rachel shrugged. "Daddy and Sarah will sing my praises. Neither of them are very good at taking care of themselves."

"What do they do when you're not here?"

"I'm hoping one of them learns through sheer necessity. I guess we'll see."

They headed downstairs together. Though Rachel

was legally blind, she knew the house so well she didn't need her support cane when walking around inside and most of the grounds outside, as well.

Duke and Sarah were likely already out doing chores, but they'd be back in a half hour or so to eat and get more coffee. Felicity set out to help Rachel make pancakes and they chatted about Rachel's art class.

It felt good and normal, and Felicity almost forgot all her worries. Everything would be fine. She had a great family. Maybe the real issue wasn't so much what had happened, but how she'd allowed herself to feel solitary and singular when she had so many people who cared about her.

Since she hadn't done anything wrong, she just had to wait out the investigation. Maybe the time off would even be good for her. She'd been so focused on having her dream job that she'd neglected her family.

She'd spend time with her sisters, with Duke, do some work around the ranch, and when she was cleared to go back to work, she'd focus more on balance.

As she turned to put the bowl of strawberries she'd just cut up on the table, she saw a truck cresting the hill to the Knight house. Not one of Duke's trucks.

"Who is it?" Rachel asked.

"Gage." Why he was suddenly the one in charge of this whole thing, she didn't know. She'd called Brady originally because she'd wanted someone to take care of it, but Brady wouldn't have just taken care of it—he would have taken over.

She'd thought she'd wanted that in the moment, but she realized as Gage's truck pulled to a stop in front of the house, she was glad Gage had included her. He'd encouraged her to speak. He believed her theories. It felt more like she was on even ground with him.

"It's early," Rachel commented. "But that doesn't mean—"

"It means he has bad news. If it's bad news, it's about the dead woman." *My sister.* Felicity really couldn't wrap her head around that part yet, so she kept pushing it away. Kept pushing the involvement of her father out of her mind. Over and over again.

Despite knowing it was coming, the knock on the door made Felicity jump.

"We could pretend we're not here," Rachel offered.

"It would only delay the inevitable. Besides, he knows we're here." Felicity steadied herself on a deep breath before opening the door.

Gage looked disheveled, which wasn't that out of character for him, but considering the circumstances it felt foreboding. His grave expression didn't help. Gage was almost never grave. He was the one who cracked a joke to break the tension or told a bizarre story to take everyone's mind off things.

Brady was the grave twin, the one who took everything seriously and was weighed down by it. She'd always admired Brady's willingness to accept responsibility.

But wasn't trying to lift the weight of a room its own kind of responsibility?

"Pack a bag," Gage said, his voice rough. "You've got five minutes before we need to be on the road."

Those harsh words, with no preamble, had Felicity frowning at him. "What are you even talking about?"

"We have to go. Now. Unless you want to spend the night, or a few nights, in jail."

GAGE SHOULDN'T HAVE put it so bluntly, but time was of the essence. He hadn't even had his coffee, which might have accounted for some of the bluntness.

"Go pack your things, Felicity," Rachel said when Felicity stood motionless.

Felicity left the kitchen at Rachel's words, and Rachel turned back to whatever she'd been doing. It looked like making pancakes.

Gage didn't know what to say in the face of a nice domestic morning Felicity should have been able to share and enjoy with her sister. This was really more of a *do* situation, and the fewer people who knew what they were doing, the better.

When Rachel turned back around, she held two travel mugs he was pretty sure were filled with coffee. *Thank God.*

She held out both to him. He stepped toward her and took them. She angled her head up, looking at him thoughtfully even though he knew she couldn't see him clearly.

The scars that had caused her loss of sight were such a part of the face he knew so well, he only noticed them now because things were bad. It made him think about all those years ago when a freak mountain lion attack had taken Rachel's sight.

Grandma had started teaching them all to shoot the next day—Wyatt brothers and Knight girls side by side, armed with various guns and starting at ten paces away from a row of tin cans balanced on a fence.

When bad things happened, you did what you could to learn how to protect yourself from the next one. That was the lesson of his life. That was why he'd become a police officer. He knew what awful, horrible things could happen—from animal attacks to cold-blooded murder—and he'd wanted to be one of the ones who set things to right.

Sometimes he had. Sometimes he hadn't. Life wasn't perfect, and being a cop didn't mean he could fix everything, even if he wanted to.

But he could fix this for Felicity. First, he had to get her out of harm's way. Then the Wyatts would work to make sure this got cleared up. But he simply couldn't stand the thought of her in a holding cell. Not Felicity.

"You'll take good care of her," Rachel finally said.

It wasn't a question, so he didn't answer it.

Felicity returned with a backpack. She'd changed into jeans and a T-shirt and was wearing her hiking boots, which was a good thing. They'd be doing some considerable hiking. "You'll need a coat. Light one, but a coat nonetheless."

"Where are we going?"

"We'll talk about it in the truck."

She blew out an irritated breath as she walked away and then returned with a windbreaker. "Good?"

He nodded.

Felicity turned to Rachel. "Duke is going to—"

"I'll handle Daddy. You be safe."

They hugged briefly, then Felicity turned to him, grasping the straps of her backpack, a grim determination on her face. "All right. Let's go."

He led her out to his truck. He'd fixed Dev's camper

shell onto his truck bed and stuffed it full of a variety of things. Hunting gear, fishing gear, ranch supplies. Hidden under all of that were two backpacks set up for backcountry camping. Brady was under strict orders to pick up the truck at the drop-off point and park it at the local airport. Make it look like he was really taking the vacation he'd lied to the sheriff about.

They reached the truck and got in. Felicity hadn't asked any questions—not that he would have answered them until they were in the truck and on their way.

She hefted her backpack into the back and folded her hands on her lap. She looked straight ahead as he started the engine.

Gage began to drive, knowing he should explain things. Instead, he took a few sips of coffee to clear his morning-fogged brain and waited for Felicity to demand answers.

"Where are you taking me?" she finally asked, which wasn't the question he thought she'd lead with.

"I figure you know some pretty isolated areas in the park we could hike to and camp without anyone finding us."

"If you backcountry camp you have to get a permit," she said primly.

He wished he could be more amused by it, but in the moment he could only be a little harsh. "Felicity. You don't honestly think I'm going to waste my time with a permit."

"It's about safety and the park's environmental integrity. We have to know how many people—"

"Well, safety and the damn environment are going

to have to take a back seat." He spared her a look, hoping it got across how dire this situation was.

"I'm a suspect," she said flatly. "We already knew that was a possibility."

God, he wished that was all it was. He rubbed a hand over the scruff on his jaw. He hadn't had a chance to shave this morning, and it didn't look like he'd be shaving any time soon.

"It's worse than that."

She swallowed. Her words were careful as she spoke, and he knew she was trying to keep her stutter under control. "How so?"

"The investigators searched your cabin."

"I d-don't have anything to hide. What does that matter?"

"They found some things anyway."

"What? How?" Felicity demanded, outrage making her cheeks turn pink. He liked it much better than the stutter, which sounded more like fear than fight.

"Someone is setting you up as a murderer." He shifted his gaze to the road. "Still want to get that permit?"

Chapter Five

Felicity didn't speak for a while after that. She let Gage drive her back to the Badlands, just as he'd driven her home from them yesterday.

Today he took the long, winding backroad to the southern portion of the park. It was far less trafficked and technically on reservation land. There would be no actual way to get into the park the way Gage was driving without doing some serious off-roading.

She looked at the grim line of his mouth and knew that was exactly his plan.

Because someone had planted evidence that she was a murderer.

A *murderer*.

The more that word spun around in her head, the more she didn't understand it. "There has to be some kind of mistake."

"What those cops found? It was no mistake. It had to have been planted, Felicity. And if it was planted, someone is purposefully trying to frame you for murder."

"It also means that poor woman was murdered."

"Felicity."

She hated the pity in his tone. *Poor, silly Felicity.* "It is still possible she just fell. It is still possible..." Yes, she was silly, because there was a part of her hoping for tragic accident over premeditated evil.

"You're the one who told me the boot in the trail was the same as the last time. Surely you knew it wasn't an accident."

"Don't you ever entertain a hope no matter how unreasonable it might be? Don't you ever think, well, *maybe* it's not as awful and dire as it looks?"

"No," he said flatly.

She didn't have to ask him why. In the silence she could hear Ace's name as if Gage had uttered it himself.

Gage had spent his formative years in the Sons of the Badlands against his will. He'd been eleven when Jamison had saved him and Brady from the gang, gotten them to Grandma Pauline. So by the time he had a real home, with an adult who truly loved him and would care for him, Gage had likely already seen too much to believe in hope.

She'd been young enough that memories of her father's beatings were vague. Sometimes she wasn't sure if they were actual memories or nightmares she'd had.

But she'd definitely been in a cast when she'd come to live with the Knights at the age of four. So, it was all true enough.

No matter her past, she could always hope for the best outcome. That's what the Knights and their love and security had given her.

"If it's Ace setting me up, I don't understand why. I don't understand."

"You said it yourself. You interfered. You helped Nina and Cody outwit his plans. That puts a big red *X* on your back, and there was already one there for being a Knight."

"But I'm not a Knight, by name or blood."

"By love you are. Which makes you a friend to the Wyatts. One who fought for us. That's all it takes to make you Ace's target."

She knew all that rationally. Though she'd assumed Ace had targeted Liza and Nina because they'd had relationships with his sons, Liza and Nina had also defied Ace's plans.

And now she'd joined their ranks.

"As for the how… I don't know how Ace does anything, let alone get hundreds of men to follow his particular brand of narcissism and contradictory insanity for years and years on end. But here we are, and you're unlucky enough to have connections to us. Maybe Ace never paid much mind to the Knights before this, but he's certainly making a case for it now."

Gage brought his truck to a stop in the middle of nowhere. Actual nowhere.

"Why are you stopping?"

"We're going to hike the rest of the way."

"And just leave your car here?"

"It'll be taken care of."

"But what if we need to get out? What if there's bad weather? Did you even pack a weather radio? Enough water? Floods, tornadoes, lightning. Rattlesnakes. You know bison are dangerous, right? And prairie dogs carry the plague."

He gave her a sardonic look and slid out of the truck without responding.

She scurried after him. There were two parts of her brain fighting it out. The one that understood he was doing what he could to keep her out of harm's way, and the part that had taken an oath to treat the park and its denizens with respect and integrity.

"Backcountry camping is serious business," she said to him in her firmest park ranger voice as he opened the camper shell on the back of the truck.

"I've been camping before," Gage replied, moving things around and barely paying any attention to her.

"Backcountry camping?"

"Yes."

"In the Badlands?"

He hefted out a sigh, stopped what he was doing and turned to her. He folded his arms over his chest, which was a distraction for a moment or two. The cuff of his T-shirt ended right at a bulge of muscle, made more impressive by the crossed-arm pose. Something wild and alarming fluttered low in her stomach.

Which wasn't important when he was talking about hiking without a permit and without taking the appropriate safety precautions.

"Sweetheart, my father left me in the Badlands for seven nights when I was seven years old. I can handle this. So can you." Then he went back to his rummaging, pulling out one backpack and then another. They were bigger backpacks than the one she'd brought— these were clearly designed for backcountry camping.

"Put anything you brought that you'll need in the

green one," he said, as if he hadn't just confided something truly awful about his childhood.

Since Felicity didn't know what to say, she did as she was told. She pulled out the things she'd need: a dry set of clothes and a sweatshirt, her knife, hat, water bottle and water treatment supplies.

They were silent as she added her things to the backpack Gage had given her. He shouldered his pack, then helped her with hers, working with her to adjust the straps so it hit her where it should.

"You ready?"

She nodded, though it was a lie. She didn't think she'd ever be ready for being framed for murder. For hiking, illegally and ill prepared, through the Badlands with Gage Wyatt.

But here she was, and she'd have to face up to it. Ready or not.

GAGE THOUGHT HE'D managed to escape the uncomfortable piece of his childhood he hadn't meant to share with her. He didn't talk to anyone about his father's rituals. The initiations, the tests. Not even Brady, because though they'd had to go through them at the same times, what with being born on the same day and all, Ace had always kept them separate.

None of his brothers had ever truly discussed it. They mentioned it and laid out the bare facts when need be. But there was no looking into what it had felt like to jump through Ace's hoops.

Gage had no interest in ever going *there*.

"Why did he do it?" Felicity asked, as though she could read his thoughts.

Gage shrugged. If he never discussed it with people who'd understand, he sure wasn't going to discuss it with Felicity. But as they hiked, using a topography map and GPS tracker and his own internal sense of the land, silence ate away at his resolve to forget he'd ever brought it up.

"He called it our initiation," Gage grumbled, stopping their progress to determine if they should head east or go ahead and climb the column of rock in front of them.

"Initiation to what?"

"To the Sons." *To the Wyatt dynasty.* Gage pointed at the map, his father's voice echoing in his ears. He had to point at the map so he didn't give in to the urge to cover his ears with his hands and block out Ace's insidious voice. "What do you think? Around or over?"

Felicity peered over his shoulder. She'd fixed a baseball hat on her head and pulled her hair through the hole in the back. She'd tied her windbreaker around her waist. Underneath she wore a dark red T-shirt. She'd always been a shade too skinny, but working at the park had packed some muscle on her.

She looked more capable park ranger than inconsequential waif. It was a good look for her, one he had no business noticing at all, let alone here and now.

"Looks like around will be better," she said, reaching over his shoulder and tapping her finger on the paper. "Best place to camp is going to be over in this quadrant."

He took her advice, ignoring the flowery scent of her shampoo or deodorant or something that shouldn't be distracting but was.

They started around the column of rock. The sun was high in the sky, beating down on them. It would have been a good time to stop for water, but it seemed like a better idea to find a good spot to camp.

As far away from this conversation as possible.

"Did you want to be in the Sons?"

"Of course not," Gage snapped at the unexpected question that felt more like a dagger than a curiosity.

"I mean, when you were little. When you didn't know any better."

"I always knew better." You didn't spend most of your childhood watching your father threaten your mother's life—knowing she got pregnant over and over to keep him from going through with it—then watch her lose everything when her body simply couldn't carry another child into this world.

And you couldn't believe it was the right way of the world when you had an older brother like Jamison, who had spent his first five years with Grandma Pauline, telling you the world could be good and right.

"I'm sorry," Felicity said after a while, her voice almost swallowed by the wind. Unfortunately, not enough for him to miss it. He didn't want her apologies, or this black feeling inside of him that threatened to take his focus off where it needed to be.

He ignored her sorry and these old memories, and focused on one step in front of the other. It wasn't the first time in his life he'd counted his steps, watched his feet slap down on scrub brush. He'd thought those days were over.

But was anything ever really over? Ace could die and

there would still be the mark he'd left on hundreds—if not thousands—of people.

And first on that list were six boys with the Wyatt name who had to live with what they'd come from.

"Do you know anything more about... It's just I never knew my mother. When they placed me with the Knights they said she was dead. I don't know how. I thought I didn't want to know. No. I *don't* want to know what happened to her or why. But this connects to my father. This half sister I didn't know I had and who's now dead. Who was her mother? Did my father beat her like he beat me?"

"Jamison's working on it," Gage said, trying to infuse his words with gentleness. What terrible questions to have to ask yourself.

"It should be me. I should go up to my father and ask him those things."

"Well, maybe you can at some point."

"Some point when I'm not going to get arrested, you mean?" she demanded irritably.

"Yeah, that's what I mean."

She sighed heavily next to him. "I don't ever want to talk to him."

Gage gave her a sideways glance. She wasn't just certain, she was *vehement*. Her jaw was set, her gaze was flat and those words were final.

"Then let Jamison do the research on the woman and your father."

She wrinkled her nose, looking at her feet as they walked. "Isn't that cowardly?"

"There's nothing cowardly about your family helping you out, Felicity. Where would Jamison or Cody be if they hadn't let each other help? Where would Cody and Nina be if you hadn't helped them?"

Felicity frowned, but she nodded. "Water," she said, stopping their hike and shrugging off her pack. Gage did the same. They took a few sips from their water bottles and passed a bag of beef jerky back and forth. When they were done, Felicity dutifully sealed the empty bag in a plastic zipper bag and stored it in her pack. Ever the park ranger.

"Ready?"

She nodded, and they started hiking again, in silence for a very long time. When Felicity spoke again, he could tell it was a question she'd been turning over in her mind.

"How do we prove I didn't do it if we're all the way out here?"

Gage didn't know exactly how to respond. He'd promised Felicity the Wyatts wouldn't take over and leave her in the dark, but the nice thing about leaving people in the dark was they couldn't take actions that might undermine what you were doing until it was too late.

Still, a promise was a promise.

"This is just step one."

"Step one?"

"When they come to arrest you, the story will be you went backcountry camping to get your head on straight. By the time they send a team out to find you—if they even do, they might wait—you'll be gone."

"Gone where?"

"That's step two. Let's focus on getting through step one."

"Gone *where*, Gage?"

He sighed. There was no way getting around it. "Back to the scene of the crime."

Chapter Six

It was a very strange thing to set up camp with Gage. As a ranger Felicity had done this with all sorts of people—friends, coworkers, strangers.

But never a Wyatt.

Which shouldn't be different or feel weird. The Wyatt brothers were her friends. She'd shared meals and *life* with them.

Trying to convince herself this was all normal came to a screeching halt when they had everything unpacked. "Wait. There's only one tent."

She looked at Gage, a vague panic beginning to beat in the center of her chest. He merely raised an eyebrow, the sunset haloing him in a fiery red that made the panic drum harder.

"Safest if we're in the same tent," he said after a while.

She wasn't sure how to describe the sound that escaped her—something strangled and squeaky all at the same time.

"Problem?"

"No. No. *No.* Of course there's no *problem.*" There

was a catastrophic, cataclysmic event happening inside of her, but no *problem*.

"Afraid I'm going to try something?"

She tried a laugh, which came out more like a bird screech. "I like Brady," she blurted, as if that had anything to do with *anything*.

"I'm very well aware."

"And you like…" She thought of the women she'd seen Gage with. Rare. He never brought girlfriends home.

Still, every once in a while for a birthday or something, the Wyatt boys and Knight girls would get together in town. Go to a bar or something. Gage's dates were always… "You like breasts."

He choked out a laugh. "Yeah. Crazy that way. Hate to break it to you, you have those."

She looked down, even though of course she *knew* she had breasts. Not ever on full display or anything, but yes, she had them. They were there. And why was *she* looking at them while her face turned what had to be as red as the sunset?

Had Gage noticed her breasts? Why did that make her feel anything other than horrified?

"If it bothers you, I can sleep outside."

"It doesn't *bother* me." She was pretty sure she'd have the same ridiculous reaction to sharing a tent with Brady. Sharing a tent was *intimate* and she didn't have an intimate relationship with…

Anyone.

But there was one tent up, and perfectly rational reasons for them both sleeping in it. It would be fine, regardless of the jangling nerves bouncing around inside of her. She'd survived those for almost her whole life, even learned to overcome them for the most part.

She was struggling today because people thought she was a murderer. Someone was trying to make it look like she was a murderer. It was messing with her brain in many different ways, not just one.

"Hungry? I can cook up some dinner," Gage said, acting as though this was normal and fine and not at all scary and weird.

"I hope you know you can't have a campfire. Backpacking stove only. We can't go breaking every park rule just because we're in trouble."

Gage didn't respond. His mouth quirked, his eyebrow raised, and he pulled a backpacking stove out of his pack.

Brady never did that arched eyebrow thing. Brady's lip never quirked in that sardonic way at her. And his eyes never went quite that shade of brown, as if there was a hidden intensity under all that...

What on earth was *wrong* with her?

She was camping with Gage to avoid being arrested for a murder she darn well didn't commit.

"Park rules are important," she insisted, though he hadn't argued. "People try to get away with all sorts of things that hurt the cultural and ecological integrity of the land and threaten the safety of the park."

"Believe it or not, I'm well versed in what people will try to get away with."

"I suppose you think your laws are more important than mine?"

He cocked his head as he set up the stove and measured out water into a pot. "Why do you assume that?"

"Because…" She trailed off because she didn't have a good answer. Gage had never given any indication he thought his job was more important than hers. Nor had any of the other significant people in her life. Certainly she'd had a few park visitors who liked to sneer at how not important she was to them, but—

"Sit. Eat. Stop…that."

She blinked at him, startled by him interrupting her thoughts. "Stop what?"

"Whatever it is you're doing standing there with your mind whirling so hard I can *hear* it."

"You cannot hear my brain."

"Near enough. If you're going to occupy yourself, might as well focus on the problem at hand, not how much more you'd rather spend a night in a tent with Brady than me."

"That isn't what…" But she couldn't explain in a way that made any sense.

She acquiesced and sat, then took the tin bowl he offered her. She *was* hungry. Tired, too. And though she knew he couldn't *hear* her brain moving, it felt like it was galloping around at rapid pace, and she wasn't sure why.

She'd sleep under the same canvas roof as Gage Wyatt. So what?

So someone wanted to frame her for murder—she had a big group of people willing to help her prove she hadn't actually done it. She had Gage to make sure she didn't spend a night in jail.

They ate in silence, watching the sun go down. It might have been peaceful, but she didn't feel any kind of peace. Just anxiety and something else. Something edgier and sharper than the sheer manic ping-ponging of anxiety.

"He doesn't get you, Felicity," Gage said quietly, staring intently at the bowl in his lap as the last whispers of light faded away. "I'm not saying that to be cruel. I just think you could find a lot better focus for your... It's not going anywhere."

It took her a minute to realize he was talking about Brady, and then another minute before full realization hit.

She couldn't find the words to argue.

"He can't ever..." Gage swore under his breath. "Brady is too noble to ever see you as anything other than Duke's foster daughter."

It should hurt. She should be outraged and embarrassed and feel horrible. Intellectually, she told herself that. But there was no crushing pain of a heart breaking. No heated moral outrage that he didn't know what he was talking about.

She was under no illusion Brady looked at her and saw the real *her*. She'd never asked herself why she liked him anyway, why she convinced herself he might someday.

It wasn't comfortable that Gage had been the one to point out having a crush on Brady didn't make much sense. Her face was on fire, and she couldn't find a way to defuse her embarrassment.

She didn't think Gage's words were cruel. In fact, she knew he was trying to be kind. Trying to show her it was never happening.

She was in the middle of the stark Badlands with

his twin brother of all people telling her things she already knew.

Because she did know. She told herself she didn't. She told herself she was holding out hope for Brady to come around, but she was aware of the truth.

Brady was safe. In more ways than one. Safe because he wasn't edgy or volatile. Because he was exactly what Gage said. Too noble to ever consider one of Duke Knight's daughters in a romantic way.

She didn't want Brady in reality. She liked the idea of him. Liked pining after him. She could tell herself she had normal feelings for a guy and never actually have to deal with it. *Know* she'd never ever have to deal with him reciprocating.

The truth was Brady was never going to break his code of honor and see her as different—and she'd known that.

She'd liked him *because* she'd known that.

"Maybe I don't need him to get me," she managed to say, when what she really meant was, *Maybe I don't want anyone to know me.*

Gage shrugged. "None of my business," he muttered.

Which was more than true. Totally and utterly true.

She couldn't for the life of her understand why he'd brought it up.

GAGE DID NOT sleep well. The tent was small, and it smelled like a woman. He'd never camped with a woman before.

Never will again.

Maybe if you were all wrapped up in the woman it would be nice enough, but with a platonic friend you had some more than *companionable* feelings for it was too crowded, too all-encompassing. Who'd want to be right on top of anyone like this?

He looked at Felicity, who was fast asleep only a few feet away from him.

She was too pale—he could tell that even in the odd cast the faint light made against the blue nylon of the tent. Her freckles were more pronounced than usual, and though she slept deeply and quietly there were shadows under her eyes.

He felt a stab of guilt, a twist of worry that he'd done something rash without fully considering the consequences. He'd put her through too much just so she didn't have to spend a few nights in jail.

Jail. Whether it was a holding cell or the facility Ace was at, she'd look worse in there. She was an outdoorsy person. Better to be hiking through the rigorous Badlands backcountry than locked in a cell, that he knew for sure.

Thunder rolled in the distance, making the tent seem all that more intimate.

Felicity's eyes blinked open, and he knew he should probably look away. Try to pretend he wasn't a creeper staring at her while she slept.

But he didn't.

Worse, she stared right back. For ticking seconds that had his breath backing up in his lungs. Her green eyes were dark and reminded him of Christmas trees, of all damn things.

"It's raining," she said quietly, still holding his gaze.

"So it is."

She pushed herself up into a sitting position. Her red

hair tumbled behind her, the rubber band she'd had it fastened back with yesterday falling onto the floor between them. She didn't seem to notice.

Gage couldn't help it. He reached out, picked up the band and held it out to her. She took it with one hand, patting the unruly state of her tangles with the other.

He watched a little too closely as she bundled it back behind her, fastening the band around it again. Then way too closely at the way her shirt pulled over her breasts.

He looked up at the top of the tent and blew out a breath. Rain pattered there and he focused on counting the drops, on considering how heavy the rain was and if they should hike today or stay put. Anything that wasn't this totally pointless, impossible attraction to the woman head over heels in love with his twin brother.

Yeah, it figured he was *that* messed up.

"If we go out today, we'll have to be very careful," Felicity said primly.

He didn't dare look at her, because something about that park-ranger-lecturing voice really did something to him.

He was *seriously* messed up in the head.

"You know, the Badlands are made up of bentonite clay and volcanic ash. Which means, when it rains the rocks become very slip—" She stopped herself, frowning at him. "What are you grinning at?"

He shook his head, trying to wipe the smile off his face. "Nothing."

"You're grinning about *something*."

"You don't want to hear it from me."

"What does *that* mean?" she demanded, hands fisted on her hips, though she was kneeling.

He should keep his mouth shut. Go outside into the storm if he had to, but that would be stupid. Almost as stupid as the words that tumbled out of his mouth. "I just remember when you couldn't string two sentences together—especially around a Wyatt—without turning bright red and running to hide in your room. It's nice you found your passion. Even if it's bentite clay."

"Bentonite."

"Right. Sure." He couldn't help laughing. "You're doing all right, Felicity. That's all I'm saying."

"Why wouldn't I want to hear that from you?"

"Anyone else notice?"

She squared her shoulders as if gearing up for a fight. "I don't need anyone to notice."

"But I did notice, is all I'm saying. And I like it." Which was better than everything he wanted to say, like *and I'd like my hands all over you.*

Their gazes met and held. She opened her mouth as if she was going to say something to that, but no sound emerged.

He should say something. A joke. God, he should tell a joke, but it was as if every coping mechanism he'd built to defuse a tense situation had evaporated simply because he'd spent the night under the same fabric roof as her.

She cleared her throat and looked away. "What's the plan? It isn't safe to stay here with a storm. You do have a weather radio, don't you?"

"I wouldn't think it'd be safe to go hiking through a

storm, either," he said, opening his pack and rummaging around until he found the radio. He tossed it to her.

She fiddled with it and he unzipped the door. They had a rain flap, and he could feel the wind blowing in the opposite direction. He could use some fresh air and a glimpse at how heavy the storm was looking.

He heard the static of the weather radio, then the low, monotonous tones of someone going on about warnings and watches.

"Gage."

"What?" He reached for his gun, sure that the gravity and fear in her voice meant there was someone coming, a physical, human threat. But as he turned to her, she was pointing at the sky.

And a very distinct funnel cloud.

Chapter Seven

For precious seconds, every training Felicity had ever received on the subject of what to do in case of bad weather simply fell out of her head. Her mind was blank as she watched the distinct form of a funnel cloud whirl on the horizon.

It was far away now, but it wouldn't stay that way.

Fear and dread skittered up her spine. She knew fear and dread—had been born into it. It was acknowledging the feelings when reality sank in—whether it was the violent look in her father's eye or a funnel cloud, first was fear.

Then, she'd learned to act.

"We need to break down the tent and get to lower ground, but not too low. More rain could come in right after it and we don't want to be caught in any flash flooding," she shouted above the sound of the wind and rain.

"You load up both packs and I'll take care of the tent," Gage said. It felt less like an order and more like two people working together to survive.

Lightning flashed, something sizzled far too close,

and thunder boomed immediately after—the hard crack echoing in her ears.

Her hands shook as she shoved the weather radio back into Gage's pack and hurried to roll the sleeping bags into their sacks. He had the tent down in record time, which left her open to the elements. She pulled up the hood of her windbreaker.

Fat drops fell from the sky on their packs and their bodies. Felicity looked at the funnel cloud. It was still there. Closer.

"Rain is a good sign," she said, knowing it was more hope than reality. "It means the funnel itself is still a long way off."

"Is it?" Gage returned, shoving the packed tent into his pack. "None of this feels like too good a sign." He settled a cowboy hat on his head and looked around. "Where to, Ranger?"

She'd looked at the topographic map when they'd camped last night and oriented herself to the area. She'd listened to the weather radio and tried to get an idea of the trajectory of the storm. "Follow me."

Though they hiked in silence, the storm raged around them. Thunder booming, lightning cracking and sizzling too close. She let out a screech against her will when she *saw* lightning strike in front of her.

"Steady," Gage said, his voice low and close to her ear. "All that slippery benzonite."

"Bentonite," she ground out as her heart beat so hard against her chest it felt like a hammer trying to break through her rib cage.

The rain slowed, the noise quieted. The air got still and the sky was tinged an unearthly green. Felicity walked, forcing herself to breathe slowly in and out as she began to shake with fear.

"Don't look back," Gage ordered.

She listened, because she knew what was coming. Especially when the still silence suddenly turned into a slow-building roar.

"We should take cover," Felicity shouted over the thundering wind. Dust swirled around them and she had to close her eyes against the debris flying into her face. "We can't keep walking."

"There isn't any cover."

"Kneel. Put your pack over your head—just like tornado drills in school."

"I—"

There was the sickening sound of a blow and a grunt. Felicity whirled around and out of the corner of her eye saw Gage go down. He stumbled, rolled and hit the ground too hard.

He was swearing when she skidded down next to him, which she'd take as a good sign. Swearing meant breathing and consciousness.

"Don't move," she ordered, still having to yell over the sound of wind and rock.

He swore some more, most of it lost to the roaring tornado around them, while he followed her instructions and didn't move.

He was bleeding from a nasty cut on his temple, but it didn't look deep enough to worry over a severe head injury.

"Can you roll onto your stomach?"

He didn't respond, but he rolled over.

"Loosen your straps," she instructed, already scoot-

ing up so she could reach his pack. "I'm going to pull
your pack up to cover the back of your head."

Small rocks and dust pelted her, seemingly from all
sides, though nothing like what had taken Gage down.
He grunted as he got the straps off his arm, and she
tugged the pack up to cover the most vulnerable part
of his head.

Then she lay down next to him and situated her own
pack over the back of her head and neck. She closed her
eyes and focused on her breathing.

It reminded her too much of a time she'd tried to forget. The first four years of her life. They were a blur and
she had always been happy to leave them that way. Eyes
closed, careful breathing, and terror ripping through her
while noise raged around her...

She could remember, clearly, hiding in the back of
a utility closet. It had smelled like bleach, and she'd
scrambled behind mops and brooms. He'd found her.
The creak of the door, the spill of light that didn't quite
make it to her.

And still unerringly he'd stepped forward and
grabbed her by her shirt and dragged her out of the
closet. For a few seconds, she was back there, struggling against her father, against the inevitable.

Then a hand closed over hers. In the here and now
and roaring winds. She opened her eyes to look at Gage.
Blood was trickling down his face since he was lying
on the uninjured side. And he was trying to give her
some comfort.

"I've survived worse," he rasped over the sound of
the tornado.

"Have you?"

"Human nature is worse than Mother Nature."

Felicity shook her head as much as she could in her prone position. "You don't know enough about Mother Nature then, Gage."

She had no idea if he'd heard her, but she didn't let go of his hand, and he didn't let go of hers. As the world heaved around them, they held on to each other.

She wasn't sure how long they lay there or how much longer after that the roar faded into a light wind and pattering rain. The rumble of thunder was distant.

Eventually she felt the groundwater begin to seep into her pants and knew they had to get up. She gave Gage's hand a squeeze before letting it go, then got to her knees. She looked around.

The Badlands stretched out before them looking no different than it had before the tornado had blown through. In the distance, the sun peeked out from the clouds, its rays shining down in clear lines.

Felicity let out a long breath. They'd survived.

"Hopefully, it stayed out here," she murmured to herself. Out here in the Badlands, nature took its course and few things were irrevocably harmed. Tornadoes and extreme thunderstorms were *part* of the shape and heart of the landscape.

But Pennington County and the reservation were in the path of the tornado. People and things could be irrevocably damaged. People and things she loved, even.

But before she could worry about that, she had to worry about Gage.

She tugged the pack off him. "Can you sit up?"

He didn't answer in words. He rolled to his side and

leveraged himself up, wincing and swearing. Then swearing some more when she moved to help him.

"Don't stand yet," she said, pushing him against the rock behind him. "Sit right here so I can clean you up."

"You're beautiful. Both of you."

She startled for a second, then shook her head, realizing he was attempting a joke despite the fact blood still oozed from the cut on his temple. "That's some head injury."

"I see double. But at least I'm not blind, right?"

"Not exactly the joke I'd make right now, Gage."

"That's my job. Make the joke no one else would make. Get a little laugh to diffuse the terror."

She felt both relief he was trying to make light of the situation and a bone-deep worry at how much blood was on his face, how deep the cut was under further inspection, and the fact he hadn't even tried to get to his feet.

She rummaged in her pack and retrieved the first-aid kit. She couldn't waste potable water on washing blood off his face, so she had to hope the antibacterial wipes would be enough. She crouched in front of him with some regret.

"Not to sound like a cliché, but this is going to hurt."

IT DAMN WELL DID. He hissed out a breath as she pressed the antibacterial wipe to the nasty wound on his head.

He didn't know what had hit him, a rock probably. It had been sharp and hard and taken him down in the same way. His neck and back hurt, probably from the fall.

And the fact you aren't getting any younger.

"I'm sorry," she murmured, wiping the blood off his face. The wound throbbed and stung in turns, but Felicity's fingers were on his face and that wasn't so bad.

"A pretty woman is patching me up. I'll survive."

Her worried expression transformed into a frown. "Stop saying that."

"What?"

"Beautiful and pretty. You don't need to suck up to me. I'm going to tend your wound either way."

"Don't you think you're beautiful and pretty?"

She stared at him for a good minute, her mouth hanging slightly open. "I… Oh, just shut up and let me do this."

He smiled, couldn't help it. Irritated Felicity made him feel better.

No matter her annoyance, her hands were gentle as she wiped up as much blood as she could and then applied the bandage. She touched his forehead and his cheekbones as if checking for more damage.

He watched her, woozy enough that he didn't even try to hide that his attention was on her face. On her, fully and wholly.

She finally looked him in the eye, opening her mouth to say something. But it evaporated before any sound came out. For seconds they simply stared at each other, silent and still, stuck in the moment.

He couldn't remember the last time he'd felt this. Middle school maybe. The desperate need to *do* something. Make a move, because it felt almost as if he'd cease to exist if he didn't. A profound fear of coming up short left him frozen in place.

Because he wasn't Brady, and Brady was always the better option. Gage was more of a backup.

Felicity deserved first prize, even if that particular prize didn't have a clue of the woman she'd become.

Felicity straightened, stepped back and wiped her hands on her pants. She looked around. The rain had tapered off, and though clouds mostly covered the sun, it occasionally broke out in soft rays as the clouds moved with the furious wind.

"We need help. We need cell service." She nodded with each sentence as if making her own mental list.

"Good luck on that front."

"We should consolidate to one pack. Your vision is messed up so your balance will be off. I'll carry one pack—water is most important. We're going to be slow moving, but I know where to go. We can hopefully get to cell range before nightfall."

"I can carry my own pack. My vision is fine." He blinked a few times. The doubling came and went, but he could walk just fine.

"No. It isn't smart. We have to be smart."

Gage struggled to his feet, ignoring the wave of dizziness and making sure not to reach out for balance. She was watching him too closely and he needed to prove to her he was fine so she didn't worry. So she didn't try to help.

"One pack," she muttered, crouching in front of the two packs, and pulling things out and shoving other things back into hers. "We'll mark this place on the map and come back for what we leave."

He watched her move—each gesture jerky. Each sentence sounded a little more... *Tight* was the only word he could think of. Like there was some invisible string pulling her in tighter and tighter.

Until she broke. Except Felicity wasn't going to break. He could see that as she babbled on and on about what they had to do. She would keep that rein on control through this whole thing, then be left with a hell of a breaking point when all was said and done.

He knew her well enough to realize she'd see that as a failure, especially if she broke in front of their family or whoever finally picked them up.

He wanted her to break now. She'd still be embarrassed that it was in front of him, but it wouldn't be as bad as Duke or her sisters or the whole Wyatt clan.

"Felicity. Take a breath."

"I'm breathing," she retorted, as he'd predicted. She made a move to sling the newly rearranged pack onto her shoulders, but he grabbed it and pulled it off her.

"Hey, I said I was going to—"

He dropped it on the ground to the side of them and stepped toward her. She scrabbled back, almost tripping in the process.

"What are you doing?" she screeched.

He didn't answer, because the more she worked herself up the better chance she had of actually letting it go.

Gently he folded her into his arms. "We're okay," he murmured. He rubbed a hand up and down her back, cupped the back of her head and held her there against him as she struggled a bit. He understood the manic look in her eyes, understood what she needed to do before they moved on. "We're okay."

"I know it," she squeaked, wriggling against his hold. But her breathing was ragged and it only took a few more seconds of holding her there for her to break. A sob, the slow surrendering of her forehead to his chest.

"That's it," he murmured, resting his cheek against her hair. "Let it out."

She did. As he held her there, hand in her hair, cheek on her hair. Soft and curling against his own skin. He wanted with an ache he didn't fully understand because it was so deep, so wide, so *nonsensical*.

Still, he held her while she cried, and though time wasn't in their favor he didn't rush her. He let her have her moment.

Finally, she pulled away with a sniffle, wiping at her cheeks with her palms. "I'm stronger than that," she muttered.

"Nothing weak about crying. I mean, I know that goes against Grandma Pauline's code of badass conduct, but I've helped too many people in too many dire situations to not know crying is essential sometimes."

"Eva always said so. More to Sarah than the rest of us."

"Sarah tries too hard to be tough," Gage returned, speaking of the youngest Knight foster.

"She comes by it honestly, between being Duke's second hand on the ranch and helping Dev when he needs it."

"Maybe we should lock her and Dev in a room and tell them we won't let them out till one of them shows an emotion that isn't categorized as pissed-off grumpy."

Felicity chuckled, which had been his hope. She sucked in a breath and let it out loudly. "All right. We've got a long way to hike."

"You're in charge."

She gave him a suspicious look. "Really?"

"You know where you're going and, frankly, you're better with that kind of map than I am. So, lead the way, Ranger. You'll get us where we need to be."

She blew out a breath and nodded. "All right. Follow me and be careful. One injury is enough."

She was right about that.

Chapter Eight

The hike was brutal. The rocks were slippery, and they couldn't find much grass to walk on instead. Added to that, no matter what Gage said, he was clearly not at 100 percent. He was slow and he'd stopped arguing about her being the only one carrying a backpack.

Felicity hated to admit it, but crying it out had certainly calmed her. She felt exhausted but determined. Worried but not panicked. They would get where they needed to go, even if Gage wasn't 100 percent.

Because she was.

She eyed the sun, and how quickly it was heading for the horizon. Maybe they'd have to hike at dark for a bit. Dangerous, but so was surviving a tornado blasting through the Badlands. Which they'd done with only minor injuries.

"How you holding up?" she asked. Though she wanted to look back and get an idea for herself, they were in a particular slippery canyon area. One wrong step would mean a nasty fall. So, she listened carefully to his response and any pain that might be threading through his voice.

"Fine and dandy, gorgeous," he said breezily.

She gripped the straps of her pack, trying to tamp down her irritation. "Stop that."

"But see, now that I know it irritates you I *can't* stop."

She kept her gaze on the landscape in front of her. If he was joking around he couldn't be that bad off. "This isn't a joking situation, Gage."

"Well, it's not a joke. It's me saying something true that irritates you for some reason," he returned so *reasonably*, as if it was reasonable when it wasn't at all. "Anything can be a joking situation if you're funny enough."

She knew there had to be a good response for that, but she couldn't find it. Not even a lecture about jokes.

Both their phones began to chirp, and they stopped in their tracks.

"We should probably keep hiking and get to the ranger station before dark," Felicity said. No matter how badly she wanted to check their phones, they were running out of good hiking time.

"People are worried about us, Felicity," Gage returned.

When she turned around to lecture him, he already had his phone to his ear. She eyed the sun again, then took out her own phone.

She had fifty text messages, ten missed calls and five voice mails. She winced, then began to type out a text to everyone at the ranch that she was okay. Something quick, then they could be on their way again.

But Gage swore, so vehemently that Felicity stopped midtap.

"What is it?"

He shook his head, held up a finger and returned the phone to his ear. "Jamison. You've got to be kidding me with that message," he said viciously into the receiver. He paused, his expression fury personified as he listened to whatever Jamison was saying in return. "Yes, we're fine. What's being *done*?"

He was silent for so long Felicity had to bite her tongue to keep from demanding answers immediately. He was getting them. She had to be patient.

"Stay put. Take care of your own. We'll handle us." He ended the conversation and shoved his phone into his pocket.

When he didn't immediately speak, she stopped holding back. "Gage. Tell me what is going on."

He shook his head, his jaw working for a few seconds before he finally spoke. "The tornado hit the jail."

Felicity felt as if the ground fell out from underneath her and she was descending through an endless canyon. Though she was standing on her own two feet, the sound of the long-gone tornado roared in her ears. "What?"

"It hit the jail in Pennington. Ace is unaccounted for."

"As in dead or as in…"

"Escaped. He's not the only one." Gage shoved a hand through his unruly dust-covered hair. "But he's the one we have to worry about."

"All right. We have to get back," Felicity said, doing her best to sound calm and sure. "Back to the ranches, work out a game plan with everyone."

"If our theory about Ace being involved in framing you for murder is correct, he's coming for *you*, Felicity."

That revelation hit hard, but she wouldn't let it show. She straightened her shoulders and firmed her mouth. "If he's behind this trumped-up murder charge, hasn't he already hurt me enough? He won't be after me—he already got me. He'll be after one of you."

Gage stared at her for a long time before finally inclining his head. "Fair point."

It felt like a victory when none of this was a victory. It was only problem after increasingly threatening problem.

"Okay, we head back to the ranch," Felicity said. "Someone can pick us up at the ranger station. It's better if we're all there, working together to keep everyone safe from Ace. Especially Brianna and Gigi." Cody and Nina's daughter and Liza's half sister had already been through enough.

"If you show up at either ranch, you'll be arrested."

Felicity tried to play off the wince inside of her. "I... I can handle that. You should be with your family." She tried to smile, though she knew it faltered.

She could handle jail. She could handle it because she knew she was innocent. It was fine. Okay, *fine* was an overstatement. But it would be bearable. She could bear it. She could. Because eventually the truth would come out.

Eventually.

"I'm not letting you go to jail, Felicity. Not ever."

She blinked at his sheer vehemence. Her entire stomach seemed to flip over at the look in his eyes.

She didn't know what that was. Didn't want to know because it scared her. It...vibrated through her. Too big and too much.

"It wouldn't be so bad," she choked out.

"If they convicted you, do you understand how many years you could be stuck in there? Do you have any idea

how long it would be before you could come out here?"
He pointed to the land around them. "Think about it—
you'll come to the same conclusion I did."

She looked around at the Badlands, at the vast gray,
moody sky. At her heart, laid out in the world around
them, even when it did things like throw a tornado at
her. "I wouldn't survive," she murmured.

She didn't need anyone to understand her, to see her
as the woman she'd become because *she* knew who and
what she'd built herself into. Being a somewhat solitary
person meant she didn't need people to constantly vali-
date her choices or tell her she was doing great.

But she hadn't realized how nice it would be to have
one person actually…get her. Not in some demanding
way, not showing off how much. Just a simple, true
understanding.

She didn't know how to fully accept that it was *Gage*,
who was nothing like her. He was all confidence, with
a certain brashness that *was* charming but certainly
nothing she understood.

How could he look at her and see…it all?

She didn't want to know. She didn't want to think
about it, but all she could seem to do was stand here
and stare at him, something big and bright and terrifying shifting in her chest.

Ace was free, and she was wanted for murder. That
was her focus right now.

Or so she told herself.

FELICITY LOOKED AT him like his understanding was some
kind of gift when it couldn't be. When his father was on
the loose, with everyone he loved a target.

Including her.

Not that Gage was *in love* with her. Liking and appreciating someone and being attracted to someone did not add up to *love*.

Besides, loving anyone while Ace existed was a pain and fear he didn't intend to take on. He'd watched Jamison and Cody survive, barely, and maybe they were happier on this side of things, but how could that fear of Ace really ever go away?

It couldn't. It didn't. Not until the man was dead. Gage was half convinced he'd never die.

"All right," Felicity said at length. She sounded shaky at first, then her voice strengthened as she spoke. "Still, you're hurt. You need to go back and have that looked at."

"Hey, I can still see. I can still walk. Cody did a lot more with a lot worse."

"Because he had to," Felicity said with a gentleness that made his skin tight and prickly.

"Are you suggesting I leave you out here on your own?" he asked, trying to keep the sheer volume of rage out of his voice. All that rage wasn't directed at her—it was at Ace, and himself—but he was in danger of losing it anyway.

"It wouldn't be the first time I've hiked, camped and survived the Badlands on my own, Gage."

"It won't be *this* time, either," he returned. "Listen to me. There's no splitting up here. No leaving anyone on their own. That isn't how you beat Ace. Haven't Jamison and Cody proven that? We have to work together best we can. And whether you like it or not, you and me are together for this one."

She didn't respond as she chewed on her lip and mulled it over. He couldn't stand the quiet, so he kept on her.

"Jamison and Cody are going to protect Liza, Gigi, Nina and Brianna in Bonesteel. The rest of my brothers will be at the ranches with Grandma Pauline and your family. It makes sense for us to keep to our plan. We have to prove you didn't murder this woman."

He took a step toward her, told himself at the last minute not to grab her hands like he wanted to. "Just think. If we prove this—we can go home to the ranches. Ace being on the loose makes things nerve-racking. But it doesn't change our objective. It doesn't change what *we* have to do."

"I don't want to be the reason you're not working with your brothers on this."

He didn't understand the things she did to him. He'd avoided personal vulnerability all his life because, good Lord, life was too tough to be worried about weakness. She was tough, but she was also…this: the broken little kid underneath all that tough exterior.

He understood it too well.

"We're in this together, Felicity. Now, how long will it take us to hike to your cabin?"

"Days."

He knew it was long, but he'd been hoping doable. They couldn't hike days. Especially after leaving one pack behind.

"Another park ranger would give us a ride if we get to the visitor center," she said, though she sounded uncertain.

"Are there any park rangers you trust? That you're willing to put in the path of both the police *and* Ace?"

She wilted. "No."

He didn't want one of his brothers making the trek, which had been the original plan. With Ace on the loose, they needed to stick together, protect Grandma and the Knights. Having one or even two come pick them up was risking too much.

"What about Cody's group?" Felicity asked. "Nina said there was some woman who helped them, and Brady mentioned a doctor who video chatted him through patching Cody up. Call Cody and see if they can help. Even if they can just offer a ride if we can meet them a little south of the visitor center."

"If they can't, he'll come himself."

"Not if you remind him his job is to protect Nina and Brianna."

It wasn't the worst idea. Besides, what would it hurt to ask?

"We have to keep hiking, though," Felicity insisted. "The minute we lose daylight, we're in for trouble. I had to prioritize water over sleeping bags and dry clothes in the pack. We can eat and we can drink, but we won't have any way to protect ourselves if another storm comes through."

He studied the sky. Another storm seemed more likely than not. Hopefully, they'd survived their one and only tornado, but rain and lightning could be just as dangerous in the wrong circumstances.

"All right," he finally acquiesced. Her plan was sound, and it was a compromise between what they both wanted to do. "I'll text Cody, then we'll get moving."

"You text him. I'm going to change your bandage." She dropped her pack and rummaged around in it while he texted Cody to ask for backup south of the visitor center.

She pulled off the bandage slowly, clearly trying to keep the adhesive from hurting his skin.

It was hard to focus on the throbbing pain when her chest was in his face and he had much more entertaining things to distract himself with.

"I'm worried about infection more than the cut itself," she said conversationally as she used another stinging wipe around the wound.

He bit his tongue to keep from hissing or groaning in pain, then let out a slow, steady breath as she smoothed a new bandage over the cut.

"There." She cupped his chin and tilted his head up as she examined the bandage. She gave a little nod, clearly satisfied with her work. She brushed at his scruffy jaw, presumably trying to get dirt and debris out of his whiskers, but her other hand gently traced the bandage.

He was sure she was making sure no dirt had gotten into the bandage, but it felt like a caress. Like she cared. And his libido certainly didn't seem to know the difference between *trying to stave off infection* and *trying to get in his pants*.

Irritated, he squirmed. "If you expect me to be able to walk straight, you're going to have to stop touching me like that."

She pulled her hand away so fast her whole body jerked and she stepped back, landing awkwardly on a rock. She started to fall backward, arms windmilling, so he grabbed her and yanked her toward him.

Which sent her bumping into him, sending *him* falling backward. Luckily, he knew how to land after a blow well enough. Unluckily, she was now sprawled on top of him.

She was on top of him, breathing a little heavily, her eyes wide and her cheeks pink. He thought not kissing her might kill him.

But she wants Brady.

"I'm going to get you out of this mess." He didn't know why he had to promise her that, to vow it here and out loud. He just had to get it out. Better than kissing her, he had to believe.

She stared at him, green eyes dark and steady, still lying on top of him, soft and warm and wonderful. "I believe you," she said quietly.

And he was doomed. So he went ahead and pressed his lips to hers anyway.

Chapter Nine

Felicity had never walked through fire before, but she was pretty sure it would feel like this. Completely enveloped by sensation.

In this case not burning to a crisp, painful and fatal, but melting into someone else entirely. Maybe it *was* fatal—she wasn't sure—but she couldn't help following it. The wild sensation of freedom like standing in the middle of grass and rock with no one else around. Just her and the wind and sky and utter glory.

Except it was Gage. *Gage.* Gage Wyatt. Kissing her. Kissing *her.*

She blinked her eyes open, trying to push herself off him. He stopped kissing her, but his hand curled around her arm, keeping her in place.

"We have to… Getting dark," she croaked.

He did his raised-eyebrow thing, and all she wanted to do was run away from him, but his big hand was still curled around her upper arm, keeping her all sprawled out against him. He was very…hard and warm and… She had to get up.

"Hike. Before dark. We need to get moving."

"You kissed me back."

"I…" She didn't know what to say to that. How to process *any* part of today. "L-let me go."

He did. Immediately. She scrabbled off him and onto her feet. She was shaky and shaken, and God knew she didn't have a clue what to say.

Gage had kissed her. Voluntarily. And…seriously. Devastatingly. Like he'd been waiting half a lifetime to do it.

Oh, boy. Oh, no.

If she went home she would be arrested for a murder she didn't commit, and Gage Wyatt had kissed her.

She *knew* she hadn't killed anyone, and as much as the world wasn't always right and good, she simply had to believe someone could prove that.

What she didn't know was how to deal with this… kiss.

She'd let Asher Kinfield kiss her when she'd worked at Mammoth Cave for a summer. It had been nothing like this. It had been kind of stiff and fumbling. Off-putting.

Not like fireworks. No, bigger than fireworks. A volcanic eruption. Destructive and totally altering.

All because of Gage Wyatt.

She looked back at him as he got to his feet. She'd jerked away not so much because of his words. More because she'd lost herself in touching him and had forgotten she was supposed to be bandaging him up, not caressing his wounds. She *had* been touching him like a lover, and she didn't know what on earth had possessed her.

Gage stared at her, his face hard and unreadable. "I'm not Brady," he said sharply.

That snapped through some of her panic. She scowled at him, insulted and maybe even hurt. She couldn't name half the feelings pulsing inside of her. "I was under no illusion you were, *Gage*."

"You sure about that?"

"Yes." She grabbed the pack and fastened it onto her back with jerky movements. She was not going to argue with him about Brady. She hadn't even *thought* of Brady until Gage had brought him up. "W-we have to m-move."

She didn't wait to see if he followed, and she refused to acknowledge her stutter. She started marching along, carefully avoiding slick spots. She was entering more familiar territory as they neared the ranger station.

She kept them away from the main road even as they approached the station. She was tired, parched and starving, but she didn't want to stop. Darkness was approaching and there was no time to stop.

So she told herself. Better than thinking about what she might have to face if they stopped.

Felicity came up short as she saw a figure in the distance. At first she thought it might be another ranger doing rounds, but the figure was wearing a baseball cap, not a park uniform.

"Just keep hiking. Act casual. Normal," Gage instructed. "It might be our ride. It might not be. If she approaches us, just act like you would with any other hiker."

Felicity swallowed at the nerves fluttering in her throat, but she nodded and kept hiking again. No matter where Felicity and Gage walked, the figure moved so their paths would cross.

When Felicity saw that she was a woman dressed all in black, with no signs of backpacking gear, she prayed to God it was someone from the secret group Cody had worked for last year.

Because if not, it was bad news indeed.

"Howdy," the woman greeted as they finally met on solid ground covered in grass. "Nice evening for a hike, isn't it?"

"Getting a little late," Felicity offered, working hard to keep her voice steady and without stutter.

"It is." The woman tipped her unnecessary sunglasses down. "You guys need a ride?" She jerked her chin in the direction of the road. "You're looking a little worse for wear, and I've got a truck not far off."

Felicity exchanged a glance with Gage.

"Sure, Shay," Gage said.

The woman smiled and winked. "Follow me, Wyatt."

Felicity blew out a breath. It was their ride, thank God. They still had a good mile walk, and exhaustion pounded at her temples. She had no idea what Gage had in mind once they got to her cabin. They'd been through a tornado, and miles and miles of hiking. All she wanted to do was sleep.

Shay led them to a big black truck with tinted windows Felicity doubted were legal. She climbed into the back of the truck anyway, Gage getting into the front seat. Gage and Shay spoke in low tones and Felicity tried to pay attention, but she couldn't stop herself from dozing as the truck began to drive.

She awoke with a start when she realized the vehicle had stopped. Shay and Gage were outside, heads together as they spoke. Felicity looked around. They were in the grove of trees not far from her cabin.

When she pushed the door open and stepped out, Gage and Shay immediately stopped talking.

Felicity frowned at them.

Gage leaned close to Shay and whispered something.

Shay nodded. "Thanks. Good luck." She smiled at Felicity as she walked back to the truck. "Especially for you."

Felicity didn't know what to say to that, but Shay was gone in a flash anyway. "What was that?" she demanded of Gage.

He shrugged, studying the trees. "Don't worry about it."

"Don't worry about... Are you... You can't..."

"Calm it down, Red."

"I'd like to punch you."

"I'd like to see you try," he returned mildly.

She was tempted. She'd convinced Tucker to teach her how to land a decent blow before she'd gone off on her first seasonal park ranger job in Kentucky. But something told her even if she threw a decent jab-cross combo, Gage would never let them land.

"Come on. Let's get to the cabin."

It was dark now, the air cool. Everything felt wrong and eerie, and she had a flash of the woman's body at the bottom of the canyon.

The woman who was apparently her sister.

She shuddered as they walked as silently as possible. The tornado clearly hadn't been through this way, though a few downed branches suggested some heavy storms. She hoped her cabin hadn't sustained any damage.

When they reached the edge of the trees and she could detect the outline of her cabin in the moonlight, she felt her stomach sink in despair. Not because of damage, though. "There's police tape," she whispered.

"Lucky for you, I'm the police."

"Gage."

He was already striding forward. He went to the back door and began untying one side of the Do Not Cross tape. Felicity stood in the clearing of her cabin and stared, openmouthed. "You can't—"

He cut off her directive. "Come on now. We've left following the rules behind. Keep up, Felicity." He motioned her forward.

SHE STOOD AS if she wasn't going to listen to him. But Gage knew there was no other way right now. Maybe they wouldn't find any leads in her cabin, but it would give them a place to sleep for the night—a place no one would dream of looking for them.

Finally Felicity moved forward.

"Got your keys?"

She didn't answer, just frowned deeper and pulled keys out of her pocket. She unlocked the door and gingerly stepped inside. Gage tied the police tape back to the banister and walked in behind her.

She stood, miserably surveying her tiny kitchen. "They moved things," she said. "Went through my home and…" She shook her head.

He gave her shoulder a squeeze, though it made her jump. Still, he couldn't stand to see that look of utter defeat on her face. She'd gotten through the past forty-eight hours on grit and determination and strength. He knew how hard it was to hold on to that when things seemed bleak.

But she needed to.

"Don't get sad. Get mad, Felicity. Someone came through here and planted evidence against you. The cops are doing their job, and it sucks that's their job, but let's focus on who's trying to make you into a murderer."

She didn't say anything for the longest time. When she finally did, she did it moving toward the fridge. "I'm hungry." She opened it, studied the contents and shook her head. She slammed the door, wrenched open the freezer, then brought out a tub of ice cream.

She grabbed a spoon, settled herself down at the tiny table in the corner and went to work.

"We might want something a little bit more nourishing."

The look she gave him could have melted that ice cream in front of her.

"I do, anyway."

"Help yourself," she said through a mouthful of ice cream, gesturing at the small refrigerator and pantry.

Gage poked around, found some mixed nuts and a beer, and helped himself. Not exactly nourishing, but maybe she was right that comfort food was the way to go tonight. He settled into the chair across from her, wondered if she ever had any cabin guests that necessitated another chair and kept his opinions on that to himself.

He lifted the beer. "You sit around drinking a lot of beer by yourself?"

"Slugs," she replied. "Kills 'em."

He chuckled. He had no earthly understanding of why he found that endearing or why he could so easily picture her putting out little trays of beer for slugs just as Grandma Pauline always had.

"I'm giving myself five minutes to wallow," she said, scooping up another large glob of ice cream. "I survived a tornado. I'm wanted for murder. A murder I didn't commit. You…" She trailed off before she finished that sentence. "I get five minutes to wallow." She shoved the entire bite of ice cream in her mouth.

"Then what?"

She swallowed and looked down at the container. "I don't know."

"I tell you what. Let's extend the wallow. Ten minutes with the ice cream, then about—" he checked the clock on his phone "—five hours of sleep in a bed."

"Then what?" she asked, echoing his own question back to him.

"In the morning, we check in with my brothers and see if they've made any progress or have any idea where Ace is. We'll go through your cabin and see if we can find anything off or missing. Then… I want to go look at where you found the body."

She shoved away from the table, abruptly sticking the lid on the ice cream and putting it back in the freezer.

"Felici—"

She whirled to face him. "Tell me one of your stories."

"Huh?"

"Those crazy stories you pull out whenever everyone's down and you want to get a laugh." She pointed to herself. "I'm depressed." Then to him. "Now, cheer me up. Make me laugh."

"I can't do it on command."

"Why not?"

"Well, for starters, it's not what you need right now."

"Oh, really. What do I need?"

He stood. He could do without the beer and they'd have a chance to eat in the morning, so he left both on the table. He walked over to her and, as gratifying as it was that her eyes got wide and dropped to his mouth, he didn't do what she was clearly expecting him to.

He simply wrapped his arms around her and gave her a squeeze. "We need sleep," he said. Much as he wanted to hold her a little closer, stroke a lot more than her hair, it wasn't the time.

He pulled back from the friendly hug and she blinked up at him. "I guess you're right," she said at length. "I have extra sheets for the couch."

He snorted out a laugh, which he tried to bite back when she glared at him. "Bad news. We've still got to be careful. We'll want to be out of here before sunrise, and we need to be close. No separate rooms, Felicity."

"Just what are you suggesting?"

"I'm not *suggesting* anything. We're going to have to sleep in the same place. Whether it's your couch or your bed, you've got a sleeping buddy tonight. So, pick your poison. My guess is your bed has more room."

"You're not going to sleep in *my* bed. With *me*," she returned, all shrieking outrage.

Gage didn't figure arguing with her was going to get him anywhere, so he shrugged and headed for the door he was pretty sure led to her bedroom. She scurried after him, blustering without forming any actual words.

He opened the door, walked over to the bed, toed off his boots, gave her a look that said *try and stop me* and settled himself onto one side.

She stood there and stared at him, mouth open, little sounds of outrage escaping.

God, he was too tired for her outrage. "You can tie me up if it'd make you more comfortable. Might give me some ideas, but if it'd make you feel better, be my guest."

She scowled at him. "I'm not *afraid* of you."

She certainly seemed it. Well, maybe *afraid* was harsh. She was nervous. Jumpy and high-strung—keeping as much space between her and him sprawled out on the bed as possible.

"Want to talk about earlier first?" He couldn't say he particularly *wanted* to talk about that kiss, but it was muddling his mind when he needed to be lucid and think about how on earth they were going to clear her.

"No!" she squeaked.

The squeak amused him even if it shouldn't. "Suit yourself."

"Fine. *I'll* sleep on the couch."

"No, you won't, Felicity. You're in here with me, if I have to tie *you* up." He might have ended it on a joke, but he was deadly serious and she seemed to understand that.

After huffing and crossing her arms over her chest, then throwing them up in the air a second later, she finally stalked to the bed. She wrenched off her boots, muttering the whole time, then lowered herself onto the bed.

In Gage's estimation, the full-size mattress was hardly adequate for one person let alone two.

No matter, she was putting as much space between them as if they were on a king-size.

It was dark in here, but it smelled like her. And if she thought *she* was ticked off about the sleeping arrangements, she had *no* idea what was going through his head.

He was almost asleep when she finally spoke.

"You kissed me," she said, as if it was some grave accusation.

"That I did." And he didn't regret it in the slightest, even if she hated him for it. She'd kissed him back.

Him. Not Brady. There might be a little sibling jealousy there, but when he'd said he wasn't Brady earlier she'd looked so shocked he had to believe she hadn't been thinking about Brady when she'd kissed him back.

"Why did you do it?" she asked, her voice soft, and he would have said *timid* if he didn't know how damn strong she was.

"Because I wanted to."

"That's hardly an answer."

"Why?"

"Because you don't just suddenly want to kiss someone after never wanting to kiss them."

"Who said I never wanted to?"

She was quiet at that, so he rolled onto his side with an exaggerated yawn. "Night, Felicity."

She didn't respond, and he fell off into a deep sleep.

HE AWOKE TO something vibrating against him and realized it was his phone.

He swore internally when he saw it was four in the
morning, but it was a text from Jamison: Call ASAP.

He slid out of the bed, tempted to spend a little too
much time staring at Felicity in the glow from his
phone. She was still dead asleep, face relaxed, hair a
mess around her head.

Prettiest damn thing he'd ever seen, and he did not
have time to dwell on this too-soft feeling going on inside of him.

He moved into the living room and called Jamison.
"What do you have?"

Jamison didn't waste time or words. "Prints came
back last night—one of Tuck's friends sent him an
email. Tuck just got off another case and called me."
Jamison was in full cop mode, and Gage didn't interrupt. "They found Felicity's biological father's prints
on the evidence they sent for DNA testing. They'd also
found his prints in her cabin. Tucker's going to go talk to
the detectives this morning, explain that Felicity hasn't
had a thing to do with her father so this is unusual.
With the tornado damage, Felicity isn't high on their list
of priorities—which is good and bad. Good, you guys
should be able to remain undetected. Bad, they're not
going to worry about dropping the warrant yet."

"Her father had something to do with it?"

"It's looking that way to me. Added to that? He's disappeared since the tornado, and I doubt he's a casualty."

"Why do you doubt that?"

"We've done some digging. The real reason I called
you. There's something bigger at play."

"Something bigger than someone framing Felicity for murder?"

"Bigger or more connected anyway. Gage, Michael Harrison visited Ace in jail. Before the murder."

"How? We've been tracking that."

"He signed in to speak to another prisoner, but after looking deeper into it, there was a switch and he managed to talk to Ace thanks to a paid-off guard."

Gage let that sink in. Felicity's biological father had visited Ace in jail. His father and hers were connected.

And he had no doubt his father was behind it all.

Chapter Ten

Felicity had never been a particularly good sleeper. Night terrors had plagued her as a kid, and while she'd grown out of those for the most part, vivid dreams still afflicted her often. Not always bad ones, just clear and real-feeling.

She opened her eyes, her body hot and heart racing, more than a little embarrassed at just *what* her vivid imagination had been up to. Steeling herself, she turned her head, but Gage wasn't there.

She told herself she was relieved, even blew out a breath as if to convince herself she was. But some echo of the dream was still thrumming inside of her and at the center of that thrumming she was most definitely not relieved.

Then from somewhere outside the room she heard Gage swear, quietly but in an uncharacteristically serious tone she knew meant bad news.

There was no rest from the true, important, pressing issues in their lives. But the words that rattled around in her head as she slid out of bed weren't anything to do with being accused of murder or Ace being on the loose.

It was Gage's voice, grave and completely unflinching, saying *because I wanted to* over and over again.

She didn't have to work to silence that voice when she stepped out to the living room, though. Gage turned to face her. The pure gentleness in his look might have totally undone her if it didn't scare her to the bone.

"What is it?"

"Why don't you have a seat?"

"What is it?" she returned, trying to do his one-eyebrow quirk.

He didn't say anything. She wasn't sure he even breathed, which made it very hard for her to.

"Jamison and Tucker have been busy," he said, with a hesitance in his voice that felt very un-Gage-like and even more disconcerting. "Looking into things and... there are things."

"Be specific, Gage."

"They found your father's prints in the cabin and on the evidence."

Felicity wished she'd taken that seat he'd wanted her to. "I don't understand."

"No one does, just yet. But I assume you haven't been entertaining your father here?"

"Here? Entertaining? I haven't had any contact with my father since Child Protection Services took me away." She crossed her arms over herself, trying to keep all the awful parts of that sentence tightly under her control instead of at the will of her emotion.

"That's what I thought. Well, he was here. Your father was *in* your cabin at some point."

"That's... If he was here, he planted the evidence." Which meant he could be the killer. Why would he kill his own child? He'd beaten Felicity herself when she'd been helpless and small, and still she had a hard time wrapping her mind around the possibility he'd gone so far as to end his own child's life. "He planted the evidence?"

"That's the angle Tucker is going to press upon the detectives, and at least that there's no good reason his prints should be here. But with the tornado, everyone's busy. This case has fallen in priority."

"My father was here?" Why would he... After all this time, why would he be causing her trouble now? And such awful, horrible trouble. She wrapped her arms around herself, trying to find some center of fight or determination when all she felt was unaccountably sad.

That's when she realized Gage remained very still, watching her with a dark hazel gaze that looked pained. "There's more." She didn't even have to put it as a question. She knew. There was more.

Exhaustion threatened despite the sleep. This was life exhaustion. This was how many blows could one person take and keep going.

The answer was always *as many as life hands you*, but that answer sincerely sucked right now.

"Jamison found out..." He cleared his throat. "Michael Harrison went to visit Ace before you found the body."

Felicity had never fainted in her life, but the room spun and faded to black and her knees went to jelly. Before she could collapse, Gage was at her side, his strong arm around her waist leading her to the couch.

Her father and Ace? It made a horrible, terrifying kind of sense. This wasn't isolated. It wasn't just her father or just Ace. It was them together. Why were Ace and her father acting together?

Gage crouched in front of her, but she didn't know what to say to him. All she really wanted to do was press her forehead into her knees and cry.

She'd cried enough. She'd wallowed enough.

But how did she keep going forward knowing that it wasn't just Ace against her, it was her own father. That the life of a woman—a sister she'd never known—was over because of her in some warped, weird way.

"You can't start blaming yourself," Gage said sharply, as if he could read her thoughts.

"You don't know what it's like to have a father who…" She trailed off and mentally kicked herself.

"Don't know what it's like to have an evil murderer for a father?" He made a considering noise. "It just so happens I know a thing or two about that."

"I don't. I never thought my father was *that* bad." There'd only been four years. Years she didn't fully remember.

"He beat you," Gage said flatly.

"I know, but…" She didn't know how the next words came out, when this was Gage, not her therapist and not her sister. But Gage. And still, the words tumbled into the silence. "Sometimes you have to… I had to tell myself it was just a bad temper. I had to tell myself it was just bad luck, extraordinary circumstances that made him snap. I couldn't make him the bad guy because what did that make me?" She realized, again, that was the worst thing to say when she looked up at him and there was a kind of desolation on his face.

Because he knew. He understood. All those feelings

she'd never been able to fully articulate in the therapy
Eva had made her go to when she'd first been with the
Knights, when she'd talked with Nina or Liza about
their less-than-stellar childhoods. She didn't even have
to articulate it for it to make sense to Gage.

Suddenly she had to know, to fully understand, the
breadth and width of Ace Wyatt. "Did Ace hit all of
you?"

"Yeah."

"And worse?"

"I don't know how to quantify worse, Felicity." He
raked a hand through his hair, a rare sign of discomfort
and frustration. "It was only eleven years."

"He abandoned you in the elements when you were
seven as some kind of initiation."

"Yeah. But see, I only had five years of that. Jamison?
He did thirteen. Each year it went up one."

"Went up one?" She could tell he didn't want to say
more, that he'd already said more than he wanted to, but
she needed understanding. For both of them. "Please,
Gage."

"You stayed on your own one night for every year of
life. It wasn't so bad. It was a week plus without Ace.
Without those people. Maybe it was hard to find food
and water. Maybe…" He shook his head, as if to shake
it all away. "It was awful. But it was all awful. Beatings, whippings, initiations. Trying to pit us against
each other. He's a terrifying man. A sociopath with
a deep understanding of people—how to manipulate
them, inspire them, twist them."

She didn't know how she understood him. What he
spoke of was longer, truly more awful than her four

sketchy years under her father's care. But she understood that he worried what all that twisting had done to him, no matter how hard he'd tried to fight it. She reached out and touched his cheek on the side of his face that wasn't bandaged. "He didn't twist his sons."

The look of anguish on his face, as if he wasn't so sure, just about broke her heart. "You're good men," she insisted. "Regardless of what our fathers are—evil sociopaths and murderers or what all—it doesn't matter. We're good." She took his large, rough hands and squeezed as hard as she could. "I know we are."

He looked at their joined hands, then up at her. He had a heartbreaking look in his eyes, as if he was the personal cause for everything bad that had ever happened.

"I hate that you're on his radar, because this will hurt. Even when we win, this will hurt."

She couldn't help feeling some bubble of hope, the curve of a smile. "*When* we win?"

"We're not going to lose, Felicity. I won't let it happen. Whatever it takes."

She had no cause to doubt him, because they'd gotten through this far. But she understood in that vehement promise, that Gage cared. Not just about himself. Not just about winning against Ace. But about her. Period.

She leaned forward and pressed her mouth to his. It was nothing like the kiss in the Badlands. She was too shy for that. Didn't know how to lead and run with all that wild heat. But she kissed him anyway, with what little skill she had. And he let her—he didn't lead her anywhere else, just kissed her back as gently and carefully as she'd kissed him.

When she pulled back, he didn't say anything. He stared, and nerves crept in to dismantle all that surety about him caring, about him wanting to kiss her for a lot longer than she'd ever thought of kissing him. "You said you wanted to kiss me."

"Yeah." He reached out, rubbed a strand of her hair between his thumb and forefinger. His mouth was curved, not in a full-blown smile, because even here there wasn't anything to smile about. But it was softer than *whatever it takes*. He looked from her hair to her eyes. "I like kissing you," he said so seriously, so simply, she couldn't do anything other than believe it was the truth.

"I think I like it, too." More than anything as simple as *like*. And it centered her, reminded her that outside all of this terrifying situation, she had a real life. Was a woman. Maybe even a woman who ended up kissing Gage Wyatt as much as she pleased. But she had to fight for that possibility first.

She was ready. She had to find a way to be ready. "All right. What's the plan now?"

GAGE SUPPOSED STAYING here and taking her to bed wasn't much of a plan when their murderous fathers were on the loose, Felicity their target.

But it was tempting.

Sadly, time wasn't on their side.

"First things first. It's nearing dawn and we've got to clear out in case any detectives stop by. I want to take a look at where the woman's body was. See if we can find any clues of our own."

Felicity winced, but she nodded.

"You don't have to—"

"I'll go with. Two people searching for clues is better than one. I guess it's just that she was my sister. I can't fully grasp it. When I try to think about it, when I try not to think about it. I don't know how to feel."

"You didn't know she existed, Felicity. I'd give yourself a break on that, and if you don't want to relive it, you don't have to."

She shook her head, her hands still in his. It was a nice weight, a sign of partnership, of some level of caring about each other.

It wasn't the time or place to delve into how much, but there was a nice certainty to being in this together.

"We shouldn't be apart. Not with Ace on the loose. Don't you think it's dangerous with him out there?"

He hated that she was right. "He wouldn't necessarily know we're here—I don't know how he could—but you're right. We should stick together. Keep an eye on each other until we know more." Letting her out of his sight wasn't an option.

"So, it's a promise. We stick together, no matter what?"

He nodded. "It's a promise."

She squeezed his hands and then released them. Her face was all determination now—the sadness and fear buried. She stood and slapped her palms on her thighs as if to say *let's go*. "I'll grab my own pack from here. You can carry the one I had. We really should arrange for someone to pick up what we left behind after the tornado."

He didn't know why her stubborn insistence on park

protocol warmed his heart like it was damn Christmas or something, but it did.

"Is there an anonymous way to let a ranger know? Hey, maybe it'd even get Ace thinking we're dead. We could have been blown away in the tornado, shattered who knows where, and all that's left is the backpack we dropped."

"What an awful thought." She shuddered. "I guess it'll be okay another few days. Go get the other pack. Grab what might work in my pantry. Load up on water. Water is most important. I'll pack mine with camping gear and bandages and disinfectant so we can keep your wound clean. That should see us through another few days if we have to."

"You didn't ask me what's next after we check out the murder site," he said, slowly standing.

She looked up at him, eyes so green and serious. "We'll go to Sons territory, of course. Ace likely went there. If my father is working for him, or they're working together—they're probably there right now. Maybe not. I don't know them, don't understand them, but we go where their power is. Regardless of whether they're with the Sons or not, someone in the Sons knows something. That's where we have to go."

"That doesn't scare you?"

"It terrifies me. But so does prison. I want to act. I don't want my fight left up to someone else. What other options are there?"

The only one he could think of involved locking her up far away, and he knew she'd never go for that. "We could just hide until Jamison and Cody figure it out."

She actually rolled her eyes as if this wasn't life and death they were talking about. "As if you could stay sane waiting for your brothers to handle everything for you. For *me*, actually. This is my mess. I'm glad you're here with me. I couldn't do it on my own, but it is my mess."

"A mess you're in because Cody called you for help."

"My father—"

"Are we really going to stand here and argue who's more to blame for a mess created by our fathers?"

"Fair point. All right. Pack up."

They went in opposite directions—her to her room, him to the kitchen. He focused on the practicalities, food and water, and trusted her to take care of shelter.

If he entertained himself by thinking of sharing a tent again, well, a man deserved some distraction from all the garbage heaped on him.

She returned to the kitchen, a pack already strapped to her body. She was wearing new khaki pants and a tan sweatshirt that would often blend right in with the landscape they'd be hiking.

She held out a similarly colored lump of clothing. "It won't help with your jeans, but it's an extra large. You don't have to wear it just yet, but it's a good idea to have. Tie it around your waist."

"Men do not *tie* sweatshirts around their waists."

She raised an eyebrow at him. He was not amused at her mimicking him. When he didn't take the sweatshirt at first, she shoved it at him.

"Take a hit on your manliness, Gage. For the sake of—oh, I don't know—surviving, maybe."

He scowled as he took the sweatshirt and tied it around his waist. "Happy?"

"Downright celebratory. Woo-hoo, time to inspect a murder scene!"

Her sarcasm cheered him even if it was at his expense. "Ready to head out?"

She nodded, and though he could see the nerves in her eyes, her hands were steady. Her expression was determined in spite of the fear.

"Oh, one thing first," she said, her expression grave as she walked toward him. She stopped in front of him, looking up at him as if he was supposed to have an idea what that one thing was.

Then she put her hands on his shoulders, rose to her toes and pressed a kiss to his mouth. It was soft, a little timid like the one in the living room, but sweet. And sweet was just as potent as anything else when it came to her.

She lowered back to flat-footed. Her cheeks were edging toward red, but her smile was satisfied even if she was embarrassed, too.

If he didn't die from Ace, he might from this.

He wanted to tell her...everything. How watching her change and find her strength had shifted something inside of him. Had set a spark to this feeling he didn't quite understand. Something bigger than himself and the fear of being Ace Wyatt's son.

He didn't have the words for any of that. So, he grinned at her and then made a move for the back door. He stepped out, his mind still fuzzy with *feelings* he didn't know how to verbalize.

He heard a shuffle, but before he could react, the cold press of steel was at his temple and his father's amused voice in his ear.

"Well, hello, son. Funny running into you here."

Chapter Eleven

Felicity tried to scramble back and run in the opposite direction, but Ace was too quick. His arm snaked in and grabbed her by the shirtfront.

"Not so fast." Ace laughed and the sound made her stomach turn in utter terror.

She wanted to fight him, but the gun pressed to Gage's temple kept her frozen in fear. Even if he didn't want to kill his own son, any struggling from her could have him pulling the trigger—purposefully or accidentally.

Then there was her own father standing in the yard, a much larger gun than Ace's slung over his arm. She hadn't seen him in years, didn't recognize him on a visual level, but she knew it was him.

Ace gave her shirt a jerk, sending her pitching forward. The weight of the backpack added to her inelegant loss of balance, and she landed hard on the ground. She struggled to get up. Maybe she could run for help? But that would leave Gage here. Alone with them.

Her father moved close and stood over her. He didn't press the gun to her temple like Ace had his to Gage, but he pointed it at her all the same.

"Can you believe it, son?" Ace was saying to Gage, grinning from ear to ear even with a gun pressed to his own son's temple. "A tornado busted me out of jail. A *tornado*. Can you understand the absolute significance of that divine intervention?"

"I'm sure you'll enlighten me whether I want you to or not."

"When my parents left me to die, it was the land that protected me, built me. Now it's the land, the fearsome power of this land, that's given me my freedom back after my sons were too weak, too soft to do what they were meant to do."

Felicity shuddered at the words, at how reasonable they sounded to her. She understood what it felt like to be made new by the awe-inspiring landscape around them. The preacher-like way he spoke those words had her listening, rapt. Understanding.

She had something in common with Ace Wyatt. What a horrible, horrible thought.

"You think it's a weakness not to be you, Ace. But you're outnumbered, because the sane ones among us consider it a strength to be able to battle back our worst impulses. To not believe ourselves the ultimate judge, jury and executioner."

Ace cocked his head as he studied Gage. "A nice story you six have told yourselves. But there are six of you. One of you will have to face the music. Or the end will come."

"Endings always come. And the most poetic ending for you will be rotting in a cell for the rest of your insane life."

"The land provides. It provides the willing and the worthy, and it has provided me my freedom, again."

He sounded so rational, so utterly sure, Felicity had to remind herself he *was* insane. Evil, surely, if he'd killed people and done some of the things the Wyatts said he did.

"Then, after the land anoints me yet again, frees and provides and gives to me, *yet again*, I'm lucky enough to stumble upon exactly who I was figuring out how to find."

"I thought you didn't believe in luck," Gage said, his voice cool and detached as if a deadly weapon wasn't pressed to his head.

Ace chuckled. "Oh, I believe in it. I also believe it favors the prepared and anointed. I am both. What are you?"

Gage muttered disparagingly under his breath. He was staring straight ahead so he couldn't see the way Ace's eyes gleamed.

Crazy. Evil. Felicity didn't know what it was, but that sheen made everything inside of her ice, made the hair on her arms and back of her neck stand up on end. All that reason she'd almost thought he'd been speaking evaporated when she looked at him.

She focused on breathing evenly in an effort to keep panic at bay. She had to find a way to survive this. A way for both of them to survive their fathers.

There wasn't much that could be done with Ace holding a gun to Gage's head and her father pointing a gun at her.

Don't panic. Don't panic. Think.

The Wyatt brothers had always said their father didn't want them dead, or they'd be dead. There were multiple theories, though most centered on the idea Ace Wyatt wanted slow, painful revenge on his sons, not just a violent death.

The likelihood of Ace actually pulling the trigger was low. And since neither had shot her, maybe they didn't want her dead, either.

Still, she could visualize Ace shooting Gage—see it happening before her, and that kept her from moving. From hoping.

Two against two might have been a fair fight if she had a weapon of her own, but all she had was a backpacking knife stuffed deep within the pack on her back. Was there any way to get it without drawing attention to herself? And even if there was, what was the point of bringing a knife to a gunfight?

"I don't know what brand-new break you've had with reality," Gage drawled, "but—"

Ace's free hand jabbed out so fast Felicity barely saw it. She wasn't even sure where the punch landed, only that it had Gage gasping for air and falling to his knees.

"You weren't next on my list, Gage. But you mixed yourself up with this one and messed up my plan. You know how I feel when people mess up my plan."

The only thing that came from Gage was horrible gasping noises as if he was struggling to breathe.

Without fully realizing she was doing it, she moved toward him. Until an excruciating pain in her hand stopped her. She looked at the source of the crushing, terrifying pain and found her father's boot pressing harder and harder against her hand.

"You stay put," he said.

She tried not to sob, not to react, but he ground the

boot harder against her hand. He was going to break her fingers with much more pressure. The only thing currently saving her was the give of the soil after the rain.

"Got it?" he demanded, jabbing her side with his gun.

She nodded, tears streaming down her cheeks. But she didn't make a noise.

The pressure eased off her hand, and she wanted to sob with as much relief as throbbing pain, but she breathed through it.

"Felicity, I need you to break your promise to me," Gage said, his voice clear and calm, which earned him another punch from Ace, right against the throat.

Her promise? Her promise. To stay together no matter what. No. No, she couldn't break it. She couldn't leave him here.

But as he gasped for air against his father's horrifying blows, she realized that in this case, splitting up was the only chance they had. Ace would have somewhere to take them, somewhere to torture them.

If she could get away, she could get all the Wyatts here. She could save Gage. She didn't want to leave him with Ace, even for a second. But when they'd promised each other to stick together that had been when Ace was out there. When the threat was from the outside, not the inside.

She couldn't save Gage with brute strength, but if she could get away she might be able to save him some other way.

She met his gaze. And nodded.

GAGE DIDN'T LET the nerves show, didn't let on how afraid he was because God knew this was going to hurt.

But she'd be safe—or safer. It was the only chance he had to survive. Maybe he wouldn't, but if she was safe that would be okay.

So, he had to make sure he did enough damage to Ace that Michael came over to save him. He had to give Felicity enough time to really run.

The two men holding guns on them would kill her, no doubt. They'd kill him, too, but Ace would want to make it hurt first. Maybe he'd want it to hurt for Felicity, too, since she'd gotten in Ace's way with Nina and Cody, but that only made her being here, in their grasp, that much more dangerous.

"Have you had your dramatic mom—"

Gage interrupted his father's comment by throwing his head backward, and straight into his father's.

It rang his bell—stars dancing and pain radiating down to his toes, but the gun dropped from his temple. Gage took the opportunity to pitch his body forward hoping his legs would hold him.

He still had the damn pack on his back and wished he'd had the foresight to drop it, but when Michael came charging at him, Gage managed to get an arm out of the strap and use it as enough of a force to knock the gun pointed at him from Michael's hands.

Gage didn't stop to look and see if Felicity ran. There wasn't time for him to look, so he just had to trust that she'd understood him and that she'd nodded because she knew she was going to run.

Michael swore at him and charged.

Felicity's father did not appear to be the smartest man, but he had fists like mallets, and was all bulk and muscle. Though he'd lost his gun, he used his body as a weapon against Gage, landing two punches to the gut before Gage could block them.

Gage was not a small man, but he felt like one for a second. Michael making him feel small only reminded him that Felicity had been small. A tiny girl and this man had used his fists on her—enough that protective services had intervened—which was a bit of a feat in isolated rural areas with low government funds.

Gage used that rage, that utter disgust to propel him forward with a blow that knocked Michael back two steps.

A gunshot rang out too close, but no blast of pain followed the noise. Still, Gage knew well enough Ace wouldn't miss twice. Even to forward his precious plans.

So Gage grappled with Michael, finally landing a knee to the most vulnerable part of his attacker. He managed to flip him off and then got to his feet, only to come face-to-face with Ace's gun barrel.

"Well, shoot me then," Gage snarled. His mouth was bleeding, and God knew what other parts of him were bleeding and broken. Every cell of his body hurt, and this was all so pointless.

Not pointless. Felicity is gone. He didn't dare look around and verify. He just *willed* it.

Ace's own face was bleeding, and Gage got morbid satisfaction from knowing his head had caused that gash on Ace's brow.

Ace's gaze whipped behind Michael, from the gun that had fallen to the ground, to the pack that had been ripped from Gage's back.

"You let her *go*?" Ace growled.

Michael was struggling to get to his feet. "He practically knocked you out. I had to—"

"You worthless moron! Go after her! Go!"

Gage couldn't help smiling even as blood dripped down his face. He wasn't sure he'd ever heard Ace sound so furiously disgusted. Usually his anger was deadly, eerie calm, but Gage had clearly put quite the crimp in Ace's plans.

Who wouldn't grin at that? Especially as Michael scrambled to retrieve the gun and then ran off more in panic than with any thought as to which way Felicity had gone.

She'd be faster and far more knowledgeable of the terrain. She was gone and on her way to find help. Gage had to believe it.

"What are you smiling ab…" Ace trailed off, rage and disgust sinking into the lines on his face.

"Jail didn't agree with you, Daddy," Gage offered, hoping to throw Ace off.

"You care about her." Ace sneered. "What is it about you boys? Where did I go so wrong? Weak. Stupid. Undone by any woman who opens her legs."

Gage couldn't keep the easy grin on his face, and it morphed into a sneer. But he bit his tongue to keep from saying anything that might give Ace more ammunition to rail against and agitate Gage into making a deadly misstep.

"What a mistake you've made," Ace whispered, a vicious fury dancing in his eyes, that Gage only remembered seeing once before—when Ace had realized Cody had escaped.

Jamison had worked hard to get Cody, the youngest of the six boys, out from the Sons before he had to go through the ritual they'd all had to survive on their seventh birthdays. Jamison had managed, managed so well Ace had assumed Grandma Pauline had paid one of his men to betray him. He'd never suspected Jamison.

At first.

That moment Ace had learned Cody was safe and out of his grip, Gage had seen this exact look. And known he'd be lucky to survive it.

But he had then, why couldn't he now?

Which was the last thought he had before pain exploded at the side of his head, and the world went dark.

Chapter Twelve

Felicity tried to keep her mind off the lack of water. Once she found cell service, she'd have help and water.

Her head pounded along with her thundering heart. She knew she could outrun her father, but he had a gun, which meant she had to do a lot more than just outrun him. She had to get away completely.

Now, Ace, he could probably catch her if he was the one chasing her. Her father was a big man, and though she remembered a certain agile precision in landing a blow, she doubted it extended to endurance running.

But Ace was tall and lean and crazy. That was the worst part, really. He seemed almost normal sometimes. She'd found herself listening too intently to what he had to say.

Charismatic wasn't the right word because that had too positive of a connotation. Compelling maybe. Even knowing everything she did about Ace—which was probably only the half of what Ace was and had done—she'd been *compelled* to listen to what he had to say.

It made her feel sick. Or maybe that was the dehydration.

She allowed her pace to slow, then stop, turning in a careful circle to study her surroundings.

She'd gone straight for the canyon land, which may not have been her smartest choice what with the lack of water, but it was better than the wide-open grassy plains. There were a million places to find cover in the rocks, crevices and caves.

And that was only if her father found her.

She was currently in a long, deep crevice. Some of the wet from yesterday's storm had dried, but there were still damp places where the sun hadn't touched. Not safe drinking water, but she considered it for a minute.

Maybe she should go back. Knife in hand. They weren't supposed to split up. This was all wrong.

She climbed up a portion of the rock wall that would allow her to see out over the horizon while still keeping her mostly out of sight. She scanned the area, the tall spires and rocky hills. The sky was a brilliant blue, as if a tornado hadn't blown through less than twenty-four hours ago.

The air was hot, but it was *Badlands* air. Home. Heart. She'd be okay.

The land provides.

The thought comforted her for a second or two before she realized it was Ace's voice. Ace's words.

She pushed out a breath, nausea stealing over her. How could a madman's words be comforting? Had she gone crazy? Was she that weak?

She shook her head. Maybe she was, but she could choose not to be. She could fight it. It was like being shy, and her stutter. Those things still existed within her, but she fought them away.

So she would fight the terrifying idea she had something in common with Ace Wyatt. Just as for years she'd fought the terrifying idea a man who'd beat his young daughter was her own flesh and blood.

And that flesh and blood had come after her, no doubt. She looked around again, a double check to make sure her eyes weren't deceiving her.

She caught the hint of movement to the east and squinted at it. Then, since she had time, she dug through her pack and pulled out her binoculars. She focused on the area where she'd sensed movement.

In between two spindly spires of red rock, a figure was moving. He was still far enough away the binoculars didn't magnify features enough for identification, but based on the size and location, she had to believe it was her father.

He didn't look like an adept hiker. He stumbled and picked his way over rock. She could continue to outrun or out-hike him if she chose.

But she would no doubt become too dehydrated to function after a while.

What were her options? He had a gun and he was clearly stronger than her. She couldn't fight him. She had no gun to ward him off. Just that knife in her pack.

She considered waiting till he got close enough and then throwing it, but she'd never thrown a knife in her life and it seemed too big a risk to just start throwing her one and only weapon.

Rocks might work. She was strong and had good aim, but he'd have to be really close for them to do any damage.

She kept watching him through the binoculars.

Maybe she wouldn't have to do anything at all. One good fall and he'd be out of luck.

One good fall. What if she *created* the fall? She could take him out. Even with him having a gun, all she'd need to do was give him a little push. Well, more than a little, but a push. Or trip him somehow. She could incapacitate him or trap him in a deep crevice.

It would be tricky and dangerous, but it would be a better option than trying to find cell service without any water to drink. If she took out her father here, she could get back to the cabin. Close enough to it and she could access her Wi-Fi and send a text.

If she was careful and quiet, she could do it without Ace even knowing she was back. Surely he wouldn't take Gage anywhere until her father returned with her in tow.

She'd hope, anyway.

In the meantime, she'd take her father out.

THE PAIN EBBED and flowed, excruciating waves of it, dulling into something almost bearable. Almost reasonable enough he could fight through, open his eyes and figure everything out.

Then another wave would take him under. Black, black, vicious black.

But then something happened, a familiar sound, a familiar panic. He found consciousness gasping for air and eyes flying open. His vision swam for a good few seconds before it cleared.

And there was Ace.

With the whip.

Gage tried to remember he wasn't seven years old

any longer. He was an adult. Whatever his father could dish out, he could take.

But that whip was the nightmare he thought he'd escaped. He wouldn't let those old memories rush into his brain. There was enough pain there. He had to focus on the present. Where he was and if Michael was here—because if he wasn't, he was still somewhere after Felicity.

Felicity. He'd focus on her and not the echoing crack of that whip.

"Good morning, son. Or should I say, good afternoon?"

Gage didn't say anything, though he wanted to demand to know how long he'd been out. He wanted to demand a whole myriad of things, but he didn't trust his voice with that whip in his father's hands.

Ace shifted it from one hand to another. "Did you think I'd forgotten? You never forget your son's weaknesses." Ace smiled, a grin that was all sharp edges and sure as hell crazy.

Except Ace always knew what he was doing. So maybe he was just evil. Maybe all his talk about being anointed and chosen and born from the dust were the things he used to justify all that potential for horror he had inside him.

Gage had never really cared to find out. Especially when that whip was involved.

He wasn't a child anymore. He was *not* a child anymore. The whip would hurt, but it couldn't break him. He couldn't let it. That was what his father wanted, so he wouldn't give it to him.

But his body wasn't getting the message. There was

the nausea, which he could blame on the concussion he had to have been given. The heart-pounding, sweaty-palmed terror making his limbs weak—that was all whip.

It's just a weapon like any other.

But it wasn't. Not for him.

"Why do you get the whip, Gage?"

Gage wouldn't respond. He wouldn't. He didn't have to give in. Not anymore. This wasn't the same game it had been when he'd been a defenseless boy.

Maybe he was tied up in what appeared to be some kind of cave…always a cave. But he was thirty-one years old. A grown man who'd fought drug addicts and arrested child molesters and done what he could, *everything* he could, to right the wrongs he came across.

He had to survive this wrong. He'd done it once, much younger but with his brothers' help.

Now he was an adult, and if Felicity had gotten away, it could be with his brothers' help again.

If Felicity and his brothers could find him.

Big, *big* if.

Ace stepped forward, still moving the whip handle from hand to hand.

"The rules are the same, boy."

Gage shuddered as if he was still that little boy. As if the years meant nothing. His size meant nothing. There was Ace and that whip, and Gage was nothing in its wake.

No.

"I ask a question, you answer it. Why do you get the whip?"

"Because my father's a psychopath?"

The crack slammed through the air the same time the stinging, breath-stealing pain lashed over his leg. He couldn't hold back the hiss of pain, despite knowing it was exactly what his father wanted.

It would be worse—get worse. His father's whip was weighted and could break bones with the right slap.

Gage could survive it. Better to survive it than give in like he'd had to as a kid.

"Why do you get the whip, Gage? You and no one else?" Ace cracked the whip between them, and though Gage cringed at the sound, no blast of pain followed it.

Psychological warfare. It wasn't enough to just hurt his sons—he wanted to break them. The problem was, if you were broken, the pain would stop.

For a time, but the war never stopped. There would always be this war between Ace and his sons, because they'd dared to be good instead of capitulate to his evil.

He'd promised himself never to be weak in the face of his father again. But giving Ace what he wanted without truly believing it wasn't weakness. It was survival.

What wouldn't Gage do to survive? To make sure Felicity had survived?

"I get the whip because I'm the smartest," Gage said, his voice already battle weary.

"Good," Ace replied in the same tone a teacher might use when a student finally succeeded with a difficult concept.

It made Gage feel slimy, slick with self-disgust and the ever-present heart-pounding fear. But if he threw up, he knew exactly what Ace would have to do.

He had to be tough. Tough enough to survive. Tough

enough so that Ace would leave him alone and torture someone else. Anyone else.

It was his own fault. If he could make more mistakes, be more of a disappointment, Ace wouldn't try to mold him, make him. If he could be less, this wouldn't happen.

Sometimes he even believed that, no matter that it was a sad, self-serving lie.

You are not a child.

But he felt it. Felt those old feelings and thoughts taking over as if they were a spirit set on possessing him. He couldn't get the words out of his head, the pleas he'd offered as a child desperate for the pain to stop.

"So much potential in you, Gage. And you failed all of it. What you could have been. What you could have done. You've failed. Just like Jamison and Cody. Did you know they could have killed me? Both of them. It'd all be over. Instead, here I am."

"Do you want to see if I'll kill you?" Gage asked, giving the bonds that held him a little jerk. "I'd be happy to oblige that little experiment."

Ace laughed. "We'll get to it. We will. I'll give you all a chance to end me, because only the one who ends me could ever take my spot."

"We don't want your spot."

"One of you will. I was chosen for a reason, Gage, and one of you will be, too. Perhaps you six are my great challenge. My cross to bear. Every leader faces them."

"I can't decide if you're crazy or just evil, but *you* barely run your own gang anymore. You're hardly a leader. Seems to me, the Sons don't need you, Ace. Hasn't jail taught you that?"

The next hit was so quick and vicious Gage howled in pain and shock. Ace's grin widened.

"The pain can end. You know how it can end."

"I'm not worried about your pa—" Another crack and painful slap, though this one wasn't as hard or unexpected. Gage breathed through it, even as he felt blood begin to trickle down his thigh inside his pants.

Based on his father's reaction, Gage knew one thing. The Sons *were* struggling without Ace at the helm. Ever since Jamison and Cody had managed to get Ace behind bars, the Sons had been sloppy.

Or maybe…

Could it be that the *Sons* weren't struggling at all. It was Ace, losing power over the group that had followed him blindly. Wouldn't that be worse to Ace—continuing on just fine without him and so many of his top men dead after a planned explosion by Cody's former North Star Group?

The thought—the utter possibility—almost made Gage laugh. It reminded him that *everything* had an end. And maybe he wouldn't live out his father's end, but his brothers would.

Felicity would.

She wasn't here, and neither was Michael. There were too many scenarios, too many possibilities of where Felicity could be and what she could be facing.

He had to survive this next little while just to make sure she survived. To make sure.

Then he did the thing he'd sworn to never do again.

Because sometimes you had to break a promise to yourself to keep a more important one to someone else.

"I get the whip because I'm the biggest. The smartest. The one best suited to take over, but the weakness of my mother needs to be beaten out of me."

Another blow, but he'd been expecting that, too. Giving in to what Ace wanted never truly offered relief. If it were that easy, life would be a heck of a lot different. For all of them.

"Isn't that how it goes?" Gage asked, failing to make his voice sound properly deferential.

"Try again. Try to mean it this time. Feel the truth. The weakness will be whipped out of you, Gage. Here. Or you'll die. Jamison won't save you this time. Brady won't save you. Even that little redheaded dimwit can't save you. It's you and me."

"And one of us will end up dead."

"Oh, son, now you're speaking my language."

Chapter Thirteen

Felicity may have lived with her father only until she was four years old, but as she waited to take him out, she realized she'd learned quite a few things from him.

Silence was the first thing. Stillness the second. If you were silent and still, it was hard to become a target. And in a house with her father, she was always a target.

He had to find her first, though.

She'd learned to fold in on herself, to meld into her surroundings with everything she had. She'd learned and honed those skills before she'd learned how to speak or walk—or so she thought. So she *felt*.

Life with the Knights, and the slow—very slow— bloom of maturity and adulthood had helped her un-learn those impulses. She'd figured out how to speak and move and dream and believe without folding in on herself. Without hiding.

But a person never unlearned their early impulses completely. As her father huffed and puffed toward her, she struggled to stay in the present. Hard when she was hiding just as if she'd been that toddler struggling to hide from another one of her father's rages.

But she had a plan this time. She had fight this time. Her father didn't get to terrorize her anymore.

She moved with his movements, keeping her body shielded by the large rock she was hiding behind. She was careful of where and how she stepped—even a pebble tumbling down the side of the crevasse she was tiptoeing around might bring his attention to her.

Though, based on all his heavy breathing, maybe not.

She kept her breathing even, that old hiding trick in full force as he passed the rock she was behind—as she moved around it so she could surprise him from the back.

She didn't even need to push him. As she jumped out, guttural scream piercing the quiet air, he jerked, tripped and tumbled down the steep cliff.

He landed with a thud, and then moans of pain that echoed and grew louder and louder. He writhed on the hard ground below and Felicity looked down at him. She felt inexplicably *furious*.

She'd won, for the moment. Done exactly what she planned to do, and still the fury swept through her like a tidal wave.

"Do you feel big and powerful now?" she called as she considering kicking some rock down on top of him. Or maybe throwing the heaviest rocks she could lift. She wanted to torture him. She wanted to cause him all the pain he'd caused her. She wanted to…

She stopped herself, and the fury. She wasn't like him—didn't want to be. She didn't need to terrorize him just because he'd terrorized her. It wouldn't solve anything or erase anything.

Still, it surprised her how badly she wanted to.

"Felicity." He said it in the same tone of voice she remembered. Pleading. Apologetic. Therapy had taught her that an abuser's strongest weapon was his ability to make himself seem truly sorry, truly sympathetic.

"Maybe you should answer the question. Do you feel big and powerful now?"

"I was only following orders, Liss. That's all. Ace is a powerful man. I had to do what he said. Please. Don't... I'm sorry. I had to."

He was a big lump on the ground, holding on to his leg. She stood quite a few feet above him. He was begging and pleading, and it was only the therapy she'd had that kept her from falling for it.

"You didn't *have* to do anything. Ace doesn't own you. You weren't..." Then it dawned on her, what she'd never fully considered. "You're *in* the Sons?" He had been. All this time. Somehow? Or was it new?

Did it matter?

No. What mattered was he'd killed his daughter—a sister she'd never known—and then tried to frame Felicity for murder. Regardless of Ace's influence, he had done those things. She was sure of it.

"You *killed* her," Felicity said, her voice vibrating with an emotion she wished she could bury for right now.

"Killed who?" His eyes bulged in horror down there in the canyon. "I ain't killed *no one*."

She believed him, for a split, stupid second when she felt a moment of relief and hope. She desperately wanted to believe her father wasn't capable of murdering his own daughter, despite all the evidence to the contrary.

But that was so utterly ignorant she hated herself for even thinking it, no matter how briefly.

"Is Ace telling people I killed somebody?" He scrambled to stand and howled in pain. Presumably he'd seriously injured his leg. "I didn't kill nobody!" he shouted, panic and desperation tinging his words.

"And yet your fingerprints were all over my cabin. *And* the evidence. You're the one who identified her body."

"I didn't! I didn't! Whose body? What are you talking about?"

Felicity faltered. Michael seemed utterly confused and lost, and it wasn't beyond Ace, even in prison, to be able to make things happen. But how could someone have impersonated her father to identify a body? How could prints be dropped without her father being culpable?

"What about your daughter?"

"You're my daughter, Felicity." He managed to get to his feet, leaning on one leg over the other. He put his hands together as if praying. To her. "Please. You gotta help me. Ace made me do all this, but I didn't kill anyone. Please."

"You beat me. I was three years old, probably younger when it started. You beat me. A little, defenseless girl."

He had the decency to drop his arms to his sides. He made a helpless gesture. "I… Yes, I did that. I know it makes me a monster. I was messed up. I still am. I get it." He didn't make the pleading motion again, but he did look up imploringly, shading his eyes against the sun with his hand. "But I didn't commit *murder*."

Maybe he hadn't. Maybe he had. She didn't know. She wasn't sure she cared.

"You deserve what you get," she said, but it was a whisper and she knew he didn't hear her down there. "You deserve what you get," she repeated, still whispering, feeling tears sting her eyes.

But it seemed more than possible that her father was just a pawn in Ace's scheme. Not an innocent one. He was in the Sons, had to be, whether he'd always been or had joined up recently. He deserved anything he got— and more than that, he didn't deserve even a second of her concern or help.

"I didn't kill anyone," he said, his voice wavering as if he was about to cry.

"Maybe," she agreed, feeling detached. As though she was floating above herself or as if there was cotton shoved into her chest instead of a heart and lungs. "It doesn't matter."

She could hear the way she sounded. Flat. Emotionless. There were emotions—she could feel them swimming under all that cotton—but she was afraid of what would happen, what she would allow herself to do if she accessed them.

She stepped back from the ledge.

"Felicity. Where are you going? You can't leave me down here!"

She took another step.

"Please! Please. I'm hurt. Don't… I'll die down here. I'm *hurt*. Please. Please!"

"I remember begging," she said. The sun was beating down on her, but all she felt was ice. Brittle, stinging ice. She had to get away from it.

Away from him.

"You'll probably die down there."

"Then it'll be you committing murder, Felicity," he yelled from his spot down in the canyon as she walked away.

"So be it," she whispered to herself.

GAGE WEAVED IN and out of the pain, out of consciousness. The blows kept coming, and would, until his father was ready to fight.

Usually at the point Gage was his weakest. But when a boy was at his weakest, that's when he fought the hardest. Or should.

According to Ace.

He'd be brought to his weakest point, then be given a weapon. A smaller, less useful weapon than his father's, but a weapon nonetheless.

Gage had survived this a few too many times to count. His own personal hell. His punishment for having a quick mind. For being born big and strong.

Gage was under no illusion he was special. Ace had picked on them all for separate reasons. Doled out punishments specific to each of his sons.

Gage had never told his brothers the whys of his personal hell. Instead, he'd worked to make himself the opposite of everything Ace said he was.

Once he'd finally got into school, he'd failed. Over and over again. He'd skimmed through graduation from high school to the police academy. He never let himself excel, and since Brady did, and so well, no one ever thought twice of the underperforming twin.

Thank God. A saving grace.

Now he was back here, in the exact position he'd escaped, the exact position he'd proved to everyone he didn't belong to be.

He couldn't think about being back in this same place he'd escaped. Couldn't think about how unfair it was.

Maybe Ace was right all along. He was anointed somehow. Chosen. Because somehow Ace always got what he wanted, even if it took years to get there.

No. No, it wasn't true. Jamison was alive and well, getting ready to marry Liza and make a family with Liza's half sister. Cody was back with Nina and their daughter Brianna, building a life in Bonesteel.

Ace didn't get everything he wanted.

Gage fought off the nausea, reminded himself not to float away from the pain because that would only prolong the inevitable.

This standoff was inevitable.

Always had been. Always would be.

And if he ended it, maybe he'd be like Ace, but maybe he'd end this for his brothers. Would that be so bad? So wrong? Couldn't he live with anything if it meant saving his brothers?

"I think you're ready, Gage."

Gage laughed. It was all so ridiculous. He'd been whipped and beaten bloody—he could feel the blood covering him. Like a film.

This was Ace's language, Ace's currency. Blood and pain.

It could be Gage's, too. If he killed Ace, by some grace of God, it would be his language, too.

He didn't want it. He'd rather die. If he just knew Felicity was safe, he'd rather die. But he wasn't sure. He had to fight to be sure.

He was tired of fighting the insanity of his own father. Tired of fighting, period. He just wanted...life. He'd taken for granted the years since his escape when Ace had left him alone thinking they'd just keep lasting.

Gage looked at the man who'd fathered him, tortured him then and now, and had no doubt murdered Gage's mother. Gage didn't understand any of it. Top to bottom. "Why didn't you just kill us, Ace? You had the chance. Over and over and over. You've always had the chance."

Ace stepped closer, looking at Gage as if he'd missed some important life lesson along the way. "What's life without the chance? You've made me into a monster in your own head, Gage. You all did. None of you ever tried to understand. I don't want you dead. I want you reborn as only mine."

Reborn. It was such insanity. As if his own mother could be erased from him even if he wanted her to be. After all, she'd been weak enough to love a monster, to keep giving birth to son after son this monster would torture. Just to stay alive. And for what? To die anyway.

In the moment, he had no warm feelings for the mother who'd allowed this, but she hadn't been a monster. She hadn't been *this*. "She was better than you, you know," Gage said, expecting the blow to follow.

It didn't. Not yet. Ace got very still. "She was weak. And so are you."

"It isn't weak to survive you, Ace."

"She didn't, did she?"

"She did. She knew who and what you were. She

couldn't break free of the spell of that, but she knew. She used to tell all of us that when she died, that when *you* killed her, you would try to make us into you. She said we never had to turn into that, if we didn't want to. She was stronger than you where it counted. We didn't escape until she was gone. Why not, Ace?"

"You really want to play the why-not game?" Ace smiled, the chaotic, gleaming smile that made Gage's stomach roil completely separately from the concussion symptoms.

If Ace was talking, though, he wasn't whipping or beating, so Gage nodded. "Yeah, let's play."

"Why didn't your mother escape? Why didn't she run you all to your precious grandma? She could have."

"Of course. She wasn't a prisoner to you *at all*," Gage said, letting the words drip with sarcasm.

"You six escaped. Why couldn't she?"

Gage opened his mouth to rage about how Ace had warped his mother, twisted her until she didn't know *how* to escape. Maybe that made her weak, but she'd given Gage himself the belief that something better existed out there. He just had to get there.

Maybe it was Jamison who had proved it, over and over again, but it was his mother's seed of truth that he'd first believed.

But he was tired. God, he was tired. And his mother was dead. What did this matter? What did any of it matter? Why couldn't he give up?

He, of course, knew the answer. Felicity was out there, and as much as his brothers would survive and thrive without him, they would blame themselves. They would want to avenge him.

"Maybe she didn't want to bring your insanity to her own mother's household."

Ace snorted. "Your mother thought as little of Pauline as I do."

"And yet Pauline lives. Thrives. She raised us. And you let her. Why is that?"

Ace's face went dark, the terrifying fury Gage had once known better than to poke at. But he couldn't hold himself back, not when his own fury was beginning to bubble under all the pain and exhaustion.

He smiled at Ace in that same way Ace was always smiling at him. "You're afraid she really did curse you." Gage laughed. "That's just sad."

A blade flicked out—Gage didn't know from where—but it was at his throat, sharp and deadly.

"I was wrong, Gage. Rare, but we all make mistakes. Even me. I thought you were the smartest. But you're the weakest, and now you'll die. Say your last words, son. Because I'm done trying to make you into something."

Chapter Fourteen

Felicity licked her lips even knowing it wouldn't help the dry, cracked texture. It wouldn't magically make water appear or make everything swirling around in her mind make sense.

She was close to her cabin. Close to water. That was all that mattered as the sun beat down on her from above.

She squinted against the sun and stopped in her tracks when she saw what sat outside her cabin in the distance.

A police cruiser.

For a moment she felt relief so potent tears stung her eyes. She started forward, then remembered she was still wanted for murder.

Even if the police had saved Gage, that didn't mean things had been cleared up.

But they could be. Wasn't water more important than getting arrested? Gage would clear it up and everything would be fine.

Eventually.

Maybe.

I didn't kill anyone.

Her father had seemed so desperate. So surprised. So confused by what little she'd said about the murder. Was it her own bias doubting he'd killed, or was it just reason? *I didn't kill anyone. I didn't kill anyone.*

Ace had to have framed him, but how could she prove Ace was behind anything when he'd been in jail? And why would she want to? Her father deserved whatever he got.

Dying of exposure?

She pushed that thought out of her head, but the roiling nausea that accompanied it stuck around.

She slowed her pace as she moved toward her cabin. There was no sign of Ace or Gage. She used as much cover as she could to creep closer and closer to the small grove of trees that had been planted on the east side to give the cabin some shade back in the days before air-conditioning.

She hid among the trees, straining to hear something that might give her an idea of why the police were here. Had they found Gage? Ace? Was everyone okay?

Or was it all much worse than that?

The vehicle was a Pennington County cruiser, so there was no chance it was one of the Wyatt brothers, who all worked for Valiant County.

She didn't realize two men were in the cruiser until the driver's side door opened, and the passenger side next.

Two men got out. They clearly weren't in any hurry. Had they just driven up before she'd crested the rise for the cabin to come into view? That would mean Ace had taken Gage somewhere before the police had shown up.

She closed her eyes against the pounding panic. She had to figure out what was going on.

"Doesn't look like the tornado disturbed much here," the taller officer said to the other as they moved slowly toward the cabin. Not out of fear, but as if they weren't in any hurry to get to work.

"Lucky for us."

"Going over the house again seems overkill, doesn't it?"

The shorter one scratched his head. "That detective from Valiant County was adamant. Hard to blame him. Seems off if it's true the suspect didn't have any contact with her father."

"Seems *convenient* more than *off*, given he's friends with the suspect." The officer stopped short and swore. "Someone's been here. The tape's off."

"Could have been the wind," the other one said, but he was already pulling on rubber gloves and reaching for the caution tape fluttering in the slight breeze.

Tucker was the detective from Valiant County they were referring to. It seemed they were here only to search her cabin again. Look for more clues.

What might they find?

Didn't matter. She had to find Gage. There was no indication they had any idea he'd been here, or that Ace had.

Before she went in search of Gage, she needed backup. She had to forget about the desperate need for water and connect to the Wi-Fi.

But she'd need to be closer than the trees. Somehow, without getting caught. She could wait them out, but how long would that be? How long could Gage survive whatever and wherever Ace had presumably taken him?

Maybe he'd fought Ace off. Maybe…

Well, she couldn't entertain maybes until she knew for sure. She had to get a message to the Wyatts, then figure out what happened.

Without getting caught.

She closed her eyes for a second, letting herself pray to anything and everything she believed in, then she grabbed her phone. She pulled up the Wi-Fi and watched the screen as she crept closer and closer.

"Come on," she muttered, waiting for her Wi-Fi name to come up. She was easing out of the trees, her gaze moving from the cabin to the phone, back and forth, back and forth.

"Someone was definitely in there."

Felicity jumped back, pressing herself behind a tree. She squeezed her eyes shut and held her breath. She couldn't hear over the pounding of her own heart in her ears. She was light-headed and afraid for a moment she might faint.

Then the engine started.

She dared peek from behind the tree and watched as the police cruiser drove away.

She nearly wept in relief. Still, she waited, making sure they were gone for good before she ran forward. She had to stop, drop her pack and dig for her keys. With trembling hands, she found them and ducked under the caution tape.

It took a while for her hands to stop shaking enough to insert the key into the lock. She pushed it open and went straight for the faucet. She flipped on the water, ducked her head under the stream and drank with messy, greedy gulps.

Once she cooled off a little bit she remembered herself and her priorities.

She pulled up the text messages on her phone and sent a group text to everyone—Wyatts, Knights.

Ace was at my cabin. Took Gage. Don't know where. Going to track. Need help.

She paused, stupidly, then took the time to explain where she'd left her father and that he'd need help and medical attention.

She couldn't be that cold to let revenge take over her.

He beat you. Gage's words, flat as they'd been when he'd first delivered them, echoed in her head.

She shook her head. What was done was done. She'd sent the text and now she had to find Gage.

She grabbed the few water bottles she had left and went back outside, locking the door behind her. She ducked back under the tape, pushed the water into her pack and studied her surroundings.

She could see a myriad of footprints. Had the cops even looked at them? She focused on them now, remembering this morning.

Ace had tossed her down, and there was the indentation in the grass where she'd slid. There was a boot print—presumably one of the cop's—in the middle of it.

She moved there, then turned to look at the house. Ace had held Gage, that horrible gun pressed to his temple, right there and—

Gun.

She bolted back into the house, knowing it would

take too long and knowing she had to do it. She got her gun and holster, then returned to where Ace had held Gage.

She tried to determine whose footprints were whose, followed the two sets that veered off behind the house. One had to be Gage's, didn't it? If her father had followed her, his prints wouldn't be aligned with Ace's *or* Gage's.

There was mud here, not sloppy mud, but slowly drying mud. Still wet enough to make deep marks, but more of a clay texture. A flurry of footprints, a few indentations she couldn't figure out, but it all ended in a set of footprints and two long trenches.

Like heels being dragged. Fear snaked through her, but she couldn't give in to it.

She followed them.

They went for a way, into the patch of grass behind her cabin. Still, the ground was soft enough she could follow it.

Until the grass gave way to rock. The millennia of wind and rain, soil and rock. Erosion and deposition in its grand, epic scale.

Her heart, stretching out before her, and the absolute worst landscape she could encounter when trying to find someone. Rock was vast, virtually trackless. Too much wind to follow any kind of idea of which way they'd gone.

Then she saw it. A little bit of fabric under a rock. Black, like the T-shirt Gage had been wearing. Just a bit of it, clearly ripped off.

You're being unreasonable. If he was being dragged away, how could he rip his shirt *and* stick it under a rock?

Unless he was doing the dragging, but wouldn't he have gotten help? Not dragged Ace off alone?

It was probably just something blown by the wind—a hiker tearing his clothes on a rock, or the remnants of a ceremonial object. Granted, those occurred more often in the southern portion of the park. Still, with the winds in the Dakotas it was hardly impossible.

But this fabric was under a rock. Specifically. Purposefully.

If she went in the direction of the piece of fabric, she'd be heading back out into the canyons and rock formations.

That didn't scare her. She was a park ranger. She was equipped, now, with water. She knew how to navigate. She knew how to get back if she went in the wrong direction.

She glanced warily at the sky. She was prepared to camp. No food, but she had water. She had a weapon now. Everything would be fine.

Because she wouldn't stop until she found Gage.

She followed the bits of fabric, almost sobbed with relief as she found a car insurance card with Gage's name on it. He had really been Hansel and Greteling it through the Badlands while Ace dragged him along.

How hurt was he, though, that he didn't fight off Ace?

She kept going, ignoring that thought as she followed the bits of Gage's things. She had to double back a few times when she couldn't find anything for a while. It was exhausting, and she should stop for water, but every time she found the next hint she pushed forward, desperate to find the next one.

She didn't touch them, hoping the Wyatt boys would be able to find them and him. If *she* could, *they* could, she was sure of it.

When she reached a clearing of sorts along a long wall of rock, she almost doubled back, but in the distance she saw something black and out of place against the tan, reddish and brown landscape.

She moved toward it, then stopped a few feet away.

It was a wallet. It sat in the open, which she thought was strange. It wasn't hiding. It wasn't under a rock— so technically the wind could have blown it.

Right above the wallet was the entrance to a cave.

Slowly Felicity lowered her pack to the ground, taking care to move quietly. She pulled the gun from the holster and crept toward the cave, her heart in her throat.

GAGE KEPT HIS gaze on his father as he waited for the pain. Would Ace slit his throat like he had the knife poised to do? Or would it be slower, meaner?

It could go either way, but for right now Ace simply held the knife there, waiting for Gage's last words.

He didn't have any. Not for his father anyway.

"Cat got your tongue? Maybe that's where I'll start."

Gage shrugged, even as he felt the blade of the knife scrape against the tender skin of his neck.

Ace paused, frowning. There was a noise, some kind of skittering like pebbles falling, toward the mouth of the cave. Likely some kind of animal, but Ace tilted his ear toward the sound.

Gage was weak, beaten, bloody, and still he knew a moment when he saw one. With enough of a push, he couldn't escape, but he could get that damn knife off his throat.

He used the bonds that held his hands tied behind his back and to whatever was behind him to hold his weight as he managed to slowly and quietly rear his leg back.

He made noise as he kicked, which was inevitable. Ace tried to sidestep the blow. Gage planned on that and managed to pivot with enough time for his kick to land, knocking Ace over, with some help from a rock formation behind him.

Ace snarled up at him. "You think you can win with your hands tied behind your back?" Ace demanded, a vicious, piping fury that overrode his usual distressing calm. *"You."* He got to his feet, searching the cave floor around them for his knife.

When he didn't see it, he began to reach for the gun at his side.

"He might not be able to. But I can."

Gage was sure he was hallucinating. The sun shone behind her like she was some kind of red-haired guardian angel, complete with firearm.

It wasn't possibly happening, but there Felicity was, stepping away from the streaming sunlight and into the dim light of the cave. She held her gun pointed at Ace.

She didn't shake. She didn't waver. She didn't look over at Gage himself. She just kept that gun pointed at Ace, her gaze cool and calm and locked on him.

Ace's sneer deepened. "You won't shoot me."

"I shot your man last month. Isn't that why you're after me now? Trying to pin a murder I didn't commit on me."

Ace laughed mirthlessly, and the sneer stayed put on his face. "Don't flatter yourself. You're a bug."

"A bug you can't squish." Her voice was so cool, so controlled, it very nearly sent a shudder through Gage. He wasn't sure he *knew* this Felicity. She was like a different person.

"Felicity—"

She shook her head, still not looking over at him. "I want you to loosen the holster, let it fall. Then you'll walk out of this cave, Ace. Hands up, walk slow. I'll follow. Then we'll all wait."

"You must have mistaken me for one of my sons. I'm not going to simper and follow along. You think that sad excuse for a gun scares me? *Me?* Do you know what I've survived? Do you know what I am?"

"I don't really care, Ace, because my finger is on the trigger and if you don't move in five seconds, you'll have a bullet to the gut."

"Let's see what you got, sweetie." He began to move for his gun—not to drop it, Gage was sure. "I'll be the nightmare you—"

The shot rang out and Ace's body jerked, stumbled, then fell.

Gage made some kind of noise—horror, shock, relief and a million other things wrapped up into whatever expulsion of sound escaped his mouth.

"Felicity."

She took a step back. She didn't seem so cool and calm now as Ace writhed on the floor. He held on to his stomach, blood trickling over his hands. She still had the gun pointed at him.

"Felicity," he repeated, trying to keep his voice calm. "Get the gun."

Ace was reaching for it, but every time his arm moved, he groaned or grunted in pain. Color and blood drained from him with equal speed.

Felicity moved forward and slid his gun out of his holster without much of a fight from Ace.

She stared down at him, both guns in her hands now.

"Felicity. Come untie me."

She didn't move. She stared down at Ace's body as if she was in a trance. Ace writhed, made awful noises, but he didn't attempt to fight Felicity. Her finger was still on the trigger, the gun still pointed at Ace.

Gage didn't know whether she planned to shoot him again, and he certainly didn't know whether he wanted her to or not, but the pale, lifeless look on her face was killing him.

"Felicity. Look at me."

Finally, she turned. A breath escaped her, shaky and pained. Then she sucked it in. She was pale, the color of death. Her eyes were glassy and her breath was coming in shallow puffs now.

He couldn't make his way to her and it cut him in two.

"I had to." She flicked a glance at Ace again.

"You did the right thing," Gage said, trying to draw her attention back to him. "Grab his knife. Then come untie me, okay? We'll figure it out. One step at a time."

She nodded too emphatically for him to feel any better about her mental state.

"Right over there. By that big rock."

"It's a sediment pile."

"Sure, sure." Hearing her using the technical term was some kind of relief. "Bring the knife here, okay?"

She nodded again, and this time actually moved for the knife. Gage glanced at Ace. He was still moving, writhing and groaning.

She'd shot him in the gut, just like she'd warned.

Felicity slid her gun into her holster, still holding Ace's in her hand. She picked up the knife, both her arms shaking now.

"Felicity. Untie me. Come on. Felicity?"

"Right." She approached him, all shaking limbs and too pale complexion. When she finally reached him, still holding the knife and gun in either hand, she met his gaze.

"God…you're… Gage." She inhaled shakily, tears filling her eyes.

"I'm okay. Kind of. I mean, I'll be okay. Look at me. I'm doing better than you, at the moment."

"You're covered in blood."

"It's okay. Don't cry, sweetheart. God, it's killing me. Just untie me. Okay. Untie me. I need you to untie me."

"I'm sorry. I'm sorry." She scrambled forward and began to work on the ropes with the knife. "My brain's in a fog. I can't seem to think."

"You're fine. You saved me. You're all right."

"Saved… I… Did I kill him?"

They looked over at Ace. He'd stopped writhing, but his eyes were open and full of hate. Directed at them.

"Get me untied, Felicity," Gage said flatly.

"I'm trying. I'm trying." She was practically chanting it, but he could *feel* her shaking behind him as she worked.

Gage kept his eyes on Ace. Ace didn't move. When he opened his mouth as if he was trying to speak, little more than a groan escaped.

All this time, Gage had dreamed of Ace's end, and he didn't know what to feel in the face of it actually happening.

When Felicity finally managed to cut and untie the bonds, Gage at least felt relief instead of uncertainty. He stumbled a little forward, shook the rope off, then turned to Felicity.

She was staring at Ace, anguish written all over her. She kept looking at Ace as she spoke. "I texted your brothers. I followed your trail, surely they'll be able to. But we should head back if we can. I don't know what to do about…" She trailed off, swallowed and then looked up at him. "You're so hurt."

He held her face in his hands and studied her eyes. Too unfocused. She was in shock and they had to get out of here. She shook underneath his palms as if she was falling apart.

He wouldn't let that happen. He pressed a kiss to her forehead. "Felicity. Hey, I'm here."

She inhaled sharply and let it out on something like a sob even though no tears fell onto her cheeks. "I left my father to die. I shot Ace. You're so hurt." She looked up at him imploringly. "I don't know what to do."

He wanted to scoop her up and carry her away, but he'd be lucky to walk out of this cave on his own. "We just gotta get out of here. You got a message to my brothers. They'll be here. Let's get out of this cave. You just need some fresh air. Come on." He let go of her face and winced at the blood he'd accidentally left there.

His body screamed in pain, but he couldn't let her see it. He took a step and tried to breathe through the shooting pain, but with the next step his leg buckled. He cursed and glared over at Ace, who'd made some gurgle of a sound. Almost a laugh.

He was smiling, but he wasn't moving. The color was draining out of his face and he just lay there, clutching the bleeding wound.

"You're going to die. A slow, painful death," Gage offered.

Ace's smile didn't die. It widened. "And won't that be funny?" Ace said, his voice a rasp. "This little girl with more strength of spirit than you worthless weaklings did what you couldn't."

Gage struggled to his feet with Felicity's help. She didn't speak as she helped him limp toward the cave opening. Gage refused to engage with his father.

Gage made it without falling again, though the opening of the cave required some climbing that had him trying to bite back groans. He wasn't successful, and by the time they were a few feet away from the cave, where he'd left his wallet, Felicity was crying, silently, the tears streaming down her face.

He couldn't stand any more, and he lowered himself to the ground in something more like a crash. She stumbled over to him, presumably to help him, but he just folded her into him.

She let out a sob, and then another, and Gage held her while she cried—while he kept an eye on the mouth of the cave.

He was pretty sure Ace was completely incapacitated, but he wouldn't put it past the man to magically heal himself and come out of that cave whole and ready to fight.

"We should head back," Felicity said, her voice a squeak.

"Not sure I can do that. Let's just wait."

"It's getting dark. They might not see the trail."

Gage held her close despite the pain ricocheting in his body. "They will. They will. Let's just rest up a bit." He felt like he was fading, but he held on to Felicity and she snuggled into him as they waited.

It didn't take too terribly long. The sun was beginning to set when he saw someone in the distance.

"There shouldn't be just one person," Felicity said, fear and concern lacing her tone. She got to her feet. "I only see one figure."

"They might have split up to track."

"I left my father, Gage. He was hurt. But it could be him. He said he didn't kill anyone. Didn't even seem to know about someone being dead."

"But Tuck said he ID'd the body."

"I know. I know. I don't understand any of this, and if Ace dies, we may never know."

"If Ace is dead, Felicity, everything will be okay. That I can promise you."

Chapter Fifteen

Brady reached them first, then was able to radio emergency services with directions. Though she protested, Felicity was whisked away to the hospital just like Ace and Gage.

She was discharged a lot quicker than they were, and then bustled away to the Knight Ranch, where Duke and Rachel and Sarah fluttered all over her before forcing her to go to bed.

Felicity hadn't slept. She tried. She closed her eyes, lay completely still and emptied her mind of *everything.* But in that numbness she couldn't find the release of sleep.

Still, she stayed in bed for a full eight hours. Awake. After that exercise in futility she was up and ready to just…do anything else.

Sarah was at her door before Felicity had even made it across the floor.

"You shouldn't be up."

"I stayed put eight hours," Felicity said, wincing at how much she sounded like a whining child.

Sarah's expression was disapproval, but she didn't push Felicity back to bed, so that was something.

"Is Gage home?"

Sarah nodded. "I just talked to Dev. They released him this morning. Brady took him home and Grandma Pauline's ordered him to bed. Tuck is staying at the hospital to make sure police are guarding Ace at all times."

"So…" Felicity had to say it, had to accept the strange dichotomy of feelings swirling inside of her. "Ace is alive."

Sarah nodded, a scowl on her face. "He went through surgery. The prognosis isn't great, but the longer he survives, the higher his chance of survival goes. Or so says Brady."

"I want to see Gage."

"Duke—"

"I'm going over there," Felicity said. She didn't know what it would do. She'd be fussed over there just as much as here, but…

She only knew what she had to do.

Sarah convinced her to take a shower first, and Felicity knew that while she was showering, Sarah was likely telling Duke what Felicity planned.

He'd want her to stay put, but she just couldn't.

When Felicity was out of the shower, dressed and ready to go, Sarah was waiting for her in the kitchen.

"I hope you're not missing chores for this."

"Chores can be made up. Besides, I'm just going to drive you over. Then I'll come back and do my work. Duke or I will pick you up later."

"You both know the doctor said I was fine."

Sarah pursed her lips as if considering what to say in response, an odd thing for outspoken Sarah. Eventually she just shook her head. "Come on."

They drove to the Reaves Ranch. Felicity insisted Sarah not walk her to the door. If it had been Rachel or Duke, insisting wouldn't matter, but Sarah understood something about a woman needing to do things on her own two feet. "Felicity?"

Felicity paused before she slipped out of the car. She looked at Sarah, who kept her head straight ahead and her shoulders hunched practically up to her shoulders. Which Felicity knew meant she was going to say something genuine and meaningful.

"I hope you know you don't have to go through this alone."

Since it made her want to cry, especially coming from Sarah, Felicity shook her head. "What I was going through is over," Felicity replied, and got out of the car.

It might have been the biggest lie she'd ever told, but it felt right to say it. She walked across the yard and stepped into Pauline's kitchen without knocking—Pauline considered knocking a grave offense among her friends.

"There's a girl," Pauline greeted, standing in her normal spot by the stove. "You're looking peaked yet."

Felicity forced a smile. "I'm all right. Where's Gage?"

"Upstairs," Brady answered from his seat at the table, a mug of coffee next to his elbow and his phone out in front of him. "Still asleep or should be."

"Can I go see him?"

"Let's give him some time yet," Grandma Pauline said, nudging Felicity into a chair. A plate loaded with a country breakfast appeared in front of her.

Felicity could hear the sounds of little girls playing in

the living room, so Gigi and Brianna were here, which meant Liza and Nina were, too.

She stared at the plate, knowing she should eat it for Grandma Pauline's sake. But despite her internal coaxing, she couldn't seem to force herself into actually doing it.

The back door opened and Dev stepped in, stomping his boots on the mat. "Any news?" he asked.

Brady shook his head. "Not since the last."

"Why are they trying to save the SOB?" Dev groused. "Worthless waste of resources."

"Doctors take a vow to heal anybody," Brady lectured.

Felicity felt numb. She didn't know why. Everything she'd done was what she'd had to do. Leave her father to die. Shoot Ace. She'd had to do all those things, and if two monsters ended up dead, didn't that make her a hero?

But she didn't feel good. She didn't even feel terrible. She felt empty, and being here didn't help.

She just wanted to see Gage. Make sure he was all right. If she did that, maybe everything would click back into place somehow. Maybe she wouldn't feel as though she were walking through a cloud.

Dev sat down and ate his breakfast, and Brady poked around on his phone and drank his coffee.

No one tried to fill the silence with conversation. The only sounds were the girls in the other room and Grandma Pauline cleaning up after breakfast.

After typing furiously on his phone, Brady set it down and cleared his throat. "Jamison and Cody are on their way back to rest up for a bit before heading out again."

"Did they find my father?" Felicity asked, even though she knew the answer. Why would they head back out if he'd been found?

"No. Not yet. A few agencies are still looking, though. And they'll keep at it."

"He should be where I left him." They'd told her they hadn't found him when she'd been at the hospital last night, but she'd hoped by morning things would change. Daylight would make finding him so much easier.

Maybe the numbness would go away once she knew what had happened to him. "I don't understand why he wouldn't be."

"It could be he tried to find a way out, a way to safety. There are a lot of possibilities, Felicity. You said your father didn't kill that woman."

"That's what he said." She had no reason to believe it, no reason not to. What did it matter? Obviously, Ace had set him up one way or another.

"We'll keep looking for him."

Felicity nodded, the knot in her stomach becoming tighter and heavier.

"If you're worried or don't feel safe, you can stay here. We can—"

"I'm not worried. There's no reason to worry." She stood and pushed away from the table with too much force—everyone in the kitchen looked at her and it made her skin crawl with the feel of their stares and assessment. "I need to talk to Gage. That's okay, right?"

Brady's brow furrowed, but he nodded. "I'm sure it'll be fine."

Felicity didn't even wait for instructions. She didn't know which room Gage would be in, but she'd figure it out. Of course, as she stepped into the living room heading for the stairs, Liza and Nina stopped her.

Liza enveloped her in a hug almost immediately. "We're so glad you're okay." She pulled back and studied Felicity's face. "You need to sleep."

Felicity tried to muster a smile. She didn't bother to lie to Liza, who'd always seen through them all with a mother's knowledge. "I tried."

It had been hard to lose Liza when she'd gone back to the Sons to save her half sister. Hard to have her back, too. Felicity hadn't fully accepted Liza's return at first—she'd still felt a little hurt and betrayed. In the moment, she couldn't access any of that bitterness.

She was just glad someone could see through her. If someone could, maybe she'd make sense of herself, eventually.

"What's wrong with Aunt Felicity?" Brianna asked, forgetting her dolls with Gigi and coming to stand next to her mother. "Did Grandma Pauline make you some magic cocoa?"

Felicity managed a smile and slid a palm over the girl's flyaway blond hair. It was amazing how quickly and easily Brianna had slid into the family. Despite spending her first almost seven years away from Cody and the Wyatts, she'd had no problem accepting he was her father, accepting the crowd of aunts and uncles she now had.

It warmed Felicity some to remember what family and love could do. "No magic cocoa yet. I'm going to go check on Gage first."

"His head got smashed," Gigi said seriously.

"Not exactly," Liza replied on the long-suffering sigh

of a frustrated parent. "The Wyatt boys need to learn to choose their words a little bit more wisely around small ears."

"Can we go up and see Uncle Gage?" Brianna asked. "I can give him my magic necklace."

"Uncle Gage has his own magic for now," Nina said. "We call them high-voltage painkillers that make him sleepy. You go on up, Felicity. I'm sure he'll be glad to see you."

Liza linked her arm with Felicity's. "I'll show you which room."

That tone, which meant *I'll drag all of your secrets out of you* had Felicity hesitating. "I can find the room. I—"

"Come on now," Liza said cheerfully, pulling Felicity toward the stairs.

Felicity had no choice. Liza pushed her in front to take the narrow staircase first, and she followed right behind.

"You know, Brady had to sedate him to keep him from charging over to the Knight Ranch and seeing you this morning."

For the first time in something like twelve hours, Felicity felt *something* pierce the numbness. Not much, but a little spread of warmth. "Oh."

"Oh."

"That's what I said. Oh."

"Felicity." Liza stopped her at the top of the stairs. "As someone who's been on the receiving end of a Wyatt man's concern, that was *not* friendly concern."

"What was it then?"

Liza narrowed her eyes and folded her arms across

her chest. A very formidable *mom* look. "Care. Serious, love-type care."

"Love." Felicity's face got hot and the word came out like a croak. She didn't particularly want to feel embarrassment, but she supposed it was nice to feel anything. "You're being ridiculous."

"Am I?"

"Yes. He just kissed me is all."

"Is all." Liza took Felicity by the shoulders before she could continue down the hall. "But you've always liked Brady."

"I…" Felicity looked imploringly down the hallway. "I didn't even really *know* Brady, you know? It was just a safe crush."

"There is nothing safe about a Wyatt."

Liza laughed at the horrified look that must have crossed Felicity's face. Then she pulled Felicity into a hug.

"Babe, you *shot* Ace. There isn't anything safe about you, either. Revel in that a bit." She pulled her back. "You saved Gage's life. But this one? It's still yours. Don't—"

"It isn't like that." Felicity didn't have the words, but she knew what she felt, what Liza was worried about. "It isn't like that. You know… How it feels like no one understands you? Deep down, I think all us foster sisters *could* have understood each other, but we were too self-absorbed to realize that. We weren't mature enough or something to access understanding, even when we had love."

Liza nodded sadly. "It's hard to see past your nose when you're that young, and that wounded."

Felicity nodded. It hurt she hadn't realized it before, but at least she understood it now. "He's the only person to make me recognize other people understand what I was feeling. To suck me out of feeling like I'm the only one who knows what certain things are like. To actually look and see all of me, not some half version. It's not transferring feelings or anything. It's… He just got me. And that matters. Does that make sense?"

Liza nodded, her eyes suspiciously shiny. "All the sense in the world."

GAGE STRUGGLED TO wake up. Something had changed. In the air. Inside of him. Something had changed, and he had to wake up to figure it out.

When he finally managed to blink his eyes open, the room swam. Back at the ranch. Last night at the hospital was a vague blur, but Brady had driven him home this morning, with strict orders to rest and heal.

It didn't sound so bad in the moment, his temples pounding and his mouth dry as dust. His body ached everywhere. He was pretty sure his hair hurt.

Then a cool hand brushed his forehead, featherlight and soothing. He sighed into it a moment, half convinced it was some guardian angel.

But God knew he didn't have one of those.

He managed to move his head, and there was Felicity, sitting on the floor next to his bed. All he could see of her was her red hair, and the arm she'd put up on his bed to stroke his forehead.

"Am I about to have an illicit dream?"

She tilted her head up, giving him a skeptical if amused look. "I don't think so."

"Darn." He tried to move, but it all hurt too much. "What are you doing sitting on the floor? I can't see you down there."

She got to her feet, moving a few steps down the length of the bed so he could look up at her without having to crane his neck.

It hit him now, safe at home in his childhood bed, in a way it hadn't back in that cave. "You saved my life." He'd been prepared to die, if she was okay, but instead she'd stepped in and saved him.

It awed him straight through. Even if she didn't seem all that pleased.

She looked down at her hands. "People keep saying that. I don't remember much of it, to be honest. It just kind of happened." She shrugged helplessly.

She was too pale. She looked frail, like she had in that cave. Shaken and in shock, though she had a better grip on it now. She still wasn't... Felicity.

"Why don't you come sit down?"

She didn't. She just stood there, staring at him as if figuring out some great mystery. "Liza said you wanted to come see me. She said you had to be sedated."

He tried to shift in the bed, but just ended up wincing in pain. "Liza exaggerates. God, you smell good. Come here." He patted the bed next to him.

She studied the small spot, lips pursed, then carefully eased a hip next to him on the bed.

"If you wanted to, you know, caress my forehead again, weep a little over my wounds, I wouldn't be opposed."

He managed to get a snort out of her. Not quite a laugh, but an improvement to the seriousness. And even better, she drifted her fingers across his forehead.

They stayed like that for a few minutes, her moving her fingers back and forth on his forehead, a kind of balm even painkillers didn't offer.

And since it was making him relax, and he was too tired, too hurt to fight it, he reached up for a handful of her T-shirt and pulled her down until they were nose to nose. Then he kissed her, with all that softness.

She kissed him back, and something in her shifted or relaxed. Lightened, like a weight lifted. At least it seemed to him.

She pulled back a fraction, green eyes studying him with a kind of meaningfulness that might have sent him running far away if he could. But he couldn't. He was pretty much stuck here, and she made him feel...

She made him feel. Which meant it was time for a joke. "Still like it without all the mortal danger clouding your judgment?"

Her mouth curved, and she didn't back away. "Yeah, it's okay."

"What's wrong, Red?"

She exhaled shakily. "I don't know. They can't find my father."

"If Ace put him up to everything, that's not so bad, is it?"

"I guess." She swallowed, searching his face as if the answers she needed were somewhere in him. "He could be dead out there. Because of me."

"You could have been dead a long time ago because of him. No matter what he did or didn't do in *this* moment. What happened to him, he brought upon himself."

She sat so still, didn't suck in a breath or let one out. It was as if she froze completely. But after a moment or so of that incomprehensible reaction, she gave a small nod. "You should rest," she said, easing away.

"You're looking a bit like you could use some yourself."

"I tried." She lifted her shoulders, then dropped them. "I can't."

He pulled her close and tugged the covers up around them both. "Give it a shot."

And they both slept.

Chapter Sixteen

As the next few days passed, everything was a bustle of activity.

Ace was going back to jail, more charges heaped on him. It would be harder and harder for him to hurt people on the outside. Though she knew no one fully believed he was powerless in jail, it was still safer having him there than in the hospital. And she knew the Wyatts were hoping the attempted murder charges would get him transferred to a federal prison.

She hoped so, too, but while they waited for the bureaucratic tape to be cleared up, Gage was healing. All the Wyatts were still insisting he stay out at the ranch instead of his apartment in town, but everyone knew he wouldn't acquiesce that much longer, nor would he need to.

The police had canceled the warrant for Felicity's arrest, which had been a relief on every level. And, best of all, she'd been cleared to go back to work starting Monday.

Added to that back-to-normal, she seemed to have come out on the other side of this whole ordeal with something almost like a boyfriend, though she hesitated to say that word aloud, especially since they hadn't exactly told anyone about them.

Still, while she stayed at the Knight Ranch and Gage healed at the Reaves Ranch and everything cleared up, they took walks, exchanged kisses and had gone for a picnic lunch yesterday.

The Wyatts treated her like some kind of conquering hero, and somehow shooting Ace, even if she hadn't killed him, seemed to get it through everyone's head that she was not still the shy, stuttering Felicity.

Everything was fine and good. Better than it had been before this whole nightmare started.

Except that her father was missing. And while there was an APB out for him, and he was considered a missing person *and* a person of interest in a murder investigation, there was no trace of Michael Harrison. Even with Jamison and Cody and even Brady spending time searching for him.

It was like being stuck in limbo. Had she killed her father, no matter how inadvertently? Or was he still out there? And would that make him dangerous?

Felicity had no answers, and no one else seemed too concerned about it, so Felicity could only pretend that life was good.

She seemed to be fooling everyone—even Liza— that she was happy as a clam. With Ace out of the hospital and back in jail as of this morning, the Wyatts were darn near jovial. So much so that they were having a big family dinner, complete with the Knights.

It was raucous and good. Felicity had hoped the large group of people in Grandma Pauline's kitchen would make her feel better. Instead, the noise and cheer was just making her feel more like she'd lost her mind somewhere in that cave.

She forced herself to smile, even forced herself to eat, though her stomach roiled and cramped at the idea.

She didn't know why she couldn't let it go. Why she couldn't have some well-deserved celebration like everyone else in the room.

Except, their father was in jail. Hers was mysteriously missing.

He had to be alive or they would have found him. Why would he be alive and hiding? Was it because he thought he'd be blamed for the murder? Was it because he'd lied to her and he *had* murdered someone—his own daughter at that?

Felicity's head pounded with all the what-ifs and emotions they stirred up. When Grandma Pauline brought out dessert, Felicity excused herself, pretending she needed to use the bathroom.

She headed away from the dining room, bypassed the bathroom, and went toward the rarely used front door, instead. There was a rickety old porch swing out there. It didn't get much use, but sometimes Grandma Pauline did her mending there when she didn't have enough people to cook for.

Felicity lowered herself onto it. She needed to get it together, but she didn't know how.

She should be happy. She should be ecstatic. Maybe concern was normal, but...

It was just that she knew the Badlands. She knew what it would have taken to survive, if hurt. He hadn't even been able to stand when she'd left him there.

Left him to die.

Somehow Ace was alive and her father, who probably hadn't killed that woman—her sister—was dead because of her.

Maybe the woman wasn't even her sister. Her father had said he hadn't identified any body. Tucker had looked into that, interviewing the morgue employees. None had been able to confirm or deny that Michael had been the one to identify the body. Might have been, or it might have been someone pretending to be him.

Felicity closed her eyes and let herself rock on the swing. She heard the dogs clatter up onto the porch and she leaned forward to pet them, trying to find some comfort there.

Something had to change. She couldn't go on pretending. Eventually she'd just explode.

But her feelings didn't seem to want to listen to her rational thoughts, and she simply felt stuck in this awful place of...

Guilt.

She turned her head toward the door when she heard it creep open, forced all her heavy thoughts away as Gage stepped out onto the porch.

He didn't seem surprised to see her there, or even confused. "Got room on that swing?"

Felicity managed her fake smile. "Of course."

Gage slid into the seat next to her, draped his arm around her shoulders and gave her a little squeeze. He petted one of the dogs that put its head on Gage's thigh. "That smile's getting a little rough around the edges, Red. You might want to just let it go."

Somehow he made it easy to do. The smile died and

she let herself lean into him. She didn't know how to explain what was going on inside of her, but he didn't seem to need her to.

"I know you're worried your father's still out there."

She wrinkled her nose. Okay, he didn't need to see through her *that* easily. "It's fine."

"If it was fine you'd be inside or enjoying even half of this shindig. Do you think he's going to come after you or something?"

Wouldn't that make things easy? Well, maybe not easy, but different. It made more sense than guilt. "Maybe."

"Ah."

She tilted her head up to look at him. "Ah what?"

"It isn't that they haven't found him, and that he may be alive. It's that he might be dead. And you'd have to blame yourself."

She blinked at him, then looked out at the late summer sunset. "Neither are particularly positive potential outcomes, Gage."

"No," he agreed. "But I'm having trouble wrapping my brain around how you're feeling guilty for doing what you had to do to someone who made your childhood a living hell. Who could have made it a lot worse if the state hadn't stepped in."

She was supposed to blame him for that. And maybe he would have been bad enough to kill her back then. She only had hazy memories of living with him. She'd done her best to push them away when she'd been younger, and now they were hard to access.

She could remember pain. Hiding. Fear and confusion, but it was hard to attribute it to a specific face.

All those reactions and impulses had come back easily enough when he'd been after her, but it still hadn't been the same.

The monster from her childhood was a faceless one. The man she'd left to die had been flesh and blood. She knew that didn't make sense, that it wasn't *right*, but it was all inside of her anyway.

She inhaled and let the breath out just like her therapist had taught her. "I—I don't like the i-idea I used the Badlands against him." The deep breathing didn't take away the stutter in the moment, but she'd gotten her feelings off her chest.

"Oh, Felicity," he said on a chuckle as he leaned his temple on the top of her head. "Leave it to you."

She slumped in the seat, but his arms stayed tight around her. "It sounds stupid," she muttered.

"No, it sounds like you. And I get it. It isn't like I don't understand. I can stand over here and think you shouldn't feel guilty that you might have left your father to the fate of the Badlands, since I know what he did to you. But I didn't experience what he did to you. Hell, everything we had with Ace is fifty kinds of warped. I wanted him to die, but I'm not sure it would have been any kind of relief if he did."

It was strange to have someone give words to feelings she didn't know how to articulate, but that's just what Gage did. When he did, it helped her find her own words. "I hate feeling this way, but I don't know how to make it stop. Not until I know for sure. Everyone expects me to be happy, and I just—"

"Sweetheart, you don't have to pretend to be happy

just because everyone expects you to be. And let's be clear, Dev never expects anyone to be happy."

She managed a true smile at that. "I should be happy."

"If you're not, you should take your time to get right inside." He squeezed her shoulders again. "Give yourself a few breaks. We clawed our way through a rough few days there—it's okay if you're not ready to jump right back into normal life."

"You are *not* my normal life." This, him… She liked it, more than liked. But it didn't feel like her life to have a hot guy want to spend time with her, to slip his arm around her, to kiss her brainless.

"I am now," he said firmly.

It didn't *fix* her problems, but that determined sincerity eased some of the tightness. She'd still have to deal with whatever had happened with her father once they found him, but she'd have someone who understood the complexity of emotions over it…right next to her.

She tilted her head up. "You sound pretty sure about that."

He tapped her chin. "I am."

It was nice. Something and someone to be sure about, so she pressed her lips to his. He kissed her back, but he let her lead. He seemed to know the difference—when she wanted to be swept away, when she needed to be in control of something.

More than that, she understood the same about him. When he was content to sit back, and when he needed to push forward on something.

She sank into that kiss. Pushing forward. She'd been sitting around sulking, basically, but that was over. She had to act. She had to grab her life—*her life*. Why did bad men get to rule her life?

Not anymore.

She pulled away a fraction. "Are you going back to your apartment tonight?"

"Um." He cleared his throat. "I wasn't planning on it."

"Maybe we should." She didn't give him a chance to answer. Instead, she pressed her mouth to his again. When he deepened the kiss, pulled her so close she could scarcely catch a breath, she figured that was a *yes*.

The door creaked open, and though Felicity jumped back, Gage kept his arms around her and gave a withering look to Brady, who was staring at them with bugged-out eyes and a wide-open mouth.

"Help you?" Gage prompted.

"Grandma Pauline told me to—um." Brady cleared his throat. "Well." He rocked back on his heels and shoved his hands in his pockets. He looked embarrassed, which was kind of funny.

Felicity couldn't remember Brady ever looking embarrassed or uncomfortable. She couldn't remember ever seeing him with *any* elevated emotion, and it solidified what she'd been finding with Gage.

Brady was, on the surface, easy and nice. But Gage was... Real. To her. Likely Brady would find someone to be real for, but it wasn't her.

"Grandma Pauline wants to shove us full of dessert," she supplied for him.

Brady did not look directly at them, still sitting on the swing with their arms around each other. "Yeah."

"Ready, Red?" Gage asked, giving her hair a little tug.

She was ready. Ready to stop wallowing and wondering and actually do something. A few somethings, in fact. She got to her feet. "You bet."

GAGE MOVED TO follow Felicity, but Brady stepped in between them, allowing Felicity to move forward and stopping Gage from following.

Gage couldn't say he expected the censure on his brother's face, but seeing it now wasn't such a grand surprise. Brady had a lot of internal rules—not just for himself, but for everyone.

"Looks like I'm staying outside to talk to my twin brother, darlin'. You go on inside."

Felicity gave him a disapproving look. "Don't do that. You don't have to do that." She turned to Brady. "And you don't have to do whatever it is you have it in your head to do."

Brady's expression remained carefully blank. "If you'll excuse us, Felicity."

She rolled her eyes, muttered something about Wyatt men and headed inside.

Gage matched Brady's pose—stuffing his hands in his pockets, rocking back on his heels. He gave a cursory glance at the dogs sitting between them, tails wagging. "Nice night," he offered blandly.

"What exactly are you doing here?"

"Well, Brady, as I've known you to do the same with a handful of pretty women, I'm going to let you spell that one out yourself."

"You shouldn't—"

Gage might have had patience for Brady's lectures if he wasn't grappling with something bigger, broader than he was particularly ready for. "She's not your responsibility. And she certainly doesn't need your protection. Not from me."

"No. She isn't and doesn't. She isn't your responsibility, either."

"And that means what exactly?"

"What *is* this?" Brady gestured helplessly. "Felicity?"

"Yes, Felicity." He didn't have doubts there. Maybe he had some doubts about himself, about how right or ready he was for what he felt, but his feelings were there. And Felicity was too important to allow himself or Brady or anyone to convince him he should run away from them.

"You can't *fool around* with one of the Knight girls. I never thought I'd have to tell you that. Duke only tolerates Cody at this point because he's Brianna's father, not because Duke *approves* of Nina and Cody. I don't think he has any reason to tolerate you fooling around with Felicity."

Gage was about to make a joke, even opened his mouth to do it. But Felicity had told him he didn't have to do *that*, and he'd known what she meant. Not to make a joke to diffuse tension. Not to be *Gage* about it, all things considered.

So, maybe instead of a joke he could just settle in with the truth, no matter how uncomfortable. This was his twin brother after all. They had survived the same things. Side by side. Two sides of the same coin. Sometimes it felt like they spoke a language no one else understood. He loved all his brothers with all that he was, but what he shared with Brady was something unique.

Surely, Brady's censure was concern. Just veiled in that very Brady disapproval. "Well, I guess it's a good thing I'm hardly *fooling around*," Gage ground out.

"What? You're in love with her or something?" Brady snorted, but it died halfway through as his jaw went slack. "Gage…"

"Look—"

"Felicity, of all damn people."

"What's it matter if it's Felicity?"

"You can be impulsive, and this is not the time to be impulsive." Brady jerked a thumb toward the door where Felicity had disappeared. "She's not the girl to be impulsive with."

Gage shook his head. He'd never felt sorry for Brady. Brady was the smartest, the most even-keeled of all six of them. Everyone liked Brady everywhere he went. He was the best of them.

If Brady didn't understand that love was impulsive and just plain inconvenient, but *there* and necessary and impossible to ignore, well, he did feel sorry for Brady and hoped his twin would learn someday what love—inconvenient, out-of-the-blue love—could do.

"She's not a girl, Brady."

"I know that."

"I don't think you get it. Even with everything she did—including save my life—I don't think you get it. That's okay. You don't need to. This is not a situation where we require your input."

Brady opened his mouth, but Gage shook his head.

"Input. Not. Required."

"Fine," Brady replied tightly. "Then I guess we should

get back to dessert." He turned for the door. "And Duke kicking your butt," he muttered under his breath.

Maybe. But it was a risk Gage would take—couldn't help taking. Still, with honesty came the need for more of it.

"Did he have a weapon—just for you?" Gage asked before Brady could go back inside.

Brady paused at the door. When he turned around it was slow and careful, his expression carefully blank. He didn't meet Gage's gaze when he spoke. "He threw knives. To teach me to expect the unexpected."

There was more to that, and Gage wanted to know it all, but they didn't have time to get that deep into it. "Did he tell you *you* were special, so he had to be harder on you?"

Brady let out a long breath, but when he spoke it was detached and rote. "He said I was stupid and worthless, so he'd do what he could to make a man out of me."

Gage could only stare at his brother at first. He'd never imagined. Brady. By far the smartest of them, at least the one who tried the hardest. He could have gone to medical school and become a doctor if Grandma had had access to the money or the understanding of how college worked.

But it made a sick twisted sense, in that Ace way things clicked together. They were twins and Ace had somehow used that against them. Make Brady work harder. Make Gage shrink away from what he was.

Brady shrugged, an out-of-character, impatient gesture for him. "We don't talk about this. What's the point?"

"I would have said there wasn't one just last week,

but now I think we should. All of us. It would make us stronger against him. When you can... When you can let it go and someone understands, it changes something, Brady. And we all understand."

Brady met his gaze then, something wry in his expression. "Yeah, maybe, but good luck getting through to Dev on that score."

"We'll work on it." Gage was certain they needed to. "And there's something else we need to work on. I want you to help me find Felicity's father. She can't rest until he's found one way or another."

"We're looking."

"I don't mean casually or leaving it up to Pennington County. I mean you and me. Really looking."

"You aren't up for it yet." Brady tapped his temple. "That concussion was serious, Gage. The rest will heal no problem, but you don't want to take chances with your brain."

"Okay, so I'll take a few days. But..."

Brady sighed heavily. "She needs closure. And you're going to make sure she gets it."

"Damn straight." She'd saved his life. He loved her, as uncomfortable as he was with *that*. He owed her something. He'd give her this. Whatever it took.

Chapter Seventeen

By the time they managed to convince everyone that Gage was well enough to spend the night on his own, and that she would be fine going back to her cabin in the park alone—though neither precisely planned on being alone—Felicity was wound tighter than a drum.

But it was good to feel something—even anxiety and a weird giddiness. She walked outside with Gage, Grandma Pauline and Brady still in the kitchen grumbling about that fool boy and his hard head.

Most of her family had already headed back to the ranch, and she'd need to have Gage drop her off so she could get her car. She couldn't very well tell anyone Gage drove her back to her cabin. It wouldn't make sense.

"You're going to have to drive me over to my car. Otherwise, everyone is going to figure out where I went."

"I don't think we were fooling Brady any. He very clearly knows."

"So does Liza," Felicity murmured, tilting her head up and staring at the giant spread of stars above. Liza, Jamison, Gigi, Cody, Nina and Brianna had all headed back to Bonesteel earlier, but Felicity had to wonder how long Liza would keep what Felicity had told her a few days ago to herself.

"So..." Gage took her hand in his as they walked to his truck.

She looked down at their joined hands, marveled at how quickly that just felt right. But with rightness meant she owed him the truth. "I'm not ready for Duke to know."

"Ah."

"It's just... All those years ago? Everything with Nina disappearing on the heels of losing Eva *and* Liza really messed him up, and we both know no matter how much he loves Brianna, he hasn't quite forgiven Cody for being part of the reason Nina stayed away with her so long. I don't want to hurt him." She owed Duke so much more than she'd ever be able to repay, and that seemed reinforced by seeing her biological father again.

"I don't think you being happy would hurt him, Felicity. Even if he shot daggers in my direction for a while."

"Maybe." Maybe Gage was right, but... "I need to do a few things on my own, *really* on my own, right now."

"You do understand that what you're suggesting by coming home with me is not something you do on your own?"

She swatted his arm, unable to contain the laugh. "Yes, I'm aware."

He took her by the shoulders, and rubbed his hands up and down her arms. "Are you sure you want to do this? Now."

She didn't hesitate, because Gage was the only thing that made sense right now. If she went after what made sense, then she'd find herself on even ground again. "Yes. I'm sure."

"Brady seems to think I'm being impulsive, and that I shouldn't be...with you."

"Well, it's a good thing Brady doesn't get a say." She saw some hesitation in him, and she knew it wasn't his own. It had been put there—that he should be careful, that she couldn't handle it.

She wouldn't let anyone push her back to that place where people thought she needed to be protected or handled with kid gloves just because she was shy or stuttered or had been abused as a child. No. "I know what I feel when you kiss me, Gage. And I know how much it means that you understand me. And I understand you. I think we both know how special that is."

He stared at her for a long time, then he nodded. "Yeah. Listen, I've got an idea. Trust me?"

She nodded.

"Get in the truck."

They both climbed into Gage's truck, and Felicity decided to relax, enjoy the nighttime drive over the short, rolling hills of the Reaves Ranch. She had a spiritual connection to the Badlands that existed for some unknown reason deep inside, but she'd been raised and loved on these rolling grasslands of the two ranches that had been her childhood. If the Badlands were her soul, the ranch lands southeast of there were her heart.

He drove out, deep into the heart of the ranch. All the way through the pasture, to the tree line that ran along what had once been a creek but rarely got a trickle these days. The Knight land was on the other side of the creek bed.

It was so distant people rarely came out here unless a cow was missing. He stopped between the old creek and the pasture fence. He turned off the ignition and made a broad gesture.

Felicity's eyes widened. "Outside?" She couldn't school the squeak out of her voice.

"Seems...right."

It did. She'd rather be out here than anywhere else, and it was coming to be that she wanted to be with him more than anyone else—even herself, a rare thought for an introvert like her.

He slid out of the truck and grabbed a blanket from the back seat, and she followed. The night was warm, though the breeze was cool. The world smelled like summer—grass and wild. And though it was very much night, sunshine lingered in the air.

He spread out the blanket, looking something like a ghost in the silvery moonlight. But he was no ghost. No apparition. He wasn't even a dream. Gage Wyatt was very real, and all hers.

Not what she'd planned, certainly. Not at all what she'd expected. And yet perfectly right, down to this. Understanding her enough to give her this.

The fog she'd been muddling through these past few days was gone, and while she still had fears and concerns and complex emotions over what had transpired, this was simple. And true.

She rose to her toes and kissed him. The stars and moon shone, the breeze slid over them, and Gage kissed her until there was only him—her own universe for the having.

He laid her out on the blanket, covered her. There

was no room for nerves—why would there be? Unlike everything else in her life, she was sure of this, sure of him.

Because he undressed her with reverence, whispered all sorts of wonderful things against her skin. He made her feel beautiful and whole and strong.

She'd always wanted to feel strong, and it wasn't that he was *giving* her strength—it was that he was showing her all the ways it already existed. And now that she saw, now that she knew, what couldn't she do?

She kissed him, touched him—tracing his bandages and the wounds Ace had marked on him with her fingers, with her mouth. She tried to imbue some sort of healing property to the touches, but when she opened herself to him, she knew what true healing was.

Acceptance. Understanding. Finding where you belonged. Building hope together.

She let herself surrender completely to pleasure and that hope, gave herself over to the wave of it. The immensity of it.

She'd been through too much for that to scare her—how much she felt, how much she wanted. There was no room for fear when he moved inside her, with her, together until a sparkling, all-encompassing pleasure pulsed through her.

He gathered her up close, wrapping them in the blanket, the stars vibrant and all but vibrating in their velvet South Dakota sky.

She snuggled into Gage, breathed the mix of him and outside. This had been the first step toward her future.

She knew what the next was, though she didn't want to think about it in the happy, sated afterglow.

Unfortunately, Gage wasn't going to like that one.

She'd ignore it for now, and she wouldn't tell him yet.

There were some things you had to do alone, no matter how nice it felt to be together.

GAGE HAD DRIVEN her back to her car so she could follow him to his apartment if only because she'd been fretful over his head wound.

He wasn't sure what sleeping out under the stars would do to make it worse, but he hated to see all that worry on her shoulders because of him. Even if he didn't mind a little fretting on her part, like she might feel some fraction of the care blooming inside of him.

Hell, it wasn't care, it was love. He kept wanting to deny it, but how could he when her red hair was spread out over his pillowcase? Her face was slack in sleep, one arm tucked under her pillow and one pressed up against his.

Felicity had spent the night in his bed, snuggled up to him like she belonged there. It felt like she did. It felt like *she* thought it did.

Still there was a sheen of anxiety to it. Whether it was her missing father, the ever-present threat of Ace—no matter how many high-security prisons they put him into—or Gage's own nerves at the idea of loving someone so…

Perfect wasn't the right word. He'd be afraid to touch perfect, but she was perfect for him somehow. Matched.

He'd never thought he'd be in love—especially not with someone who'd been hung up on his brother not all that long ago. He'd never thought he'd find himself dreaming of a particular kind of future that wasn't: be a cop, have fun, protect his family from Ace.

He touched the bandage on his head. He was still achy and knew he wouldn't be cleared to work for a while yet. Maybe he could be doing desk hours by the end of the week, but Gage hardly looked forward to that.

So, he wouldn't look forward. He'd enjoy his present.

Felicity moved, yawning and stretching as she rolled into him. Her eyes blinked open, that dark, intoxicating green. Her mouth curved. "Morning," she murmured sleepily.

"Morning," he replied, his voice rusty—and not from sleep.

She pressed a kiss to one of the scratches on his arm. She didn't fuss over the marks Ace had put on him. Instead, she treated them with a kind of reverence that made him feel vulnerable, but not in that fearful way he had as a child. This was something else. Not weakness, not fear, but hope and love, he supposed.

"I need to get up and get going," she said, yawning again as her eyes seemed to focus and engage.

He had no doubt Felicity Harrison was a morning person.

"What's the rush?"

"I want to give my cabin a good clean, and I need to get my uniforms ready for tomorrow." She gave him a quick peck and slid out of bed. She grabbed her T-shirt from the floor and slid it over her head.

A pity.

She shook out her sleep-and-sex-rumpled hair and then began to separate it into sections. It was mesmerizing, but his brain kicked into gear over what she'd just said.

"Are you sure you should be out there all alone?"

She pushed out a breath and began to braid her hair. "No. But I think I have to. I can't live scared Ace might get through again and…" She paused twisting the band around the end of her braid and looked at him, a heartbreaking desolation in her gaze. "I haven't said this to anyone, but I don't think my father could have survived, Gage. I really think he has to be dead. Which means they might never find him. Not if animals got to him. It's so big, so vast, and I just have to live with the uncertainty I guess, but I'm mostly certain."

It killed him that she blamed herself, but he knew how sneaky and hard to shake blame could be. He got out of bed, didn't bother with his shirt and just pulled his boxers on. "Okay, but I want you to take one of those button things Cody makes. The emergency call. You shouldn't be out there without cell service. Regardless."

She frowned at him as he crossed to her. "I'll have my radio when I'm on duty."

"I'm talking when you're off duty, babe. It's a drive from here to there."

She wrinkled her nose and finished with her hair. "I do not like *babe*."

"Sweetheart, honey, darlin'." He tugged the tight braid. "Red."

Her mouth curved. "Red's okay."

And it was that, her standing there in a rumpled T-shirt, her hair smoothly braided and her smile still sleepy that did it, completely and irrevocably. "I love you, Felicity." He hadn't meant to say it out loud, or if he had, he hadn't thought it through. Things were different for her. He'd been halfway in love with her for something like two years, and she'd been mooning over his twin brother, no matter the reasons. "You should take some time with that. I've had longer to think about it."

She stared up at him as if she'd frozen when he'd said those words. She blinked once but, other than that, didn't move. But he knew she was thinking, taking it in, in that rational way of hers. "B-but l-love doesn't really have to do with thinking," she said thoughtfully, eyebrows knitting together. "Accepting it does, I guess, but love is there, either way."

"I don't know."

"You wouldn't have *chosen* to love me, Gage."

"Why not? You're beautiful and sweet and smart, and kind of a badass, if you haven't noticed."

She nearly grinned at that. "You're all of those things, too, you know." She inhaled deeply, keeping her gaze steady on his. Her hands curled around his forearms, and he was almost certain she was about to let him down gently.

"I love you, too," she said, instead. "Maybe I need to think some about what to do with that, but I feel it, either way."

He had to clear his throat to speak. "Well, same page then, Red."

She nodded, still staring up at him. "You know, when I got that first summer internship at the National Park Service, I didn't let myself really dream about someday getting the full-time position here at home. When

I finally got it, I told myself I'd believe that my dreams could come true if I worked really hard."

"I think you ended up with the wrong twin," he half joked.

She shook her head. "No. Brady was a nice enough placeholder, but I didn't want *him*. I wanted someone kind and good who understood me and made me feel like…this. That was never him, not really. But it's been you."

"Well. Hell."

She grinned up at him, brushed a kiss over his mouth. "Come on, I'll make you some breakfast before I go."

He slid his arms around her waist, pulling her close, nuzzling into her hair. "I have some different ideas."

She leaned into him for a second, then gave him a little push. "I'm hungry." She laughed, sounding a bit bewildered, as if she couldn't quite believe this was all happening. "But maybe after."

Chapter Eighteen

It took a few days to work out, especially without any of the Wyatt boys being tipped off. They wouldn't let her do this thing, and she had to do it.

It required a secrecy she wasn't very good at, and then waiting for her own day off to align with when she could accomplish the task.

Getting back to work had been good. It kept her mind busy, and though she struggled to forget everything that had happened at her cabin or on the trails, it was better to struggle than to avoid.

Routines were good. Having a plan was better.

Now she was going to enact it. She felt sick and nervous leading up to it but it had to be done. When it was over, maybe she would tell Gage, even if it made him mad.

She couldn't tell him before. He'd stop her, and she would not be stopped on this.

Luckily, Gage was back at work, though he was relegated to desk duty until he had his checkup next week. He'd grumbled about it all morning. Felicity had let him grumble, made him breakfast, then sent him on his way.

It was a bit like… Well, she didn't like to think about it too deeply, but waking up with him, whether at his apartment or her cabin, felt a bit like living together.

She shook her head as she got out of her car. Thoughts for another time. Today wasn't about Gage or how good she felt there. It was about closing the book on the unfinished chapter that still weighed on her, even if Gage allowed her to take a considerable amount of that weight off at any given time.

She tried not to think too hard about Gage as she pulled into the jail parking lot. He would hate this. He wouldn't understand it, and he was going to be so ticked off when he found out.

He had no one to blame but himself, though. He'd been the one to tell her she didn't have to be happy just because everyone expected her to be. He'd been the one to help her find the courage to do this.

He'd hate that even more.

Now she was here, and she was ready. She'd close the door on this, if she could, and then her life wouldn't feel like it was in an awful limbo.

Felicity stepped into the jail, followed the instructions to be a visitor, and then was taken into a room with plexiglass partitions. She took a seat and waited. She breathed through her nerves and focused on portraying a calm, unflappable exterior.

It didn't matter if she was a riot of nerves inside. If Ace didn't see it, it wouldn't matter at all.

It didn't take long for Ace to be escorted to the other side of the glass. He was handcuffed and in a prison uniform. He looked haggard and pale, his face more hollow than lean in that dangerous predator type of way.

He wasn't having the best recovery from his gunshot wound here in jail.

Good.

When their gazes met, he smiled just like he had back at her cabin, as if he had all the control and power in the world.

She wouldn't let that rattle her. She had the power now. She kept her expression neutral and her posture as relaxed as she could muster. "Hello, Ace."

"Felicity Harrison. This *is* a surprise. My would-be murderer wants to speak to me. I could hardly resist my curiosity."

"You mean the opportunity to try to mess with my mind?"

Ace's smile didn't dim. If anything it deepened so that he looked normal. Like a kind man happy to see someone. Not even a prisoner happy to have a visitor to talk to, but like a man at a family Christmas dinner.

The fact it could look real was far more chilling than him calling her his would-be murderer.

"Care to take a guess as to why I'm here?" she asked. She'd practiced this. Perfected what she would say, how she would broach the topic. Being too direct would give him a kind of ammunition. She didn't know what Ace could still do to her, especially with his impending move to a federal facility, but she wouldn't take any chances.

"So many reasons. But I note you're alone, which means not one of my sons, and probably not one of your little Knights, knows you're here. They wouldn't let you do this alone."

"I'm not afraid of doing anything alone." It wasn't totally true. She'd told Cecilia. Just in case something happened, though she couldn't think of anything that would. Still, she'd realized that someone needed to know, and Cecilia was the only one who'd be true to her word not to tell anyone unless she needed to.

Ace didn't need to know that. Let him think she was alone. Let him know she could handle it. "I shot you without anyone's help."

"Good. That's good." Ace leaned back and chuckled. "I like you, Felicity. I do." His gaze sharpened. "You don't like that, though. Gage wouldn't be too keen on me liking you, would he?"

Her blood ran cold, but she kept her mouth curved and forced a little laugh out herself. "Yeah, he's that gullible. He'd drop me because *you* said you liked me. And I'm that pathetic, I came here to talk to you about your son."

"Fancy yourself a strong woman now?" Ace's smile got a sharp quality that no one would be fooled into thinking was kind. "You shot me, Felicity. But I'm still here."

"Yeah. Looking a little rough around the edges, though." Felicity leaned forward, trying for his fake kind smile. "Not sure how federal prison is going to agree with you, but I can't wait to find out."

"I can't wait to drag you into a long, painful trial. You and Gage. It'll be a real joy. To taint your lives for years. To always be the dark cloud over your future. To twist and bend the law to my will until I'm walking free again. And when I am—"

It sent a cold shudder through her, but she kept her expression neutral and shoulders relaxed. "The law can be tricky, it's true, and it fails a lot of people."

"When I'm free—"

"But we won't let it fail you. Trust me on that."

Ace yawned, gave an exaggerated stretch. He pushed away from the table in front of him. "Well, if that's all."

She knew she shouldn't blurt it out, but he was standing up. She should let him go. Come back another time. Play his little game, because if she didn't, he'd end up playing her.

But she had to know. She had to.

"My father didn't know about the dead woman."

Ace stood there, smiling like he'd just been crowned the King of England.

Felicity had to swallow at the bile rising in her throat. She'd lost. Already. She should give in and leave.

But she had to know. Mind games or not, she had to know.

Ace sat back down and leaned forward. He clasped his hands together on the little table in front of him and pretended to look thoughtful. "Did you two end up having a little chat?"

She refused to answer.

"Was it tearful? Did your heart just swell right up, being reunited with your daddy?"

She couldn't affect nonchalance, but she could keep her mouth shut, and she did, even if she looked at him with a black fury coating her insides.

"The state never should have taken you away. Is that what you'd like to think? He was misunderstood. It was just the once. He really, truly loves you deep down underneath all his problems."

It stung because once upon a time that *had* been her fantasy. That there'd been a mistake. That her memories were made up. The way Ace said it made it seem so possible.

But she remembered now. That hike in the Badlands, hiding from her father, it had reminded her of a truth she'd known and hadn't wanted.

She knew what her father was.

She just had to know for sure what he'd done. "He said you forced him to help you. He didn't know about the murder. He didn't know what I was talking about."

Ace sat back into his chair, lounged really, rangy and feral even with the sick pallor of his skin.

She'd shot this man and he still held the cards.

"So, you've come in search of the truth," Ace said thoughtfully. "Without my son."

"It's my truth." He wouldn't use it against her. She wouldn't let him.

"He won't see it that way. You and I both know that. Nothing is yours once you're involved with a Wyatt. They fancy themselves better than me, but they're the same. Their name means everything. Their vengeance is all that matters. Every woman they've ever brought into the circle gets swept right up into the Wyatt drama— don't they? Liza and Nina, your *sisters*, banished because of your boyfriend's brothers."

It wasn't true, but he voiced it so reasonably. Because he believed it. In his warped brain, that was true, and love and duty had nothing to do with it.

Because he had no love, and no duty other than his own evil. It would be sad if he wasn't such a monster.

"My father came to visit you here," Felicity said, keeping her voice bland and steady. She would get to the bottom of things, no matter Ace's tangents. "Before you two showed up at my cabin to enact your little failure. You have a connection."

Ace inclined his head. "He did come. He did indeed. Came to visit. We had a good chat about some things. Then, as fate would have it, Michael was the one who helped me out when the tornado, my divine intervention, set me free. Michael has been a good friend."

"If the tornado was divine intervention, what was that bullet I put in you?" she asked, and didn't try to smile or laugh. She let the disgust—and her win over him—show all over her face.

Ace smiled. "The divine requires payment. Suffering. I didn't become what I am until I had been abandoned, until I suffered and nearly died. This is only my second coming, Felicity. I hope you're prepared."

She shook her head. He struck fear in her and she hadn't come here to be brainwashed. To be made afraid. She'd come here for answers, and that had been stupid. Ace would never give her real answers. Which made her more tired than afraid.

"You know what? Never mind." She had started to get up, when Ace spoke. Quickly and hurriedly as if, for once, desperate.

"Two possibilities, right, Felicity? One, your father was the bumbling idiot he portrayed himself to be. I used his weakness and stupidity to get to you. He didn't murder his own daughter. It was all me and I framed you both, or at least the people who work for me did. It's a nice story. I know it's one you'd like to believe. But I think you know... I think you know there's another story. Another truth."

She should walk away. He was lying. He had to be lying.

"Once upon a time a man came to visit me. I owed him a favor, from a long time ago. Your father wasn't so much *in* the Sons as he was an associate, one who'd saved me from a particularly bad run-in once. I knew your mother."

She made a sound. Couldn't help it. She knew nothing about her mother, except that she had died. But Ace, this monster, had known her.

"I knew your mother very well."

She almost retched right there.

"But I digress. Your father, excuse me, this *man*, came to see me in jail a few weeks ago. He'd been holding out asking for the favor returned until he really needed it. Apparently, he'd accidentally, or so he said, killed his daughter. He needed an alibi. A sure thing so it never came back to him—murder would certainly put him in jail for the rest of his life. He wanted me to use my Sons influence to make sure that didn't happen."

Felicity absorbed his words. She didn't want the second story to be true, and maybe it was a lie. Ace was nothing if not a liar.

But it made more sense. Unfortunately, the dead body in this scenario, and her connection to Felicity and Michael, made the most sense out of anything.

"Well, I left him to die," Felicity said, knowing her voice wasn't as strong as it had been. "So I suppose it doesn't matter."

"Nightmares never die, little girl. I'm living proof of that. Your father played the fool well, but he was no fool. The truth is, I don't know the truth. I know I didn't kill that girl. Whether she was your sister or not, I don't know. Michael and my resources collaborated to try and make it look like you did it, sure, but you deserved a slap back after getting involved in Wyatt business. As for the murder itself." He held up his hands. "All I know is it didn't have a thing to do with me. So, I guess you'll have to have a conversation with him."

Ace grinned when Felicity said nothing. "Oh, I forgot. He's missing. Very convenient."

"He's dead," Felicity said flatly. She believed that. She did.

Or had. Until talking to Ace.

"That'd be easy, wouldn't it?"

Felicity knew those words would haunt her, and that was her cue to leave. Maybe she didn't have answers, but she'd gotten what she'd come for.

Her father was no hapless pawn of Ace's. But he was dead. Had to be.

GAGE CHUGGED THE bottle of water he'd pulled out of his pack. He wouldn't admit to Brady his head was pounding and that he wished they'd quit two miles ago. Not when he'd been the one to insist on another two miles.

The search for Michael Harrison was fruitless. Worst of it was, he hadn't told Felicity that's what he'd planned on doing today. He didn't want her getting her hopes up. He'd made a good choice there. This was utterly useless.

"Need a break?" Brady asked mildly.

"Nah. We can head back. Rest up. Try again tomorrow."

"I have to sleep sometime. Some of us aren't on desk

duty. And you're not coming out here alone. Not until that doctor clears you."

Gage wouldn't be stupid on this, though it was tempting. "I'll see if Tuck or Cody can come with me."

"Be sure that you do. That is, if you make it through the hike back."

"He's got to be out here somewhere," Gage said, using his sleeve to wipe the sweat off his forehead. "Even if he's dead…he didn't just evaporate."

"You've got the winds, animals, caves. Plenty of people disappear without a trace in plenty of places. Especially if they're dead."

"You've always been Mr. Positivity."

"Reality isn't often very positive. You know that, Gage."

Gage followed Brady's path back, scanning the area around them. Not a hint of Michael Harrison where Felicity had left him—or in the miles around where she'd left him, and the worst part was Brady was exactly right.

There were a lot of ways to disappear—dead or alive.

Gage just wanted to give Felicity some piece of closure. It ate at him that he might not ever be able to and that it would weigh on her. Forever.

Gage sighed. Life sucked sometimes. He'd accepted that a long time ago. It was harder to accept for the people you loved, he was coming to find. Growing up, there'd been nothing to do about Ace. Even now there was only so much to be done. He was who he was and his sons were what they were. There was no option of shielding or protecting his brothers—that ship had sailed probably before Gage and Brady had been born.

But finding Michael for Felicity felt doable, and the fact he couldn't do it might drive him crazy.

He could tell when he and Brady got into cell range because both their phones started sounding notifications like crazy.

"That can't be good," Brady said grimly.

Gage pulled his phone out. Ten texts. Five missed calls. Three voice mails. "No. Not good." He opened the texts, read them. Listened to his messages, all variations of the same theme: call me.

What he couldn't figure out was why they were all from Cecilia. She was a tribal police officer on the rez, and spent way more time there than out at the ranch. Of all the Knight girls, Gage had the least to do with her on a personal level, though sometimes their lives intersected on a professional one.

Maybe it was that. Maybe it was something to do with one of her cases on the rez. Relief coursed through him at the solid explanation. "I'll call her, assuming all your messages are from Cecilia."

"Yeah."

He hit Call Back and Cecilia picked up before the first ring had finished sounding. "Gage."

"Hey, Cecilia, what's up?"

"Don't be mad." She sounded breathless and worried, which was the antithesis of Cecilia's usual demeanor—which was either cool as a cucumber or hotheaded as all get-out. Cecilia had no in-between.

His nerves were humming. "Gee, that's a good way to ensure that I'm going to be really, really mad."

"Felicity's missing."

Gage went cold, despite the oppressive heat of the day. "What?"

"She went to visit Ace. I—"

He gripped the phone so hard it was a wonder it didn't crumble. "She did *what*?"

"I can't get it out if you don't listen to me. She went to visit him in jail. That all went fine. But after? She was supposed to call and check in. She didn't. I can't get ahold of her. I already called Tuck, and Jamison for that matter. We've checked in with the jail, and they're working to figure out what happened between leaving the jail and...not coming home. We're handling it, but I knew you'd want to know."

"You're handling it?" He wanted to rage and punch something, but all he could do was grip the phone. "It's hardly handled if she's missing."

"Gage."

"You knew about this. You knew and—"

"I don't have time for you to berate me. She needed to do this," Cecilia snapped. "Alone. And she knew I was the only one who wouldn't—"

"Keep her safe?" Gage replied.

There was an intake of breath and the call ended. Gage swore, but he didn't stop moving. They still had a good quarter of a mile before they got to Brady's truck.

"Well, I heard all that," Brady said grimly, following after Gage. "Felicity's probably back at her cabin. Upset. Visits with Ace are upsetting. She forgot to check in. Took a shower, maybe."

Gage kept walking at the breakneck pace he'd set for himself. "She wouldn't. She just wouldn't." If she told someone, she'd be sure to say she was all right.

Why did she tell Cecilia?

"We should check," Brady insisted.

He had no patience for his brother's calm reason. "No time."

"Don't you think we should be sure before we go anywhere with guns blazing?"

Gage wanted to whirl on his brother and pound some sense into him, but there was no time. Instead, he broke into a jog, no matter how it made his head ache or his stomach roil. "What happened to Nina and Cody after their visit to Ace? They about got themselves killed, but they had each other. She's alone. And she put a bullet in Ace, which means he won't rest…"

Gage swore again. He hadn't fully grasped how much of a target Felicity had made of herself.

All because of him.

He reached the truck and held out his hands for the keys.

Brady had jogged after him, but he stopped resolutely out of reach. "I think I should drive."

"Don't fight me on this."

Brady hesitated, then handed him the keys. "Where are we going?"

"The jail."

Brady winced. "I was afraid of that." But he got in the truck and didn't lodge one complaint when Gage drove like a bat out of hell. Luckily, they'd already been out in Pennington County rather than back at the ranch, where it would take way longer to get to the jail.

Gage parked haphazardly, taking up two spots. He saw Brady eyeing the bad parking job. Gage tossed him the keys. "Here. Fix it. I want to do this alone."

"What exactly?"

"I'll kill him this time. No qualm."

Brady put his hand on Gage's shoulder. "In the jail? Gage. Take a minute. You have to think before you act. Going in there with murder on the brain is a recipe for a whole new disaster we most certainly don't have time for."

Gage shrugged off Brady's hand. "I'll think once we know where she is."

"We know she isn't *here*."

But Ace had to know where she was. What had happened. Why the hell had she thought to do this on her own? Why had Cecilia *let* her?

She should have told him, and he couldn't deal with the hurt of that when she was God knew where. Gage strode forward, about to wrench open the front door of the jail entrance, badge at the ready, but Tucker stepped out of the door first.

He came up short, looked from Gage to Brady. "Well. You got here fast."

Gage only growled.

Tucker held up his hands. "Listen, we've got a few leads. Her car is still in the lot, so wherever she went, it was with someone else."

"How is Ace doing this?" Brady asked, too much bafflement and not enough fury.

Gage wanted to whirl on him, rage at someone, but it was only the impotent terror building inside of him. He couldn't let it win because it was clouding all rational thought.

"He's not," Tucker said grimly. "At least, it seems

really unlikely. The security footage seems to point to a van. No windows. No plates. We've got an APB out."

"And that's not Ace because?"

"Because…" Tucker sighed. "We went over the past few days of security footage, and that van was here every day for the past four, only during visiting hours. No one ever got out. The only time the van moved before the end of visiting hours was today. It moves after Felicity enters the jail. We caught a quick glimpse of the driver. It's not… It's not a clear shot, and there's room for interpretation, but I'm about sixty percent sure the driver is Michael Harrison."

Chapter Nineteen

Felicity had spent the first ten minutes trapped in the back of a van berating herself for her stupidity. She'd been so shaken when she'd walked out of the jail that she'd turned to the sound of her name rather than run from it.

She'd been pushed into the back of the vehicle before she'd had a chance to get her footing. Before she'd had a chance to fight or run or scream—the doors had closed on her.

She was an utterly worthless fool.

The back of the van was completely black. She'd spent most of the drive feeling around, trying to find a handle or some way to get the door open. She could tell the car was going fast because every time it turned she'd tumble around like loose change.

If she could find a door, and open it, she would jump out regardless. Even if he were driving 100 miles per hour. Anything was better than being at her father's mercy.

He was alive. Alive and well from the looks of it. He certainly hadn't been trapped or lost in the Badlands for the past few days.

The van came to an abrupt stop and she pitched forward, painfully banging her elbow and hip against who knew what.

She didn't let the jarring pain stop her from hurrying back to her feet, crouched and ready. He'd have to open the doors, and he hadn't tied her up or hurt her. Maybe he'd taken her somewhere terrible. Maybe he had a gun.

But she wouldn't go down like she had in that parking lot. Stupid and off guard. No. Absolutely not.

She didn't let herself think about how he'd survived or why he'd come for her. It didn't matter.

She'd fight him no matter what.

He'd taken her purse, and that stung, because she'd been dumb enough to put Cody's little button in there. When Cody had given it to her, he'd told her to wear it on her person. She had, every day, but she hadn't wanted questions about it when she'd been searched at the jail, so she'd put it in her purse before heading inside.

Everything that was happening was because of stupid choices she'd made out of arrogance or ignorance or something. Desperation? Why couldn't she have left it all alone? For her own stupid, pointless conscience.

That line of thought did nothing to help her. She wouldn't let it be the end of her life. She had to be smart. She had to fight her way out of this.

Beating herself up could—and *would*—come later.

The van was still stopped, so she remained crouched in a fighting position. But when the doors opened, the light was blinding and she winced away from it out of instinct.

Nothing happened as she adjusted to the light. She

clenched her fists and blinked as her father came into focus.

He stood outside the van looking grim. "Never could leave well enough alone. You should have let it go, Felicity. Gone back to your life. But you just had to keep poking."

She stayed back in the van, fists clenched as she got used to the light pouring in. "You're the one who dragged me into this. You killed her, and you had me framed."

He sighed. "Ace going to blame it all on me? Typical. But he's in jail and I'm not."

"You killed her," Felicity repeated. She would get his confirmation—if she had been stupid enough to be caught here, she would get his confirmation.

"Yeah, I did. But she had it coming. Did you believe me, Felicity? I ain't killed no one. Oh, I'm so hurt. Don't leave me here to die." He scoffed, not even pleased with himself. Just disgusted. "I'll give you credit for leaving me there to die, but you should have finished off the job if you really wanted me dead."

It dawned on her how much he'd fooled her. Not just about the murder, but about everything. "You weren't hurt."

"Man, you're dumb. Come on out now." He gestured her forward.

The fact he expected her to listen to his directive made it seem like he, in fact, was the dumb one. She wasn't about to scuttle out there to die just because he told her to.

She stayed where she was, crouched and ready.

"Going to make this harder on yourself." He groaned

like an inconvenienced teenager. "Fine. But I warn you, I like a struggle. You won't."

"You'll have to drag me out of here, kicking and screaming," she replied, ready to do whatever it took. He would physically overpower her, no doubt, but she wouldn't make it easy.

He shrugged. "No problem there." He leaned forward, his big body and long arms giving him the reach he needed. She kicked, scratched and bit, but it was no use. He got ahold of her arm and dragged her out. If she landed any blows, he didn't so much as grunt. He jerked her arm so hard and violently she wasn't altogether sure her arm was still in the socket.

Pain radiated through her and for a moment she was too bowled over by it to fight. He dropped her onto the ground, a patch of gravel in front of a run-down trailer.

She tried to breathe through the pain, tried to stand. She managed to get to her knees. He stood over her and reached a hand back, as if he expected her to cower and take the blow.

No. She wasn't a little girl anymore.

She used everything she had to push forward and crash into his knees. Apparently, it was enough of a surprise to knock him backward, and he tripped over the edge of the gravel, sprawling onto his back with a grunt.

She stumbled on top of him. He immediately fought her off, trying to pin her to the ground. He was bigger, but she was faster. She was slithering away when he caught her by the ankle and dragged her back across the hard, painful gravel.

She kicked out, tried to shake off his grasp. He kept pulling her toward the trailer and she knew she couldn't wind up inside. She watched his legs move, timed them and then managed to kick her heel out to strike his ankle. He tripped and lost his grip on her.

She jumped up, knowing she could outrun him. She had to. But before she'd made it three strides, he grabbed her by the shirt.

She'd never grappled with anyone before, let alone someone nearly twice her size, but she didn't let that stop her. She knew the important thing was getting in as many blows as possible. So she punched and kicked and kneed, while his breath wheezed out.

She gave him a nasty blow to the nose, which had blood spurting out. Triumph whirred through her, but it was only a second before his meaty fist connected with the side of her face, sending her sprawling.

Her vision blurred, and her mind seemed to echo in on itself.

Get to your feet. Get to your feet. She could feel her mind telling her to do it, but her limbs took forever to cooperate.

She struggled to her feet again—and she would keep doing so. No matter how many times he knocked her down or got in her way—she would fight.

Fight!

Dizzy and bleeding, pain radiating through her, she stood there ready to fight him off again. There was nowhere to run behind her. It was all rock wall and trailer. But there had to be a way to get past him.

Except Michael didn't come after her again. He leaned into the passenger side of the van and came back out with a gun.

"See, if you didn't fight me, Felicity, you would have avoided this. I didn't want to kill you. Well, not with a gun. It's hard enough getting away with one murder—two would be pushing it." He laughed a little. "But now you're hurt. And you've got my DNA on you, so no wandering in the Badlands till you die for you."

She was woozy and out of it, but she knew one thing for sure. "I'd never have died in the Badlands."

"I'd have made sure of it," he replied, turning the gun on her.

He'd shoot her. No matter what. She could run, but there was nowhere to go that a bullet wouldn't find her. So she wouldn't run. At least not away.

Instead, she ran toward him. If he killed her, at least she'd gone down fighting for her life. At least she'd tried.

She rammed into him just as the shot went off. She didn't feel the piercing pain of a bullet, but the blast of sound next to her ear made it feel as though her head had exploded. She pressed her hands to her ears, trying to somehow ease the horrible sound and pressure.

It was a heck of a lot better than being shot, but the pain was still a shock to her system. Such a shock she couldn't think past the fact she couldn't seem to hear. Everything was a buzz. She looked around, trying to understand…

Fear gripped her, and in that fear, he won.

He wrenched her arms behind her back. She could feel him tying something around her wrists. The blow must have knocked out more than just her hearing, because it didn't occur to her to fight him off.

She knelt there in the gravel, rocks digging into her knees, hands being tied behind her back and just… prayed.

GAGE TAMPED DOWN the panic. He'd had a lifetime of doing that. Danger had been the story of his first eleven years, and if he was able to survive that, to survive that cave with Ace, he could do it.

His profession had given him the skills to disassociate. To focus on one step at a time to get someone to safety.

He could find Felicity. He would.

He had to.

There had been different sightings of the van, giving different possible directions. Tuck had asked a few deputies to go check Michael's last known place of residence, though no one expected him to be there.

And he wasn't.

Gage had wanted to go, but he knew himself well enough to know his temper wasn't suited for searching. Not for clues. He wanted to be searching for *her*. But he needed a lead, a damn plan.

"We could head back to the Badlands, where she left him," Gage offered to Brady as they drove down a highway someone had claimed to have seen the van driving on. "It's what Ace would do."

"He isn't Ace," Brady replied. "Did you look at his record?"

Gage shook his head. He hadn't given a thought to Michael Harrison other than finding his body so Felicity could rest easily. Quite frankly, when he hadn't been searching for Michael, he'd been headfirst lost in

Felicity and what having a normal life with a woman he loved felt like.

"Threats. Assault. Battery. Over and over again. Dude can't control his temper, and thanks to lawyers and judges, never stays behind bars for very long. Which I know isn't exactly a comfort, but I don't think he's enacting the kind of poetic justice Ace is always after. This is just vengeance."

"Why? Felicity didn't do anything to him," Gage returned resolutely. Because if it was just vengeance, she might already be gone. At least with Ace you always knew you had a chance to save someone while he showboated his anointed routine.

"Felicity left him to die and, from what Cecilia said, confronted Ace about his role in that woman's murder." Brady's calm faltered. "He did it. I think Michael killed that poor girl. Not Ace."

"And Ace is innocent?" Gage asked incredulously.

"No. But I think Ace got involved for different reasons, and I think once we've got Felicity back, you'll be able to think the same thing."

"Getting Felicity back is all I care about." Who cared about the reasons. Who cared about anything except her safety.

He looked out at the highway, analyzing every rare vehicle that passed him by. This was going to drive him slowly insane. Not that he could stand anything that wasn't finding her. If this was all he could do... Well, maybe it'd help him come up with something else.

"You sure you want me to ride shotgun on this?" Brady asked, squinting out the passenger seat window.

Gage blinked at his brother—his twin. "Why wouldn't it be you?"

Brady shrugged. "Because you're mad at me for being calm."

"Any of you would be calm," Gage returned, and though disgust laced his tone, he was glad someone could be. Without Brady and Tucker's calm, he would have already done a hundred stupid things.

"Dev wouldn't be calm," Brady offered.

"I don't need Dev making my worst impulses even worse," Gage muttered, frustrated with the conversation. "I need you, Brady. Ticked off at your calm or not, I need it."

"You got it."

Gage blew out a breath. It didn't ease his fear, but it calmed some of the ragged edges. They were the Wyatt twins. They had a whole army of Wyatts looking for her.

They'd find her. Who knew. Maybe she'd already saved herself. She could face down Ace, surely she could take down Michael.

Gage's phone rang and he answered it tersely.

"Don't get too excited just yet," Cody's voice said without preamble. "But I think I've got a track on her." Gage hadn't heard from Cody this whole time. Gage had figured it was because he was all the way in Bonesteel and not law enforcement in any licensed capacity.

But Cody knew tech and computers.

"Explain," Gage snapped.

"I didn't want to say anything until I was sure it would work. But the button I gave her... Even though she didn't hit it, I'm tracking her. At least the button. If it's on her, I can tell you where she is."

"Then do it." He tossed the phone at Brady, then followed Brady's instructions as to where to drive.

It was a good twenty miles from the jail. Gage didn't let his stomach curdle at the thought of how long she'd been gone, and how little of it would have been in transport.

He focused on action, on reining in his temper. Felicity was in danger. True, mortal danger. He couldn't let his temper be the thing that killed her. "We can't go in guns blazing."

He felt Brady's surprise more than saw it.

"He has her," Gage said, keeping that tight control on his rage, because fear and rage were too dangerous a combination. "We can't risk her. We'll stop here. Go the rest of the way on foot."

Brady nodded. "Stick together until we have our target, then split up if she's not immediately visible."

Since that was exactly what Gage had been thinking, he slowed the truck to a stop. "Ideally, backup is here before we have to engage, but I can't make promises on stopping if she's hurt. I need you not to get in my way. She's too important to me. I need you to understand that."

Brady didn't nod at that. He didn't even agree. But he didn't argue. "Be smart. For both of you—not just her."

Gage flashed a smile he didn't feel. He couldn't promise his brother he wouldn't lay down his life for Felicity. He wouldn't be able to live with himself if he didn't. "We'll see."

Wordlessly they silenced their phones, unholstered their weapons and slid out of the truck. The location of the button was one mile due north. Gage had parked the truck outside a cluster of trees. He and Brady moved forward—two men, one unit, one purpose.

The trailer came into view slowly. It was settled in among thick trees, a rock wall at its back.

Hell of a spot to hide out—but also a hell of a spot to get trapped. Not many ways to escape. The van was parked on a patch of gravel and the back doors were wide open, as was the passenger side door.

It was eerily quiet.

Brady nodded to the right, and Gage gave assent, peeling away to head to the left. If Michael and Felicity were still here, they were in the trailer.

He didn't let himself consider what might have happened if they weren't here.

The windows were covered on the inside with thick curtains, on the outside with dust and grime and a collection of dead bugs.

There was no way to see inside. No way to tell if they were in there. Gage moved slowly, quietly, gun trained on the trailer. He skirted the side of the trailer, looking and listening for any sign of people.

As he came to the back, Brady appeared from the other side. There was a narrow yard, if one could call it that, between the trailer and the steep rock face. If he and Brady could block both sides, there'd be no way for Michael to escape.

If he was in there. If they could get him out here instead of him running out the front and to the van.

Gage studied the back of the trailer. It was the same situation. The few windows there were covered. The door didn't have any kind of window in it. And everything was quiet.

If they weren't in there, they were somewhere on foot. Unless Michael had another vehicle at his disposal.

Based on this setup, Gage doubted it. They had to be in there. The quiet threatened his ability to stay calm. There was nothing good about quiet—too many awful possibilities.

He wouldn't let himself think about any of them. He crept forward, Brady moving to flank him. Both had their guns drawn and ready for anything.

When shouting from the inside started, Gage gave Brady a look. Brady nodded. Gage eased the storm door open, wincing at the squeak and hoping the shouts covered the sound.

He had one chance. One chance to get in there quick and clean and without putting Felicity at more risk.

He counted to three in his head, then kicked as hard as he could, the door splintering open.

Inside things were dim and dingy, and a metallic smell clung to the air. Felicity was on her knees in the corner. Clearly, her hands were tied behind her. She looked up at him like he was a ghost, but Gage had his eyes on the gun in Michael's hand.

"What is it with you Wyatts?" Michael gave a bit of a shrug, and Gage had been in enough situations to know what that shrug meant. He wasn't going to fight his way out. He was giving up.

But not before he killed everyone he could.

So, Gage pulled the trigger. It was the only thing to do—the only way to save Felicity—he had no doubt about that. Blood bloomed on Michael's dirty T-shirt and he jerked back, crashing into the wall. But his face went hard and he got off his own shot before falling to the ground, the gun clattering out of his grip.

The shot didn't hit Gage, but he heard a crash behind him. "Brady." He whirled.

Brady had fallen, but he was struggling back to his feet, swearing a blue streak as he held his shoulder.

He glared up at Gage. "Get her out of here, damn it."

Brady had been shot. Fresh rage swept through Gage, but if Brady was on his feet it couldn't be all that bad, and they had to get Felicity out. Get all of them out. He rushed forward, putting his arms around Felicity.

"Come on, sweetheart. Can you stand up?"

She struggled to get to her feet, even with his help. Gage had to work hard to tamp down the impotent fury raging through him.

"I'll untie you when we're outside. Come on, sweetheart. Red, let's move outside."

She didn't move except to shake her head. "I can't hear," she shouted, making him wince as her mouth was close to his ear.

Michael's gunshot must have gone off close to her ears. He bit back a curse and nodded. "Okay. Okay. That's okay. It'll wear off." He tugged her toward the door, giving one look at Michael, who'd gone still.

Good riddance.

Chapter Twenty

By the time the doctors were done with her, she could hear a little bit. If the room was quiet and someone was close enough, speaking slowly. Her ears still rang, and the ibuprofen they'd given her helped her headache but didn't eradicate it completely.

She much preferred thinking about all that than the fact her father was dead, and worse—she'd be dead if it wasn't for Gage.

And Brady, who was currently in the ER having his gunshot patched up.

All because she'd been stupid. She sighed. She kept trying to work up enough blame and guilt to think this was all her fault, but she couldn't muster it. If she went back, she'd do the same. Maybe put up a bit more of a fight in the jail parking lot, but she still would have gone to see Ace, without telling any of the Wyatts.

Would that have changed anything?

It might have changed everything.

But she'd done what she'd done, and she couldn't really hate the result. Except Brady being shot.

She wanted to go home. She wanted Gage. Most of her life when tragedy had struck, she'd wanted to be alone, to deal in peace and without having to worry if she looked weak or stupid or whatever.

But Gage had showed her that it didn't really matter how you looked, especially when the other person understood. He'd understand the complicated feelings at her father being dead.

She wasn't so sure he'd understand her decision not to tell him she was visiting Ace, but she didn't know how to deal with that, so she just kept pressing forward.

She walked through the hospital, the buzz still in her ears, but she could hear some things. She could understand people if they were close enough and talked directly to her.

The doctors had said the hearing loss would likely wear off, but she had to come back in a week to be checked out again. It had been a relief to know her hearing wasn't irreversibly damaged, but she would have accepted that. Accepted anything over being dead.

She found Gage exactly where she knew he would be, in the waiting room of the ER. She wasn't sure she could accept it if he was angry enough at her to want to end things.

She swallowed. He looked desolate. Pale and lost. But when his gaze moved to her entering the waiting room, he tried to hide that away.

"How's Brady?" she asked.

He spoke in low tones, looking down at his hands.

When he was done, she tapped his arm and then her ear. "Sorry, I didn't catch all that." She slid into the seat next to him.

He shook his head and forced a pathetic smile. "That's

okay. He's okay. You're okay." He touched her cheek and slid his palm over her hair. "It's all okay."

She put an arm around his shoulders. "Then why do you look so miserable?"

He shook his head and looked down at his hands for a while, until she tipped his chin toward her so he had to look at her.

"It should have been me," he said simply.

"Why?"

"He wouldn't have been there if it wasn't for me."

"And you wouldn't have been there if it wasn't for me." He gave her a look and opened his mouth to argue, but she shook her head. "You can't play it only the way you like. Either we blame the people who are actually responsible, or you have to blame me."

"Why didn't you tell me?"

It was hurt that chased across his face before he shook his head again and tried to turn away, but she kept a firm grip on his chin. "I should have," she said, hoping her voice sounded as strong as she wanted it to. "I knew you wouldn't like it, so I didn't tell you. I wanted to handle it on my own, thought I had to. Thought you wouldn't let me. But I should have told you. I shouldn't have been... If I was determined to do it, I shouldn't be afraid to tell people. I can't be afraid to disappoint people. If you had been mad at me, I would have dealt with it. I should have told you. Things would be different if I had."

"Well, hell, Felicity, you make it real hard to hold on to a mad."

"You weren't mad. You were hurt." He tried to turn away again, but she wasn't done. "You saved my life. You really did. He was going to kill me. The only reason it took so long was he was trying to find a way to make sure it couldn't be connected back to him. It wouldn't have lasted much longer. He was losing his patience."

He blew out a breath like she'd physically hurt him. "Well, guess we're even, Red."

She swallowed at the lump in her throat. "I'm sorry Ace isn't dead."

"I'm not." He brushed a hand over her hair. "I wouldn't want that on your conscience." He pulled her in, so she leaned on his shoulder.

She wasn't sure it would have weighed all that heavy, certainly not any heavier than him being alive to wreak havoc.

"So, you're not…" Felicity didn't know how to put it. They hadn't been dating in any traditional sense. It had been a relationship, of course, but the words of how to describe anything failed her. Still, she had to be sure. "We're okay?"

It was his turn to take her chin, tip her face up and make her look him in the eye. He brushed his mouth against hers. "You and me, Red? We'll always be okay. One way or another."

She wouldn't cry at that, though she wanted to. So, she looked away. "Where is everyone?"

"Brady told me not to call anyone. Said he was fine and—"

Felicity made a noise of outrage. "What! They're going to hear it through your cop grapevines? I don't think so. If you don't call them, I will."

"You can't hear well enough to make a phone call."

"We'll see about that." She made a move to grab her phone, then realized her purse was still somewhere in her father's van. Dead father. She shuddered. It was necessary, but that didn't mean she'd have the images from today out of her head anytime soon.

Gage handed her his. "Here you go, tough girl."

She took it primly, then wrote a text because Gage was right—trying to talk to anyone on the phone would be difficult.

When she handed it back to him, he was just staring at her. So serious. Everything inside of her jittered with nerves.

"I love you. It would have killed me, just killed me, if he'd hurt you. And I can't promise you that Ace will never come after you again. Worse, I think if we're together, that'll make it more... He'll take it as a challenge to hurt us. All the ways he can. I don't know how to live with that."

She reached out and pressed her palm to his cheek. She'd known he was a good man, but she thought he didn't have that core of nobleness that Jamison and Brady had, which was often more annoying than impressive. Like this was. "You'll have to find a way, because I love you, too, and I'm not going to be shaken off that easy. Ace can try to hurt us."

"Feli—"

"No. You don't have a choice. Quite literally. I won't live my life afraid of Ace. Neither will you. If he tries to hurt us again, we'll fight again. Together. So, just shut up."

He managed a chuckle. "All right. Sounds good."

"Good." She let out a breath and leaned against him. "You're probably going to have to marry me, too, but we can talk about that later."

She felt him stiffen underneath her, but it made her smile. It'd give him something to be anxious about besides his brother and trying to protect her, so that was good.

A nurse came in and smiled kindly. "Gage. You can go back and see your brother now." Felicity stood, too. "I'm afraid you'll have to stay out here, ma'am."

Gage gave her arm a squeeze. "By the way I'm telling him it's your fault when everyone shows up."

"That's just fine."

Since he still looked haunted, she reached up on her toes and brushed her mouth against his. "It's over, and it's okay." She was ready to believe it.

BRADY WAS LAID out in a bed. He was pale, but at least he looked pissed. It took energy to be pissed.

"Hey. How's it going?" Gage asked lamely, hanging by the door rather than stepping farther inside.

"You know, I'm a trained paramedic. I know a thing or two about medicine. You think any of these doctors or nurses will listen to me?" Brady grumbled.

"So, it's true. Medical professionals really are the worst patients."

Brady grunted as he eyed Gage. "I'm not going to shout all the way over there to have a conversation with you, and you can leave the guilt right there. I'm fine."

"You won't be able to work for weeks."

Brady pulled a face, but then he lifted his uninjured arm. "It happens. It's what we risk every day we work, isn't it?"

"It wasn't work. You didn't have to be there."

"Where else would I be?" Brady shook his head. "Reverse it, Gage. Where would you have been?"

Much as he didn't want to admit it, he would have been right behind Brady. Always.

"I don't think you realize what you did," Brady said, once Gage got closer to the hospital bed.

"Let you get shot?"

"Gage. You stepped in front of me. We both saw what Michael was going to do. We've both been there before. The only reason I couldn't get off a shot, too, was because you'd stepped in front of me, blocked me. Damn stupid. But that's what you did. The only reason I got shot was because...well, bad luck really. Your shot got off first and his aim was off."

"I don't—"

"Maybe it's not how you remember it, because you were focused on Felicity, but that's what you did. I'm not going to argue about it. I'm tired and my shoulder hurts and they keep wanting to pump me full of medicine I don't want. So, if you can't get over it, get out."

Get over it, maybe not. But he could set it aside.

"It isn't like you to play martyr," Brady said with no small amount of disgust.

"I'm not—"

"And since it's me, why don't you just say what you're really all wound up about."

Because it was Brady, it was hard to pretend he wasn't right on the money. "I guess I know what she felt like after she left Michael to die. I thought I did. I did, in a way, but not like this. I know I did the right thing."

"There's not a doubt in my mind he would have killed her."

"Mine, either. Or hers. But, Brady, if this was all Michael, those charges don't get used against Ace."

"Ace tried to kill you. Himself, not through some two-bit lackey. You can testify to that. Even if we can't get him on murder, he'll go to a higher security prison for attempted murder."

"If he doesn't, Felicity is in even more danger."

"Then I guess you're pretty lucky to have each other's backs, huh?"

Gage didn't know if he'd go so far as *lucky*, but it was certainly a blessing to have…this. His brothers, his family. Everyone would rally around and protect. It was what they did.

"We know how this goes, I think. He took a swing at Jamison, then Cody. It doesn't work, then he moves to the next. If he finds a way to go after one of us again, it's probably not going to be Felicity."

Gage looked at the bandage on Brady's shoulder. They left it unsaid, but it was pretty clear that if Ace found a way to manipulate the system again, Brady would be the next target. He was weakened.

"He said he had a list. A list and I'd messed it up. I wasn't supposed to be next. Which means, we could—"

Brady shook his head. "I'm not here to out-manipulate Ace. If we ever beat him, really beat him, it won't be using his own tactics."

Gage looked down at his hands. "Growing up, Ace told me I was smart, and could take his place, so I did a lot to prove I wasn't and couldn't. He told you you were stupid and weak, so you did a lot to prove you weren't." Gage had never believed he was his father, though sometimes he'd been afraid he could have inherited his impulses. But he fought them and that was all that mattered. He'd never considered that his father might have stamped him in different ways. "Did he shape us?"

"Are we running the Sons? Come on, Gage. If he shaped us, if he left a mark on us, it only got us here. We help people. You saved Felicity. Whatever he did, didn't work. We're the good guys."

Gage looked up at his brother, pale but alive and irritable. He smiled a little. "Felicity saved me first."

Brady chuckled, then winced. "Your ego can take the hit."

Gage studied his twin. "Thank you," he said, letting the words have the weight they deserved. Brady opened his mouth, and Gage had no doubt it was to argue. He shook his head. "You were there. It means something. Thank you."

"Fine. You're welcome. Now leave me alone."

Gage nodded, headed back to the door. He stopped there, knowing exactly what Brady needed. "Oh, by the way, Felicity notified the cavalry, so expect some visitors."

Brady swore and Gage laughed. It felt good to laugh, though it died when he reached the waiting room and Cecilia was standing there with Felicity.

She was still wearing her tribal police uniform. When she saw him, she squared her shoulders and lifted her chin, like she was ready for a fight.

"I came to—" she made a face like she was forced to swallow something bitter "—apologize."

"Don't."

Cecilia frowned, looking at Felicity. "That's what she said, too."

Gage smiled at Felicity. It was good to be on the same

page, to understand without discussing. He turned back to Cecilia. "If you thought she'd be in danger, if either of you thought that, I know it would have been different. We all know if she *hadn't* told you, and you hadn't told us right away things weren't right, everything would be different." He swallowed at the horror that tried to get through, but it hadn't happened. "We can't change anything. We just have to… Look, this takes away the charges against Ace. And…"

Felicity slipped her hand into his. "It just means we have to look out for each other. Together. And we agree no more trying to do things on our own. Not when it comes to Ace."

Cecilia didn't say anything to that.

"You want to go in and see him?" Gage asked, nodding back toward the door he'd just come out of.

"Uh. Well. I mean, I guess," Cecilia replied, looking uncharacteristically unsure.

"I'm going to take this one home. She needs some rest."

Cecilia nodded. "You both do."

Gage gave Felicity's hand a squeeze and they headed for the exit. Felicity looked back at Cecilia, who was straightening her shoulders again, all soldier ready to go into battle.

"What?" Gage asked.

"I don't know." She tilted her face toward him and smiled. "Just…should be interesting."

"What should be interesting?"

She laughed as they walked out of the hospital, into daylight and freedom and hope. "You'll see."

Epilogue

Trials weren't fun, even when you won. It had been grueling days of testimony—including Felicity's own and Gage's. On the stand she'd had to relive shooting Ace, and she wasn't particularly thrilled about it.

Especially with what else was twisting inside of her, uncertain and scary and huge.

But it was over now, Ace guilty of too many charges to count and being moved to a higher security prison much farther away.

It was relief, even if it wasn't full closure. They walked out of the courthouse, a group of four Wyatt boys and three Knight foster girls who'd survived Ace's influence. Out into a sunny day that felt completely right.

Gage's hand slid over hers. Her stomach jittered with new nerves, because now that the trial was over she couldn't ignore her suspicions. And she could hardly not tell him.

Still, she smiled easily and exchanged hugs and goodbyes with her sisters. They shared something now, and even without that, Felicity had come to understand some things about growing up the way they had that made it easy to forgive Liza and Nina their choices to leave. And embrace their decisions to come back.

Gage said his goodbyes and gave Brady a gentle hug. He'd had a setback with his gunshot wound, an infection, that had left him on desk duty for way longer than any Wyatt should have to endure.

Still, she liked to think the trial's outcome had taken a bit of a weight off his irritation.

She and Gage went to Gage's truck and slid in. He would drive her home, and spend the night in her cabin, but he'd be gone before she woke up—to get back to Valiant County and his job.

Her stomach jittered more. Things would have to be different. She hadn't figured out a way that would make them both happy.

"Nothing quite like testifying together, right?"

She forced a smile. "Better than doing it alone, I think."

"You think right," Gage said, patting her knee as he pulled out onto the highway.

Gage chattered the whole way home, and though Felicity tried to keep up, she was caught in her own loop of thoughts and worries and what she had to do.

Gage pulled to a stop in front of her cabin and she quickly slid out, afraid if they dawdled she'd blurt it out.

It needed more finesse, and she should be sure.

But Gage was right behind her, his arm around her waist as she walked up to the door. "All right. What's up, Red? Something's freaking you out, and it's not the trial. Tucker himself is going to oversee the jail transport. Ace won't—"

"I think I'm pregnant." She closed her eyes as the words fell out. Flopped there in between them as they stood awkwardly on her front stoop.

He didn't say anything. Didn't move. And she just stood there with her eyes squeezed shut, not having a clue what to do.

She'd tried to plan it out, tried to know what else to say and how to handle his reaction, but she always reached this point and then shut down. She could only wait, eyes closed and panic keeping her frozen.

"I guess it's a good thing I applied for the opening at Rapid City."

Her eyes flew open. "What?"

"Rapid City is hiring. I was tired of being that far, and you could hardly leave your dream job."

"But you work with your brothers, and now..."

"And now, God willing, I'll get the position, and we'll be in the same county and...and..." He inhaled sharply. "You sure?"

"No." She shook her head a little too emphatically. "I bought a test, but I didn't want to take it until the trial was over. I should have taken it first. I just had to tell you."

"Well, hell, go take it," he said, all but pushing her toward the door.

She nodded. Her keys shook in her hands, but she finally opened door and went into the bathroom to take the test. She went through the motions, set the timer on her phone and then let Gage into the bathroom.

"We have to wait three minutes."

"Okay." He swallowed, looking down at her, but the concern and worry in his expression slowly changed into something else. Then he pressed his mouth to hers in a gentle, calming kiss. "I love you, Felicity."

"I know, but before we know for sure, I don't want you to feel like… Duke isn't going to hold a shotgun on you. I mean, he might, but you don't have to marry—"

"I applied for that job for a reason, Felicity. Yeah, to be closer, but because I wanted to start getting things situated for the future. And maybe I was waiting for a little kick in the butt—but here it is. I was getting there before this."

"This is faster."

"Yeah. But I think we can do it." He lifted her hand and pressed a kiss to it. "I *know* we can do it. And so do you."

The timer on her phone went off and they both jumped.

"Okay." She *did* know they could do it, but it helped to hear. Helped to be steadied by someone else. She took a deep breath and looked at the test sitting there.

"Translate for me," Gage said, his voice a bit strangled. "What does two lines mean?"

"Pregnant," Felicity said, staring at the results window, where there were two lines clear as day.

"Pregnant," he repeated. Then he laughed and lifted her clear up off the floor, still laughing. Happy.

"You're happy," she murmured, because he was a constant marvel. She knew they were good together, knew he'd want to do the right thing, but she wasn't sure he'd jump right to happy.

"Yeah, hell of a thing, but yeah." He put her back down on her own feet. "Are you happy?"

Since her throat was clogged with tears, she could

only nod and rest her forehead on his chest. *Happy* didn't seem a big enough word. But there was reality, too.

"He might get out some day. That trial wasn't the end. God knows he'll appeal. Ace touching our lives isn't over."

"Maybe not," Gage agreed.

It was scary, especially with this new life growing inside of her, but he was holding her. They were in this together. She lifted her head and looked up at him. "But we'll have even more to fight for, right?" She put her hand over her stomach. It was impossible to believe something was there—a life. Impossible to fully grasp, and yet true.

And right. So right.

"We have everything to fight for," Gage agreed, sliding his own hand over hers. "And we already have, so we know we can again." He pulled her close, tucked her hair behind her ears. "So, you going to marry me? Before the baby, just in case Duke gets any ideas about making me disappear."

She tried to say yes, but her throat was too tight with tears. And hope. And joy. So, she nodded, and he kissed her until she thought her knees might dissolve.

"It's going to be a good life," he said, a promise and a vow.

"Yeah, yeah, it is."

* * * * *

BADLANDS BEWARE

For the family secrets that never get told.

Chapter One

Rachel Knight had endured nightmares about the moment she'd lost the majority of her sight since she'd been that scared, injured three-year-old. The dream was always the same. The mountain lion. The surprising shock and pain of its attack.

Things she knew had happened, because what else could have attacked her? Because that was the truth that everyone believed. She'd somehow toddled out of the house and into the South Dakota ranchland only to have a run-in with a wild animal.

But in the dreams, there was always a voice. Not her father, or her late mother, or anyone who should have been there that night.

The voice of a stranger.

Rachel sucked in a breath as her eyes flew open. Her heart pounded, and her sheets were a sweaty tangle around her.

It was a dream. Nothing more and nothing less, but she couldn't figure out why twenty years after the attack she would still be so plagued by it.

Likely it was just all the danger that her family

had been facing lately. As much as she loved the Wyatts, both sturdy Grandma Pauline and her six law enforcement grandsons who owned the ranch next door, their connection to a vicious biker gang meant trouble seemed to follow wherever they went.

And somehow, this year it had also brought her foster sisters into the fold time and again. Putting them in jeopardy along with those Wyatt brothers—and then culminating in true love, against all odds.

All of their tormenters were in jail now, and Rachel wanted that to be the end of it.

But something about the dreams left her feeling edgy, like the next dangerous situation was just around the corner.

And that you'll get thrust into the path of one of the Wyatt boys and end up...

Rachel got out of bed without finishing the thought. Just because four of her five foster sisters had ended up in love with a Wyatt didn't mean she was doomed. Because if she was doomed, so was Sarah. Rachel laughed outright at the thought.

Sarah was too much like Pauline. Independent and prickly. The thought of her falling for *anyone*, let alone a bossy Wyatt, was unfathomable. Which meant it was inconceivable for Rachel, too. She might not be prickly, but she had no designs on ending up tied to a man with a dangerous past and likely even more dangerous secrets.

So, that was that.

Rachel went through her normal routine of showering and getting ready for the day before heading downstairs. She didn't have to tap her clock to hear the time to know it was earlier than she usually woke up.

She was—shudder—becoming a morning person. Maybe she could shed that with the coming winter.

It was full-on autumn now. Twenty-three was creeping closer and while she knew that wasn't old, she was exactly where she'd always been. Would she be stuck here forever? In the same house, on the same ranch, nothing ever changing except the people around her?

Teaching at the reservation offered some respite, but she was so dependent on others. If she moved somewhere with more public transportation, she could be independent.

And yet the thought of leaving South Dakota and her family always just made her sad. This was home. She wanted to be happy here, but there was a feeling of suffocation dogging her.

Maybe *that* was why she kept having those dreams.

Weirdly, that offered some comfort. There was a reason, and it was just feeling a little quarter-life crisis-y. Nothing…ominous.

She held on to that truth as she headed downstairs. Inside the house she never used her cane, even after the fire this summer. They'd fixed the affected sections to be exactly as they had been, which meant she knew it as well as she knew Pauline Reaves's ranch next door, or her classroom, or Cecilia's house on the rez where Rachel stayed when she was teaching.

She wasn't trapped. She had plenty of places to go. As long as she didn't mind overprotective family everywhere she went.

Rachel stopped at the bottom of the stairs, surprised to hear someone in the kitchen. Duke's irritable mutterings alerted her to the fact it was her father before she could make out the shape of him.

Big, dark and the one constant presence in her life, aside from Sarah—who was the opposite of Duke. Small, petite and pale. She couldn't make out the details of a person's appearance, but she could recognize those she loved by the blurry shapes she could see out of her one eye that hadn't been completely blinded.

"Daddy, what are you doing?"

"What are you doing up?" he returned gruffly.

Rachel hesitated. While she often told her father everything that was going on with her, she tended to keep things that might worry him low-key. "I think my body finally got used to waking up early," she said, forcing a cheerfulness over it she didn't feel.

"Speaking of that..." He trailed off, approached her. His hand squeezed her shoulder. "Baby, I know you've got a class session coming up in a few weeks, but I think you should bow out. Too much has been going on."

Rachel opened her mouth, but no sound came out. Not teach at the rez? The art classes she held for a variety of age groups were short sessions and taught through the community rather than the school itself. She only instructed about twenty weeks out of the year, and he wanted her to miss a four-week session? When teaching was the only thing that made her feel like she had a life outside of cooking and cleaning for Dad and Sarah.

"Just this session," Dad added. "Until we know for sure those Wyatt boys are done bringing their trouble around."

It felt like a slap in the face, but she didn't know how to articulate that. Except an unfair rage toward the Wyatts.

Rachel took a deep breath to calm herself. She never let her temper get the better of her. Mom had impressed upon her temper tantrums would never get her what she wanted. "I don't have anything to do with their trouble."

"I might have said the same about Felicity and Cecilia, but look what they endured this summer. It won't do."

"Dad, teaching those classes—"

"I know they mean a lot to you. And I am sorry. Maybe you could do some tutoring out here?"

"I'm an adult."

"You're twenty-two. I know this is a disappointment, but I'm not going to argue about it." His hand slid off her shoulder and she heard the jangle of keys.

Rachel frowned at how strange this all was. Maybe she was still dreaming. "Are you *going* somewhere?"

There was a pregnant pause. "Just into town on some errands."

Her frown deepened. Sarah took care of almost all the errands now that it was just the two of them left living with Duke. Her father almost never ventured into town. And he never gave *her* unreasonable ultimatums.

"What's wrong, Dad?" she asked gravely.

"I want my girls safe," he said, and she heard his retreating footsteps as though that was that.

She fisted her hands on her hips. Oh, no, it was *not*. And she was going to get some answers. If they wouldn't come from her father, they'd just have to come from the source of the trouble.

TUCKER WYATT HAD always loved spending nights at his grandmother's house. Though he kept an apartment in town, he'd much rather spend time with his family at the Reaves ranch.

Until now.

He sighed. Why had he ever thought his current predicament was a good idea? He was *terrible* at keeping secrets.

Case in point, he was about 75 percent sure his brother Brady had figured out that Tucker *accidentally* stumbling into a situation where he could help save Brady's life from one of their father's protégés wasn't so accidental. That it was part of his working beyond his normal job as detective with the Valiant County Sheriff's Department.

And, since their youngest brother had been kicked out of North Star Group just a few months ago, it didn't take a rocket scientist to figure out what group Tucker might also be working for.

He was going to have to quit. The North Star Group had approached him because of his ties to Ace Wyatt, former head of the dangerous Sons of the Badlands, and a few of Tucker's cases that involved other high-ranking officials in the Sons.

Cases Tuck had been sure were private and confidential. But those words didn't mean much to North Star.

They'd wanted him on the Elijah Jones investigation, but then Brady and Cecilia Mills, one of the Knight girls, had gotten in the way.

The only reason Tucker hadn't been kicked out of North Star, as far as he could see, was because the

North Star higher-ups didn't know his brother and Cecilia were suspicious of Tucker's involvement.

Which didn't sit right. Surely they didn't think his brother, a police officer, didn't have questions about a mysterious explosion that took Elijah Jones down enough to be restrained, hospitalized and, as of today, transferred to prison.

It had been a mess of a summer all in all, but things would assuredly calm down now. Ace was in maximum-security prison and Elijah was going to jail, along with a variety of his helpers.

But as long as Tucker was part of North Star and their continued efforts to completely and utterly destroy the Sons of the Badlands, he wouldn't feel totally settled *or* calm.

The back door that came into the kitchen swung open—not all that unusual. Grandma Pauline always had people coming and going through this entrance, but Tuck was surprised by the appearance of a *very* angry looking Rachel Knight.

She pointed directly at him, as if he'd done something wrong. "What's going on with my dad?"

Tuck stared at Rachel in confusion. She looked… pissed, which was not her norm. She was probably the most even-keeled of the whole Knight bunch.

While her sisters had all been fostered or adopted by Duke and Eva Knight, Rachel was their lone biological daughter. She didn't look much like her father—more favored her late mother, which always gave Tuck a bit of a pang.

His memories of his own mother weren't pleasant. He'd had Grandma Pauline, who he loved with his whole heart. Her influence on him and his brothers when they'd come to live with her meant the world to him.

But Eva Knight had been a soft, motherly presence in the Reaves-Knight world. Even if she'd been next door and not their mother, she'd treated them like sons. He'd never seen anything that matched it.

Except in her daughter. Tall and slender, Rachel had Eva's sharp nose and high cheekbones and long black hair. The biggest difference were the scars around Rachel's eyes, lines of lighter brown against the darker skin color on the rest of her face.

She could *see*, but not clearly. It always seemed to Tuck that her dark brown eyes were a little too knowing.

At least on *this* he wasn't keeping a secret—and failing at it. He had no idea why she'd demand of him anything about Duke Knight.

"Well?" she demanded as he only sat there like a deer caught in headlights.

"I haven't the slightest idea what's going on with your father. Why would I?"

"I don't know. I only know it has something do with *you.*"

By the way she flung her arms in the air, he could only assume she didn't mean him personally but the whole of the Wyatts.

"Why don't we sit down?" He took her elbow gently to lead her to the table. "Back up. Talk about this, you know, calmly."

She tugged her elbow out of his grasp, clearly not wanting to sit. "He doesn't want me teaching this fall. He's worried about our safety. I know it doesn't have to do with *my* family. So, it has to do with yours."

Tucker held himself very still—an old trick he had down to an art these days. Letting his temper get the best of him as a kid had gotten the crap beaten out of him. Routinely.

Ace had told him his emotions would be the death of him if he didn't learn to control them. Hone them.

Tucker refused to *hone* them or be anything like his father. Which meant also never letting his temper boil over. He pictured a blue sky, puffy white clouds and a hawk arcing through both.

When he trusted his voice, he spoke and offered a smile. "I guess that's possible." He didn't allow himself to say what he wanted to. *Your sisters seem to be getting my brothers in trouble plenty on their own.* "I'm not sure specifically what it could be that would have Duke worried about you teaching at the rez. Did something happen? Maybe Cecilia would know."

"What would I know?" Cecilia asked, walking into the kitchen. She was in her tribal police uniform, likely on her way to work. Though she was still nursing some wounds from her run in with Ace's protege and hadn't been cleared for active duty, she'd started in-house hours this week.

Though Duke and Eva Knight had fostered Cecilia, like Rachel she was a blood relation—Eva's niece. But she had been raised as "one of the Knight girls" as much Rachel's sister as her cousin.

"Has there been any new trouble at the rez that might make Duke nervous about Rach teaching her upcoming session?" Tucker asked.

Rachel scowled at him. "I wasn't going to bring her into it, jerk."

Cecilia's brow puckered. "I haven't heard anything. Dad doesn't want you teaching? Kind of late to have concerns about that, isn't it? Doesn't your session start the first of the month? And why didn't you want to bring me into it?"

Rachel sighed heavily. "Yes, it does, and yes, it's late." She looked pointedly in Tucker's direction, but when she spoke it was to Cecilia. "I wasn't going to bring you into it, because obviously it's not about *you*. I don't think it's about the rez, either. I think it's about the Wyatts."

"Look, Rach, I know the Wyatts are an easy target, no offense, Tuck. But if something bad was going on over here, Brady would have told me."

Because Cecilia and Brady now shared a *room* at his grandmother's house, a simple fact Tucker wasn't used to. Four of his brothers all paired off. And with the Knight girls of all people. It was sudden and weird.

But he just had to keep that to himself. Especially when Brady and Cecilia lived here now. "Well, I'll let you ladies figure this out. I've got a meeting to get to," Tucker said, quickly slipping past Rachel even as she began to protest.

Whatever was going on with Duke and Rachel was not his business, and he had to meet with his boss at North Star to nip this whole mission in the bud. It wasn't for him. He was a detective, and a damn good one, but he would never become adept at lying to his family.

He got in his truck, and drove to the agreed upon location. A small diner in Rapid City. Tucker had never met Granger McMillan, the head of the North Star

Group. He'd been approached by field operatives and dealt with them solely.

Until now.

Tucker scanned the diner. Granger had said he'd know who he was, and Tucker had thought that was a little over-the-top cloak-and-dagger, but the large man in a cowboy hat and dark angry eyes sitting in the corner was *quite* familiar.

The man he was sitting across from turned in his seat, looked right at Tucker and gestured him over.

Tucker moved forward feeling a bit like he'd taken a blow to the head. Why was Duke here? What *was* this?

"You two know each other," the man, who could only be Granger McMillan, said. Not a question. A statement. "Have a seat, Wyatt. We have a lot to discuss."

Chapter Two

Rachel didn't get anywhere with Cecilia. Falling in love had certainly colored her vision when it came to the Wyatts. It was a disappointment, but one that was hard to hold on to when Brady had come in and he'd exchanged a casual goodbye kiss with her sister.

She would have never put Brady and Cecilia together, but when they were together, it seemed so *right*. Two pieces clicking together to mellow each other out a bit.

But even if that softened her up, Rachel wasn't ready to give up on being mad at the Wyatt brothers. So, she sought out someone she knew would back her up.

Sarah wiped her brow with the back of her arm. She'd been hefting water buckets into the truck to move them to a different pasture while Rachel laid out her case.

"Yeah, it's weird Dad took off, but what do you want me to do about it? I'm kind of running a ranch single-handedly here while he's doing whatever." Dev Wyatt's dogs raced around Sarah and Rachel. "My biggest concern is why I suddenly have two dogs. I did not consent to these dogs."

Rachel patted Cash on the head. Sarah talked a big game, but Rachel had overheard her just last night loving on the very dogs she was currently irritated over.

With a pang, Rachel missed Minnie, her old service dog. She knew she should start working on getting another one, or maybe even work on training her own, but it just made her sad still.

"What do you need help with?" Rachel asked, feeling guilty about unloading on her sister when she was so busy. The Knight ranch wasn't the biggest operation in South Dakota, but Duke and Sarah had to work really hard to make it profitable, and with all the danger around lately, hiring outside help felt like too big a risk.

"It's fine," Sarah replied, hopping off the truck bed and closing the gate. "Dev's coming over this afternoon to help. Maybe he'll take those stupid mutts back with him."

Even if Sarah could convince the dogs to go back with Dev, Rachel knew Sarah was all talk. She'd be bribing the dogs back over by suppertime.

"Well, I'll go make up some sandwiches for lunch. Want some pasta salad to go with it?"

"Yes, please."

Rachel walked back to the house over the well-worn path along the fence that led her to and from the stables. She moved through her normal chore of preparing lunch for Sarah and Dad, though Dad still wasn't home.

Rachel set the water to boil for pasta salad and frowned. It wasn't like her father to run errands on a ranch morning, even more unlike him to be gone for hours at a time. Cecilia had seemed concerned, but not enough to miss work. Plus, now she was going to tell

Brady and he'd talk about it with his brothers and Rachel was fed up with Wyatts interfering.

Ughhh, those Wyatts. Rachel let herself bang around in the kitchen. She supposed Cecilia was a *little* right and Rachel was *maybe* projecting some feelings on them because it was safer than being upset with her father.

But Rachel didn't really care about being fair or balanced in the privacy of her own thoughts. Pasta salad and sandwiches made, she set them in the fridge and went to handling the rest of her normal chores, grumbling to herself the whole way.

Duke and Sarah were terrible housekeepers, so Rachel was often the default cleaner in the house. She didn't mind it, though. Having things to do made her feel useful. She tidied, swept, vacuumed, even dusted. She went upstairs and made the beds. Once she was done, she tapped her clock for the time.

The robotic voice told her it was nearly noon. Still no Sarah and even worse, no Dad. Rachel headed downstairs, wracking her brain for some reason her father would be gone this long without telling her.

She stopped halfway down the stairs. A horrible thought dawned on her. What if he was sick? Like Mom. What if he was at the doctor getting terrible news he wanted to hide?

The thought had tears stinging her eyes. She couldn't do it. She couldn't lose her mom and her dad before she was even twenty-five. Before she found a significant other. Before she had kids. Dad had to be around for that. Mom couldn't, so Dad *had* to be.

Rachel marched toward his room, propelled by fear

masked as fury. If something was wrong, she'd find evidence of it there.·

She stepped inside. He'd moved down to the main floor with Mom when she had gotten sick. He'd never moved back upstairs. Sometimes Rachel worried about him wallowing in the loss. Now she worried the same fate was waiting for him.

No. I refuse.

She tidied up, deciding it was an easy excuse to poke around his things. Which wasn't out of the norm. When she deep-cleaned the house, she took care of Dad's room. She didn't find anything out of the ordinary, though she wouldn't be able to read any of the medicine bottles to tell if there was something off there—but based on the number and size there didn't seem to be anything more than the usual over-the-counter pain-killer and heartburn medicines.

She'd need Sarah to read the labels to be sure, but then she'd have to bring her sister into this and Sarah had enough to worry about with the ranch.

She pondered the dilemma as she made Dad's bed. As she adjusted the pillows, she felt something cool and hard. She reached out and touched her fingers to the object. It was a black blob in her vision, but she quickly realized she was touching a gun.

Rachel stood frozen in place for a good minute, pillow held up in one hand, her other hand grasping the gun. It wasn't that her father didn't have firearms. He had a few hunting rifles, kept in the safe in the basement. He had one hung above the back door because after reading the *Little House* books to her, he'd decided that's where one needed to go.

But this was a small pistol. Like the ones the Wyatt boys carried when on duty. And it was under his pillow. Carefully she picked it up and felt around some more, getting an idea of the gun model before she checked the chamber.

Loaded, which seemed very unsafe in his *bed*. Rachel didn't know what to make of it, but his whole talk about safety sure made it seem like he was worried about some kind of threat.

What on earth kind of threat would Duke be facing?

"Rachel?"

She nearly dropped the gun at Sarah's voice. Luckily, it came from the kitchen, not from right next to her. She quickly slipped the gun back under the pillow, left the bed unmade and tiptoed into the hallway.

"Coming!" she called, trying to steady her beating heart. Sarah didn't need to know about this. Not just yet. First, Rachel had to figure what was going on.

"So, WHAT YOU'RE telling me…" Tucker raked his fingers through his hair, not knowing whether to look at Duke or Granger "…is Knight ranch was a witness protection hideout."

Duke's gaze was patently unfriendly, which was odd coming from a man he'd always looked up to. Tucker had grown up in a biker gang surrounded by nothing but bad. Ever since he'd gotten out, Duke had been there. Grandma Pauline and Eva had been mother figures. Duke had been the father figure.

But Duke clearly didn't want Granger letting Tucker in on his past. His *true* identity. How did Duke Knight of all people have a *true* identity?

"And the girls don't know?"

"Why would they know?" Duke asked, his voice a raspy growl. "I left that old life behind over thirty-five years ago. Met Eva two years later, and we built this family on who I was *now*, not who I was *then*. Then was gone, and has been for a very long time."

"A cop." Duke Knight had been a cop. A cop who, in his first year on duty, had taken down a powerful family of dirty police officers. And then had a bounty put on his head and had to be moved into WITSEC.

A ranch in the middle of nowhere South Dakota sure made sense, and feeling safe enough to find a wife and build a family here made even more sense. But Tucker didn't know how to accept it.

"Grandma Pauline… She had to know."

Duke shrugged. "Don't know if she did or didn't, but Pauline never asked any questions. Never poked her nose into my business." He looked pointedly at Granger.

Granger, who was here for a current reason. That somehow involved Tucker. "Why would this group want to come after you when thirty-five years have passed? Wouldn't it be water under the bridge?"

"You're Ace Wyatt's son and you really have to ask that question?"

Tuck was chastened enough at that. When fear was currency, the years didn't matter so much. Only proving your strength, your ability to destroy did.

Tucker turned to face Granger across from him at the diner table. "And how does this connect to North Star?"

"We've been working under the assumption Vince MacLean was casing your grandmother's ranch because of the Wyatt connection, which is why we brought you in," Granger said. Facts Tucker was well aware of.

Granger was a tall man, dressed casually. A layperson might not think anything of someone like him, sitting in a diner, having a friendly cup of coffee. But Tucker saw all the signs of someone on alert. The way his gaze swept the establishment. The way he filed away everyone who entered or exited.

"We couldn't quite figure his role out. But the information you've passed along to us, plus what we already had, started to point to the fact there might be a different target." Granger nodded toward Duke. "We started looking into not just who Vince was directly reporting to, but who the people he was reporting to passed information to and so on. What we found is a connection to the Vianni family."

Tucker didn't need to be led to the rest. "Who were the family of dirty cops you took down?"

Duke nodded.

"We started digging into the family, into possible connections, and figured out Duke's. Since he was the target, we brought him in. And now we're bringing you in. The Sons connecting to the Vianni family is an expansion. It gives both groups more reach, and makes them stronger than they were."

"The Sons have been weakened."

"You can keep throwing their leaders in jail, Wyatt, but that doesn't end their infrastructure or ability to regroup."

"What does?" Tucker returned.

Granger's gaze, which had been cool and controlled up to this point, heated with fury. But his voice remained calm as he spoke. "We need Duke to help us. Which means he has to disappear for a little while. Duke's not too keen on leaving his ranch or his daughters."

"Nor should he be," Tucker snapped, his own temper straining. "Have you been paying attention these past few months? Duke being gone doesn't make the threat go away." He turned to Duke, who was sitting next to him in the booth. "You're leaving them to be a new target, that's all. And you—" Tucker faced Granger "—you're caring about your own North Star plots and plans without thinking about innocent lives."

Tucker didn't wilt when Granger lifted his eyebrows regally. "Watch your step, boy. I know more about protecting innocent lives than you could even begin to imagine. But Duke is our key between the Sons and the Viannis, and without him, more innocent people get hurt. A lot more."

Tucker whipped his gaze back to Duke, too angry to be chastened by Granger's words. "You didn't tell any of us? This whole time you knew you were a target and you didn't think to give us a heads-up so we could help?"

"I didn't want to bring you or your brothers into it. I don't want my daughters brought into it, and that's all your brothers seem capable of doing." Duke nodded toward Granger. "His father is the reason I have the ranch I do. The life I do. When Granger here came to me… I might not like it, but I owe the McMillan family, and I owe it to the other people the Viannis have hurt after I bowed out."

Tucker snorted in derision. Maybe he should have felt sorry for Duke, but all he could think about was

Rachel already coming to him worried about her father. "You think your girls are going to buy you *leaving*?"

"It'll be your job to convince them," Granger said matter-of-factly, like that was a mission anyone could accomplish. He pushed a manila envelope over to Tucker. "This includes a letter to the daughters from Duke, a packet of fake vacation itinerary. You'll take it to Sarah and Rachel and say you found it—where and how is up to you." Then Granger slid a phone across the table. "You'll also take this. It's been programmed with your cell number, as well as a secret number that will allow contact with someone at North Star directly. We'll reach you through this if we need you. It's also got access to security measures set up around the Reaves and Knight ranches, thanks to your brother. He has no idea you have access to any of this, and no one in your family or Duke's can know, either. Is that understood?"

Tucker looked at the folder and the phone. None of this made sense, and how on earth was he going to convince Sarah and Rachel—and the rest of either family for that matter—that Duke, who'd barely left the ranch even for errands throughout all their lives, was going on vacation. Suddenly, and without warning. "You can't be serious."

"Oh, I'm deadly serious, Wyatt. And so is this."

Chapter Three

"Something has to be wrong." Rachel stood in Grandma Pauline's kitchen, Sarah next to her. She could hear the dogs whining outside, but Grandma Pauline did not allow dogs in her kitchen.

"If he'd come home before dinner, I wouldn't think *too* much of it. But he still isn't back and he won't answer his cell," Sarah said, wringing her hands together.

"I called Gage," Brady offered. "He's going to head over to Valiant County and see if he can sweet talk them into putting some men on it before the required hours for a missing person. Then he'll look himself. Cecilia said she's going to ask around town after her shift, too. If he's around, one of them will find him."

"What do you mean *if*?" Sarah demanded. "Where else would he go?"

Which echoed the fear growing inside of Rachel. "Do you think something happened to him?" she asked, straight out. Because if Brady Wyatt thought something had happened to him, his instincts were most likely right.

Brady's response was grim. "Duke left the ranch of his own volition, but you were concerned about him being worried about danger. Maybe there's something he wasn't telling us."

The door opened and Tucker entered. Aside from Brady and Gage, Rachel could tell the difference in the Wyatt brothers by general shape. Even though they were all tall and broad, they had a different presence about them.

If she took a lot of time, she could figure out Gage and Brady, but being twins made it a bit more difficult, and she could always tell from their voices.

But Tucker was always a slightly…lighter presence. His hair wasn't so dark, his movements were always a little easier. But something about the way he entered the kitchen now was all wrong.

"Hey, all. What's going on?"

Rachel frowned. He did *not* sound his usual cheerful self. Something was weighing on him, and that was clear as day in his voice.

"Duke's missing," Sarah said plainly.

"Missing?"

"We can't find him. He hasn't come back to the ranch since this morning."

"You're sure he's not out in the fields?" Tucker asked.

"No. I'm worrying everyone because I didn't look around the ranch," Sarah replied sarcastically. "Don't be an ass, Tuck."

"I'm sure there's a rational explanation. If you're all worried, I can—"

"We've already got Gage and Cecilia on it," Brady said.

There was something off about Tucker. Something… odd in the way he delivered his responses.

"Oh, I picked up your mail," he offered as if it he'd just remembered. "It was falling out of the box."

Rachel assumed he put it into Sarah's hands before he moved over to the table. "I didn't have a chance to get dinner. You got any leftovers, Grandma?" He moved farther into the kitchen, still acting…strangely. But no one else seemed to notice, so maybe she was taking her worry about Dad and spreading it around.

There was a thud and the flutter of papers. "There's a letter from Dad," Sarah screeched. The sound of the envelope being ripped open had Rachel moving closer even though she wouldn't be able to read it.

Sarah read aloud. "Dear girls, I know you probably won't be able to believe this, but I've decided it's time for a break. If I don't go right now, I know I never will. I've included my vacation itinerary so you don't worry, but this is something I need to do for myself. Take good care of each other. Love, Dad."

"There's no possible way," Rachel croaked, panic hammering at her throat. "Maybe he wrote that, but not because he wanted to take a vacation. Not of his own volition." Nothing would drag her father away from the ranch, away from his daughters. Not even temporarily.

"And he'd never leave without someone here to help me," Sarah added, her voice uncharacteristically tremulous. "I can't handle the ranch on my own."

"We'll work it out," Dev said gruffly. "Don't worry about the ranch. Brady—"

"We'll tell Gage the latest development," Brady said before Dev could instruct him. "He can—"

"Let me look into it," Tucker said. "I'm the detective. We don't need to get Valiant County involved or have Gage and Cecilia asking around."

"We can *all* look into it," Brady said evenly.

"Yeah, but if we all start looking into it, and something *is* wrong, we've alerted everyone we know. But if I look into it, pretend like I'm just researching one of my cases, we might be able to unearth whatever trouble there actually is without causing suspicion. *If* there's any trouble at all."

"My father did not go on a *vacation.* Period. Let alone without telling us. What kind of trouble would he be in?"

"I don't know, Rach. Let me look into it. If there's trouble, we'll find it."

"Yes, you're very good at finding it," she replied caustically.

"Now, now," Grandma Pauline said, and though the words might have been gentle coming from most grandmothers, from Pauline it was a clear warning.

Rachel blew out a breath.

Tucker's voice was very calm when he spoke, and she could easily imagine him using that tone with a hysterical person on a call. He would promise to take care of everything no matter how upset the person was.

She swallowed at the lump of fear and anxiety in her throat. Tucker could do that because he wanted to help people. She wanted to blame him for all the trouble right now, but deep down she knew it wasn't his fault or his brothers' faults.

The Wyatts were good men who wanted to do the right thing, and she had to stop sniping at them. Division was not going to bring her father home.

"What can we do? While you're looking for him?" she asked of Tuck. "We can't just sit around waiting."

"Unfortunately, I think you *should* sit and wait. If there's danger, and we're not sure there is, we want to know what kind before we go wading in. What we do know is that even if he is in danger, he's alive. He left of his own accord. He's made *some* kind of decision here."

"He could have been threatened to leave," Sarah pointed out. "Blackmailed. Though over what I don't have a clue."

"Yes," Tucker agreed equitably. "If that's the case, someone wanted him to leave of his own accord. Think how easy it would be to ambush a man like Duke. How often he's out in the fields or barn or stables alone. This is more than Duke being in life-threatening danger. It's deeper and more complicated. *If* it's anything other than a mid-life crisis."

Rachel scoffed simultaneously with Sarah.

"He's not wrong," Grandma Pauline said. "Duke hasn't been himself lately. Wouldn't be unheard of for someone in their late fifties to have a bit of a personal crisis."

Rachel felt like the world had been upended. Why were her and Sarah the only ones freaking out about this? How could Grandma Pauline stand there and say her father was having a *personal crisis*?

"I'll head back into the office right now. Get the ball rolling on an investigation. I'll update you all in the morning."

No one spoke, not to argue with Tucker or demand more answers. Rachel had to believe they were in as much shock as she was. This couldn't actually be happening.

And Tucker wasn't acting right. She couldn't put her finger on what was wrong, just that something *was*. She heard him exit, the normal conversation picking back up. Sarah and Dev discussing ranch concerns, Brady on the phone with Jamison, the oldest Wyatt brother, giving him an update, and Grandma Pauline fussing around the kitchen cleaning up.

Didn't any of them feel it? Didn't any of them... She shook her head and slipped out the kitchen door. She couldn't make out Tucker's shape in the low light of dusk, but she didn't hear a car engine so he hadn't made it that far yet.

She took a few steps forward until she could make out the shape of him. "What aren't you telling us?"

She could tell he turned to face her, but she didn't have the ability to read his expression. Still there was a lot in that long careful pause.

"If there was anything I could tell you to make sense of this, I would."

She wasn't sure why that made her want to cry instead of yell at him. Which left her unsure of what to say.

He stepped close, then his hands were giving hers a squeeze. "I'm going to do everything I can to bring him home safe, Rach. Whether he's in trouble or not. You believe that, don't you?"

She wasn't sure what she believed in the midst of all this insanity, but in her heart she knew Tucker was a good man and that he loved her father. Maybe none of this made sense, but he wouldn't promise to do everything he could and then not.

"Yeah, I do."

He gave her hands one last squeeze, released them. "Good. I'll have an update in the morning. I promise." Then he left her standing in the cool evening, unsure of how to work through all her emotions, and all her fears.

It was a lot of work. Not looking for Duke, and trying to undo all his brothers had already set in motion. Tucker couldn't very well have the entire Valiant County Sheriff's Department out searching for Duke. Even if North Star hid Duke or used him for whatever their plan was, having people sniffing around just wasn't going to be good.

Tucker scrubbed his hands over his face. Granger hadn't given him much to go on. Just that he had to make sure the Knights thought Duke was on vacation while they did the hard work.

When North Star had first approached Tucker, it had been through a lower operative. The woman had told him they had reason to believe Vince MacLean was gathering intel on the Wyatts, and to do whatever he could to find out who Vince was reporting to.

It had been a simple mission, straightforward and in Tuck's own best interest to help his family. And it had, in fact, helped his family a great deal as his following Vince had led him straight to Brady and Cecilia when they were in trouble.

Tucker locked up his office and headed for his car. He'd have liked to head back to the ranch, but it was two in the morning and he needed to catch a few hours of sleep.

He didn't know how he was going to face Rachel. He hadn't lied to her. He *would* do everything he could to bring Duke safely home. Tucker just didn't know how much of a say he had in things. But the one thing he *did* know? That he was never going to convince her Duke had taken a vacation of his own accord.

He headed for his car. The night was dark, the station mostly deserted. Still, the feeling of being watched had him slowly, carefully resting his hand on the butt of his weapon strapped to his belt.

"No need, Wyatt."

He didn't recognize the female's voice, but when she materialized out of the dark, he recognized her as the woman who'd originally contacted him about North Star.

"What now?" he muttered. Instead of stopping, he kept moving for his car. He wasn't too keen on being accommodating to the North Star crew right now, considering they were making his life unduly complicated. He kept one hand on his gun for good measure.

"There's chatter. Some people know Duke's missing."

"Yeah. Like his entire family? They're worried about him, because no one in their right mind is going to believe Duke Knight left South Dakota to go on *vacation*."

"Like the Sons. From what I've been able to gather, they think the Viannis got him. While they think that, there are certain parties who are going to be interested in friends of the Wyatts being unprotected, so to speak."

Tuck tossed his bag in the passenger side of his car. He was tired and irritable and this wasn't helping. "And who's fault would that be?"

"Look, I'm trying to be friendly here. I know enough about the setup from your brother. Someone needs to keep an eye on the Knight ranch. Just because the Viannis are focused on Duke, doesn't mean the Sons won't focus on a weakness in the Wyatts' armor if they can find one. Last I heard, the Knights are a weakness."

"I'm pretty sure I told your boss to be just as worried about Duke Knight's daughters as he was about Duke. He didn't seem too concerned."

"Yeah, because his concern is the mission."

"And what's your concern?"

She muttered something incomprehensible under her breath. "Watch their backs, huh?"

"Why don't you go talk to my brother about it?"

"Because your brother got kicked out, pal. You, on the other hand, are in the thick of things. So, grow a pair." She melted back into the dark shadows before he could retort.

Which was for the best. No use taking his nasty mood out on someone who was trying to help.

Especially when she was right. Sarah and Rachel alone in the Knight house, even with Dev's dogs, just wasn't a good idea. He wouldn't be surprised to hear that Cecilia had decided to spend the night over there herself, and she was trained law enforcement.

She'd also been injured not that long ago, and Brady still wasn't on active duty due to his injuries. They'd saved an innocent child from being taken into the Sons, but they hadn't come out unscathed.

So, sending him over there to spend the night with Cecilia wasn't enough of a comfort. Dev would be helping out with ranching duties, but he'd been a cop for all of six months before he'd sustained serious injuries that left him with a limp.

Thanks to dear old Dad.

Jamison and Cody both lived in Bonesteel, and while he knew they'd all pitch in to help, it'd bring Cody's young daughter and Jamison's even younger sister-in-law into the fray and they deserved to be as far from danger as possible after what they'd endured when Ace Wyatt had come after them and their families. The only other option was Gage and Felicity, who both worked almost two hours away. Not to mention, Felicity was pregnant.

Which left him. He didn't mind that. He was happy to protect whomever needed protecting. It was the convincing the women involved they *needed* protecting that was going to be the headache. On top of the one he already had.

Tucker slid into his car. There was no going to his apartment now. Even if it was the middle of the night, he needed to head to the ranches. He had to figure out a way to convince Rachel and Sarah it was best if he stayed with them for a while.

As he drove through the thick of night, he considered just telling everyone the truth. What could the North Star Group do to him? He didn't owe them silence. And with the whole Wyatt clan in on things, wasn't it possible they could help take down the Viannis and the Sons themselves?

The list of reasons not to have his brothers spend the night at the Knight house went through his head. Because for all the same reasons, it didn't feel right to bring them into this. They'd built new lives, survived their own near-death injuries. And what had he done? All this time, all these months of danger and threats from Ace and the Sons, and he'd *investigated*. Between his brothers and their significant others, they'd all been tortured, shot, temporarily blinded and more.

Tucker had fought off a few Sons goons, but had mostly emerged unscathed.

So, no, he couldn't tell them. It was his turn to take on the danger, take on the Sons. His turn to protect his family, and the Knight girls.

Whether they wanted protecting or not.

Chapter Four

Rachel woke up from the nightmare in a cold sweat. The recurrence so soon after the last one made sense. She was stressed and worried. Of course, she'd have terrible dreams to go along with those terrible feelings.

But there'd been no mountain lion in this nightmare. She sat up and rubbed her eyes and then hugged herself against the chill.

The mountain lion had been a man. She could still visualize him. Blue eyes glowing, burn scars all over the side of one face. She could hear his voice in her head, rough and growly with an odd regional American accent she couldn't place.

She shuddered. It was a *dream*. Yeah, a creepy one that was still lodged in her head, but it was fiction. Dreams weren't real.

Though this one had felt particularly, scarily real.

She got out of bed even though it was still dark. She didn't bother to check the time. Too early. She'd just go downstairs and get a drink of water. Hopefully, it would help settle her.

She was safe. Maybe Dad wasn't, but she was. Here in this house, with Cecilia and Sarah down the hall. Though she felt a little guilty that Cecilia had insisted on spending the night since Brady had to stay at Grandma Pauline's due to his leg injury.

She wished she could say her and Sarah could handle it, but while they could manage anything around the ranch, they weren't trained law enforcement, and they didn't have any background or experience in fighting off bad guys.

Cecilia did. In fact, *everyone* else did. Rachel blew out a breath as she tiptoed downstairs. She stopped at the bottom, frowning at the odd sound. Like the scrape of a chair against the floor.

Her breath caught, pulse going wild as panic filled her. Someone was in the kitchen. Someone was—

"What are you doing up?"

Tucker's voice. Coming from the kitchen table. The *Knight* kitchen table. Long before sunrise.

"What are you doing here? It's...dark still."

"Honestly? I got a little tip that I shouldn't be letting you two be here alone. A friendly tip, but still. I thought it was better if I headed over here rather than stayed the night in my apartment."

"You didn't need to do that. Cecilia's here. We have our law enforcement contingent."

"Good." But he made no excuses to leave. Instead, they stood there, together in the dark.

"Which means you don't have to stay," she continued. She wasn't sure why she'd said that. It was a nice thing he was doing, and she should be thanking him. But she was braless in her pajamas and Tucker Wyatt was in her kitchen. She crossed her arms over her chest.

"Unfortunately, I don't agree."

She scowled in his general direction, whether he could see it or not. "A penis is not the protector of womankind, Tucker."

He sighed heavily. "I never said it was, but Cecilia is still recovering from her injuries. It's good she's here. She'll be able to notice and address a threat, but will she be able to neutralize it? No one heard me pick the lock, did they?"

"You picked the lock?" she screeched.

He immediately shushed her, which did not do anything to make her feel better about the situation. "It's just a precaution. Regardless of what's going on with Duke, the Sons know he's missing. We don't want them looking at you as easy pickings."

"Because I'm blind," she said flatly.

"Because we don't know where this threat is coming from, if it's coming. I don't think Sarah should be out in the fields alone, and I don't think you should be in this house alone. And before you lecture me about sexism, it isn't about your gender, it's about numbers. When there's danger, two is better than one."

"Then I can accompany Sarah out in the fields, and *you* aren't needed."

"What do you have against me, Rach?" His voice was soft. Not sad exactly, but there was a thread of…hurt in his voice. "I thought we were friends, but you seem to have something very specifically against *me* right now."

"I don't."

"You're sure acting like you do."

"I…" She felt like an absolute jerk, which wasn't fair. She wasn't acting like she had anything against Tucker. He was just…

She felt him approach and his hands rested on her shoulders. "I know it's a tough time. I'm not trying to make it tougher. I'm honestly just trying to help. Can you let me do that?"

There was no way to say no and maintain that she was a reasonable human being, which she *was*. Plus, he was giving her shoulders a squeeze—a kind, reassuring gesture. He smelled like stale coffee and she wondered if he'd been up all night worrying over Duke and his girls.

It made her heart pinch. Here he was, doing all he could to find out what was going on with her father, and she was taking out her fear and anxiety on him. She sighed. "Of course I can," she said gently. "I'm not trying to be difficult. I'm just scared."

He gave her a light peck on the temple. It was something he'd always done. Tuck was the sweet Wyatt brother, if you could call any of them sweet. He had an easy affectionate streak, and he often comforted with a hug or a casual, friendly kiss.

But his hands lingered, even if his lips didn't. Rachel didn't know why she noticed…why she felt something odd skitter along her skin.

Then he cleared his throat, his hands dropping as he stepped away, and she didn't have to think about it any longer.

"I think it'd be best if I stay here," he reiterated. His voice had an odd note to it that disappeared as he continued to speak. "It'll help my investigation, and after the fire, we can't be too careful about threats that can get through Cody's safety measures. Everything I've found points to Duke leaving of his own accord."

Before Rachel could object to that, Tucker rolled right on.

"I'm not saying he left because he wanted to. I'm just saying he did it on his own two feet. No one dragged him away. Even if he didn't take a vacation like he's saying, there might be a reason. One that doesn't mean he's in immediate danger. It could be he's trying to protect you girls."

"You don't really think that."

"Actually, so far? It's exactly what I think. You don't have to agree with me, Rach. You just have to give me some space to stay here and keep an eye on things, and maybe go through Duke's room."

"And if I say no?"

"Well, I'll go through the rest of your sisters until someone agrees."

She huffed out an irritated breath. Of course he would, and one of her sisters would. But he could have barged in there and done it without any permission, so she would have to give him points for that. "I guess you could stay in his room, and if you poke around, it wouldn't be any of my business."

"Great," he said, sounding a mixture of pleased and relieved. "Hey, you should go back to bed. It's three in the morning."

"Yeah, I just came to get a glass of water."

"Here, I'll get it for you."

"I'm perfectly capable of getting my own water, Tucker."

"I know you are, but there's nothing wrong with letting someone who's closer to the glasses and the sink do something for you, Rach."

Rachel didn't know what to say to that, even when he handed her the glass of water. So she could only take it, and head back upstairs, with those words turning over in her head.

TUCK WAS NOT in a great mood. Usually when he felt this edgy, he kept himself far away from his family. He wouldn't take his temper out on anyone. Ace Wyatt might be his father, but he didn't have to be like the man. He got to choose who he was and how he treated people.

He was very afraid he wouldn't treat anyone very nicely in this mood, and quite unfortunately he had to deal with Wyatts and Knights all day long.

Tuck hated lying to his brothers. He didn't relish lying to the Knights, either, and last night with Rachel he'd felt like a jerk. She was afraid for Duke and Tucker knew he was fine, but couldn't tell her.

Then there was that odd reaction to touching her bare shoulders and inappropriately noticing that Rachel's pajamas were not exactly *modest*…

Nope. He wasn't thinking about that. Rachel was and always had been off-limits. Him and Brady had always felt like any attraction to a Knight girl was disrespectful to Duke. A good, upstanding man, great rancher, excellent, loving father, helpful and compassionate neighbor. Next to Jamison, Duke had been the Wyatt brothers' paragon of what a man should be.

Of course, Brady had broken that personal rule. Now here he was, in love with Cecilia. Planning a future together once they were healed.

Tucker shook his head. Brady might be the most

strict rule follower Tucker knew, but that didn't mean Brady slipping up on one personal tenant meant Tucker would. Or could.

He focused on the fact Brady was coming up to the Knight house, which no doubt meant Tucker was in store for a lecture from his older brother.

"You look rough," Brady commented, limping toward the porch where Tucker was standing, trying to get his temper under control.

"Yeah, you, too," he replied, then immediately winced. Brady had been shot in the leg just last month. He'd made great strides—this wound healing a lot quicker than his previous gunshot wound had.

Because Brady had been beaten to hell and back over the course of this dangerous summer, and what had Tucker done? Not a damn thing. "I updated Cody."

"I'm not here for an update." He took the stairs with the help of his cane. "I'm here to see Cecilia before she heads in to the rez."

"Shouldn't she be going to you?"

"Walking is part of my physical therapy, Tuck," Brady replied mildly, standing in front of him and putting all his weight on one leg. "What crawled up your butt?"

Tucker scraped his hands over his face. "Running on no sleep. Sorry. Dev's out with Sarah, but I've got to stick close for Rachel. Making me a little antsy."

"How are you going to stick around when you've got work?"

"I've got a call with the sheriff this morning about doing some remote work, and leaving field work to Bligh for the time being."

His brother frowned. "I can help out around here. Just because of the bum leg doesn't mean I can't be of some use."

Tucker could easily read Brady's frustration with being out of commission. He couldn't imagine the feelings of futility, especially since Brady had been dealing with months of healing, not just weeks. "A lot of it's just research and following leads from the computer. Once I've got a decent thread to tug on, I'll share it with you." Which ignored the fact his brother could help with the watching out around the ranch, but Tuck didn't want to go there.

Brady nodded, then studied him a little too closely for Tuck's comfort. "I'm trusting you, Tuck." He nodded toward the house. "I always have. It hasn't changed."

Tucker shoved his hands in his pockets. He knew Brady was referencing last month when Tucker had called in backup to get Brady and Cecilia out of a dangerous situation. There'd been some aspects of that rescue mission that Tucker had had to lie about to keep his involvement with North Star a secret, and he knew Cecilia hadn't trusted him at all. But when push had come to shove, Brady had. It meant a lot. "Well, good. You should."

"I haven't said anything, and I won't. But maybe you could talk to Cody…"

Tucker couldn't let him finish his sentence, since he had a feeling it was about North Star. "This is my thing, Brady. Let it go."

Brady opened his mouth to say something, but the door behind them swung open.

"I thought I heard you." Cecilia came out in her tribal

police uniform, smiling at Brady. She crossed to Brady first, gave him a kiss.

Tucker looked away from the easy affection. It wasn't that it bothered him. His brothers deserved that kind of good in their lives, and if they were happy, Tuck didn't have any problem with their choice of significant other.

He just didn't really want to...*watch* it. It caused some uncomfortable itch. At first when Jamison and Cody had hooked up with their ex-girlfriends, both Knight fosters, he hadn't felt it. But something about Gage and Brady falling for Felicity and Cecilia respectively made things...weird.

Rachel stepped out onto the porch, and Tucker's gut tightened with discomfort. Something he *refused* to acknowledge when it came to Duke's daughter who was a good eight years younger than him.

"Who all needs breakfast? I'm making omelets."

"I got fifteen minutes before I need to head out," Cecilia said. She patted Brady's stomach. "Don't tell me you actually snuck away from Grandma Pauline without getting stuffed full of breakfast."

"Mak was doing his crawling demonstration. Grandma was distracted, so I made a run for it." He had his arm casually wrapped around Cecilia's waist. An easy unit where one hadn't been before. They'd helped Cecilia's friend keep her infant son, Mak, safe, and now both lived at Grandma Pauline's, as well.

"All right. Tucker, since you're our sudden houseguest, you can come help me with setting the table." Rachel smiled sunnily, then turned back into the house.

Cecilia and Brady's gazes were on him, a steady, disapproving unit.

"Whatever is going on, she needs to stay far, far away from it," Cecilia said solemnly. "I'll give you the space to handle it, Tuck, because it seems that whatever's going on needs that, but I'm holding you personally responsible if anything happens to Rachel."

"She's not so helpless as all that," Tucker replied, trying not to let his discomfort, or the weight of those words, show.

"You know what I mean, whether you admit you do or not. Now you better get in there and help out."

Tucker had a few things to say in response, but he'd get nowhere against these two hardheads. Better to just save his breath. He had enough of a fight ahead of him—he'd just avoid the ones that were pointless.

He stepped into the kitchen as Rachel sprinkled a ham, cheese and pepper mixture into a pan.

"Let me guess, Cecilia was saying how you need to watch out for me or she's going to leave you in the middle of the Badlands chained to a rock with no water."

Tucker couldn't help but smile—at both the colorful specificity and how well she understood Cecilia. "It was a little less violent than all that, but the general gist."

"I don't need to be babied."

"Believe it or not, that's what I told her."

Rachel made a considering sound and said nothing else, so Tucker set out plates and silverware. He couldn't understand why she was cooking for everyone. "Why do you go to all this trouble?"

"It isn't any trouble to make breakfast."

"You and Grandma Pauline. Cereal isn't good enough. A frozen pizza is an affront. I happen to subsist just fine off of both when I'm at my apartment."

"That's because you have us to come home to."

Come home to. He didn't know why those words struck him as poignant. Of course, Grandma Pauline's was home. It was the place he'd grown up after escaping the Sons. It was the first place he'd been safe and loved.

"I guess you're right."

"Grandma Pauline taught me that you can't solve anyone's problems, but you can make them comfortable while they solve their own."

"What about when *you* have problems?"

She paused, then expertly flipped an omelet onto a plate next to her. "We aren't the ones out fighting the bad guys," Rachel said, and he could tell she was picking her words carefully.

"That doesn't mean you're without problems."

She inhaled sharply, working on the next omelet with ease and skill, but she didn't say anything to that.

Like Grandma Pauline, she was so often at the stove it seemed a part of her. Yet she'd been blinded at the age of three, lost her mother at the age of seven. Maybe she hadn't survived a ruthless biker gang like he had, but she had been scarred. Now he had to stay under the same roof as her and *lie.*

Not just to protect her, though. He was also protecting Duke, and the life he'd built. As long as North Star brought him back in one piece, did the lies matter?

Still, he stood frozen, watching her finish up the omelets, as Cecilia and Brady strolled in, still with their arms around each other. A few moments later, Sarah and Dev came in from the fields, bickering with the dogs weaving between them.

The North Star worked in secrets, in following the

mission regardless of feelings, and he'd made a promise when he'd signed on with them. He wouldn't break it.

But it was a promise to be here, to be part of these families, too. He couldn't break that, either.

So he had to find a compromise.

Chapter Five

Conversation around the breakfast table flowed the way it always did when Wyatts and Knights got together. Rapid-fire subject changes, people talking over each other, Sarah and Dev constantly disagreeing with each other.

They avoided the topic of Duke, though it hung over them like a black cloud. Still, Rachel appreciated how hard they all tried to make it seem as though this were normal. In a way it was. They'd eaten hundreds of meals together over the years. Usually not in her kitchen, though.

"You going to eat that, Tuck?" Sarah asked through a mouthful of omelet.

Rachel frowned. Why wouldn't Tucker be eating? "I can make you a different kind if you'd like."

"No, it's fine."

She heard the scrape of fork on plate and was sure Tucker had just taken a large bite. He needed to eat. He hadn't slept, that much she'd known when she'd woken up and there'd been coffee before Sarah had even come down.

"I'm just thinking," he continued. "Something about this whole Duke thing doesn't…match."

Whatever chatter had been going on around the table faded into silence at the mention of her father. Rachel's appetite disappeared and she set down her fork.

"Duke left of his own accord," Tucker continued. "Maybe he's being blackmailed in some way, but he left on his own two feet. With everything that's happened this summer, I'd assume it has to do with the Sons, but there's no evidence that it does."

"What else could it have to do with?" Cecilia demanded.

"That's what doesn't jive. Maybe there's something in Duke's background we're missing."

Dad's *background.* "Just what exactly are you suggesting about my father?"

"Nothing bad, Rach. Just that there's more to the story than we've got."

"I don't see how we can rule out the Sons," Cecilia returned. "Not when four of Duke's foster daughters are hooked up with four of Ace's sons."

"I'm not saying rule it out. You can never rule out the Sons. I'm saying, look beyond them, too. Look at *Duke.* Not just where he's gone, but why. He wasn't taken. His house wasn't set on fire. This is different than the times the Knights have been caught in the crossfire of the Sons."

Rachel heard the voice from her nightmare echo in her head. Silly. It was just a dream, and it had nothing to do with what Tucker was talking about.

"What could Duke be hiding? We've been underfoot

forever," Sarah said. "Wouldn't we know if he had some deep dark secret?"

Secrets always hurt the innocent.

Rachel squeezed her eyes shut, trying to push the dream out of her head. It had no bearing on the actual real conversation in front of her. That voice was made up, born of stress and worry and an overactive imagination.

She stood and pushed away from the table, abruptly taking her plate to the sink.

"Rach—" But Cecilia was cut off by someone's phone going off.

Cecilia muttered a curse. "I have to get to work."

There was the scraping of chairs, Dev and Sarah arguing over what work they had to get back to, Brady offering thanks for the breakfast as he left with Cecilia. The voices faded away, punctuated by the squeak and slap of the screen door.

And though he didn't make any noise, Rachel knew Tucker was still there. Likely watching her as she cleaned up the breakfast mess.

"Do you have something to say?" she demanded irritably, which wasn't like her. Nothing about the past week or so felt like *her*. She wanted to yell and rage and punch somebody and make her life go back to the way it was.

Weren't you just complaining about your life staying forever the same?

Rachel stopped washing the pan she'd used to cook the omelets and let out a pained breath. She'd wanted change, yes, but on her terms. Not the kind of change that put her father in danger.

"Did something I say upset you?" Tucker asked carefully. Like she was fragile and needed careful tiptoeing around.

"Do you assume everything is about you? That's pretty self-centered of you."

He was quiet for a long time, then she could hear him stacking dishes and placing them next to her so she could finish loading the dishwasher.

"It's just a theory, that this has something to do with Duke and not the Sons. It's not the only theory. I'm just struggling to find any evidence that ties to the Sons."

"I'm sure that struggle has nothing to do with how little you want to tie your father's gang to my father's disappearance."

"Don't be a child, Rachel," he snapped, with enough force to make her jolt. And to feel shamed.

"I wasn't—"

"I'm more aware of everything my father has done than you'll ever know. He's also in maximum-security prison because my brothers put their lives on the line to make it so. And so did some of your sisters. Let's not pretend I'm under any delusion that I could ever erase the effect my father has had on your family, through no fault of your family's."

The shame dug deeper, infusing her face with heat. "I'm sorry. I didn't mean—"

"You meant to slap at me, and I get it. You want to take out your fear and your frustration on me and I'm usually a pretty good target. But not today. So back off."

Fully chastened, Rachel reached out. She found his arm and gave it a squeeze. "I am sorry."

She could hear him sigh as he patted her hand. "I

am, too. I didn't sleep worth a darn, and I'm not handling it well."

Silence settled over them, her fingers still wrapped around his arm, his big hand resting over hers. It was warm and rough. Despite being a detective, Tucker helped out at the ranch as much as he could, which was probably where he'd gotten the callouses. The big hands were just a family trait. All the Wyatts were big. She was a tall woman, but Tucker's hands still dwarfed hers. If she flipped her hand over, so they were palm to palm—

Why was she thinking about that? She pulled her hand away from under his, and only the fact she was at the sink kept her from backing away. She had dishes to finish, so she turned back to them, ignoring the way her body was all…jittery all of a sudden.

"My theory about Duke seemed to upset you," he said, in a tone she would have considered his detective voice. Deceivingly casual as he tried to get deeper information on a topic. "Do you know something about what's going on? About Duke's past?"

She laughed, with a bitterness she couldn't seem to shove away. "No, I don't know anything."

"You're acting like you do."

She blew out a breath. Mr. Detective wasn't letting it go, so she had to be honest with him even if it was embarrassing. "I had one of those nightmares last night that felt real. I can't seem to shake it."

"Why don't you tell it to me?"

She shook her head. How embarrassing to lay out her silly, childish dreams for him to hear. He'd tell her they were natural. She'd had a traumatic experience as a young child and her brain was still dealing with it and blah, blah, blah.

"Grandma Pauline always said if you explain your nightmare, it takes away its power."

She couldn't help but smile at that. Grandma Pauline had something to say about everything, and wasn't that a comfort? "Did that work?"

He was quiet for a minute. "With the things that weren't real."

The word *real* lodged in her chest like a pickax. Sharp. Painful. Both because Tuck probably had plenty of real nightmares after almost eight years raised in a terrible biker gang, and because hers wasn't real. No matter how much it felt that way. "It wasn't real," she insisted.

"Then lay it on me."

TUCKER HAD NEVER seen Rachel quite so…wound up. He understood this situation was stressful, but they'd been in stressful situations all summer, and she'd kept her cool.

Did she know something? Was the dream some kind of distraction? Something wasn't adding up.

He'd brought up Duke's past because it was a possible answer. If Brady or Cecilia stumbled upon those facts on their own, without him telling them specifically what, then he wouldn't have betrayed his promise to North Star.

They probably wouldn't see it that way, but the more he felt the need to comfort Rachel as she came slowly unraveled, the less he cared about North Star's approval.

They'd put him in an impossible situation. All because he wanted to do what was right. Well, getting some of his own answers was right.

Rachel hesitated as she did the dishes. Finally, she shrugged. "It's silly. I just… I've always had nightmares about the night I was attacked by that mountain lion."

"That makes sense."

"It does. Usually they're few and far between. Especially as I've grown up. But something about the last few weeks has made them an almost nightly occurrence, and they're morphing from memory into fiction. But the fiction feels more real than the memory." She frowned, eyebrows drawing together and a line appearing across her forehead.

She really was beautiful in her own right. Much as she could remind him of Eva, the older she got, the more she was just… Rachel. He knew her sisters sometimes saw her as the baby of the family, the sweet girl with no grit, but that was her power. A softer Grandma Pauline, she held everyone together. Not with a wooden spoon, but with her calm, caring demeanor.

And *why* was he thinking about that? He should be thinking about what she was saying. "Well, what's different? Between the real dream and the fiction dream?"

She took a deep breath and let it out slowly. She looked so troubled that he wanted to reach out and hold her hand. He curled his fingers into his palm instead. Touching seemed…dangerous lately.

"Instead of a mountain lion, there's a man. He has blue eyes, and half his face is scarred. Not like mine. Not lines, but all over. Like a burn, sort of. He's carrying me. We're…" Her eyebrows drew together again, like she was struggling to remember. "It was the hills in one of the pastures. I don't know which one, but that's where the mountain lion attack happened. Outside one of the pastures."

"Do you remember if that's where the mountain lion attack happened or is that just what you've been told?"

She stopped rinsing a plate. "What does it matter?"

"For the purpose of your dream. Is that part real—what you actually remember when you're awake. Or is it what you've been told so that's what your subconscious shows you?"

"I... I guess I'm not sure." She put the plate in the dishwasher then turned to him.

He'd hoped getting it off her chest would ease her mind some, but she seemed just as twisted up. Like the more she talked about it, the more it didn't add up.

"Mom and Dad didn't like to talk about it, but I remember sometimes they'd mention something and it didn't...match with what I thought had happened. But I was only three. Their memory would be more accurate."

"Okay, so in your dream the mountain lion usually takes you somewhere?"

"No. I'm already there. He jumps out of nowhere. I see the glint of something sharp and then I wake up before it swipes at me. But...the dream last night was more involved. I was being carried away. The man's talking. And the thing glinting in the moonlight isn't claws. It's some kind of knife."

She whirled away abruptly. "It's a *nightmare*, Tuck. It's happening when I'm asleep. It's nothing and I'm tired of it making me feel so unsettled."

He watched her agitated pacing, decided to hold his tongue and let her get it out. Maybe she needed a full-on breakdown to be able to find that center of calm that was so inherent to her.

"But I can't get that *fictional* man's voice out of my head. The way he talks. There's an accent. Like New York or Boston. Why is that so clear to me? What can't I shake this stupid dream?"

She raked her fingers through her hair, and Tucker desperately wanted to offer her some soothing words and a hug, but over the past day any physical offers of comfort had gone a little weird. He needed to keep his hands to himself.

"Secrets always hurt the innocent." She dropped her hands, wrapping them around her body instead. "I keep hearing this voice say that. *Secrets always hurt the innocent. Curtis Washington is going to learn that the hard way.*"

Tucker's entire body went cold. He didn't know that name, but having a specific name, a specific voice in her dreams…

Dread skittered up his spine.

"Who's Curtis Washington?"

"I don't know. I've never heard that name before. It's just in my head."

Tucker had to work to keep his breathing even. To maintain control and a neutral expression rather than let all his theories run away from him in a jumble of worry.

She gestured toward him. "Say something."

He had to be careful about his words. About how he approached this horrible possibility. "Mountain lions aren't particularly aggressive."

"No, but I was three. Who knew what I was doing."

"You were three. Why were you so far from your

parents? Duke and Eva weren't exactly hands-off parents."

"They...they didn't like to talk about it. I probably wandered off. Accidentally. Not because they weren't paying attention. You know how toddlers are. It's possible... It just happened."

She didn't seem so sure.

"This voice...this man..."

"It's stupid. All my life the dream has been a mountain lion. The man is a recent change, Tuck. It's a new morph on the old nightmare. If something else happened that night, why would I only dream about it now?"

Because Duke was in trouble, in danger. And this was his WITSEC life. Which meant he had another name.

Could it be the name in Rachel's dream?

Chapter Six

Tucker made himself scarce after Rachel had told him her dream. She could hardly blame him. Why was she coming so unglued over a nightmare? It made no sense, and if it was irritating to her—she could only imagine how annoying it was to the people around her.

She wouldn't bring it up ever again. Not to Tucker, not to anyone. Her dreams were her problem.

She went through the rest of the day without seeing him, though she knew he was there. Then he popped in for dinner, chatting cheerfully though she could tell he was distracted. He helped clean up after dinner, then he disappeared into Dad's room.

Door shut.

She had to admit, she didn't feel babysat, even though that's why he was here. Still, it helped that he wasn't hovering. Which meant she had the space inside herself to recognize Sarah's irritation simmering off her in its usual fraught waves.

Rachel had never been to the ocean, but she always associated Sarah's moods with the slapping waves and whipping winds of a hurricane.

While Sarah's moods were often operatic in nature, Rachel couldn't blame her right now. She was carrying the entire ranch on her shoulders, even with Dev's help.

"How about an ice-cream sundae?"

"I'm not a child, Rach," Sarah replied grumpily. But Rachel heard her plop herself at the kitchen table.

Rachel got out all the fixings for a sundae. Her conversation with Tucker from breakfast repeated in her mind.

Grandma Pauline taught me that you can't solve anyone's problems, but you can make them comfortable while they solve their own.

What about when you have problems?

She supposed her comfort was making other people food, and she supposed she'd gotten that from Grandma Pauline. She'd never fully realized how much she'd adopted the older woman's response to stress or fear, or wondered why before.

It wasn't hard to put together, though. Grandma Pauline was the last word around here. You didn't cross her, but everyone loved and respected her. They spoke about Grandma Pauline with reverence or loving humor.

"What do you think about what Tucker said?" Sarah asked.

Rachel blinked, remembering she was supposed to be making a sundae. Heck, she'd make one for herself, too. "Which part?"

"This being more about Dad than the Sons?"

Rachel scooped the ice cream, poured on chocolate syrup and sprayed on some whipped cream. She set one bowl in front of Sarah, then took her seat at the table with her own bowl.

They were the two youngest Knight girls, often sheltered from danger. Not just because they were the youngest or because Rachel was blind, but because they hadn't come from the dire circumstances their sisters had. Rachel had been born happy and healthy to Duke and Eva, their miracle baby. Sarah had been adopted at birth, so Sarah didn't remember or know anything about her birth parents.

Neither Rachel nor Sarah had ever left home. No tribal police or park ranger jobs for them. Rachel's part-time job as an art teacher was a challenge, and Sarah being a rancher was definitely hard work, but they were home. Still sheltered from so much of the *bad* in the world.

So, if Rachel could be honest with anyone, it was Sarah, because more than everyone else they were especially in this together. "I really don't know what to think of it."

"He's a detective," Sarah said.

"It doesn't make him infallible."

"No, but it gives him some experience in putting clues together. He also knows the Sons, and much as I hate to agree with Dev, he's right. The Sons have left Duke alone for all this time." Her sister released a breath. "So why would they start poking at him now? Especially with Ace in jail. Ace is the one with the vendetta against the Wyatts, not the Sons in general."

"I don't imagine they feel kindly toward the boys who escaped, or the men who put their leader in jail."

"Maybe not. I'm not saying it can't possibly be the Sons. God knows almost all our problems this summer have come from that corner of the scummy world. But… Dad never talks about his parents."

Rachel frowned at that. Surely that wasn't true. But no, she couldn't remember any stories about Dad's parents.

"It never really dawned on me that it was weird since we had Grandma and Grandpa Mills. And I always *assumed* this ranch was passed down, Knight to Knight, because Dad's so proud of it, but…wouldn't there be stories? Heirlooms?"

"What are you trying to say?" Rachel demanded, panic clutching at her.

"We don't actually know anything about Dad, and we never asked. As far as stories I've heard, and just being around Dad, his life started when he met Mom. And that can't be true."

Rachel couldn't eat another bite of ice cream. What was there curdled in her stomach. Sarah was right. She couldn't think of a thing Dad had ever told her about his life before he'd met her mother.

"So, you think he's running from something in his past?"

"Or running *to* something in his past."

Rachel thought of the gun under his pillow. About Dad not wanting her teaching. "He didn't want me to teach this session. He blamed it on the trouble with the Wyatts, but I taught all summer through all that danger."

"So, he was afraid. Something was *making* him afraid. I can't imagine Dad leaving us if he thought we were in danger. Unless…"

"Unless what?" Rachel demanded.

"What if he did something wrong? What if there isn't

danger so much as... I mean, he could have run away from something bad."

"Dad would never. He wouldn't... No, I don't believe that."

"He wouldn't have left us in danger, Rachel. So one of these things he would never do *has* to be what he's done."

What a horrible, horrible thought. Maybe it was true, and maybe she was naive, but she refused to believe it of the father she loved. This man who had been a shining example of goodness and hard-working truth. "What if he thought only he was in danger? Just like Cecilia and Brady when they were trying to save Mak. They thought staying here would bring trouble to our doorstep, so they took off trying to draw the danger with them."

Sarah didn't respond to that. They sat in silence for ticking minutes.

"We have to tell Tucker he was right," her sister finally said. "That we don't know anything about his life before Mom. The answer is somewhere in there, and Tuck can find it. He's a detective. He has to be able to find it."

Rachel wasn't so sure. If her father had kept this secret for over thirty years, maybe no one could find it.

"Rach." Sarah's hand grasped hers across the table. "We have to help in whatever way we can. We're always swept off to the sidelines. But who put out that fire last month? We did. Who always holds down the fort? Us. And we're damn good at it. But Dad's gone. He can't protect us like he's always trying to do. Whether he's running away or hiding or *whatever*, it's just us. We have to step up to the plate."

Rachel knew Sarah was right, and she didn't understand the bone-deep reticence inside of her. It felt like they were stirring up trouble that would change *everything*, and she didn't want everything to change. Maybe she'd wanted a *little* change, but not her whole world.

"I can talk to Tucker myself. If you don't want to—"

"No…you're right. It's just us. We have to work together. It's the only way to make sure Dad's safe."

"He's a tough old bird," Sarah said firmly, and Rachel knew she was comforting herself as much as trying to comfort Rachel.

"He is. And we'll bring him home."

TUCKER CALLED EVERY North Star number he had in his arsenal over the course of the day, and no one would answer. He was too annoyed to be worried that was a bad sign. He needed to know if Curtis Washington was Duke's real name.

It would change things. For North Star, too. He barked out another irritable message into Granger's voice mail, then threw his phone on the bed in disgust.

He'd searched Duke's room, too. No hints to a secret past. There'd been plenty of guns secreted throughout the room, which led Tucker to believe Duke was a man who'd known his past would catch up with him eventually.

No. He'd fostered five girls, raised one daughter of his own. Duke had been certain he'd left that old life behind. Something must have recently happened to lead him to believe he was in danger.

And it tied to the Sons. It shouldn't make Tucker feel guilty. Just because he'd been born into the Sons didn't make him part of them. His life had nothing to do with Duke's secret past.

But the guilt settled inside of him anyway. Luckily, a knock sounded at the door and he could pretend he didn't feel it.

"Come in," he offered.

Sarah poked her head in. "Hey, can we talk to you in the kitchen for a second?"

"Uh, sure."

He followed her out of the room and down the hall. Rachel was already in the kitchen, washing out some bowls. He wondered if she ever stepped away from that constant need to cook and clean for everyone. He wondered if anyone offered a hand, and doubted it very much. He knew from experience how little kitchen work held appeal after a long day ranching.

Maybe that explained it. This was her way of helping her family, the ranch. It was how she felt useful.

When she heard them enter, she turned and smiled. "Did you want some dessert?"

"No, thanks. What did you want to talk about?"

Rachel took a seat at the table, but Sarah paced, wringing her hands together. "We were thinking about what you said. About Duke's life, and the truth is…" She looked at Rachel, so Tucker did, too.

Her expression was carefully blank, calm, which told him all he needed to know. Inside, she was anything but.

"We don't know anything about his life before he married Mom," Sarah continued. "He never talked about parents or siblings. Where he was born or if this ranch was passed on. We just…assumed. And we had so much family, and everything with losing Mom, and

Liza and Nina disappearing and… Well, you know. It just didn't come up. Until now."

Liza's stay with the Knights had been brief, but her returning to the Sons had hurt all of the Knights, and Jamison. Liza and Jamison had since patched things up after saving Liza's half sister, but it had taken a long time.

Nina's disappearing had been the only time in Tucker's life where he thought Duke might actually cut all ties with the Wyatts. He'd personally blamed Tucker's youngest brother Cody, Nina's boyfriend at the time. It had taken a long time for Duke to get past it. When Nina had returned—injured and with her daughter in tow—Tucker had been sure Duke would be furious all over again, but the reconciliation of Cody and Nina had soothed some of his anger.

Some.

There was the guilt again, darker this time. Tucker *knew* Duke had a secret life. He'd put the idea in their heads. Now he was going to lie to them as if he didn't know what it was.

Where does your loyalty lie? North Star or your friends?

Two very different women stared at him. Rachel, dark hair, eyes and skin. Tall and slender. Sarah, petite, curvy, with baby blues and flyaway blond hair.

He wanted to tell them the truth. He couldn't think of a good reason not to, except Granger had told him not to. Duke hadn't argued with it. There might be a very good reason Sarah and Rachel should be kept in the dark.

What might they do if they knew the truth?

"I'm…looking into it. His past, that is. Best I can. To see if it connects to anything that's going on." He did his best not to cringe, not to show how utterly slimy he felt for the flat-out lies. "I haven't gotten very far because I don't have a lot to go on. I don't suppose you have any ideas?"

Sarah shook her head sadly. "That's just it. Who *never* talks about their parents? Or where they're from. Dad's got to be from South Dakota. How else would he end up with all this?"

Tucker really hated that he knew the answer to that question. He forced himself to smile reassuringly. "I'll keep digging. I—"

He was interrupted by his phone going off. It wasn't his regular ringtone. He frowned at the screen. It must be a North Star number. "I have to take this," he said, pushing away from the table.

Both women looked at him with frowns, but he lifted the phone to his ear and stepped out of the kitchen. "Wy—"

Granger was barking out questions before Tucker even got his last name out of his mouth. "Where'd you get that name?"

Tucker felt shattered, and he didn't even fully understand why. He looked back at the kitchen. No one had followed, but he still slid into Duke's room and closed the door. "So, it's true. That's his real name."

Why was Rachel dreaming about Duke's real name? A man instead of a mountain lion?

"I asked where you got the name, Wyatt."

Tucker hesitated. He had the sinking suspicion if he mentioned it was in Rachel's dream, she'd be dragged into this. Maybe North Star would keep her safe. Maybe they even needed to know that she knew something. But...

He couldn't bring himself to utter her name. It felt wrong, and beyond that, he doubted very much Duke wanted his daughter dragged into this even if she did know something.

And his loyalty *was* to his friends over the North Star Group. Even if they were doing something good in trying to take down the Sons, and that *was* important. But so was safeguarding Rachel.

So, he lied instead. "I did some research on dirty cops in Chicago. You did give me enough information to go on to make an educated guess."

"Wyatt. Your job is to keep your families from getting suspicious while we handle the real threat. I don't need any misdirected people wading into this. Keep your side out of it. No more digging. Do you understand me?"

Tucker wanted to say *or what*, but he had a feeling Granger McMillan was dangerous enough to make *or what* hurt. "All right, but it seems to me it'd be more helpful if I knew the whole story."

"I don't need your help. I need you to keep your families out of it. That's it. If you can't do that, I'll bring in someone who can, and you will be dealt with accordingly."

Tucker opened his mouth to tell Granger to jump off a cliff, but the line went dead.

Probably for the best. He let out a long breath.

Rachel knew her father's real name without knowing that's what it was. Which meant, she'd had *some* encounter with *someone* who'd been a part of Duke's previous life.

If that someone was still out there, if that someone was behind this connection to the Sons, it meant Rachel was as much of a target as Duke.

Chapter Seven

Rachel didn't have the dream. She woke up feeling rested for the first time in days. It might have put her in a good mood, but as long as her father was missing, there was no real good mood to have.

Tucker had promised to look into Duke's past, but she had to wonder if it wouldn't end up being...catastrophic somehow. She didn't want to believe her father was involved in something bad, but how could she ignore facts?

He'd left of his own accord, sort of. She still believed he'd been forced to leave, but he hadn't been carted off or held at gunpoint. His little disappearing act and fake vacation *had* to be born out of threats, or something like that.

Rachel got dressed, trying to remind herself there wasn't anything she could do about it. She had to trust Tucker and the Wyatts to look into her father's disappearance. And Cecilia. Cecilia wouldn't sit idly by. None of her sisters would. Sarah would ranch, Nina and Liza were busy with their children but would probably help Cody and Jamison in whatever ways they could.

Felicity should be concentrating on growing her baby, but she would likely discuss with Gage what was going on.

And Rachel would be left to cook and clean. She tried not to be disgusted with herself. After all, if it was good enough for Grandma Pauline, it was good enough for her.

But Grandma Pauline was eighty. Rachel also had no doubt she'd pick up that big rifle she kept hidden in the pantry and take care of whatever intruders might deign to invade her ranch.

What could Rachel do? Scream?

No. That really wasn't good enough. She needed to learn some basics about getting away or fighting back.

She'd insist Tucker teach her. If he had to be underfoot, the least he could do was be useful. She headed downstairs and to her normal routine of making breakfast, but she stopped short at the entrance to the kitchen.

Tucker was in her kitchen. She couldn't tell what he was doing, but she could make out his outline. She could hear the sounds of…cooking.

"What are you doing?" she demanded, maybe a little too accusatorily to be fair.

"Thought I could take breakfast duty since I'm staying here," he replied, continuing to move around *her* kitchen as if she were just some sort of…bystander.

"But… I always make breakfast."

"Don't tell me you've completely morphed into Grandma Pauline and can't stand someone else carrying some weight?"

"That isn't…" She had to trail off because it was silly to be upset someone had beaten her to breakfast. She'd been complaining for years that Duke and Sarah never even tried to figure out their way around the kitchen.

She should be grateful someone was lending a hand, even if it was Tucker. But mostly she felt incredibly superfluous and useless. "I guess I'll—"

"Have a seat. It's almost ready. I don't want you picking up after me. I can do my own laundry, keep Duke's room tidy and all that. I'm not your houseguest, so you don't need to treat me like one. I'm here to help. That's all."

"Being here to help does technically make you a guest," Rachel muttered irritably.

"Well, this guest can take care of himself." As if to prove it, he slid a plate in front of her. "All I did was bake some of Grandma's cinnamon rolls you had in the freezer and cut up a melon. Hardly putting myself out."

"But what if your coffee sucks?" she asked, trying to make light of how small that made her feel. When did she get so pathetic that she needed to make a meal to feel worthy of her spot here?

He slid the mug in front of her. "It doesn't. And, I already doctored it. You're welcome."

The coffee didn't suck. She might have made it a little stronger for Sarah, but he had indeed put in cream and sugar just how she liked it. She wanted to make a joke about keeping him around, but it sat uncomfortably on her chest so she couldn't form the words.

It was a little too easy to picture. She knew it would be…difficult to find a significant other. Not so much because of her scarring and lack of sight, but because she just didn't get around much and lived in a rural area.

But she'd always had that little dream of a husband and kids in this kitchen.

To even picture Tucker filling that role was *embarrassing*. So she shoved a bite of cinnamon roll in her mouth instead. Even after being frozen, Grandma Pauline's cinnamon rolls were like a dream.

"You know, Sarah and Duke would mess up even reheating frozen rolls," she offered, trying to think of anything else than what was currently occupying her brain.

He took the seat next to her, presumably with his own plate of food and mug of coffee. "If that's what you want to tell yourself, Rach, but I don't think you give them much space to figure out how."

She frowned at that.

"I'm sorry," he said. "I wasn't trying to be a jerk. Maybe you're right and they can't."

But she could tell he didn't think so, and worse she knew he was right. She complained about how little they did, while never ever giving them even an inch to do it for themselves.

She ate her feelings via one too many cinnamon rolls, then started on the fruit. She could wallow in…well, everything, or she could do something. She could act. She could *change*.

"Tuck, I want you to teach me how to fight."

"Huh?"

"I can't shoot. But I could fight." She pushed the plate away, ignoring the last few bites of melon. "I want to be able to defend myself. Maybe nothing bad happens here, but I want to be ready if it does."

"Rach, you don't have to worry about that. We're all—"

"Tucker." She reached across the table, found his arm. She needed that connection to make sure he understood this was more than just…a suggestion. She needed it. Needed to feel like she could contribute or at least not make a situation worse. "I could fight. I want to be able to fight." She gave his arm a squeeze.

He hesitated, but he didn't immediately shoot her down again. "I'm sure Cecilia—"

"Isn't here. You are. Didn't you teach some self-defense class at the Y for a while?"

She could hear him shift in his chair, a sense of embarrassment almost. "Well, yeah, but—"

"But what? What's different about that and this?"

After a long beat of silence, he finally spoke. "I guess there really isn't one."

"Exactly. So, you'll do it." She didn't phrase it as a question, because she wasn't taking no for an answer.

"I guess I could teach you and Sarah a few things." He didn't sound enthused about it, but she'd take agreement with or without excitement.

Rachel heard Sarah stepping into the kitchen, and then her small bright form entered Rachel's blurry vision.

"What things are you teaching me?"

"Self-defense. Rachel wants to learn how to fight."

Rachel noted that, while he didn't sound sure of teaching her anything, he didn't seem dismissive or disapproving. Maybe he didn't like teaching was all.

Well, he'd have to suck it up.

"Good idea," Sarah said around a mouthful of food. "But I can shoot a gun. And kick your butt, if I had to."

"Kick *my* butt?" Tucker replied incredulously. "You're five foot nothing. If that."

"I also wrestle stubborner cows than you, Wyatt. I could take you down right here, right now."

"All right." There was the scrape of the chair against the floor. "You're on."

"Oh, you don't want to mess with me."

Rachel could see the outlines of them circling each other. "You aren't really going to…"

There was the sound of a grunt, a thud and then laughter. It was a nice sound. Comforting. Like having her family home. Except Dad wasn't here, and they were pretending to fight.

"All right. Sarah gets a pass," Tucker conceded. "Though I maintain you did not kick my butt."

"Whatever you gotta tell yourself, Tuck," Sarah replied cheerfully. "Dev's truck is already out there." The cheer died out of her voice. "I could wring his neck. I told him to wait for me. Leave me a cinnamon roll to heat up," she called, already halfway out the door.

The door slammed.

"Did you let her win?" Rachel asked.

"It wasn't about winning. I just wanted to see what she's got. Good instincts and a nice jab. She's scrappy and mean, which is good in a real fight. Besides, she's right. She can shoot."

"Are you saying I'm not scrappy and mean?"

Tucker laughed. "I wasn't saying that, but we both know you're not. Which is why I'll teach you a few self-defense moves, if it'll make you feel better."

"It will. When do we start?"

AUTUMN IN SOUTH DAKOTA meant anything could happen. A nice sunny day. A sudden blizzard. Today was a pleasant morning, thank God. The yard in front of the Knight house would be as good a place as any to teach Rachel a few moves.

Rachel had changed from jeans and a T-shirt to something…he couldn't think too much about. It was all stretchy and formfitting, so he kept his gaze firmly on the world around him and not on her.

"Shouldn't we have padding or something? I don't want to hurt you."

The fact she wasn't joking was somehow endearing. Before he'd moved to detective, he'd been on the road. Fought off the occasional person too high on drugs to feel pain, quite a few men larger and meaner than him, and more than one criminal with a weapon.

"We're just doing a few lessons. Learn a few rules and moves. You're not going to be beating me up quite yet."

"But shouldn't I be able to?"

"Sure. But we'll have to work up to it. You can't learn everything there is to know about self-defense in a day."

She wrinkled her nose. "Is it *that* complicated?"

"It's not about being complicated. It's just…something you practice, so it becomes second nature. So you're ready to do it. But listen, Rach. You're not going to need to, because I'm here and—"

She shook her head. "I don't want to feel like the weak link. Like the person everyone has to protect. Maybe it isn't much, but I just want to be able to land a punch or get away from someone if I need to. That's all."

She more than deserved that. He just wished he didn't have to be the one to teach her. It would involve touching and guiding, and she was… Hell, exercise leggings and a stretchy top were not *fair*. He was *human*.

Human and better than his baser—and completely unacceptable—urges. Because he'd shaped himself into a good, honorable man. One who did not take advantage of a young woman who meant a lot to his family.

And to you.

Because what he could forget when he didn't spend too much time one-on-one with Rachel was that they had a lot in common. What she'd said inside about wanting to feel useful echoed inside of him. Her surprise and irritation that he'd help out around the house made him want to do it all the more.

Take care of her and—

He cleared his throat, forced himself to focus. To treat this like any other lesson. "Rule number one. Always go for the crotch."

She made an odd sound. Like a strangled laugh. "I'm not going for your crotch, Tucker."

Jesus. He could *not* think about that. "Thanks for that. I just meant, in real life, that's your target. Crotch. Eyes. The most vulnerable points." He hated the thought of her needing to do *any* of that.

"Okay."

"You have to be mean."

She fisted her hands on her hips. "I know how to be mean."

"*Really* mean. Channel your inner Sarah."

"I'm going to channel my inner Grandma Pauline and whack you with a rolling pin."

Tucker laughed. "All right, killer. Show me how you'd punch."

He walked her through the proper form for a punch. Tried to talk her through aiming even though her sight was compromised. He instructed about grabbing anything she could make into a weapon. How to kick with the most effect.

Her form wasn't bad, and it got better the more she practiced. He offered to quit or take a break at least five times, but she kept wanting to go on. Even as they both ended up breathing heavily.

"The problem is I'm not going to be in a boxing ring. If *I'm* going to be in a fight, it's probably going to be because someone's trying to hurt me or someone I love. But they'd underestimate me. Either by ignoring me or just grabbing me."

"Maybe, but you have to learn the basics."

"But I can practice punching and kicking form on my own. We need to practice like…how to get away if someone grabs me. I know you don't want to hurt me, and I don't want to hurt you, but it has to feel more like an actual fight."

"You don't have to worry about hurting me."

"Because I'm that weak?" she demanded.

"No, because I'm a professional at dodging a punch, Rach. I've been a cop for almost nine years. I've been learning to not get hit my whole life." He hadn't really meant to say that last part, or wouldn't have if he'd known she'd get that…sympathetic look on her face.

Nothing to be sympathetic about. He'd survived eight years of Ace Wyatt and the Sons of the Badlands. All his brothers, except Cody, had survived more time than him. Jamison hadn't gotten out until eighteen, after working hard to get Cody out before his seventh birthday. Tucker had followed not much later when he'd been eight. Gage and Brady had been eleven, and Dev twelve.

Tucker had gotten off easy, like he usually did.

She opened her mouth to say something—likely something he didn't want to hear, so he spoke first. "Come on then. If I'm coming at you, land a punch."

She got in the stance he'd taught her, made a good fist. As he moved forward, she swung out. He easily pivoted so she didn't land it.

"That's good."

"I didn't hit you!"

Tucker laughed. "Don't sound so disappointed." He took her still-clenched hand by the wrist and held it up. "This is your dominant hand, so you want it to do the big work." He took her other hand and brought it up. "But this one needs to do the work, too. Make a fist."

He walked her through using both hands to punch. Using her arms to block. He let her land a few punches. She wasn't going to ward off any attackers with her fists—she'd have better luck kicking a vulnerable area or grabbing something to use as a weapon. Still, if it made her feel as though she was more prepared, that was what mattered.

It wasn't so bad all in all. It felt good to teach her something useful. A little *uncomfortable* teaching her to break holds by holding on to her against her will— but an important skill nonetheless.

Until he had the bright idea to teach her how to get away from someone who grabbed her from behind. Which necessitated…grabbing *her* from behind.

They went through the drill a few times. Slow, with pointers, and he tried very hard not to think about anything related to his body. He told her how to position her hands, how to maneuver her body. All while pretending his was made of…ice. Or plastic. Whatever kind of material that was not moved by a woman's body.

She was…lithe. Graceful.

Hot.

That was a really, really unacceptable thought when it came to Duke's daughter. Duke's daughter who's safety he was being entrusted with.

The strangest part was he'd scuffled with Sarah just this morning, and it hadn't felt any different than wrestling with his brothers. Familial. Funny.

But this was *none* of those things and he hadn't the slightest idea why.

"Do that again."

"I don't think—"

"Do it again," she insisted. "Come at me from behind."

He allowed himself to curse to his heart's content silently in his head. Rachel turned her back to him.

He just needed to enact a quick, meaningless grab around the waist.

The problem was he didn't like putting himself in the mind-set of an attacker. And he didn't like staying in his own mind-set, which was way too aware of how the exercise clothes she wore molded to every slender curve.

But who else could he be?

He gritted his teeth and tried to think about times tables as he wrapped his arm around her waist. She lifted her right hand to keep it from being held down by his grab, but he used his free hand to ensnare her arm.

She mimicked a kick to the insole and twisted in his

grasp. He gave a little, as if stepping away from her kick. It gave her room, but kept his arm slightly around her, palm pressed to her stomach.

He wanted to tell her to pull her arm down in the way he'd shown her earlier, but he was afraid his voice wouldn't come out even. Or that he could manage to unclamp his jaw.

But she paused there, in this awkward position. His hand was on her abdomen, the fingers of his other hand curled around her wrist. He could feel the rise and fall of her breathing because her back was against him, her butt nestled way too close to a part of him he could *not* think about right now.

She tilted her head, and though he knew she couldn't see out of one eye and only general shapes out of the other, it felt as though she were studying him.

And then there was her mouth. Full and tempting. She wasn't trying to get out of his grasp, and she definitely wasn't putting any distance between their bodies.

She smelled like a meadow, and everything they were doing faded away. There were two aches inside of him—one he fully understood, and one that didn't make any sense. They both grew, expanded until there was only his heartbeat and the exhale of her breath across his cheek.

The sound of people arguing interrupted the buzzing in his head. He dropped her abruptly, moving away clumsily.

"Tucker..."

He didn't like the soft way she spoke, or the way her breath shuddered in and out, or that look in her eye, which he could not in any circumstances think about or consider.

"Hey, there's Sarah and Dev. We've been at this a while, huh? How about a break? I'm starved, you know?"

Sweet hell he was *babbling*. He cleared his throat. He was a grown man. A grown man with an inappropriate attraction, but that just meant he knew what to do with it. Scurrying away and babbling were not it. Getting himself together and *handling* it was what he needed to do. Would do. Absolutely. *Obviously.*

The dogs raced over first, so Tucker focused on them, squatting to scratch them both behind their ears. He spoke to them in soothing tones and tried his damnedest to get that *ache* coursing around inside of him to dissipate.

"How goes the self-defense?" Sarah asked.

"Great," Tucker said, far too loudly. "Going to take a break now."

"Yeah, us, too."

When Tucker looked up, Dev was frowning at him, but Tucker reminded himself that his brother's resting face was frowning disapproval. That was all.

Besides, he had enough frowning disapproval for himself. He didn't need anyone else's.

Chapter Eight

Rachel went through the rest of the day with an odd…
buzz along her skin. Like the precursor to getting poison ivy. It was uncomfortable. Not quite so painful as
a rash, but uncomfortable. Definitely.

She knew it was all Tucker's fault. Though she
couldn't figure out why. Had he read her mind? He
had been horrified that she'd kind of enjoyed him manhandling her. Or, had he enjoyed manhandling her and
was horrified?

Either way, there was some horror. And then locking
it all away and acting his usual genial self.

Except that he avoided her at all costs.

Which was probably for the best. Or was it? She got
ready for bed, edgy and worked up. There was just too
much going on. Her father was missing. She was having recurring nightmares. She was apparently attracted
to a man she'd always looked at as family. Sort of. And
worse than being attracted to *him* was the wondering if
he was attracted to her right back. Or oblivious.

She groaned and flopped onto her bed. She needed
to talk to someone. With most problems, she confided

in Sarah or Cecilia. Sarah would be no help with this one, and Cecilia… She'd be too blunt. Too…forthright.

Rachel needed someone with a softer touch. So she called Felicity.

"Hey, Rach. Everything okay?"

"Yeah. Nothing new to report on our end."

Felicity sighed. "I really hate all this waiting. Gage keeps fluttering around me, trying to distract me from my stress, but all he is doing is stressing me out even more."

Rachel smiled. That was sweet. And also the perfect segue. "How did you end up involved with Gage?"

"What kind of question is that?"

"Not a mean one. I just… I wondered." Rachel rolled her eyes at herself. She sounded like an idiot. A transparent one. But at least of all her sisters, Felicity would never call her on it.

"Is this about Tucker?"

Rachel forced out a laugh. She was afraid it sounded more like a deranged array of squeaks. "What? No."

"You're a terrible liar. And even if you weren't, this is completely transparent."

Rachel pouted in spite of herself. "Of course it is. But you weren't supposed to call me out on it!"

Felicity laughed. "Sorry. Normally I wouldn't, but you're strung tight. I know Dad's whole disappearing act is scary, but you're usually calm in the midst of a crisis."

"I'm calm." Aside from the dreams. Aside from Tucker *touching* her. "Tucker believes Dad left of his own accord. Whatever prompted it, he doesn't think he's in any immediate danger and I have to believe that."

"I do, too. And so does Gage for that matter." Felicity paused. "So…why are you wound up?"

Rachel could blame it on the dreams. Some of it *was* the dreams, and the possibility of Dad being…far more complicated than she wanted him to be. But she didn't want to lay either of those things at Felicity's feet, where she'd worry needlessly.

"I think there was a moment. With Tucker. When he was teaching me some self-defense moves."

"Define *moment*."

"I don't know. Like…like…an awareness of each other. As a man and a woman. Not…family friends. As people who…"

"Might want to have sex?"

Rachel squeaked, her face getting hot, even though she was alone in her room and no one but her sister had heard that word. "Oh my *God*, Felicity."

"Sorry. It's just that's what moments usually lead to with the Wyatt boys."

"Why? I don't get it. I don't get why we're falling like dominoes for that lot of…"

"Really good guys who also happen to be hot and smart and caring? Who want to protect you, not because they think you're weak or need protecting, but because it's just who they are. On a cellular level."

Rachel expelled a breath. "I don't… I'm twenty-two."

"Is that commentary on the age difference or on being too young to have a serious relationship?"

"Neither. Both. I don't know! Why are we talking about relationships? It was like a moment of…lust. Fleeting lust. Very fleeting."

"Let me tell you this, Rach, lust over a Wyatt is never

fleeting. I wasn't exactly planning on doing this whole baby thing yet. But then Gage came along and…boom, lust. And love."

Love. That was *terrifying*. "Just because you four did it, doesn't mean I will."

"Of course it doesn't. You're your own person, and so is Tucker. I'm just trying to say it's normal to be attracted, and to be confused by it since you haven't always had those feelings. Danger and worry has a way of…stripping away our normal walls. When it does that, we can see someone as they actually are instead of how we've always perceived them to be."

"I don't have any walls."

Felicity was quiet for a few seconds. "Okay." She did *not* sound like she agreed. "But Tucker does. Even knowing how awful that childhood before Pauline must have been, I don't think I fully understood it until I saw Gage in that cave with Ace. Knowing Ace would have killed him and felt…justified. It isn't just viciousness and abuse they were raised with, it was…well, insanity."

Felicity paused, and Rachel shuddered. She hated to think about what Gage would have gone through. As a child and as a man. Tucker seemed so…not as afflicted as the others. She knew the older ones had spent longer being at the mercy of Ace Wyatt, but Tucker's eight years were nothing to ignore.

"The point is, being scared churns things up," Felicity continued. "That's okay. It doesn't mean you're weird. It doesn't mean you're not worried about Dad. It just means you're human. And Tucker is hot."

That shocked a laugh out of her. "Aren't you supposed to only have eyes for Gage?"

"Heart and soul for Gage. Eyes for anyone else. Things will be clearer when this is over, and Tucker and the rest of them are working hard to figure out what's going on so Dad can come home."

Rachel wanted to believe her. More than belief, though, she heard something in her sister's voice she wasn't sure she fully ever had before. Felicity had grown up nervous and shy, and she'd slowly come into her own the past few years. But Gage and this pregnancy had really given her an even bigger strength that she'd been afraid to believe in growing up. "You sound happy, Felicity."

"I am. And I'm mad at Dad that he's adding worry to my happy, but that's life. Happy and worry and even attraction can all pile up on each other in the same moment. I'm learning to accept that. I think the the thing is…we were raised right. We've got good instincts. Don't question your instincts."

Rachel let that settle through her. Wasn't that what she'd been doing? Or maybe she'd been questioning her worth or usefulness but it all kind of added up to the same thing. "Thanks, Felicity. This helped."

"I'm glad. Try to get some rest, Rach."

"You and baby, too."

They said their goodbyes and Rachel climbed into bed. She didn't feel any more clear on the whole Tucker thing, but she felt…more settled.

Don't question your instincts.

She'd be thinking about that a lot over the next few days.

She fell asleep, hopeful for another restful, uninterrupted night. But in the shadows of night came the noise. The rustle. The unearthly glow of cat eyes.

Were they cat eyes? They weren't human but…

Secrets always hurt the innocent. Curtis Washington is going to learn that the hard way.

He had her. He was holding her too tight and she couldn't wiggle away. The eyes weren't his, but they followed. Animal.

The human who had her was someone entirely different. She could hear the hum and scuttle of night life. Could see the moon shining bright from above. But she couldn't see the shadow who carried her too quickly and too easily away from everything she loved.

She squirmed and tried to scream, but she was squeezed too tight—both by the man's grip and her own fear.

When he stopped, it was worse. He wasn't squeezing so tight, but she couldn't breathe at all as he lifted the thing he always lifted, glinting silver in the moonlight. Some kind of…pronged knife. Slashing down at her face.

Run. Wake up.

She always did. Until now.

This time she felt the searing pain of the knife. But a growl, and a thud kept the knife from scoring too deep. It was painful. So painful she thought she might die. She was bleeding and her eyes felt like they were on fire, but the man didn't have her anymore.

TUCKER TOOK THE stairs two at a time, the safety already off on his gun. Rachel's blood-curdling scream had woken him from a fitful sleep, and he'd immediately jumped out of bed and run upstairs.

"Tucker." Sarah stood in the hall in her pajamas, holding a baseball bat.

"Go back to your room," Tucker hissed at her. The screaming had stopped. He inched toward Rachel's room, keeping his footsteps light. He controlled his breathing, pushed all the fear away and focused on the task at hand.

Save her. Now.

He could bust the door open, which was his first instinct. But he didn't know who was behind it, and if he could go for stealthy, he had to. Carefully, he reached out and placed his hand on the door. He willed the slight tremor away with sheer force.

He couldn't afford to be emotional right now. He had a mission. Slowly, carefully, he turned the knob and eased the door open inch by inch.

The room was bathed in light. Rachel sat in the middle of her bed, head in her hands, but Tucker didn't see anyone else.

He immediately swept the room. "Where is he?"

"Tucker." She wrapped the blanket around herself. "What are you doing?"

"I... You screamed." He slowly lowered the gun, belatedly realizing she wasn't in trouble at all. All the fear drained out of him until his knees nearly buckled. "Hell, Rach. That scream could have woken the dead."

"I'm sorry. I'm..." She inhaled shakily and he finally realized she'd been crying. Tears tracked down her cheeks even as she spoke calmly. "I had a bad dream, that's all. I didn't mean to scare you. I…" She shook her head. "Did Sarah wake up?"

"Yeah, but—"

She picked her phone up off the nightstand. "Text Sarah. I'm okay. Bad dream." She dropped her phone, and Sarah burst into the room a few seconds later.

"Oh my God. Rach. How awful. What do you need?"

"Noth—" She seemed to think better of it. "I think I could use a drink."

"I'll be right back." Sarah scurried away.

Tucker studied Rachel. She was shaking, and though she made no noise, fresh tears leaked out of her eyes.

"I'm sorry to have woken you up. I—"

"Stop apologizing," he said, and he knew his voice was too harsh when she winced. But he felt…ripped open. That scream and all the most terrible scenarios that had gone through his mind even as he'd shoved them away to do what needed to be done had taken years off his life.

He let out his own shaky breath. She was okay. Well, not okay. She was crying. Upset. He moved for her bed. "Are they all like this?"

She shook her head, pulling the blanket up to her chin. "No. Usually I wake up before…" She took a steadying breath and he just couldn't take the fear still in her eyes, in her voice. He sat on the very edge of the bed, putting his hand on her shoulder.

She took a deep gulping breath. "It's just I usually wake up before he hurts me. But tonight the knives slashed across my face."

He rubbed his hand up and down her arm. She

seemed to need to talk about it, and he had some sus-picions now about these dreams. "Knives?"

"A man. He had me. He had this knife or knives with multiple points. He…" She couldn't seem to swallow down a hiccupped sob. She shuddered, so he pulled her closer until she leaned into him.

She let out a little sigh, and some of the shaking sub-sided. "I could feel it. The pain. The blood. I don't know if it was a memory or made up, but it felt real. And I was small. I had my adult brain, but he could cart me around easily. It was a man, but there was also an ani-mal. I don't think it was a mountain lion. It was more… doglike. And he jumped on the man when he hurt me. That animal saved me, I think."

She shook her head. "It doesn't make sense. I don't want it to make sense." She buried her head in his shoul-der. "I want the dreams to go away and I want Dad to be home."

"Of course you do, sweetheart." He rubbed his hand up and down her back. "So do I." He tried to keep the grimness out of his voice. But this situation was grim. The more she explained the dream, the more he had to wonder if Rachel knew more than she understood.

And he had to wonder if *Duke* knew that. If that was half of why he'd agreed to disappear with North Star on such short notice. To keep Rachel out of it.

"I heard that name again. Curtis Washington. Do you think that's a real person?" She pulled back from him, her gaze meeting his. Her complexion was a little gray, and the faded pink of her scars seemed more pro-nounced against the brown of her skin. She looked at him earnestly, even though he knew she couldn't see him clearly. "Why am I dreaming this name? I've never thought my dreams were real, but…"

"It keeps repeating. And getting worse."

She nodded. Her face was close to his. Their noses would touch if he leaned just an inch forward. His arm was still around her and she was leaning into him.

In her bed.

Tucker let his arm slip away from her, though he stayed seated at the edge of her bed. He inched even closer to that edge so that, though he was close, their bodies were not in danger of touching, and berated himself for even the second of inappropriate thought that gripped him.

She was shaking, crying and scared.

And very close to a truth he wasn't supposed to let her know about.

"I think we need to look into that name. Don't you? Maybe it has something to do with Dad. Maybe—"

Sarah bustled into the room carrying a tray full of glasses. "I didn't know what kind of drink so I just kind of brought…"

"Everything." Rachel smiled indulgently. "Thank you, I think I'll take the water."

Tucker slid off her bed. He needed to let Sarah take care of this. Comfort her. He needed to escape before she asked him to do what he wasn't supposed to do.

He eyed Sarah's tray, took the shot glass off it and downed the whiskey. He put the glass back, then tried to disappear.

"Tuck, I want to look into the name. I think we have to."

How could he say no to her? "I'll see what I can do."

Chapter Nine

Rachel knew that Tucker would look into the name Curtis Washington, and he was a detective so he'd be able to do far more than her. Still, that didn't mean she couldn't aid him in his search.

If the name connected to everything that was going on, that meant it connected to Dad. And if the dream connected to everything that was going on...

She didn't know what it would mean.

It scared her. That it might be terrible. That it might be buried deep in her subconscious...

"There's a lot of junk up here, Rach. I don't know how we're going to go through it all," Sarah said.

Rachel could tell Sarah was antsy to get outside, to do her work on the ranch, even if it was a rainy, dreary day. But when Rachel had mentioned going up to the attic, Sarah had insisted on helping.

"I know it's overwhelming, but I can't sit around waiting for Tuck to figure it out. I know it was a dream. This is probably insane, but—"

"Look, that's some dream. Maybe normally I'd brush it off, but everything is off right now. Dev is being *nice* to me." The horror in her tone had Rachel smiling.

"That's sweet of him."

"It's creepy as hell." Sarah moved through the attic, and Rachel figured she was doing what she had asked—reading labels of boxes and pulling out anything that seemed relevant. "Speaking of creepy, Tuck was totally checking you out last night."

Rachel nearly stumbled over what she assumed was a box. *"What?"*

"One hundred percent checking out your rack, sis."

Rachel sputtered, and she could feel heat creeping up her face. "Geez, Sarah…"

"I can tell him to knock it off if you want."

"What? No. Oh my God, don't do that!"

"Why not?"

Rachel tried to work through this insane turn in the conversation. "Because that's embarrassing and weird."

"So, not because you'd *like* Tucker to be checking you out. Tucker Wyatt."

"I know who Tucker is," Rachel replied, all too shrilly.

"That doesn't answer my question."

"Did you actually have one?"

"Yeah. Are you creeped out Tuck was looking at your boobs, or do you like it?"

Rachel opened her mouth but no sound came out. She wasn't creeped out, but she wasn't sure if she liked it, either. She was just… "I don't know."

"I mean, in fairness it wasn't like super creeper ogling. It was like…noticing. Your boobs."

"I need this conversation to be over," Rachel muttered. Her face was hot, her heart was hammering and they had way more important concerns at hand. "Whatever we're looking for, it's not going to be in a box. If it's such a secret that Dad had to disappear, it's going to be somewhere…like in the wall. Or out in the stables or something. It'd be hidden."

"But who would go through all this stuff? Wouldn't hiding it in plain sight work just as well?" Sarah asked, thankfully moving away from the subject of Tucker.

"Not if you expected someone to go looking for your secret stuff. If Dad *had* secret stuff—the kind you run away from so your children aren't in the middle of it—it'd be hidden somewhere. Which means there's not going to be a box labeled *secret stuff*. It's going to be harder than that. Sneakier than that."

Sarah blew out a loud breath. "I really hate this."

"Yeah, me, too."

They worked in silence for a while. Sarah went through reading labels on boxes and checking the contents of those unlabeled. Rachel went around the attic perimeter feeling the walls, trying to determine if there was any place that could be hiding something.

She was about to give up when her hands landed on something metal in the corner by the door. It was some kind of box, but instead of cardboard or plastic, it was a heavy metal.

"What's this?"

"Huh." Sarah stepped closer. "It's a locked cashbox type deal, but there's a little piece of masking tape on it that says *buttons*."

"Who would lock up buttons?"

"Mom loved collecting buttons, but I don't think there'd be any reason to lock them up. Here, give it to me."

"If it's locked, how will you—" Rachel began.

There was a squeaking sound and then a crash—like tiny buttons falling across the floor.

"Oops," Sarah said. "Lock was a little easier to break than I thought. But it is just…buttons. Everywhere now. Here, take the box so I can pick up the ones that fell."

Rachel took the box back. She let her fingers trail over the buttons. Mom had loved to collect them. Old grief welled inside of her, though it had been enough years now that she knew how to push it away.

Still, touching something of her mother's had her eyes and nose stinging with unshed tears. She blinked them back as she dug her fingers into the buttons— and touched something with a sharp edge. She cradled the box in her elbow and pulled the item out of the buttons. Using both hands, she felt around the edge of it. Much bigger than a button. Maybe an oddly shaped belt buckle?

"Sarah?"

"Wh— Oh my God."

"What? What is it?"

"It's a police badge." It was snatched out of Rachel's hand. "It says *Officer. Chicago Police.*"

"Chicago? Why would there be a Chicago police badge in a box full of buttons?"

"A *locked* box full of buttons," Sarah pointed out. "If we're looking for secrets, I think we might have found one."

"Are you guys up in the attic?" Tuck's voice called from below.

Rachel felt Sarah press the badge back into her palm.

"Your call. You want to hide it, I will. You want to tell him, I'll be right behind you."

"Why are you leaving it up to me? He's your father, too."

"They're your dreams, Rach. And Tucker seems to be your thing. Let's face it, you're the calm, rational one between the two of us. Whatever you want to do is what we should do."

Tucker's form appeared in the doorway. "Hey. Dev's looking for you, Sarah. What are you two doing up here?"

Sarah didn't answer him. Because she'd put it all on Rachel.

"We wanted to poke around and see if we could find something of Dad's. Get some idea of what he might be keeping a secret." She held the badge behind her back, the box of buttons in the crook of her arm. What else might be in there?

And did she want Tuck to know about it?

"I'll go find Dev. See what he wants."

Rachel heard Sarah's retreat as she let her fingers trace the outline of the badge. Chicago Police? Could she picture her father as a police officer?

Or had he had some kind of run in with a police officer? Was this darker? More awful? Should she *want* to hide it from everyone so they never knew?

But how could she bring her father home without help? Without *Tucker's* help. Why wouldn't she trust Tucker Wyatt with everything she found? He was…a Wyatt. He was a good person. He didn't lie. He was a detective who searched for the truth, who's father's sins weighed on him even when they shouldn't.

He was a good man.

Tucker was totally checking you out last night.

"You okay?"

She nodded and cleared her throat. "We found a box of my mom's buttons."

His hand was on her shoulder, giving her a friendly squeeze. "That's a nice thing to have. Even if it makes you sad."

She nodded, because she agreed. Because she knew he didn't have anything from his mother, whatever complicated feelings he might have had about her. And he wouldn't want anything from his father. She had two good, supportive, loving parents who hadn't just loved *her* but had fostered or adopted five other girls over the years and made them all a family.

"I miss her most around this time of year," Tuck said, his voice gentle. "She was always rounding us up, trying to help Grandma Pauline get us ready for school rather than show up the first day looking like feral dogs."

"She used to say you boys needed love, education and a hardheaded woman to keep you on the straight and narrow."

He laughed. "Grandma Pauline did all three. So did your mom."

It was strange to talk to Tucker about her mom. She knew Eva Knight had considered the Wyatt boys part of her own brood. She'd helped Grandma Pauline corral them as much as she could. Mom had loved them. She'd cared about people who needed help, and love, and she'd given hope to those in the darkest places.

Rachel didn't have any dark places. Not really. Even her dreams were just dreams—even if they were pointing to *something*. She wasn't like Liza and Jamison who had survived the Sons, or Felicity who'd survived an abusive father both as a child and then as a woman. She wasn't any of the Wyatt boys with the horror they'd grown up with and escaped.

She'd had a good, mostly easy life. So, Mom had always tasked her with helping, providing for, being the hope.

If there was any hope in this situation with Dad, it was that they could get him home. Secrets wouldn't do that. Being suspicious of Tucker wouldn't do that.

Rachel took a deep breath, feeling around the edge of the badge one more time. Then she held it forward. "I found this in the box of buttons."

TUCKER STARED AT the badge held out in Rachel's hand. Chicago PD. He didn't know how to react. He knew, of course, that it was Duke's, though Rachel probably didn't. Wouldn't.

He wanted to tell her. Not just about her father's past but about everything. North Star and where Duke was.

An equal part of him wanted to laugh it off, stop her from probing into this, from entwining herself in trouble. He wanted to wrap her up in a safe bubble so she didn't have to worry about all this.

But he remembered all too well that terrifying scream that had woken him in the middle of the night. Some of this mystery and danger was inside her subconscious somewhere. No matter what he did—he couldn't protect her from that.

"It's a police badge," he said, his voice a shade too rough.

"Yes. Sarah told me it says *Chicago Police*." She pressed it into his palm. "It has to mean something."

Boy, did it. "Did you check the rest of the box?"

"I haven't had the chance. We'd just found this when you came up."

He frowned over that. "Why didn't Sarah say anything?"

"She said she'd give me the choice whether to tell you or not."

"Why wouldn't you tell me?"

Rachel shrugged. "I did tell you, though."

He wasn't sure that was much of a comfort, but he supposed it had nothing to do with the issue at hand. He set the badge aside, then took the box of buttons from her. He found an empty mason jar to dump the buttons into. As he poured them into it, he let the buttons fall over his fingers. There was nothing else big, but as he came to the end of the buttons, a key fell into his fingers.

He held it up, looking at it on both sides. "Nothing else in there except a key."

"A key to what?"

"I don't have a clue. It's just a key."

"It can't *just* be a key."

"Well, no. It was in with the buttons and the badge so it has to be something, but there aren't any hints as to what." Tucker examined the box. It was a rusted out cashbox, nothing special about it. No space for any kind of false bottom.

"A badge and a key. A missing father. Dreams that

feel way too close to real." She blew out a breath. "Anything else life wants to throw at me?"

"Please don't go taunting the universe like that."

Her mouth curved. "You don't honestly believe in curses and jinxes?"

"*Believe* might be a strong word. Let's say I have a healthy respect for the possibility."

Rachel shook her head, though she was still smiling. A beam of sunlight shone in front of her, making dust motes dance around her face. He'd always *known* she was pretty, but something about doing all this made him *feel* it.

Maybe he wholeheartedly believed in curses and jinxes, because his sudden attraction for Rachel felt like both.

She frowned. "Did you hear that?"

He hadn't heard much of anything except his own stupidity. "What?"

"I'm not sure. Like an engine, but…" She trailed off and he strained to hear what she heard. Everything was silent, but he felt the need to hold himself still, and continue to strain to hear long after the moment had passed.

Creak.

Rachel's frown deepened, and she opened her mouth, presumably to say something, but Tucker laid his hand gently over her mouth.

She'd heard an engine. He'd heard the creak of a floorboard under the weight of someone. If it was any Wyatt or Knight, they would have announced themselves—or they'd know which boards to avoid.

Tucker scanned the attic. Maneuvering Rachel to hide her would make noise. Everything would make noise, and whoever or whatever had creaked the floor-board had gone silent again. He was too far from the tiny window letting in the light to see through it and scan the surroundings.

He didn't wear his gun around the house because he was afraid it would make Sarah and Rachel nervous, and now he mentally kicked himself for caring more about feelings than safety.

He'd have to fight off whoever was at that door. He'd need the element of surprise. And to do it all while keeping Rachel out of the way.

There was only one way to do it, since once the attic door opened it would open this way and give whoever was on the stairs clear sight of Rachel.

But if he hid on the other side of the door, he could come at whoever it was from behind. They might know he was up here, but Rachel would be a momentary dis-traction he'd use.

He pressed his mouth as close to her ear as he could. Spoke as softly as humanly possible. "You're going to stay right here. Don't move unless I tell you to. Squeeze my hand if you understand."

When she squeezed, he squeezed right back. He was loathe to let go of her, to do what he knew he needed to do. He wanted to promise her things would be okay. He wanted to be a human shield between her and hurt.

But he had to stop doing what was most comfortable, and start doing what was the safest. He moved in abso-lute silence to the opposite side of the door.

He waited, counting his heartbeats, keeping his breathing even. Rachel's life rested in his hands, so he could not focus on panic or worry or that heavy responsibility. He could only focus on eradicating the threat.

The door squeaked, the narrow opening slowly growing. He saw the barrel of a gun first. It was pointed down at the ground, but he couldn't take any chances.

He waited until he actually saw an arm, then pushed the door as hard as he could. The gun didn't clatter to the ground as he'd hoped, but the intruder had stumbled back onto the stair.

"Get down, Rach," he commanded, moving through the door and closing it behind him. A figure in all black was on the stairs. The figure didn't raise the gun, but that didn't mean it wasn't dangerous.

The figure struck out, and Tucker managed to block most of the blow. They grappled, exchanging punches and elbows and kicks. Eventually they both stumbled, crashing down the first flight of stairs and onto the landing that would go down to the second floor.

Tucker banged up his elbow pretty good, and he'd landed on the side with his phone in his pocket so not only did a shooting pain go through his hip, but he was pretty sure the phone was crushed.

He swore, and so did the figure. Tuck frowned. It was a woman. He noticed blond hair had escaped the black ski mask she wore. He scrambled to his feet, recognizing her as the woman who'd first approached him on behalf of North Star, then again outside his office.

"You." Why was the woman from North Star sneaking through the house? Pointing a gun and fighting with him?

The woman glared up at him, then landed a kick to his stomach, and he cursed himself for being caught off guard. She made a run for it to go up the stairs, but Tucker got his breath back quickly enough to grab her by the foot. He heard her let out a curse as she crashed into the stairs.

"Why are Wyatts always ruining my life?" she demanded, kicking back at him.

"What the hell are you doing? North Star is supposed to be the good guys."

She stopped kicking and fighting him off and gave a derisive snort before rolling onto her back. Tucker had the sense she could easily kick him down the stairs and there wouldn't be much he could do about it.

"I have my orders, from those *good* guys." The woman jerked her chin toward the attic "She knows something. She needs to come with me or our mission is compromised. Granger knew you'd be difficult about it."

"How do you know she knows something?" Tucker demanded. How on earth could they know about Rachel's dreams?

The woman gave him a withering glare. "We know everything, Wyatt. Haven't you caught on?"

It didn't matter. It couldn't. "Screw your mission. She's got nothing to do with it and you know it. You're going to drag an innocent into the midst of this? Via kidnapping?"

The woman's expression went grim, but Tucker thought he saw a flash of conscience. "I have my orders," she repeated.

Which told Tucker she didn't particularly want to follow those orders.

"Excuse me?" Both he and the woman he'd fought

looked up at the top of the stairs. Rachel stood with her arms over her chest, expression furious. "Maybe one of you could tell me what's going on and I, the woman in question, can decide for myself?"

Chapter Ten

Rachel was shaking, but she'd wrapped her arms around herself to keep it from showing. She was at the top of the stairs and from what she could tell, Tucker and…some woman he knew were on the landing in the middle of the stairs having an argument about her.

"Rach."

"No, I don't think I want you to tell me," she said, holding on to her composure by a very thin thread. Tucker had been lying to her, that much was clear.

"Listen. My name is Shay. I'm with the North Star Group. Tucker and Cody Wyatt have worked for us. Your father's past connected to ours, so we're helping him out. If you come with me—"

"What a load of bull. You're not helping him. You're using him," Tucker said disgustedly. "If you're taking her against her will, you're not in this to protect anyone."

"No one said it was against my will, Tucker."

She heard him take a few stairs. "She was damn well going to, Rachel. She snuck in here, and she fought me—"

"You started that," Shay interrupted.

"She was going to kidnap you. Because you know things about your father's past. Not because she wants to protect you or Duke, but because they'll do anything to bring down the Sons. Including letting innocent people get hurt."

There was a heavy, poignant silence.

"Don't have anything to say to that?" Tucker said scathingly to the woman.

Who still didn't say anything. Rachel didn't understand any of this, but she understood one thing. "You have my father."

"We're helping your father," this Shay person said. "It's what we do."

"What does this have to do with the Sons?" she asked. Because of course it did. Tucker had lied to her and her father was in danger because of the Sons of the Badlands.

What else was new?

"Rachel, listen to me—"

"You knew where he was, who he was being protected by and *why*, but you didn't think to share that with me?" Her throat closed with every word, until the last one was a squeak.

"Rach." He sounded pained, hurt.

But she couldn't have any sympathy for him. He'd lied to her. Let her worry and fear and… He'd used her. Even if he was right about this North Star Group using Dad instead of helping him, Tucker had used her. Knowing…everything.

"If I go with you, what happens?" she said, addressing Shay.

"I'd take you to your father."

"Oh, that's low," Tucker said sourly. "She would not. They would interrogate you about your dreams until they got the information they wanted. If you give them what they want, they *might* let you see Duke, but considering they're using him as bait, I don't think that's happening anytime soon. They need him. They need the information they think you might have. What they don't need is a father–daughter reunion. And who knows, they might use you as bait, too. You can't go with her, Rachel."

"She's coming with me. Whether she does it willingly or not, my mission is to bring her back. So I will."

But Rachel noted they were standing in the attic staircase having this conversation. Shay wasn't making a move to fight Tucker anymore. She hadn't yet attempted to take Rachel against her will like she was saying she would.

"Can you promise my father will be okay if I go with you willingly?"

There was a hesitation. "I…can't promise that. Your father's in a dangerous situation."

"Think, Rachel," Tuck implored her. "I know you're mad at me. Maybe you'll never forgive me. I get it. But think about your father. What would he want you to do?"

"I don't care as much about what he'd want me to do as what I can do to protect him."

"They'd use whatever you gave them to complete their mission. You and Duke would be collateral damage." Tucker sounded so…desperate. So intent. It wasn't his usual self.

But his usual self had been lying to her. Should she

have seen it? There had been hints. Hesitations. A care-fulness.

The woman was suspiciously silent at Tucker's ac-cusation. "Is that true?" Rachel asked quietly.

There was a long silence. "It's not...untrue."

"So, you're both liars who don't care about anyone?"

"Your father wanted you safe," Tucker said, and while he was being contrite, so to speak, there was a thread of steel in his words. "You and Sarah. Why do you think I'm here? He—"

"You saw him. Before he disappeared. You saw him and you lied to all of us."

She couldn't see his expression, but she knew all those accusations landed like blows. Unless he was a completely different man than she'd always believed. Which maybe he was.

"He wanted you and Sarah protected," Tucker re-peated, and his voice was rough. She wanted to believe that was emotion. Guilt.

She just didn't know what to believe about him any-more. He'd seen her father. He'd let her worry.

He'd comforted her after her dreams. Stepped in and made meals, cleaned up. He'd taught her self-defense and...maybe he'd tried to ease some of her fears. She thought of the badge, the key.

"Were you lying about looking into the name?"

Tucker was silent for ticking awful seconds where she wanted to curl into herself and cry. Just...disap-pear from this world where the man she trusted was such a liar.

"I wasn't lying. I looked into it. I was told to leave it be."

"In fairness, he didn't leave it be," Shay said. "Which is why I'm here."

"You guys are keeping some kind of tabs on me?" Tucker growled as if he was both surprised and disgusted by the information. "What the hell is this?"

"It's business, Wyatt. The business of taking down the Sons."

"I'm so tired of people trying to take down the Sons," Rachel said, her voice growing louder with every word. "I'm so tired of people getting hurt because of the *Sons*. My father and I have nothing to do with them. Why can't you leave us alone?"

"Listen, you can dismiss me and all, but neither of you actually have a say. If I don't take you, they'll send someone else. You're a part of North Star's mission now. They won't just take no for an answer. It'd be easier if you just came with me."

Rachel didn't know why that was the straw that broke the camel's back. "And I am really done doing what's *easier* for everyone else."

Tucker had to ignore the searing pain in his chest. The slick black weight of guilt. He had to focus on getting Rachel out of this mess. Once she was safe… Well, he could self-flagellate and she could hate him forever.

He rubbed at his chest.

"If you don't come with me of your own volition," Shay said in a careful, emotionless voice, "I'll take you by force."

Tucker had already positioned himself between Shay and Rachel. He was ready to fight. He didn't think Shay would use the gun against him. At least he hoped not.

"She is an innocent bystander. Whatever she knows is wrapped up in nightmares she can't untangle." He thought about the badge, the key he'd slid into his pocket. He could give that to Shay as a peace offering. It might even help Duke, and it wasn't that he thought North Star was evil—they just didn't care about people. They cared about their mission.

As for him, he cared about too many people involved to let this go so far as to touch Rachel. The key might be some kind of insurance if he kept it. So, he had to.

Tucker turned to Rachel. She held herself impossibly still, her expression mostly blank. Except her eyes. They were hurt. Betrayed.

And he'd done the betraying.

He had to get her out of this. Maybe she'd never forgive him, but if he could get her out of this, maybe he could forgive himself.

"Your father wanted me to protect you from this. Keep you separate."

"But I'm *not* separate. If they're here about my dreams, there's something real in them." Her eyebrows drew together. "It has to be real."

"That doesn't mean you have to put yourself in danger. It doesn't mean you have to go with this group who doesn't care about you."

"This group has my father."

"You going there doesn't help him. It helps *them*." He wouldn't let her go. Even if she wanted to. But maybe he could assuage at least some of his guilt if she'd just understand the truth here. A truth he hadn't fully understood until now.

Maybe North Star wanted to take down the Sons, but they didn't care enough about the innocent collateral damage involved.

"Oh, just someone punch me," Shay said with no small amount of exasperation.

"What?" Tucker demanded, turning from Rachel to face her.

"In the face." She pointed to her nose. "Make it good, too."

"What are you talking about?"

"I can't go back to Granger unscathed *and* with you having gotten away. You need to make it look like you beat me. Literally and figuratively."

Finally, what Shay was saying got through. She was...letting them go. "I... I can't punch a woman."

She rolled her eyes. "I can punch you first if it gets you going."

"That's not—"

"I'll do it," Rachel said, walking down the stairs. She stopped on the stair right above Shay.

"No offense, but—"

Rachel squared like he'd taught her, curled her fist and landed a blow right to Shay's face.

Swearing in time with Rachel, Shay gingerly placed her palm on her jaw, working it back and forth. Rachel shook out her hand, then cradled it.

"Well, that'll work," Shay said. "Hell."

"You really think one punch is going to convince them?"

"I can handle the rest, but I couldn't punch my own self in the face." She gave Rachel a once-over. "Not half bad. Keep working on that and you might be one hell of a fighter." She moved as if to leave, but Tucker stepped in front of her on the stairs.

"I should take your gun."

She grimaced, clearly loathing the idea of losing her weapon.

"They can't think you got back in one piece still armed, can they?"

"Yeah, yeah, yeah." She handed over the weapon.

Still, Tucker couldn't move out of her way. "Will they kick you out?"

She shrugged. "Not if I quit first."

"Why would you do that?"

"Because you're right, Wyatt. I'm not in the business of hurting innocent people for the sake of a mission. North Star didn't start out that way, but lately... Doesn't matter. It's getting old and maybe this is my last straw. You're going to need to run, though. Whether I get kicked out or quit—they'll keep coming for her. She knows stuff." Shay let out a sigh. "That phone Granger gave you?"

Tucker pulled it out of his pocket. It was in a couple pieces after his fall down the stairs.

Shay nodded. "That's good. Leave it here."

It dawned on Tucker that meant Granger had been tracking him, maybe listening to him. He'd know about everything up to the fight on the stairs. He nodded grimly at Shay, tossing the phone onto the ground. He smashed it once more under his heel for good measure.

Shay looked back at Rachel, then leaned close to whisper to Tucker. "Get her out of here ASAP. Whatever she knows, they'll use it. Not to help or protect Knight, but to get the Sons. I want the Sons destroyed as much as anybody, and I imagine you do, too, but good people shouldn't be used as bait to take them down."

"If you don't quit, if you don't get kicked out, you could help keep Duke safe. From the inside."

She smiled wryly. "That's a lot of ifs."

"Like you said, we both want to bring down the Sons. We just don't want innocent people hurt in the process. We could work together on this."

She shook her head. "You and your brother. Two peas in a dumb, naive pod."

"Is that a yes?"

She blew out a breath. "Look, I'll do what I can. That does *not* mean we're working together. Be clear on that."

He wasn't sure he believed her, and when he held out a hand for a shake, she shook her head. "We are *not* partners. Be best for you both if you get out of here before I do."

Tucker nodded and looked up at Rachel. Her expression was grim. But Shay was right, they had to get out of here. He didn't know where yet, but he'd figure it out.

What he wasn't so sure he was going to figure out was how to live with what he'd done.

Chapter Eleven

Tucker stole a horse.

Maybe it was harsh for Rachel to consider it stealing, considering it was *her* horse, and she was one of the people riding it, but it felt like stealing. It felt like lying and scaring the people she loved by disappearing.

Like Dad did?

She didn't even have time to wallow in the betrayal of it all because Shay was absolutely telling the truth, no doubt about it. Someone else would come for her, because her dreams were true.

True.

They rode Buttercup away from the ranch—in the opposite direction of the pasture Dev and Sarah were working in this afternoon. It felt really stupid to be riding a horse named Buttercup when trying to escape a group that was trying to bring down the Sons—which was what she wanted.

How could two groups of people want the same thing and disagree so fundamentally on how to get there?

She didn't speak as Tucker explained everything from the beginning. His helping out North Star. Being ready to quit before he walked into a diner with the North Star guy and her father.

Her father. Who'd brought down dirty cops as a young man and was somehow paying for it over thirty years later.

Her father wasn't who she'd thought. Tucker wasn't who she'd thought.

Oh, that probably wasn't fair. In fact, it was really quite *Wyatt* of Tucker to want to save the day without telling her. Still, no matter how justified, the fact he'd lied to her and she'd bought it hook, line and sinker… It hurt.

Maybe his deception was necessary, but how easily he'd fooled her made her feel stupid. And weak. Now she was riding a horse, with Tucker's hard body directly behind her, through the rolling hills of southeastern South Dakota like she was some kidnapped bride on the prairie.

Rachel didn't say anything as they rode, and after he'd told the whole story, neither did Tucker. She didn't know how many hours they rode in silence, how many miles they covered. She didn't know where they were going and she didn't ask.

Because she was too afraid he'd offer another lie, and she'd believe it as gospel.

"Sun's going down," Tucker said, his voice rusty with disuse. "We should camp."

"Camp," Rachel echoed. Up to this point, she hadn't been afraid, not really. In the moments Tucker had been fighting Shay, yes, but after that there'd been too many other feelings. Sadness, fury, hurt and the ache in her hand from punching Shay had taken up too much space to be truly afraid.

But now the idea of camping had those beats of panic starting in her chest.

"I'm sorry. It's the only way," Tucker said gently. He brought the horse to a halt and he got off. Since she couldn't see the ground, she had to let him help her dismount.

Rachel immediately pulled away from his grasp, though she kept her feet in the same place since she couldn't be sure she wouldn't trip and fall.

"So, what's the plan?" she asked flatly.

He handed her something. Her cane. It took her a moment to register that and to take it. They'd left in such a hurry, but he'd thought to grab her probing cane.

After lying to you about everything.

"Right now? The plan is to keep you away from North Star."

"For how long?" she asked.

"As long as we need to."

"We're just going to camp in the hills until someone magically alerts us to the fact North Star no longer needs me?"

"You still have your phone," he reminded her.

"It doesn't have service out here." She was completely alone in the wilderness with a man who...who she'd trusted and who'd lied to her. About the most important things. "Sarah is going to be worried sick."

"She would be worried sick if you'd stayed—because Shay would have taken you, or someone else would have come and finished the job. At least she'll know you're with me."

It was true, but that didn't make it comforting. Maybe because she knew Tucker would have stood up for her. He would have fought and protected her against all the people North Star sent. Liar that he was. "I don't camp."

"I know," he said, with enough weight that she figured he understood it was because it reminded her of that night. Of her memories or dreams. She'd been alone in the wilderness when the mountain lion had attacked, or at least that's what she'd believed until lately.

"I'm sorry this has touched you, Rachel. I wish I could make it not."

She wanted to ask him if that was another lie, but she understood in that statement that while Tucker had lied to her about facts, he'd never lied to her about feelings. He'd promised to try to keep her father safe—and he had been working to do that. He'd promised her father to keep her out of it.

He'd failed, and likely was busy heaping all sorts of guilt on himself. She wished that made her feel better, but it actually deflated some of her anger.

"He's my father. It was always going to touch me no matter what you did, Tucker."

He didn't respond, and she could hear the sounds of him making camp. He'd gotten her out of the house so quickly she didn't know how he'd had time to gather supplies, but he seemed to have enough.

"I know you don't want to camp. I wish there was another way," he finally said, so grave and... It wasn't fair. She couldn't be mad at him when he was beating himself up.

"You know, the same thing would have happened even if you'd told us the truth from the beginning.

Didn't Shay basically say that phone North Star gave you was tracking everything?"

"Maybe if I'd been a better liar, you'd be just fine at home."

"Is that what you want? To be a better liar?"

He expelled a loud breath. "No."

"That's why you were going to quit. Well, Dad threw a wrench in your plans, and so did my dreams."

"That sounds a lot like absolution. And misplaced blame."

"It's neither. You did what you had to do. And I can't control my dreams."

"You should be mad at me."

"Oh, I am," she told him. "I'm mad at you. I'm irritated with myself. I'm downright furious with Dad. I don't want to camp. I don't want to run. I don't want any of this."

"I'm sor—"

"I don't want your apologies, either. I want the lies to end. And I want Dad back in one piece. So, we have to figure out how we're going to do that. We can't wait. We can't play the hide-Rachel-away-in-a-safe-corner game. We have to fight. For my father. We have to help him. However we can."

RACHEL SOUNDED FIERCE, and looked it, standing there in the fading daylight, probing cane grasped in one hand, the other clenched in a fist. Her expression was hard and determined.

He wished he could agree. Immediately support her. "If I knew how to do that, I would have already done it."

It was humbling to admit. He'd seen no real way to

help Duke except protect Rachel and he'd failed. He'd brought her more into the fold by not suspecting Mc-Millan might be listening in.

The bastard had listened in on private conversations. Rachel's dream aftermath. Talking about her mother and the buttons.

He fingered the key in his pocket. Duke already knew his past. There were no secrets to be uncovered. Whatever the key unlocked, Duke knew about it. Had locked something up. It wouldn't help him now. In fact, it was probably best if it stayed buried.

"Dad's being threatened by this Vianni family, through the Sons, according to North Star."

"It's not just North Star's story. Your father was there when McMillan told me about it. It's true."

She nodded sharply. "Okay. It's true. North Star is supposed to keep him safe, but both you and Shay acted like they're trying to use Dad as some kind of bait to get enough evidence on the Sons. But to what end? To arrest them all? Kill them all?"

"I'm not privy to North Star's plans."

"No, but Shay said that it's gotten too mission focused. They're not caring about people. I don't want Dad to be collateral damage."

"I don't either, Rachel."

"I know you don't." She moved forward using her cane to avoid the dips and bumps in the ground.

Tucker had found the flattest, most even ground he could, but he'd wanted to stay in the hills and trees as much as possible.

"But North Star knows everything about Dad, and

presumably they know a lot about the Viannis and the Sons. They don't *need* him there."

"They're protecting him."

"Are they?" she returned. "Or did they say that to you, maybe even to him, but what they really meant is they're using him?"

It was a horrible thought. Even if he didn't agree with everything North Star had done, he believed in their mission. "Your Dad went to them willingly. He had some connection to their leader. Or the leader's dad. Something about him being the reason he had this WITSEC life here. He had to believe they were going to…fix things or he wouldn't have gone."

"But I don't. I don't believe that at all. When one of their own, a woman sent to take me, let's us go instead… Something is very, very wrong. I want my father out. Screw their mission. *You* said that."

"I did. And I meant it in regard to Shay's particular mission of kidnapping you. But I don't want to sabotage North Star. Even if I don't approve of their methods, I approve of what they're doing. I *support* what they're doing." How had this gotten so messed up? "Bringing down the Sons is important."

"It is. Should my father die for it?"

"I don't think North Star would let that happen." But their attempted kidnapping of Rachel made him uncomfortably concerned.

"You don't *think*."

Tucker raked his hands through his hair. "People are after him. Dangerous people. Regardless of the Sons or North Star, your father was a target."

"Because he did something right. Don't you know what that's like?"

It snapped something in him. That leash on his temper and his emotions he fought so hard to keep tethered. "Yeah, I do. I know it's living your life in fear, wondering when it shows up to take you down. I know it's watching your brothers get hurt over and over again by this thing you escaped, while you can't do a damn thing about it. Knowing you don't even rate to be a target because apparently you're not that much of a threat to their kind of evil. I know what it's all like, Rachel, and I'm telling you, *we* can't do anything about it."

She blinked. "Tuck—"

He was so horrified by his torrent of words that had nothing to do with her or this situation, he turned his back on her. "No. It's not about me. It's about Duke."

"Tucker—"

"I said no. I won't steal your father out of the North Star's hands, not with you. I can't protect you both from all the different forces after you. I got you out of there so they can't use you, can't use your dreams. Because Duke would have wanted me to keep you safe and because it's the right thing." Because the thought of putting her in any more danger just about ripped him in two.

He had to stop this…*emotion.* It was weak. It was…

Wasn't that what Ace told you? Emotion is weak? Caring is weak?

"Would you do it without me?" Rachel asked firmly, breaking through those old memories of his father.

He'd promised to not let himself lose control. The whole tirade about the Sons and his brothers was bad enough. He wouldn't say anything else stupid. But how could she say that? How could she think he'd leave her behind? To think he'd ever, *ever* let her be a target.

He moved to her, telling himself to keep it locked down. He didn't lose his temper. He didn't lose control. Not because emotions were weak as Ace had always said, but because he had to handle this.

But he wanted to grab her by the arms and shake her. He wanted to do all manner of impossible, disastrously ill-advised things.

Instead, he stood in front of her, maybe a few inches too close, and kept his voice ruthlessly controlled. "Let's make one thing very, very clear. There is not a damn thing I will do without you right now."

She stood very still. The sun had disappeared behind the hills, though there was enough light to still make her out. She wouldn't be able to see anything, even shapes in this light. Still, she moved unerringly into him, wrapping her arms around him.

A hug. A comfort.

He couldn't return it. He couldn't push her away. He could only stand there still as a statue, her arms around him and her cheek pressed to his chest.

"Hell, Rach. Be mad at me. Hate me. I can't stand you being nice to me right now."

"I guess it's too bad for you, because I can't stand to be mad at you right now." She pulled back, tilted her head up toward his. "If you told me right now, promised me right now, that you won't lie again, I'll believe you."

Even knowing he shouldn't, he placed his palm on her cheek. "I'm sorry. I can't do that."

Chapter Twelve

Rachel didn't move away from his hand, even though Tucker's words were...not what she'd expected. At all. She liked the warmth of his calloused palm on her cheek, and she liked how close he was as night descended around them.

She shouldn't be concerning herself with warmth. Or how nice it felt. When he was telling her that he wouldn't promise not to lie.

"Why not?" she asked, and the fact it came out a breathy whisper surprised her, as much as the fact he didn't remove his hand. Instead, his thumb brushed back and forth over her cheekbone.

A sparkling heat shimmered underneath her skin, in her blood. She didn't understand it. Not when it was Tucker touching her, but she could hardly deny it existed. The feeling was too big and real and potent.

His voice was low and rough when he spoke. "I can't promise to never lie. I lied to Brady and Cecilia last month. It was one of the hardest things I've ever done—to lie to my brother like that. Knowing they were both suspicious of me. But I'd do it all over again. I'd have to. Because I was trying to accomplish something good and right. If I had to lie to protect you, Rachel, I would. Any of you. Your sisters. My brothers. Your father. Anyone."

She might not have believed him, except she knew from Cecilia he had definitely lied to Brady. His own brother. Even when Cecilia had been convinced he'd been turned into a Sons member, Brady had trusted him. Even with the lies.

If his own brother could—did—how could she not?

"Okay." She didn't dare nod because he might take his hand away. "Okay."

"We'll camp tonight, and maybe in the morning we'll have a clearer idea of what to do. I managed to grab enough supplies for a day or two for us and Buttercup. This is temporary. Until we figure out how to fix this."

She had no idea how they were going to do that, but it didn't feel so impossible with Tucker touching her. Despite everything, she believed in him. He'd gotten them this far. He'd fought off Shay. Convinced her to let them go.

"I want my dad to be safe. I don't want this awful thing to come back and hurt him. He did the right thing, and he had to give up his whole life. It isn't right that he managed to build a new one and they want to take it away from him."

"No, it isn't. If I knew what to do… If I had any clue, I'd do it. *That* I can promise you."

She nodded, the scrape of his rough hand against her cheek a lovely, sparkling distraction from the fear and confusion roiling inside of her.

He didn't need to promise her anything, but of course

he would. She had a plethora of *good* men in her life, and it often insulated her to the fact that bad people like Ace Wyatt and whoever was after her father existed. She so seldom remembered what an enormous miracle it was that Tucker and his brothers had escaped the Sons and become...them.

Good men, determined to do good in the world. Maybe not perfectly. He had his issues. That whole spiel about not being worth the Sons' notice because he wasn't a threat.

If anything underscored all her hurt, it was *that*. Tucker put on a face for the world that he was perfectly adjusted, a good detective, brother, man. And he was those things.

But he didn't think he was.

She didn't know how to make him believe he was all the things *she* thought he was. She could only lean into his hand, lean into *him* and this feeling.

She still didn't know how she felt about being attracted to Tucker, about the possibility he felt the same way. She didn't want to be a domino of Knight girls falling in a line for the Wyatt boys.

But everything swirled inside of her obscuring what she didn't want. She could only think of what she did.

"If they don't think you're a threat, they don't understand you. Caring about people isn't a weakness, Tucker." She placed her hand on his chest when the moment didn't evaporate like she'd been afraid it would. "You don't need to be in North Star or putting yourself in mortal danger to be as strong as your brothers, as important. You solve problems. You take *care* of people. That's just as important as putting your life on the line."

He inhaled sharply, but his hand was still on her face. He was so close, their bodies brushing in the increasing darkness around them. "Rach, I don't know what to say to all that."

His voice was as rough as his hand. He was as strong as she'd said, standing there so close. She couldn't resist tipping her mouth up...wishing for something she'd promised herself she couldn't possibly want.

Then his mouth touched hers. Featherlight. No one had ever kissed her before, and she'd always figured it would take some miracle—getting off the ranch, away from her overprotective father and sisters, into a life that was independent and hers, and when would *that* ever happen.

But it was Tucker Wyatt. She didn't need to convince him she was independent—even when he was protecting her, it was only because that's what he *did*.

It ended far too quickly. The kiss. His hand on her cheek. The sound his footsteps made had her thinking he stumbled back and away, as if he'd realized whom he'd kissed.

"We should get some sleep," he said, his voice tight.

She barked out a laugh, couldn't seem to help the reaction. He'd *kissed* her and he was talking about going to sleep. He was ignoring it. Coward. "You kissed me."

"Forget it. It was... Just forget that."

"Forget it? Why would I?"

"Wrong place. Wrong time. Wrong everything."

She frowned at that. Intellectually, he was probably right. Wrong time certainly, which went along with place. But... "It didn't feel so wrong."

"Well, it was," he said firmly.

So firmly that she thought maybe she was missing something. "Why?"

"*Why?* Because…"

She waited impatiently for him to come up with this reason she was missing. "Because?" she demanded when he was just silent.

"Because you're…you're like a sister to me."

She snorted. It was such a pathetic grasping at straws. "Then you're a pervert, Tucker. You don't check out your sister's boobs and then kiss her."

"I didn't! I never…"

"Sarah said you did."

"I…"

"Maybe you can't promise to lie to me, but if you lie to me about *this*, I won't forgive you. Period."

He was quiet for a long stretched-out moment. "I don't know what you want me to say."

"Why did you kiss me?"

"You want the truth? Here and now of all places? Fine. Maybe I owe that to you after all this. Yeah, I'm attracted to you. I don't have a clue as to why…why *now*. I just am. It's just there. Then you had to go say all that stuff, looking up at me like you meant it."

"I can't see," she pointed out, hoping to lighten the moment.

"You know what I mean," he replied gruffly.

"Yeah, I think I do." Unfortunately that made her all the more gooey-hearted when they had much more important things to deal with. Still, truth for truth was only fair. "I meant it, Tuck. I did. And I…guess I'm attracted to you, too."

"You guess," he muttered disgustedly.

Which almost made her smile. "I'm still working through all that. I haven't exactly had a lot of experience with this."

He groaned. "Please God, tell me that wasn't your first kiss."

"Okay, I won't tell you."

He swore a few times, and she had no idea why that made her want to laugh.

"Look. We need to…go to sleep. Tomorrow, we'll come up with a plan. No more of…this stuff."

"This *stuff*?"

"Whatever this is, we'll figure it out when we're not camping in the South Dakota wilderness, with absolutely no plan on how we're going to accomplish what we want. For now, we get some rest and focus on the important things."

She nodded as though she agreed with him, and let him lead her into the tent.

TUCKER WOKE UP in his own personal nightmare. He had to come up with a plan to save Duke, to keep Rachel safe. To outwit North Star, the Sons and some other group of people out for blood.

All knowing he'd kissed Rachel. And now she was curled up next to him. Because he'd only had time to grab the pack out of his truck—which was outfitted for one person. A tiny tent and *one* sleeping bag.

It was edging far enough into fall that nights were cold, so he'd had to let her cozy up next to him and fall asleep. All while pretending that kiss had never happened.

It was the only way to survive this. Put a brick wall around his own personal slip-up. Seal it off and forget it.

But he'd never in a million years be able to forget the feel of his lips on hers. Simple kisses weren't supposed to…do that. Make you forget who you were and what was important: safety. Hers most of all.

But he'd forgotten everything except her for those humming seconds—not just the kiss, but her talking to him like she understood him. When it felt like no one did.

He knew his brothers saw him as an equal. They couldn't understand that he didn't *feel* like one.

Right now in this warm tent, Rachel's hair curling against his cheek, the soft rise and fall of her chest matching time with his… Well, he supposed Rachel seeing through his issues was a better line of thought than how good she felt here against him.

She shifted, yawned, her eyes slowly blinking open. Even though she wouldn't be able to see in the dim light of the tent, he could see. The sleep slowly lift. Realization and understanding dawning.

And the way she definitely did not try to slide away or disengage from him, but seemed perfectly content to cuddle closer.

There was a very large part of him that wanted to test it out, too. To see what it would be like to relax into her. To touch her face again. To recognize the soft curves of her body as they pressed to his. To kiss her and—

No. Not possible.

Carefully, he disengaged from her arms and scooted away from her as best he could in the tiny tent.

"Maybe we should go back. I've got nothing. My

brothers might have some ideas. They're better at this than I am."

She was quiet for a while as she pushed herself up into a sitting position. "Are they better at it, or were they just put in a position you weren't?"

"You don't need to keep defending me. I don't have low self-esteem. I—"

"You've got issues, Tuck. Good news is, we all do. Better news, you have someone around who's not going to let you believe the crap you tell yourself. So..." She yawned. "I don't suppose you have any coffee?"

He didn't know how to stay in this tiny tent with her looking sleepy and rumpled and gorgeous, talking about how everyone had issues. "I've got some instant. I'll go warm up some water." He didn't *dive* for the tent opening, but he got outside in record time.

The sun was just beginning to rise and the grass held the tiniest hint of frost. It was cold, made colder by the fact that the tent had been so warm. He shivered against the chill as he zipped the tent back up.

A piece of paper fluttered to the ground next to him. Tuck whirled around, scanning the area. But there was nothing except the soft whisper of the wind against the rolling hills of ranch land.

He crouched down, studied the note on the grass. It was wet from the dew, and all he could figure was that it had been left on the tent, and opening the flap had knocked it off.

He looked around, scanning all he could see for any sign of human life or movement. But the world was quiet, with only the interruption of birdsong.

He picked the paper up and opened the fold. Water

had smudged the first word, but Tucker could figure it out and read the rest clearly.

Rachel knows the key and the lock.

Tucker flipped the paper over. Nothing on the back. Nothing else on the front. Just one sentence. That didn't make any sense.

The key and the lock? He thought of the key in his pocket. But what did it unlock? And Rachel definitely didn't act like she had any idea what the key was to.

"Rach." He unzipped the flap again and stuck his head in. She was crouched over, rolling up the sleeping bag. He could tell she'd already tidied what few things were inside. "I found something."

She yawned again. "I take it not coffee." She sighed. "What is it?"

"A note. I… I think this is Duke's handwriting." He frowned, studied it. He wasn't a handwriting expert, and he'd never spent much time scrutinizing Duke's writing, but it certainly looked like his typical slanted scratch.

Tuck looked around the campsite again. He hadn't heard anyone so it was near impossible Duke had left the note for them. He was a big man, and even if he'd been a cop in a former life, stealth was not Duke's current skill. "It was on the tent, then when I opened the flap it fell to the ground."

The only one who knew enough, and had enough access to Duke to get a message to them, was Shay. "Shay must have gotten it to us. She must have."

"Is there any way it's a trap or a trick?" Rachel asked.

"It wasn't addressed to us. There's no signature. It's written in *some* kind of code. So, it might not be from your father, but it's Duke's handwriting." He cleared his throat. "As of yesterday, North Star still had Duke. It could be from North Star. They could have made him write it, but I have to believe if they went through the trouble to track us down, they would have just taken us. You especially. Or written a more specific note."

"Here. Let me see it."

He handed her the paper, though he wasn't sure what she was going to do with it. She felt the corner of the paper. "It's Dad. And not like someone made him write it, either. That's an actual note from him."

"How can you tell?"

"We developed a little system when I was in school. If he had to sign something and he'd done it, he'd poke a little hole in the corner. If there was no hole, I knew I needed to ask him again." She held up the paper, and sure enough there was a small hole in the corner. "What does it say?"

"Rachel knows the key and the lock."

Her eyebrows drew together. *"Me?"* She shook her head. "I don't know anything about that key we found. Let alone what it would unlock."

They were silent for the next few minutes, Rachel frowning as if searching her mind for an answer. Tucker studied the note again, wondering if there was more to it. Something he wasn't seeing. Something more… abstract.

He looked up at Rachel. She'd gone back to tidying up the tent. It was less smooth than how she did it at home since she was going by feel rather than lifelong knowledge of a place. Still, she had the inside of the tent all packed up in no time.

Duke thought she knew what he was talking about, Tucker assumed. Rachel didn't think she knew anything about the key or its lock.

"Maybe it's about your dream. If you know, but you don't actually *know*, maybe the answer is in your subconscious."

Chapter Thirteen

Her dream. Rachel's arms broke out in goose bumps. As much as she was slowly coming around to the idea her dream might be more reality and memory than fiction, she wasn't comfortable with her subconscious knowing something she couldn't access.

Especially when it came to this.

"Dad doesn't know anything about my dreams changing. He still thinks they're about a mountain lion."

"Did you tell him about your dreams?"

"When I was a kid. When I first started having them. He…" An uncomfortable memory had her chest tightening, like she couldn't breathe.

Tucker was immediately at her side. He rubbed a hand up and down her back. "Hey, breathe. It's all right, sweetheart. Take a deep breath."

She managed, barely. The panic had been so swift, so all encompassing, it was hard to move beyond. "I don't know if this was the first time I had the dream, but I remember being little. I still… I may have even still had the bandages on my face. Dad would sleep on the floor of my room. Mom would try to get him to come to bed, but he would insist. He said he was afraid I'd wander away again."

Tucker kept rubbing her back, and it gave her some modicum of comfort as her body seemed to chill from the inside out.

"I remember telling him about the nightmare and he told me not to tell Mom. That whenever I had nightmares or felt scared, I should tell him. Only him. He said so Mom wouldn't worry, but…"

"If your mother didn't know…"

"How…how could she have not known? How could he have lied to her? How could he have had *me* lie to her?"

"He was in WITSEC, Rach. I'm not saying it was the right thing to do, but you're supposed to leave your old life behind. Entirely."

"It's his story. The mountain lion. He made that up." The horror of that almost made her knees weak. He'd pushed her into the mountain lion story, made sure he convinced her the dreams were of that.

Even when they weren't.

"Are you sure?" Tucker asked gently.

"No. How can I be sure?" Her throat closed up and she refused to cry, but how was she expected to have an answer from a dream? "Everything is wrapped up in a dream that suddenly changed on me!"

"Hey. Maybe it's not about your dream. Maybe I've got this all wrong."

She shook her head. "You know you don't. You're a detective. You know how to piece things together." She wrapped her arms around herself. "What else would I know that I don't think I know? You're right. It's something about my dream, but I don't know *what*."

"Okay, then let's work through this like I'd work through any case. We start at the beginning. What's the very first part of your dream you remember?"

"Do you really think the answer is in my dream?" she asked.

"I don't know. I really don't. But it might help. To lay it all out."

Rachel didn't think that was possible. She'd spent most of her life knowing this dream might pop up. Except the dream had morphed. From what Dad had pointed her to—to the truth? It was impossible to know for sure.

Maybe she'd never get rid of the nightmares, but maybe she could find the truth in the way it had changed… Maybe.

"I'm not sure I know where to start," she said, her voice rough and her chest tight.

Tucker's arm came around her shoulders and he gave her an affectionate squeeze. "Sit. No use crouching around."

"No, no. I need to…to move. To be doing something."

"Okay, so we'll go out and break down the tent while you talk. Sound good?"

She nodded. He helped lead her outside, then led her to the first stake.

"Do you mind if I do it myself?"

"Whatever you need, Rach."

She nodded once and pulled out the stake. Then she felt around the tent, slowly taking it apart. She didn't like to camp, but she and Sarah had often put tents up and down around the ranch as forts or playhouses, so she was familiar with the process of breaking down the tent even without her sight.

Tucker didn't push. He didn't ask questions. Nor did he jump in to help take down the tent. He waited until she started to speak herself. "I'm not sure I know exactly where it starts. When I wake up, when I try to remember, it's just that I'm suddenly aware I'm being carried away."

"Carried away from where?"

"Home. I don't see home, but I know he's taking me away from home." Even knowing she was safe with Tucker, the fear and panic clawed at her. She focused on the tent. "He's taking me away from…lights. I think there's a light behind us and he's going into the dark."

"Lights on in the house maybe?"

"I think so." Even though it was silly since she couldn't see anyway, she closed her eyes. She tried to bring the nightmare back to her. She'd seen for the first three years of her life. There were things she could remember, and this dream had always been one of them.

"Or maybe it's the stables." She opened her eyes, frowning. She could tell light was beginning to dawn in the here and now, but she still couldn't fully make out Tucker's shape. "It isn't windows. It isn't a glow like if it was home at dark. It's more one lone beam of light. I think it's the light outside the stables."

"So, he's taking you away from the stables," Tucker said. His voice was calm and serious and believing. He took everything she said at face value and put it into the puzzle they were trying to work out. "The light on the stables is on the north side. If you're moving straight away from it, that's heading into the north pasture."

"Or toward the highway." She felt how *right* it was, more than saw or knew. Going away from one lone light, heading for the dark of the highway. "The new dream, the changed dream, he's holding me so tight I can barely breathe. I'm too scared to scream. He's talking, but I can't make sense of the words. In my head, they're just a jumble. I just want my mom."

Tears welled up because she still just wanted Mom and couldn't have her. Couldn't find comfort in her. She'd been gone for so many years now. Rachel folded the tent poles and blinked back tears, fought to make her voice steady. She appreciated that Tucker didn't rush her.

"At some point I notice eyes watching us. They glow a little."

"Mountain lion?"

"At first, that's what I thought. As me. Adult me." She frowned. "I think Dad convinced me that's what I was seeing when I told him about the dream. But when I think about how I saw the eyes move, how it jumps out... I think it was a dog. We used to have dogs then. Lots of them."

"Yeah, four or five, right?"

Rachel nodded. "If this is all real—if it isn't my three-year-old brain getting things mixed up, or dreams mixing with reality, I think it was one of the dogs."

"And it just follows you while the man is carrying you away?"

"Yes. I'm not scared of the eyes. I'm scared of the man. He's holding me too tight, and he has..." She trailed off. This was where she didn't want to go, even knowing she had to.

"Last time, you said he had some kind of knife."

Rachel nodded, folding the tent with shaking hands. "It's either a knife with prongs, or multiple knives. It's sharp, and it keeps flashing in the moonlight." She brought a hand to her scars, and could feel the smooth lines. "It could have made this. Not claws, but this special knife he's carrying." Her breath whooshed out of her. "How is it possible?" she whispered. "And what does any of that tell us about a key?"

"I don't know yet, but let's focus on what you do remember. On the dream."

"That's all I remember. The last one I had, the one where he actually cut me? That's the first time I remember getting that far. Even when I was a kid, he never hurt me in my dream. I woke up before. But in this one, the dog jumps out. The man slashes the knife down and it cuts into me. I can feel the pain and the blood, and hear the dog—barking and snarling. But the dog isn't the one hurting me."

Tucker collected the tent and the poles. She could hear him wrapping it all up and putting it into his backpack. He said nothing.

"Thank you for letting me take down the tent."

"Thank you?"

"Most people can't stand to watch me do something myself, at a slower pace than they would go. They have to jump in to help to speed things up."

"We've got all the time in the world right now, Rach."

But Tucker didn't understand that time didn't always matter. People's compulsion with accomplishing tasks made it hard for them to step back. So, she'd just appreciated that he hadn't needed to do that.

He didn't press about the key, or if she remembered any more of her dream. He simply gave her the space to work through it.

"Do you know where my father is? Where they're keeping him or hiding him or whatever?"

"No."

"Would Cody know?"

Tucker hesitated. "It's possible."

"I don't have the answer to this, Tuck. And Dad clearly wants me to, or thinks I do. He sent us a message, and if Shay was the messenger, it probably wasn't sanctioned by your group."

"No, probably not."

"I need to talk to him. It's the only way."

TUCKER COULDN'T LET his own personal feelings or issues, as she'd call them, rule his thoughts or actions. Though it was hard to ignore how much it hurt, he couldn't do this without bringing his brother into the fold.

His brother who'd actually fought the Sons. On multiple levels. And won. Beat Ace. Beat those who would have hurt Cody and his daughter.

Cody. His *baby* brother.

"Tucker?"

"Sorry. I'm just trying to figure out how that would work. We'd have to get to a place that has cell service, and we don't know for sure that North Star doesn't have ways of tracking your phone, too."

"Maybe we should head back to the ranch. Surely

North Star doesn't think we'll go back. They'll think we're on the run. We go back. Get word to someone without phones, and have Cody meet us somewhere? We could hide on the ranch. That's smart, don't you think?"

Tucker had to pause and work very hard to keep the bitterness out of his voice. "Yeah, smart."

"Unless you have a better plan?"

"No, Rachel. I don't." How could he?

He continued to clean up the campsite, leaving Rachel standing there with her cane. She ran her fingers over her horse's mane.

She made quite a picture there, dark hand moving through the cream-colored mane of the horse. Her hair was a mess, but it haloed her face. The sun was rising behind her, making the rolling hills sparkle like some kind of fairyland. Her, the reigning queen of it all.

She made a face. "I can tell you're staring at me."

"Maybe I'm staring at the scenery."

"Maybe. But I don't think you are. Why are you staring at me, Tuck?"

"Maybe I think you're pretty, Rach." Which wasn't what he should have said, even if he meant it. Even if her looking pretty was something akin to a punch in the gut. There wasn't room for this—not just because of the current situation—but because of the *always* situation.

"You could kiss me again," she said, very seriously.

She had no idea what it cost him to sound unaffected. "I could, but I don't think that's such a good idea."

"Why not?"

"I can't imagine what Duke would say if I happened to mention it took us so long to help him because I was busy making out with his daughter after spending the night in a tent together."

"After keeping me from being taken by this North Star Group, who are supposedly good guys but condone kidnapping." She huffed out a breath. "I don't understand why you joined them in the first place. Why you worked for people who made you lie."

"Sometimes lies aren't the worst thing in the world."

"I suppose not, but you're not comfortable with them. The weight of that guilt weighs a little heavier on you."

She was right, somehow always seeing right through him. Which meant it seemed honesty was the only option—especially if it kept him from talking about kissing.

"I've been working with them because... I thought I could do something. My father never thought much of me. Not as a threat or as a successor, and mostly I've been grateful for that. But I thought I could do something, like Cody and Jamison did. Like Gage and Brady did. Hell, even Dev stood up to him." He scowled. It hadn't ended well for Dev at all, but he'd tried. "I've done nothing. I thought I could be a piece of what brought my father down, so I did what North Star asked even though it hurt."

She dropped her hand from the horse, used her probing cane to move forward until she was close to him. Too close. "Until they wanted to take me." She looked up at him, her eyes dark except where they were damaged.

To think it had been a man not a mountain lion made it all worse somehow. The end result was the same, but someone had done that to her on purpose. When she'd only been three. All because her father had done the right thing decades ago.

"You didn't deserve to be dragged into this."

"No. I'm not sure you did, either." She reached out, resting her hand on his arm.

He wanted to touch her hair, her face. He wanted to somehow take those scars away from her, which was a stupid want. This was the life they had. He could only make the right decisions now.

Which meant he had to keep his hands off her. "The Sons connect to me. They connect to this. Don't they always?"

"Only if you let them." She moved onto her toes, leaned into him. She brushed her lips across his jaw, though he imagined she'd been going for his cheek or mouth. Still, it rippled through him. No matter how he told himself to block it away.

"Dev'd probably be a better option for all this," he said, voice tight. She'd be good for Dev. All light and hope to his dark and hopeless.

She wrinkled her nose and fell back onto her flat feet. "Dev's even older than *you*. And so grouchy. Dev is better suited for a life of inherent bachelorhood. Grandma Pauline told me once all her uncles were bachelors, and she wouldn't be surprised if the lot of you ended up just like them."

"Did she now. Well, four out of six proved her wrong, didn't they?"

"You won't be a perennial bachelor, Tucker. You're too sweet."

"Gee. Thanks."

"You think that's some kind of slight, but it's a compliment. It's a miracle, actually. The way you were brought up. To have any sweet. I think that's pretty amazing."

She almost made him believe it.

"We should get back. Time isn't on our side. The North Star Group has a lot of skills, technology and reach. We can only avoid them for so long, even with Shay's help."

"All right, but you're not getting out of this so easy."

No, he didn't think he was.

Chapter Fourteen

The ride back to the ranch was quiet. Not tense, exactly. There was a certain comfort to just riding Buttercup, Tucker's strong body behind her. A companionable silence as they both thought through what was next.

She had to believe Cody would know enough about North Star to figure out where they'd be keeping her father or what they'd be doing with him. She had to believe he'd give them the location, Tucker would find Dad, and they'd get him away.

Then what?

Well, the key. Dad would know what the key opened and maybe it would...end everything.

Of course, she thought if it would end everything Dad would have handed it over to North Star, told *them* about the key and the lock. But maybe he just didn't trust them. Maybe he could only trust her.

Rachel wished she had any idea what the key was for. There was nothing to unlock in her dream. There was only darkness and fear. Pain and relief all mixed into one powerful, messy, emotional experience.

Tucker zigzagged through rolling hills. "I'm going

to head up along the north pasture, come down to the stables that way. Maybe the route will remind you of something."

"I can't see, Tucker."

"I know, Rachel," he said with an endless patience that dug at her. "But I'll tell you where we are, what I see. It can't hurt to try to reenact the moment. And if it doesn't jog your memory, all we've done is add a little time I would have probably added anyway to make sure we aren't being followed."

She didn't say anything to that. Going through the dream once already had left her emotionally drained. Then there was the fact Tucker had refused to kiss her.

Though she wasn't convinced it was because he didn't *want* to. She figured there was something more about honor or loving her dad or something twisted up. Because he watched her. She couldn't see and she could *tell* he looked at her in ways he hadn't before.

She could feel the tension in him when she'd touched him. That quick little sigh of breath he'd tried to hide when she'd tried to kiss his mouth and ended up just touching her lips to his jaw.

Maybe she'd missed, but that had been nice, too. The rough whiskers against her lips. There had been an exciting friction in that.

Tucker Wyatt and exciting friction. She might have laughed at the thought of those two things going together, but it just seemed…right, when it never had before.

"We're on the hill outside the north pasture gate. I can see the top of the stable. From here I can see the light. If it was dark and the light was on, it'd be visible this whole stretch."

Even though she didn't want to, she brought to mind her dream. The light. "Where's the highway in relation to where we are?"

"We're facing south. The highway is due east."

"And how far would you be able to see the light in that direction?"

He clicked to the horse, and they moved. "Let's see. If you were headed for the highway, but looking back toward the house or stables…" He trailed off and the horse moved in a gently swaying motion beneath them. "Most of the way. The main gate is just coming into view and I can see the very top of it. Which means if the light was on, I'd be able to see it clearer."

The main gate led to a gravel road, which led to the highway, but it all made sense. The light had gotten smaller as the man had taken her. Like it was slowly being enveloped—or in this case, hidden by distance, direction and hills.

"I think that's where he was taking me."

"On foot, right? So, probably heading for a vehicle. Then the dog saves you."

Rachel brought a hand up to her scars. Her mother had never let her feel much self-pity over the loss of sight, over the scars. Rachel supposed her age helped with that. She didn't remember all that much before, so it wasn't a comparison or ruminating over what she'd lost.

But the dog *saving* her felt like too strong a word. She hadn't been saved fully. She'd lost something that night.

"Tuck…" She swallowed at the sudden emotion clog-

ging her throat. "Why do you think he did it? Lied to
me. To my mom. Made us think something had happened when it hadn't. I know he had to keep his former
life a secret, but... I love him, I do. Nothing changes
that, but I'm having a really hard time not being mad
at him for warping my nightmares to keep this secret."

"Can you imagine how he feels? He did something
right. *One right thing.* He did his job, and he had to leave
his entire life. Then he starts a new one and this right
thing he did not only haunts him, it hurts and perma-
nently injures his daughter. I lied to you, Rach. Because
I thought it would protect you. You and Sarah and...
everyone. I can't imagine his lies were any different."

"But they are. He made me think something completely different happened than actually did. It wasn't
just a lie of omission or hiding something. He *warped*
something I actually experienced."

"What's worse? Believing a random act of Mother
Nature hurt you, or that your father's past was out there,
just waiting? I know what that's like. To know at any
point your past could pop up and ruin your life. I mean,
Grandma Pauline gave us a good life, a good child-
hood once we got out of the Sons. But we always knew
Ace could pop up—hurt us, hurt her. We always knew
Jamison sacrificed eighteen years to get us out of there.
It's a hard, heavy weight."

Rachel didn't know what to say to that. She certainly
couldn't argue with it, and as much as it hurt that her
father had lied to her in such a devious way, she understood that Tucker thought Duke had given her a gift.
Maybe he had. What would life have been like if she'd
always been afraid?

Tucker had come through it okay, but she was realizing he had deeper scars than he ever let on.

Tucker's body went suddenly tense, not just behind her but his arms holding the reins around her. Everything in him was iron and she was encompassed in all that strength. "We're going to get off the horse."

"What? Why? What's happened?"

"There's a man watching us." He'd slowed down Buttercup, but they were still moving. "We have to do this quickly. I'm going to swing you off with me. I'll point you in the right direction. Then you run for the stables. I'll send Buttercup off as a distraction, and I'll run for him. Three different directions, and he'll either focus on the horse or me."

"Is it North Star?"

Tucker was quiet for a long moment. "I want you to run to the stables. Hide in there. That's it."

"But—"

"I need you to do it, Rach. If I need help, I'll yell, okay?"

He wouldn't. She knew he wouldn't. But he couldn't protect himself, or her, if she didn't listen to him. He'd try to play the hero even more than he already was.

If he wasn't answering her question about North Star, well, that was worse. So, she'd run. If she made it to the stables, she could make it to the house. She could call for help. She didn't have her cane, but once she got to the stables she'd know where she was. She'd be able to move around the ranch without it.

As long as she didn't fall on her run to the stables.

"On my count. One, two, three." She let him swing her off the horse, and he helped her land a lot more gracefully than she might have alone. He turned her by the shoulders in the right direction.

Then, she ran.

TUCKER POINTED RACHEL in the right direction, gave Buttercup's reins a flick, then ran himself. There was no cover until he got a lot closer, so he couldn't pretend like he was doing anything but going after the man behind the fence.

Who had a gun. If it was North Star, he wouldn't shoot.

If it wasn't…well…

The sound of the gunshot had him hitting the ground. When nothing hit him, he took a chance to look toward Rachel. She was still running, as was Buttercup, so no one had been struck.

Tucker got back to his feet, went back to running toward the man, but this time in a zigzag pattern. If he could get to the copse of trees that followed the creek, he could use some cover to get closer.

Another gunshot. Tucker didn't dive for the ground this time. Based on the angle of the gun, he was almost certain the man was shooting at him, not the horse or Rachel. He didn't have time to pause and look, though. He had to keep going.

He reached the cluster of trees and pulled his gun out of its holster. Clicking the safety off, he gave himself a moment to hide behind a tree and steady his breathing. His chest burned with effort, his heart pounded with fear and adrenaline.

The creek was nearly dry, but the trees were thick

and old. When the third gunshot went off, it hit a tree way too close to Tucker for comfort.

The fence the man had been crouched behind was due east of the tree Tucker was behind. Still, moving enough to see and shoot would put him at risk.

It was only a gut feeling, not fact, but Tucker sincerely doubted the man was part of North Star. As much as they might prioritize mission over innocent life, they weren't the type to shoot first and ask questions later.

That was more Sons territory. But what would they be doing just lurking around waiting for Tucker and Rachel to appear? How would they know they'd disappeared in the first place?

Unless it was coincidence.

Tucker couldn't mull it over much longer. He had to act so whoever the gunman was didn't get it in his head to go after Rachel.

He slid from one tree to another, working the angles to keep as much distance between him and the shooter as possible.

Another shot went off, but it was way more off target than the last one. Tucker got the glimpse of movement out of the corner of his eye, quickly changed direction to get behind a tree. The gunman was coming toward him just as Tucker tried to move toward the gunman.

He was somewhat hesitant to shoot someone not knowing where they came from or why they were shooting at him, but when the next bullet hit the tree he was standing behind, he figured it was time to do what needed to be done.

Tucker used the tree as cover, listened for the man's movements, then when he thought he had a clear idea of where the man was, stuck his arm out to shoot. He didn't need it to hit, just needed to catch the man off guard.

Immediately after the first shot, he peeked out from behind the tree. The shooter had ducked behind a bush, but as he slowly rose again, gun aimed, Tucker managed to get off a shot first.

The man stumbled backward. Tucker immediately charged. He didn't think he'd hit anything vital, which meant he had to get the gun away from him.

The assailant had lost his gun—a long high-powered looking model—after Tucker had shot him, but he was curling his fingers around the barrel as Tucker approached. He had to lunge to get to it before the man could lift it.

It was narrow timing, but Tucker managed to grab a hold of the handle. They grappled, pulling and jerking like a life-or-death game of tug-of-war. Which gave Tucker the idea to take the dangerous chance of letting the gun go.

Since he'd been pulling hard, the attacker fell backward, the gun winging out of his grasp as Tucker had hoped. Tucker immediately leaped on him.

Even with the gunshot wound, the man fought hard. The bullet must have only glanced his side, even with the amount of blood staining his shirt. Tucker had to fight dirty to win, so he landed the hardest blow he could at the spot with the most blood.

The man howled, grabbing the injured section and rolling away. Tucker managed to pin him, face down, hands pulled behind his back. With pressure on the injured side to keep the man from fighting back, Tucker looked around for something to tie the man's hands.

Which was when he noticed the man was wearing a utility belt. Tucker went through the pockets, found a phone and tossed it as far into the creek bed as he could. Next he discovered a plastic bottle of some kind of clear liquid wrapped in a cloth—he disposed of that in the same way—and then happened upon the perfect answer to his problems. Zip ties. He quickly got them on the man's wrists, then had to fight to get another one around the man's legs.

The man swore and spit and kicked, but there wasn't much he could do with his arms tied behind his back and his legs bound together. Tucker got to his feet and rolled the man over onto his back.

Tucker didn't recognize him—not that he'd recognize every Sons goon. Still, there was something different about him. About the way he dressed and held himself, as though he wasn't quite used to the rough terrain.

Sons members were too local, too used to living in the elements and outside of society. This man didn't even have a knife on him. Just the high-powered gun, some zip ties, the phone and a tiny bottle of something Tucker assumed was a knockout drug.

All the tools for kidnapping.

Tucker's stomach roiled, but he didn't let it show. He sneered down at the man.

"I assume you're with Vianni."

The man spit at him.

Tucker didn't flinch, didn't jump away, as the spit missed him entirely. He kept his sole focus on the assailant. "Who are you here for?"

"Not you."

"I guess I could just leave you here, all tied up, and

never let anyone know." Tucker looked up at the sky. "Might be fall, but sunny day like this? Going to get pretty hot."

"Bud, so much worse is coming for you if you don't let me go. I don't even care *what* you do."

Tucker leaned in, smiled. "Oh, you're going to care."

Chapter Fifteen

The gunshots had Rachel pulling out her phone. She was afraid to speak too loudly, but her phone was having trouble picking up her voice with her shaky whisper. "Call Cody," she finally said with enough force.

"Rachel? Where are you?"

There was a sharp command in his voice that calmed her. Because he would know what to do when she didn't.

"I'm in the stables at our ranch. Tucker saw someone and went after them. There's been gunshots. I know you're in Bonesteel—"

"I'm going to get off the line and call Brady. He's right next door."

"No! Listen. I mean, you can call Brady, but you have to know North Star is mixed up in this somehow. They have Dad. Tucker was working for them. Then this woman helped us—helped *me* not get taken by North Star and… I don't understand what's going on."

There was a brief pause. "I'm calling Brady to help Tuck. As for North Star…" Another pause that had Rachel holding her breath. "The woman? Was her name Shay?"

"Yes."

"All right. You stay put. I'll get back to you on the North Star thing." The connection clicked off and Rachel slipped her phone back into her pocket. Sure, Brady could maybe take care of things, but he was hurt, too. Likely Dev was out in the pasture somewhere with Sarah.

Would they have heard the gunshots? Surely, they'd have had to. Wouldn't they come running? Call their own reinforcements?

She couldn't just stand here, though. Tuck could have been the one shot.

She heard the door creak open and she pressed herself against the corner.

"Rach?"

"Tuck." She raced forward too quickly and tripped, but arms grabbed her before she could fall face-first. She was too relieved he was okay to be embarrassed. She held on to him as he helped her back to her feet. "You're okay."

"Yeah. We have to get out of here."

"No, it's okay. I phoned Cody. He was calling Brady and figuring out the North Star thing and—"

"What did you do that for?" he demanded, his voice sharp and unforgiving. He released her and she stood in the middle of the stable, feeling unaccountably chastened.

"What do you mean, what did I do that for? A man was out there. I heard gunshots. What was I supposed to do?"

"Just hide here like I told you to."

"You don't get to boss me around, Tuck. Certainly

not when there are *guns* going off. We agreed to talk
to Cody about—"

"About where your dad might be. Not drag my brothers into a lethal situation."

"Why not? You got dragged into Brady's thing.
Brady was dragged into Felicity's. It's what we do. Get
dragged into each other's dangerous run-ins. And it always goes a little better with help, doesn't it?"

He was silent.

"Besides, it's too late. Cody is calling Brady and he's
going to look into the North Star thing. He knows Shay."

"Well, he used to work for them."

"But he knew who she was even before I said her
name."

"Sit tight," Tucker said, like he was about to leave her
alone again. *Oh, no. Not going to happen.* She lunged
forward and managed to grab his shirt.

"You will stop this right now." He tried to tug her
hand off his shirt, but she only held on tighter. "I don't
know what the damn key unlocks, Tucker. I don't understand anything Dad said in that letter. Now there's
a man after us. Don't brush me off. Don't tell me to sit
tight, and don't act like a child because we need help. I
can't even do the *one thing* Dad seems to think I can."
Emotion rose up in her throat, making her words squeak
when it was the last thing she wanted. "If we need help,
it's because of me. Not you."

"Rach." Instead of tugging her hand away again, he
drew her close and smoothed a hand over her hair.
"None of this is your fault."

Wouldn't that be nice? She leaned into Tucker, wondering if she'd ever fully believe that when the letter had

said she was the key. It helped that he'd said it, though. That he'd take the time to give her a hug.

Someone cleared their throat from over by the door. "Uh, sorry to interrupt but I was just wondering if I should ask why there's a guy in zip ties lying next to the creek?" Dev said.

"What are you doing here?" Tucker demanded, releasing her abruptly.

"What am I doing here? You know how sound travels, right? Gunshots ring out while I'm tending to my cattle, and I'm left figuring out who the hell is shooting things. I sent Sarah over to Grandma's to round up help."

"Tucker's being very childish about help."

Dev made a sound that *might* have been a laugh, if he wasn't perpetually grumpy Dev who almost never laughed. At least not without a sarcastic edge. "Yeah, we Wyatts get that way sometimes. Should I leave the guy where he is?"

"Yes," Tucker said.

"And there aren't others?"

"Not yet."

"Who is he?" Rachel demanded.

There was a pause and Rachel didn't have to see to know *something* passed between brothers.

"I guess I'll go head over and stop Sarah and Brady and whoever else off at the pass."

"Have Brady call local police—ones he'd trust to keep it as quiet as possible—to pick up the guy."

Dev didn't say anything to that, but she heard him retreating so she assumed it was some kind of assent.

"What exactly are we going to do?"

"We're going to follow the original plan. Sort of. The next step is getting Cody to see what he might be able to tell us about North Star and Duke, but I want to keep the rest of the family out of it as much as we can. Not because I need to do this on my own, but because the more people we drag into this, the more targets they have. The wider it gets, the harder it is to fight."

She supposed that made sense. A gunman had been waiting on the ranch. What if Sarah had happened to drive by on her way to town? Or what if Dev had come that way instead of across the pasture where Knight land butted up against Reaves land?

If she and Tucker went off on their own, maybe they'd be able to keep the focus on them, not their families.

"So, we're heading to Bonesteel on Buttercup?"

"Not exactly. The guy has to have a car around here somewhere. And it just so happens, I grabbed his keys."

TUCKER LED RACHEL toward the front gate. He imagined Vianni's man had hidden the car somewhere on the gravel road. There weren't very many places to hide a car, so it should be easy enough to find.

"It still doesn't make sense," Rachel said, one arm hooked with his as he helped her walk. Though this ground was a little more familiar than not, she didn't spend a lot of time walking this far past the main buildings.

"What doesn't?"

"Dad's note. I've gone over and over my dream. There's never been anything about a key. Or a lock. Not in old dreams and not in the new ones. Dad wouldn't even know about the new ones. I never mentioned it to anyone until you. In fact, the more I think about it, the more I don't think he knew I still had the nightmares. I didn't tell him. I didn't wake up screaming. For all he knew, they went away."

It made Tucker's chest ache that she'd continued to be tormented by the dreams and hadn't told Duke, or anyone else. Just dealt with them. As they slowly morphed into something real.

"What else could it be?"

She shook her head as they walked. "I don't know, but we've only focused on my dream. Maybe it's something else..."

"Okay, so the note said you know the key and the lock. We've been focusing on the key, since we found that. Maybe we should think about locks. Are there any locks in your dream?"

She shook her head. "No keys. No locks. Nothing even symbolic of a key or a lock."

"So let's think about Duke. Do you remember anything about keys and locks you specifically associate with him?"

They reached the gate and Tucker looked down the gravel lane. He wanted to get out of here before the police arrived. Avoid answering any questions they'd have so he and Rachel could move on to the next step.

He wasn't looking forward to bringing Cody into this, but there didn't seem to be another option. Brady was involved now. Dev as well, to an extent.

It ate at him that he'd failed so spectacularly at keeping them out of it. He'd wanted to let them heal and protect their families and instead...

"Wait." Rachel stopped abruptly. "Key and lock. It wouldn't have to be…literal, would it?"

"I mean, we have a key. That's pretty literal."

"Or it's not. It's not about the dream. It's not about the key. It's about Dad. Take me to the cemetery."

"I'm sorry…*what*?"

"The cemetery. Where Mom's buried. It's not far from here. Dad always said… Mom was the key to his lock. Like, always. It was one of his favorite sayings before she died. He doesn't say it much anymore. But he used to. Key and lock."

"Okay," Tucker said gently. "But…"

"Maybe it's nothing. I know it sounds crazy. But Dad wrote that letter and it says, *Rachel knows the key and the lock*. Well, if he's the lock—she's the key."

Tucker couldn't imagine what might be hiding at the cemetery, let alone at Eva Knight's grave, but it was hard to refuse her request. Even knowing it was beyond a long shot.

"We have to find the car first." He opened the gate and led Rachel through. The Knight ranch was the last turn off on the gravel road. If Tucker had been trying to hide a car, he'd have gone past the gate, then tried to hide the car in a ditch.

They walked down the side, Tucker keeping an eye and ear out for any cars that might be coming.

Just as he'd predicted, he found the car just a ways down, half in a ditch. You'd only see it if you passed the gate and likely their little spy had been counting on no one going that far.

Tucker helped Rachel into the car, then slid into the driver's seat himself, adjusting the seat. It smelled a little too much like cigarettes and cheap cologne, so he rolled down the windows.

Keeping his eye out for a police cruiser, he took the backroads to the cemetery where Eva Knight was buried. The parking lot was empty, which was good. "We can't spend too much time here."

"I know. I just need to… I don't know. If she's the key…"

"I get it." He thought it was too symbolic and metaphorical, but she had to look. Hell, even he had to look or he'd wonder if he'd missed something. He got out of the car, then went over to Rachel's side and helped her out, leading her through the archway of the cemetery entrance.

He didn't have to lead her any farther than that. She'd clearly been here plenty, since she walked around the other graves with unerring accuracy, before stopping in front of her mother's.

Eva Knight. Loving wife and mother to all her girls. 1970–2006.

She'd been more than that little epitaph. She'd been the only calm, gentle presence across the Knight and Wyatt ranches. Until Rachel had taken on that mantle, and maybe Tucker had tried to be some of that as much as he could.

"I miss her," Rachel said softly.

"Me too." Missed her, and felt suddenly ashamed he'd let Rachel get so involved in this. Eva would have expected him to keep her safe. Keep *all* the girls safe. "She'd want you to be safe. At home."

"No. No, she wouldn't." Rachel smiled at him, and though there were tears in her eyes, they didn't fall.

"She wanted everyone to treat me like an equal. Even if it hadn't been for the blindness, I was their only biological daughter and she never wanted the other girls to feel less. She was careful. So careful to treat me like everyone else. To give me the same responsibilities and expectations. Honestly, I think that's why... Well, Dad and Sarah, they kind of treat me like a maid. They don't mean to. It's just, I was always supposed to pull my weight. Mom wanted me on equal footing." She took a deep shaky breath. "I *am* on equal footing. Maybe you have the eyes and the police skills, but I know the key and the lock. What do you see?"

"Just the grave. Just the grass around it. There are some flowers in the holder."

"Fresh?"

"Yeah, they're drooping a bit. Maybe been here a few days, but fresh enough."

"So, Dad's been here recently. Before he left."

"It could have been one of your sisters."

She shook her head. "No. They always tell me if they're going so I can go, too. It had to be Dad. And it was in the last few days. The key *has* to be here."

Tucker didn't remind her that technically they had a key, and they were essentially just searching for a lock. Still, he would do it for her because... Well, his leads were nonexistent. He went around the grave, looking for anything. He even pulled out the flowers and looked into the water holder. He laid his hands over the stone, and it was only as he moved his palm over the side of the grave that he felt something odd under his foot.

Unsure, he stood. "Wait. This is..." Tucker toed the grass with his boot. A whole section of it moved, like a square of sod had been placed down over dirt. Coincidence, no doubt. Still he let go of Rachel and crouched down. He pulled up the square of sod. Underneath was freshly unpacked dirt. Tucker poked his finger into it. Not far beneath the crumbles of dirt was something hard.

"What is it?" Rachel demanded.

He began to dig in earnest. It was just a tiny metal tube, but it had a lid and Tucker screwed it off. He pulled out a slip of paper. It only had numbers on it, but it was clear what they were. "I found a piece of paper buried in the ground. There are numbers on it. It's a combination. Like to a safe."

"The only safe I know of is…"

"Grandma Pauline's," they finished together.

Chapter Sixteen

They drove to Reaves ranch in silence. Rachel felt a little raw as she always did after visiting her mother's grave. She'd only been seven when Mom had died, but she had worked so hard to live up to that memory that it felt like her mom had been around longer.

Which was nice.

It was also strange that Tucker had said Eva would have expected him to keep her safe, and suddenly she understood her place in her family a little better. Mom had done her best to make her an equal for two very different reasons—biology and her blindness—and both had worked. She was an independent, equal individual in her family.

If she'd felt trapped before this all started, or scared her future was never going to change, maybe that was just normal adulthood stuff—not the result of her blindness.

"What are we going to do?" Tucker muttered. "Just barge in and demand Grandma Pauline let us open her safe?"

Rachel didn't think he was actually asking her, but she answered anyway. "She knows something, Tuck. If this leads to *her* safe, Dad certainly didn't hide it there without her knowing."

She could sense his frustration. She wasn't sure exactly what it was toward, so she reached over and rested her hand on his arm. It was tense, and she imagined he was gripping the steering wheel hard enough to break it.

"If Grandma hid something about this, you should be angry with her," he told her.

"I'll save my anger for when I know what actually happened. You're only angry because you're scared."

"Scared?" he demanded.

"Your brothers can take care of themselves, even if they're injured or have kids to protect. You have a certain comfort in knowing they're all law enforcement and know how to deal with these issues. But your grandmother?"

"Raised the six of us, put the fear of God into Ace so he never came after her, and taught us all how to shoot way better than any law enforcement training. I'm not scared for her."

Rachel wasn't so sure. Sometimes you could know someone was strong and good, like her father, and still worry something had changed. Or something had been there that you'd never known.

She sighed as Tucker slowed the car. "How are we going to play this?"

"We're going to go in and tell her we're going to open the safe."

"You've met your grandmother, right? You go in there demanding things, she's going to knock you out with that wooden spoon."

Tucker didn't say anything to that, so she opened the car door and slid out. "You let me handle it," she said decisively. She closed the car door and started striding for the house. Tucker hadn't parked in his normal spot, so once she reached the house she had to feel around for the door.

She didn't knock. She stepped inside, and she could hear Tucker striding quickly behind her as if he meant to beat her to the house and take over.

No. Not on this. "Grandma Pauline?"

"What on earth are you doing here?" Pauline demanded.

Rachel could make out her form over by the sink or oven. "We need to get into the safe."

Tucker closed the door behind her, and she could feel him standing next to her. She couldn't see Grandma Pauline's expression, but she could feel the hesitation in the silence.

Rachel nodded toward Tucker. "We have the combination. Because Dad gave us a clue. He wants us to get into the safe."

Grandma Pauline sighed. "All right, then. Follow me."

"That wasn't exactly asking nicely," Tucker muttered into her ear. He took her arm as if he meant to lead her, and though she didn't need it in this house, she didn't mind her arm in his hand.

"I can say things like that to her. *You* can't," Rachel whispered back as Grandma Pauline led them down into the basement.

Rachel had to trust Grandma Pauline and Tucker to open the safe. To tell her what was inside. She knew from hearing everyone talk about it that it was a giant safe. The boys used to joke it was where Grandma Pauline hid dead bodies.

Rachel shuddered at the thought.

"Bottom shelf there. That's Duke's," Grandma Pauline said in her no-nonsense way.

Tucker let go of her elbow. There was the sound of shuffling and scraping. "It's another safe," Tucker said, sounding wholly baffled. "Not small, either. What on earth is happening here?"

"Is it another combination?"

"No. This one has a lock. I'm assuming that's what the key you found is for."

"Well, open it," she urged. Surely this safe wouldn't lead to yet another. *Surely* this was the last step.

Rachel had to wait more interminable seconds. She could hear Tucker fitting the key into the hole on the lock. The click. A squeak as the safe opened.

Tucker swore. Not angrily but more shock. More... fear. Rachel even heard Grandma Pauline's sharp inhale of surprise.

"What is it?" Rachel demanded when no one spoke.

"Rachel..."

"Tell me," she insisted. "*Now.*"

Tucker sighed. "It looks like... It looks like the knife you described in your dream. And there's...there's old blood on it."

Rachel couldn't even make sense of that. "I don't understand."

"He kept the weapon that injured you. Kept it locked away." There was a ribbon of hurt in Tucker's voice that finally made the words sink in.

Except, how…

"He kept the knife. That hurt me. On purpose."

"You knew," Tucker accused, and Rachel understood he was talking to Grandma Pauline.

"No. Not in the way you think," Grandma Pauline replied. Though she didn't betray any emotion, she didn't speak with her usual verve. "After the accident, Duke was distraught. He needed… Well, he felt alone. Guilty. Responsible. Now, you've both dealt with the Sons enough to know that it wasn't his fault. It was those awful people's fault."

It was an admonition disguised as fact—Grandma Pauline's specialty. It didn't make Rachel feel any better about anything, though.

"He asked me to hide something for him and not to ask questions. I didn't. He called it insurance. That's all I know about it. Timing-wise, I knew it connected to what happened to Rachel, but not how or what."

"It doesn't make sense. If he had what hurt me, he would have taken it to the police. He would have used it." She turned toward Tucker's form. "Why wouldn't he have used what he could to put them in jail with this when it happened?"

"I don't know, Rach."

He sounded immeasurably sad, which of course made her feel worse. Dad had kept a weapon that had blinded her at the age of three. Locked it up like he was protecting the people who'd hurt her.

"I know it's hard, but let's not jump to conclusions."

"Not jump to conclusions?" Rachel couldn't tell where Grandma Pauline was standing in the dark with her own heart beating so loud in her ears. "I was blinded

by a man with that knife when I was *three years old*. I
might have been killed. I'll jump to every damn conclusion I want."

And because all she wanted to do was cry, she
marched back the way she'd come and up the stairs.

"WELL, DON'T JUST stand there, boy. Go follow her."

"Grandma…" Tucker couldn't wrap his head around
it. He didn't know how this could have gotten so much
worse. "This is…"

"You don't know *what* it is. And before you get all
high and mighty on me, I don't know what it is, either.
I took the safe and put it in my own because a friend
asked me to. I didn't ask any questions, because I'd
been around enough to understand some things are better left alone."

"He made her believe—and all of us believe—she'd
been mauled by an animal."

"Any person who'd use that knife on a child *is* an
animal. That's the truth of it. You don't know Duke's
truth or what he's done or escaped or how this might
have been him protecting her. Don't you think I've done
some shady things to protect you and your brothers?"

It was a horrible thought. She'd raised them to do
what was right. To uphold the law after watching their
father break it, try to destroy it for the entirety of their
childhoods. And she was admitting to *shady* things to
keep them safe.

"Rachel's hurting. She feels betrayed. Fair enough.
But you're protecting her, which means you've got to
think beyond her hurt. Duke's a good man. You know
it and I know it."

"Maybe he's not as good as we think he is."

"Or maybe, good isn't as simple as you want it to be. Now, go after her."

Tucker did as he was told, in part because it was habit and in part because he was worried what Rachel would do next. *He* knew what it was like to feel like you could never understand or believe in your father, but she never had.

She wasn't in the kitchen and the door was ajar, so he stepped outside. She was pacing the yard. He had a feeling that constant movement was what kept her from losing the battle with tears.

"We need to keep moving. Stay on plan."

She shook her head. "The plan? To save him from those people when he…" She just kept shaking her head as if she could negate the truth. "He shouldn't have that. I can't think of one good reason he'd have it locked up."

"Then let's go find out the reason," Tucker said gently. "We find your father. We have our answers."

"What if the answers are… What if he's…"

She couldn't get the words out, so he supplied them for her. "Not the man you thought he was?"

Her lips trembled, but she gave a sharp nod.

"Nothing he's done changes two very simple facts. One, we know he helped bring down dirty cops. Whatever he's done, he fought for the right thing and probably out of a need to protect his family. Two, he's been a great father and a good man for as long as I've known him. If he made a mistake, it might have been for the right reasons. Or maybe it's forgivable. Or maybe, it wasn't a mistake at all. We don't know until we talk to

412   *Badlands Beware*

him." He took her by the shoulders, trying to give her a certainty he didn't fully believe. "He gave you the clue. You figured it out. No matter what…we have to see this through. If only so you can have some answers."

"Answers. What possible answer could make this not awful?"

"I don't know. But that doesn't mean there isn't one."

She leaned into him. They didn't have the time, and yet he couldn't rush her. Not when she was grappling with what he knew too well was… He hated his father. Always had. Yet even with all that hate, it was complicated knowing he was related to someone so awful.

Duke wasn't awful. Grandma had that right. Whatever mistake he might have made, it wouldn't have been done out of cruelty. Tucker had to believe that, and with answers, they'd all be able to move forward.

"Come on. Let's head over to Bonesteel. We'll meet with Cody and come up with a plan to get to Duke. He wanted us to find this, Rach. Maybe it's useful. Important."

"Should we leave it with Grandma Pauline if it's so important?"

"She'll keep it safe. That's why it's here in the first place."

"Tucker…" She pulled away, and tilted her head toward him. Her eyebrows drew together and she opened her mouth but didn't say anything, as if she was struggling to come up with the words.

She needed reassurance, and Tucker didn't feel very sure, but he wanted to give that to her. Wanted her to be able to believe in Duke and trust that they were doing the right thing trying to save him from North Star, the Viannis *and* the Sons. "It'll be okay. I'm not saying it will be easy, but it'll be okay. I know it."

It had to be.

Chapter Seventeen

Tucker had to lead Rachel to Cody and Nina's door. Rachel had been to their house in Bonesteel a few times, but most family get-togethers were at one of the ranches. She didn't know her way around very many other places.

Tucker had explained he was parking around back, so she knew she was being led to the back door, which opened into a kitchen. Since it was the middle of the day, Nina was probably teaching her seven-year-old Brianna and Liza's half sister, the just-turned-five Gigi. Her and Liza traded off homeschool-teaching duties.

The door squeaked open. Immediately Nina went, "Oh," as if she knew exactly what was going on.

Then Rachel was quickly being ushered inside and greeted by her enthusiastic niece.

"Aunt Rachel! I didn't know you were coming over. Are you good at adding?"

"Brianna," Nina said in that warning tone moms always seemed to have. "No having Rachel or Tuck do your math while I go get your father."

"Where's Gigi?" Rachel asked as she heard Nina retreat.

"She's sick. I heard Aunt Liza say she threw up *everywhere*," Brianna said with some glee. "If you had three hundred and twenty-four...um, apples. And then Uncle Tuck brought you fifty-seven more—"

"Brianna!" Nina yelled from somewhere deeper in the house.

Brianna humphed. "Why are you guys visiting in the middle of the day?" Brianna seemed to suddenly realize it was odd timing. "Is there trouble again?"

Poor girl. She was way too intimately acquainted with trouble. Rachel forced a reassuring smile. "Just a little, but it's a problem for Uncle Tuck and me. Nothing for you to worry about."

"You need Daddy's help?"

"Only for a few minutes," Tucker interjected. "He won't even have to leave home."

Brianna sighed with some relief. "So are you guys going to get married then?"

Tucker seemed to choke on his own spit, and Rachel found herself utterly speechless.

"What now?" Tuck finally managed, though his voice sounded croaky at best.

"Well, when Mommy and Daddy were in trouble, they ended up getting married. And same with Aunt Liza and Uncle Jamison. Then Uncle Gage and Aunt Felicity are getting married and having a baby. Uncle Brady and Aunt Cecilia aren't getting married yet, but I heard Mom say that it was *inevitable*. Now you two are in trouble. So..."

"No, sweetheart, that's not...how it works...exactly." Tucker sounded so pained it was almost funny.

There was the sound of footsteps and low murmurs.

Then Nina's voice. "Get your math book, Bri. We'll go finish up in the living room."

There was a long suffering sigh and the shuffle of books, papers and feet.

"Say goodbye to your aunt and uncle."

"Aren't they going to stay for dinner? We could order pizza." Nina must have given her a significant mom look because Brianna groaned and stomped away.

Rachel felt Nina's slim hand on her arm. "I'm sure Cody and Tucker can take care of whatever this is."

Rachel slid her arm away. "Don't do that to me. You didn't let Cody and Jamison handle your thing."

"Rach, I'm just saying… You're not a part of this. You could go home and—"

"I *am* a part of this. I'm the only reason we've gotten this far. Isn't that right, Tucker?"

There was a hesitation, like he might refute her so Nina could whisk her away and keep her safe. But there was no safety here. Whether she helped get Dad away from North Star or these other groups or not, Dad had still lied to her—to all of them.

She wanted to believe there was a reason for it. Maybe she had to do this so she could actually…see it. If someone just told her, even Dad, that it was for her own good…

She'd never be able to forgive him.

"Rachel's right," Tucker finally said. "We wouldn't be this far without her. If we're going to get Duke away from North Star—"

"Woah, woah, woah," Cody's voice interrupted Tucker. "What makes you think you're getting *anyone* away from North Star?"

"They tried to kidnap me," Rachel said.

"Rach, if they tried, you'd be kidnapped."

"No, she's right," Tucker told him. "They sent this woman named Shay to take her. They must have been listening in somehow and knew she was getting clues about everything from her dreams. Shay and I fought—"

"No offense, Tuck, but Shay'd take you down in a heartbeat."

"You know her that well?"

There was a pause. "I worked with her quite a bit. She's helped me out of a few jams."

"I have to go help Bri," Nina said softly. "Just…be careful. Both of you." Rachel felt arms wrap around her and squeeze, then heard the sounds of Nina exiting the room.

"I pointed out to Shay that kidnapping an innocent bystander wasn't necessary," Tucker said. "That I wouldn't let anyone put a mission above her life. Eventually, she agreed with me."

"So, she let you go."

"Yeah. Because she knew I was right. She knew that what North Star has been doing isn't what I signed up for."

"What *you* signed up for?"

Tucker huffed out a breath. "What? You don't believe they'd tap me for some help? I'm not North Star material?"

"I didn't say that," Cody said evenly.

Rachel wanted to defend Tucker, but it wouldn't change the fact he felt slighted by his baby brother. Still, she understood a little too well what it was like to be overlooked. Underestimated. To not fully realize it until the crap hit the fan.

I'm sure Cody and Tucker can take care of whatever this is. Nina meant well, because she loved her. Because they were sisters. But it still hurt.

Silence remained. Tucker and Cody were likely having some nonverbal conversation she'd never be privy to.

Rachel could be mad about that, and pout, or she could take matters into her own hands. "After we ran from Shay, after she let us, Dad sent us a note, through Shay. It led us to the weapon that did this to me." She pointed at her face. "We could hand that over to North Star, but what would they do with it?"

Cody didn't answer for a few seconds. "I couldn't say."

"But you know as well as I do that it wouldn't be used to save my dad or keep me safe. It would be used to take someone down."

"Taking those people down *would* be keeping you safe."

"Would it? Because Ace is in jail. So is Elijah and Andy Jay and all the Sons members who've come after you all this year. They're all in *jail*. Am I safe, Cody? Are you?"

Cody didn't have anything to say to that, either.

"Dad sent me this note in secret. He wanted me to get that evidence without North Star knowing. What does that tell you about what North Star is doing? Shay let us go and she *works* for North Star."

"Look, you avoided getting kidnapped because Shay let you. Maybe you're right and North Star can get a little…people blind. Regardless, you can't get into North Star and get Duke out. You just can't. They're too well organized."

"You know where he's being held?" Tucker asked.

"I have an idea. You wouldn't make it within fifty yards without them picking you up. Then they'd have Rachel like they wanted in the first place. And you're right, mission comes first. It has to or they can't do what they do."

"I don't care what they do, Cody. I care about my father. I care about the fact someone did this to me when I was *three*, and I won't let them do anything else to my family. Maybe I'm not a detective or a secret operative, but I sure as hell am in the middle of this thing."

"She's right," Tucker said softly. "She remembers things. She knows Duke. North Star wanted to kidnap her. She's smack dab in the middle of this."

"Why are you, Tuck?"

"Because North Star asked me to be. But they've taken a wrong turn, and I won't let that hurt Duke. They asked me to keep his daughters safe—so that's what I'm going to do."

"If I tell you where Duke probably is, like I said, it's not going to go well. I can't tell you how to sneak in. They'll know you're coming a mile away. I can't help you get in there. I'm not part of North Star anymore, and as much as I know, they know I know it. They'd have protections against it if they wanted to keep me— or someone related to me—out."

"You know how to get in touch with Shay."

When Cody spoke, his voice was firm. "I won't get her kicked out."

"She didn't sound like she was in it for the long run," Rachel said. "She got us the note. Surely you can get in touch with her and give her the option of helping us."

"That won't be necessary."

It was a woman's voice, and Rachel could only assume it was Shay herself.

"So, you'll help us?" Rachel demanded.

"Yeah, but you're not going to like how."

TUCKER HAD TO blink to make sure that was indeed Shay entering the room from where Nina and Brianna had disappeared earlier. "How…"

"I figured you'd hit up Cody once you figured out Duke's note. The weapon that did that, huh?" Shay said, nodding toward Rachel's face.

Tucker glared at Cody. "You didn't tell me she was there," he gritted out.

"He didn't know," Shay said with a grin. "Nina's the one who gave me the heads-up."

"I never should have let you two become friends," Cody muttered. "You'll get kicked out. This would be the last straw."

"I've been saying that for months now. Apparently, Granger loves me. Also, you didn't *let* me become friends with your wife."

"What aren't we going to like?" Tucker demanded, wanting to keep the focus on what needed to be done.

"My brother do that?" Cody asked with some surprise as he noticed Shay's bruised cheek.

Shay shook her head. "He wouldn't hit a woman," she said as if that was a *bad* thing. "Rachel did it."

Cody let out a low whistle. "Nice work, Rach."

"Can we focus?" Tucker demanded.

"So, all you Wyatts are wound that tight, eh?" Shay said to Cody, earning a frown from both Wyatts in question. "Duke's not going to talk to me. Even if I said I was in cahoots with you. Why do you think that letter I smuggled out was in code? We need to get Rachel to him."

"Or we need to get Duke to Rachel."

Shay shook her head. She was still dressed all in black, but no mask or hat. Her blond hair was pulled back in a tight ponytail and she stood there, legs spread, arms folded across her chest like some kind of special ops soldier.

In a way, Tucker supposed she was.

"We're not getting Duke out of there. It's not possible unless they're distracted by something they need more than Duke's knowledge of the Viannis and the Sons." Shay looked meaningfully at Rachel.

Even though it didn't change what she'd said, Tucker moved in between Shay and Rachel. "No."

"Don't say no," Rachel told him. "Not *for* me. You'll tell me what you mean, and *I'll* say no if I see fit."

"She wants to use you as bait," Tucker said disgustedly.

"And what's wrong with that?" Rachel returned.

He, of course, couldn't answer that. What he thought was wrong with that wouldn't be appreciated.

"How would we do it?" Rachel asked calmly.

Tucker didn't know how she could be calm. Maybe because she hadn't actually seen that knife that had been used to take away her eyesight, sitting there grotesquely in a box. Maybe because she didn't fully grasp what the Sons could do on their own, let alone with another dangerous group of criminals.

Or maybe she was calm because she lived that night over and over again in her dreams and she had no control over that. This…she felt like she could act on.

How could he not support that?

"I take you to headquarters," Shay began. "I'll say I tracked you down and convinced you to ditch Tucker. You'll say you want to help your father in whatever way you can. Which is all true."

"Except it's sending her into the lion's den."

"Only one, and the less dangerous of the three," Shay returned. "While they're focused on getting information from Rachel, it'll give me a chance to slip out and grab Tucker. We'll work together to get Duke out."

"Except Rachel is stuck in there then."

"It might not matter," Rachel said. "Depending on what the full truth is."

"No, it'll matter," Shay corrected. "The whole point of me going against the group I've dedicated six years of my life to is to help keep you and your father from being caught in a crossfire that's got nothing to do with you, and only a little to do with your father. Tucker will take Duke. I'll go back in and get Rachel."

"It'll be your last hurrah. You take people out of North Star custody, no amount of Granger liking you keeps you in North Star," Cody said gravely.

"I'm okay with that. I wasn't at first. But this whole thing… It's been different since you left, Cody. Since Ace has been in jail. It should have made it easier, but we're going at it harder and caring less and less who gets caught in the middle. I won't be party to it any longer."

"All right, what do you need from me?" Cody asked.

Cody and Shay discussed some technical stuff to do with the North Star security systems and Tucker turned to Rachel. She had her chin set stubbornly. It was stupid to try to convince her to back out of this, but…

"You're risking your life. I want you to understand that."

"Duke already risked it," Rachel replied. "Risked Sarah and me, all of us. Didn't he? By going with them."

"North Star brought me in because he wanted you protected. I was there to make sure you weren't brought into the thick of things."

"Maybe, but we're here. In the thick of things. I won't be swept into a corner. Maybe what we found in the safe hurts my feelings. It…hurts. Even if my father has a good reason, to know that's there is painful. But you were the one who told me it doesn't change the fact he's a good man who's always been a good father. He loved my mother. He loved me and my sisters. He raised us when she died, and all the while…" She blew out a breath. "You've all lived with terrible things. Now, I'm living with mine. I won't back down. You wouldn't. None of my sisters would. None of your brothers would, and I know my father wouldn't. So. Why should you expect me to?"

"It's not that I expect you to, Rach. It's that I care about you and I want you to be safe." Which he would have said before kissing her. Of course, he cared about her—about all the Knights. But it felt heavier in his chest, even in this kitchen with his brother and a North Star operative a few feet away.

She reached out and he took her hand. She squeezed

it and smiled at him. "We're all doing this because we care about each other."

Which wasn't exactly what he'd meant or felt. He'd meant *her* in a very uncomfortably specific way.

"It's a risk, but it's not like I'm walking into Sons territory. I'm walking into a group who wants to take down two very bad groups of people. It's the lowest risk I could take. You're taking a bigger one trying to get Dad out." Her hand slid up his arm, shoulder, until her palm cupped his cheek. "So, we both have to support each other taking risks to end all this danger. I'd like to have my life back. I'm sorry I ever wanted something different. It was perfectly nice. Well, mostly." Her thumb moved across his jaw, then she dropped her hand as if she remembered there were other people in the room.

"We should move immediately, right?" she asked.

"Right," Shay agreed. She gave Tucker a considering look but crossed to Rachel. "I'm going to give you a panic button of sorts. It's tiny and easy to lose, so I'm going to sew it into the sleeve of your shirt. Okay?"

Rachel nodded and held out her arm to Shay. Shay worked on sewing the tiny button into the inside of Rachel's sleeve, and Tucker was not at all surprised his brother pulled him away from Rachel and into the hallway.

"It's not really going to go down like this."

"What isn't?" Tucker muttered.

"You and Rachel? Don't think I didn't notice that little moment. That's five for five."

Tucker shrugged uncomfortably. "It's not like that... exactly."

"Yeah, *exactly.*" Then Cody laughed. Loud and hard. "Jesus. Dev and Sarah."

"Not in a million years," Tucker said, managing a small laugh of his own. "They'd eat each other alive first."

Cody shook his head. "Don't bet against it."

Chapter Eighteen

Rachel did her best not to act nervous. She knew Tucker didn't approve of this plan, but he was going through with it because of her.

So she had to be brave. She had to be sure. Too bad she was wholly terrified.

Shay had sewn a *panic button* into her shirt, instructing her that it had to be pressed three times to send a signal. Which would go to Cody, who would no doubt send the whole Wyatt clan after her.

After *her*, because she was going to be the distraction. The bait. She was going to walk into North Star and demand to see her father.

Shay warned her they wouldn't let that happen. That they'd likely put her in an interrogation room, holding the carrot of seeing her father over her head until she answered all their questions.

She was supposed to refuse. Give them bits and pieces to keep their attention, but mostly be difficult, and lie if necessary. So that all eyes were on her while Shay and Tucker snuck in to get Duke out.

It was a lot of pressure, and while her family treated

her as an equal more often than not, no one had actually ever put *pressure* on her. The hardest thing she'd ever done up to this point was demand to teach art classes at the rez. There had been some pressure to succeed so no one pitied her for failing, but not like this.

"Okay, you'll drop us here," Shay instructed Tucker.

The car came to a halt. Rachel was seated in the back. She hadn't realized until this moment she was going to have to trust Shay implicitly, not just to be telling the truth but to guide her through a completely unknown setting.

When the door next to her opened, Rachel had to fight the desire to lean away. To refuse to get out. She stepped into the autumn afternoon instead.

"Don't be afraid to speak up if I'm walking too fast or something. Better to get there in one piece than worry about hurting my feelings or whatever."

The no-nonsense way Shay took her arm and said those words had Rachel's shoulders relaxing. Maybe it was scary, but at least Shay wasn't going to be all weird about her being blind.

"Let me talk to her for a minute," Tucker said briskly.

"All right," Shay said. She let Rachel's arm go and Tuck's hands closed over her shoulders. He gave them a squeeze.

"You be smart. Take care of yourself first. I couldn't…" He let out a ragged breath. "I don't want you hurt, Rach."

"Tuck…" She didn't know what to say. There wasn't time to say anything. So, she could only give him what he'd given her. "I don't want you hurt, either."

"Then we'll stick to the plan, and everything will be okay."

"You don't actually believe that," she said, both because she didn't and because she could hear it in his voice that he didn't, either. "We'll stick to the plan, and hope for the best. And if the best blows up in our face, we'll just have to fight like hell."

He chuckled softly. "Yeah, you got that right."

Then, before she could say anything else, he kissed her. It wasn't sweet or light. It was firm, a little fierce and had her heart beating for an entirely new reason aside from fear. "Stay safe, Rach."

He released her, and she was passed off to Shay. It was disorienting for a lot of reasons, but the whole being shuttled between people in foreign settings certainly undercut the happy buzz of that kiss.

"They all like that?" Shay asked, leading her forward.

"Like what?"

"Like…gentlemen, but not wimps about it. Think of women as equals, and aren't too keen on using them as a punching bag. Kiss like that and then walk away to save your butt—while you're also busy saving your own butt."

Rachel had to smile. "Pretty much."

Shay didn't say anything else to that, just kept leading Rachel forward.

"Can you describe it to me? Give me some kind of idea of where they're going to take me and how to get out?"

"Good idea." Shay explained that it looked like a hunting cabin from the outside. Inside, they had different holding rooms, a medical center and a tech center. She explained the layout, which room Duke was in and what room they'd probably take her into.

"So, if for whatever reason you want to run, they're going to be able to track you until you get off the property. Not much use in it. But, to get out the door, you'd just need to remember how to get to the hallway."

Rachel filed all that away, tried to bring her own picture to her mind. It would help if she found herself needing to escape.

Shay brought her to a stop. "All right. Here we go."

Rachel expected her to knock or buzz in or something, but the sound of the door opening was the first thing she heard once they stopped.

"This is an interesting turn of events," a male voice said. "Where's the guard dog who gave you that shiner?"

"I got to her without Wyatt," Shay returned. She spoke differently to the man. Sharp. All business. Any hint of the woman who'd asked if the Wyatts were all like that was gone.

"How?"

"Everyone has to take a bathroom break now and again, Parker. Now are you going to step aside or what?"

The man grumbled, but Rachel was being led forward so he'd clearly allowed entrance. "Wait here for McMillan."

Rachel listened as the footsteps quieted.

"McMillan is my supervisor," Shay said in a whisper. "He's all bark and mostly no bite. I imagine since he's been handling Duke, he's going to be the one who questions you. If not? Be as difficult as possible until they bring McMillan in."

"All right."

"Shay."

Rachel had assumed Shay was the woman's first name all this time. But the way her superior barked it out, Rachel had to wonder if it was actually her last name.

"Sir. A little late, but better late than never."

"How'd you manage what you failed at earlier?" He emphasized the word fail as though failure was the absolute worst thing a person could do.

"Followed them. They were on the run, off their home territory. Wyatt let his guard down and I convinced Rachel to talk to us. She's willing, if you let her see her father."

"Dymon!" the man yelled.

More footsteps, a few hushed words, then someone took her other arm. Shay's grip tightened and Rachel felt a bit like she was in the middle of a tug-of-war.

"Who's that?" Shay asked, suspicion threading through her voice.

"Your replacement," McMillan said, his voice so chilly Rachel thought to shiver. "Shay. You're done here."

"Sir, I think a woman should—"

"I said you're done here," McMillan said, and this was no bark or yell. It was cold, a succinct *or-else* order.

Shay slowly released her arm, and Rachel was being led away. The grip on her other arm was unnecessarily rough. She remembered what Shay said about being difficult. "You're hurting me," she said, trying to tug her arm away from the too-tight grasp.

"Oh, you have no idea what's in store for you, little girl," the voice hissed.

Rachel's entire body went cold. She recognized that voice.

It was the voice from her dream.

"SOMETHING ISN'T RIGHT."

Tucker whirled, gun in hand. It was only Shay, but she'd snuck up on him soundlessly. Still, he didn't have time to worry about that. "*What* isn't right?"

"New guy. McMillan isn't in the habit of hiring new guys."

"He hired me."

"Not the same. You're not an operative. You're like a…liaison. This guy I've *never seen* is in the South Dakota headquarters of North Star, and I've never heard his name or even heard whispers of a new guy." She rubbed a hand over the back of her neck. "Something isn't right."

"You left Rachel in there? When something wasn't right?"

"Calm down," Shay said sharply. She pulled her phone to her ear. "Wyatt? Yeah, I need you to do some spying for me." She sighed heavily. "Yeah, yeah, yeah, you ask your wife if she thinks you should stay out of it when her sister is in North Star headquarters with a stranger." Another pause. "Yup, that's what I thought. Someone named Dymon. Get me anything you've got on him." She hung up, shoved her phone in her pocket.

"Are you sure they're not tracking you through that?" he asked.

"Do you think I'm dumb? I had your brother take care of all the tracking devices when we were there."

"It never occurred to you that a group that tracked your every move might not be on the up and up?"

"Look. You don't know anything about North Star, or McMillan for that matter," she snapped. "Like that your father was responsible for his wife's death."

Tucker didn't say anything because he hadn't known that. At all.

"Grief does funny things to people. He's not a bad guy, and whatever is going on doesn't make him one. It makes him…human. And, hell, aren't we all?"

Tucker didn't want to think about how human they all were. Not when being human meant making mistakes, and they couldn't make any with Rachel inside North Star.

"Let's move. The less time she has to be in there, the better."

Shay nodded. "On that, we can agree."

It was Shay's plan since she knew the headquarters— what from the outside looked like an upscale hunting cabin. They bypassed the front, and Shay would occasionally pause to do something on her phone that allegedly moved the cameras or turned off security or whatever else North Star had in place.

"You sure you know all of those?"

"I installed them. I sure as hell should." They finally got to the back door, which was next to a garage of sorts. "I'm going in. I imagine everyone knows I got the boot, but I've got stuff in there. So, I'm going in to collect my stuff. When no one's watching, I'll open this garage and the door inside. You'll head straight for it. If I don't have Duke waiting, you move back into the garage. Check at five-minute intervals. Once he's there, you sneak him out the garage, go in the direct route we came and get to the car. Once you're there, you'll give me fifteen minutes. If I don't show up with Rachel, you get Duke out. I'll contact you or your brother with the next step once I've got Rachel. And whatever you do, don't go all Wyatt on me."

"What does that mean?"

"Don't play the hero. You may hear or see something you don't like, but you focus on Duke. You're going to want to barge back in here and get Rachel, but I've got it handled. You trust me and I trust you."

"That's asking a lot."

"Yeah, it is," she agreed. "For both of us. You up for the challenge?"

He didn't want to be. Trusting someone he barely knew was like tossing a coin with Rachel's life on the line, but hadn't he already done that? Besides, Shay didn't strike him as a stupid woman and she was putting at least some of her safety in *his* hands. It was a risk they both had to take.

"How long do I wait until I open the door?"

"Minute the garage opens you're in. You hear a whistle—I don't mean a sharp whistle, I mean like me whistling a tune—you go back and hide in the garage. We'll keep trying till it's clear."

Tucker nodded. "All right."

Shay nodded in return, then she slid in the back door. Tucker stood in the corner next to the garage, doing his best to hide his body in the way Shay had instructed. When the garage door opened, almost soundlessly, he slipped inside. Then immediately located the door inside and headed for it.

He turned the knob, eased it open and himself inside. He was in a basement that bizarrely looked like any house's basement might. A TV room in a little finished alcove, a laundry area on the opposite side. The hallway was dark.

Tucker remembered what Shay had said and went back to the garage, waited the aforementioned five minutes, then went inside again. He kept his mind blank. Thought of it like detective work—often boring and tedious…until it wasn't.

Fifteen minutes had passed, and finally Duke appeared. Duke studied him there at the end of the hallway and didn't budge. That was when Tucker realized Shay was standing behind him, with a gun to his back, and he only moved forward toward Tuck when she poked it into his back again.

"He's being difficult," she hissed. "Fix it. I've got maybe ten minutes before Parker comes back. Maybe."

Fix Duke Knight's hard head? Yeah, in what world? Still, Tucker moved forward. "We have to get you out."

"Why should I trust you? I trusted Granger and look what happened. Now I've got two North Star operatives trying to sneak me out? That smells like a setup, boy."

"We're trying to help you. It's because of *you*, and what they want to do with your family, that we're turning our back on North Star."

Duke didn't respond to that. "Who's watching the girls?"

Tucker hesitated. "We're all doing what we should be

doing," he said carefully, already knowing that wouldn't fly. His hesitation spoke volumes.

Duke narrowed his eyes. "You've always been a crap liar. Where's Rachel?"

"She's…" Tucker couldn't tell Duke under any circumstances. If he knew Rachel was upstairs, he'd charge up there like an angry bull.

"She's upstairs keeping them busy," Shay said.

Tucker nearly groaned, but he had to leap in front of Duke as he charged for the stairs. Though Tucker was taller, Duke was thicker, and he'd been a cowboy for thirty some years so he was no slouch. Still, Tucker had been trained to deal with threats bigger than him.

Tucker managed to shove him a step back. "You don't know what will happen to her or you if you barge in there. Trust that we've got this under control."

"That's my daughter you're risking," Duke said, and though his voice was ruthlessly controlled in volume, his eyes bulged and the tendons in his neck stood out like he was about to explode.

Tucker couldn't blame him if he did.

"She risked herself, buddy. For you. So maybe you make it easy on us so I can get her out without causing a storm where someone gets hurt," Shay said with absolutely *no* finesse.

Which was apparently what Duke needed to hear. He moved forward, though his scowl was still in place. Tucker passed him up to get to the door first. As he did, Duke he full-on sneered.

"I'm holding you personally responsible."

"As if I'm not," Tucker muttered. He glanced back at Shay.

"Take him out, just like we said. I'll go get her."

Tucker nodded. He led Duke into the garage quietly. Then out. Tucker had to hope Shay remembered to close it.

"Shay will bring Rachel to us," Tucker told him, moving in the same direction they'd come. Shay had disabled the cameras, but they could have come back on. Still, he had to trust she'd handle it.

"I can't believe you'd be this stupid," Duke muttered, though he followed behind Tucker.

Tucker looked over his shoulder and raised an eyebrow. "That's really how you want to play this? When we found the weapon that blinded your daughter in Grandma Pauline's safe? I had to beg your daughter to understand that you *must* have had a good reason for that. So—"

Tucker's phone vibrated. He shook his head and kept walking. When it vibrated again, he swore under his breath and pulled the phone out of his pocket. They were finally in some tree cover, but not to the car yet. Tucker saw it was Cody calling and answered.

"Cody—"

"Shay didn't answer, but this is important. I got into North Star's system to look up this Dymon guy. I managed a quick glimpse into the files before they figured out I was hacking in and kicked me right back out. This guy's got connections to Vianni. I suppose he could be a double agent—helping out North Star. Sort of like us."

"Except we never worked for the Sons or our father." Tucker thought about everything Shay had told him. About this whole lead up. "He's working for Vianni.

They're so hung up on taking down the Sons, they don't care who they go to bed with."

"Maybe," Cody replied gravely. "Either way? I'd get Rachel out of there ASAP."

Chapter Nineteen

Fear paralyzed Rachel, but all the man from her nightmares had done was drag her deeper into the building and then shove her into a chair. He was almost immediately followed by someone else, and once that person spoke, she knew it was the head guy. What had Shay called him? McMillan?

At least she wasn't alone with her nightmare—but would this man be just as bad?

It didn't matter. As long as she was in this building, she had a chance of survival. Dad was here. Shay was here. Tuck was here. She would survive.

Rachel studied what she could of the room. She reached out and felt the table in front of her. So she was sitting on an uncomfortable chair at a table. The man across from her was McMillan. He had a big dark presence and he appeared to move in such a way that she figured it meant he was sitting down at the table, too. The other man was dressed all in dark colors, too, but not as broad as McMillan. Not as…still.

She remembered that about him from her dream. A need to move. He stood next to McMillan, a vibrating presence. In the vague way she saw things, they appeared to be a unit.

Did McMillan know? Was North Star actually in bed with Vianni? It was a horrible thought. If they were, she was dead. Shay and Tucker were likely dead, too, and God knew her father was already dead.

Except he wasn't. They'd gone to rescue him. So, surely North Star didn't know.

Unless they needed that knife, and that was the only reason her father was still alive.

Rachel swallowed. "I just want to see my father," she said through a too-tight throat, terror making her feel like lead all the way through. But she couldn't just lie down and die.

She had to figure out a way to fight.

"That's understandable, Ms. Knight. Your father is here under our protection. Just how much do you know about that?"

She didn't let her eyes drift to the man standing. He had to know she knew who he was. Didn't he? Or would he assume because she was blind that she didn't? But he had to have felt how afraid she was. Her reaction to his voice.

He had to know she knew.

"Miss?"

Rachel sucked in an audible breath. McMillan had asked her a question. "I'm sorry. I… I don't know. I know Shay tried to kidnap me at the ranch. She and Tucker fought and Tucker got me away from her. She followed us, I guess. She…" Rachel had never been a good liar, but she let the genuine fear she felt consume her. Her voice shook. She shook. They'd believe it was a result of fear of the situation, not her lies. "She found me later. While Tucker was… Anyway, she said I could see and talk to my father if I came with her. That everything would be explained if I came with her."

"Our operative was sent to retrieve you because of the dream you've been having. Can you tell us about that?"

"I…" Rachel trailed off. They likely knew everything at this point. God knew the man from her nightmare did. If they'd been listening to Tucker before Shay's arrival, they had the full account of how her dream had morphed.

"It was just a nightmare. Just a…memory of what happened to me." She gestured at her face. "I don't see what it has to do with anything."

"You never dream past the moment you were hurt?" McMillan asked.

He made it all sound so clinical, but he couldn't see the nightmare, the reality in his mind like she could. "I was three. A madman slashed my face up and I was saved by a dog. What more would I know than that?"

"What about the knife?" It was the other man's voice. The voice from that dream, and she couldn't help but flinch at it.

"What knife?" she managed to whisper.

"Dymon." It was a warning from the man. "You're not involved in the questioning. If you can't remember that, you can step outside."

She could all but *feel* the tamped-down energy humming off the nightmare man. Still, he didn't say anything else.

But he wanted to know about the knife. The knife in

Grandma Pauline's safe. One thing she knew for certain, she couldn't tell them about that.

"I don't know what you're talking about. I told you about my dream, now I want to see my father."

"What do you know about your father's past?"

"None of your business," Rachel snapped. She wouldn't play the cowering victim anymore. Not when she couldn't decide if the man in front of her was good or bad or some mix of the two. But, regardless, she didn't have to be nice to him.

"The group who's after your father has aligned themselves with the Sons. You've got quite a few in-laws who are former Sons members, don't you?"

"If you think being held in that gang as a child against your will is being a *former member*, you're a monster."

The man sighed, like a disappointed teacher or parent.

"Miss, it'd be easier on you if you simply answer our questions. Once you tell us the truth, we'll take you to your father. I understand you're not part of this, but Duke Knight is in a very dangerous situation. He's trying to protect you, but it's not getting us anywhere. It seems this knife might be the answer to some of our... *problems*. I'm sure you want to help him, don't you?"

She thought about what one of her more smart-mouthed sisters might say in this situation. She managed a sneer and did her best impersonation of Liza. "Go to hell."

She thought about laying her cards out on the table. Lifting her chin and saying, *Is that why you've got some-*

one associated with the Viannis in this room with us?
To protect him and help him?

But her father had gone willingly with this group.
Shay and Cody, both people who'd helped her and other
people, had worked for North Star believing in its mission. Tucker had helped them. Surely, they weren't evil.
They couldn't be evil and fool so many good people.

But the Viannis and the Sons *were*. Didn't that mean
someone could have infiltrated North Star without them
knowing? Maybe North Star was smart, even good at
helping people, but they hadn't brought down the Sons
fully yet—and how long had it taken them to put Ace
in jail?

They'd needed Jamison *and* Cody to do that. So it
was plausible, especially by partnering with the Viannis who were more of an unknown, that the Viannis
had in turn tricked North Star.

She wanted to believe that—needed to—because the
alternative was too bleak to bear.

Rachel hitched in a breath. She had to find a way to
tell the man across from her that the man standing be-
side him had been her would-be kidnapper—the man
who'd blinded her. But she couldn't write a note. And
she couldn't just come out and *say* it either, because if
the man across from her truly didn't know, he'd likely
be killed, no matter what kind of operative he was.

"Why don't I go get you some water? Give you some
time to think about what direction you want to go in.
Dymon here will watch you until you're ready to talk."

It wasn't threatening exactly. Nor was it friendly. A
mission. It was all about the mission.

She could hear his chair scrape back as if he was

going to get to his feet. As if he was about to leave her with her nightmare. She reached forward in a desperate attempt to grab him. She managed to do just that, both her hands clasping McMillan's arm before he fully stood.

"Please, wait."

Cody had taught her Morse code when they'd been in middle school. She'd been feeling bad about something—she couldn't even remember what it was now. But he'd cheered her up by teaching her Morse code. They'd made a game of it that summer.

She didn't remember it all, and there wasn't time to stumble. Still, she had to try. She *had* to.

"Miss. Let go of my arm," McMillan said, not totally unkindly.

It gave her an awful hope, that glimmer of kindness.

So she tapped what she could think of, in the most succinct terms she could manage.

Danger.

My face.

Him.

He didn't say anything, but he also didn't pull his arm away. He didn't tell her to let go, so she tapped out the code again. The same code. The same words.

He withdrew his arm, but instead of getting up or doing something dismissive, he laid his hand on top of hers and gave it a reassuring pat. "All right," he said, his voice low and controlled. "Dymon, why don't you go get the water? I'll stay here with Ms. Knight."

"I'm sure you've got better things to do, boss."

"You're still new. I wouldn't push your luck," McMillan warned.

"I did pass all your tests. You hired me. You have to trust me to do this stuff when you've got more important things to do."

Rachel held her breath, but the one thing that steadied her the most was McMillan's hand over hers. A reassuring weight that he'd gotten her message, and wasn't going to leave her alone with this man.

"You told me you hadn't had any personal experience with the Knights," McMillan said quietly. "That you were too low on the Vianni totem pole to know more than a few stories about Curtis Washington and his new life in South Dakota."

"That's right," the nightmare man agreed.

"Is that the story you want to stick to right here and right now?"

There was a long tense silence. McMillan's hand was still atop hers, and he began to tap. It took Rachel the second time through to figure it out.

Duck.

And then a gunshot went off.

There was a scuffle, a moan and then Rachel's arm was jerked as she was pulled out from under the table. "Wrong move, little girl."

Her nightmare had her again.

But this time—she would fight.

TUCKER SLID THE phone back into his pocket. He had to remain calm, because Duke was there and Duke wouldn't remain any kind of calm.

They had to head back to the house and get Rachel the hell out of there, even if he had to fight the entirety of North Star to do it.

"How familiar are you with the area?" Tucker asked, careful to keep his voice calm.

"Who was that on the phone?"

"I need you to get to the car. It's parked—"

"Oh, hell no," Duke snarled. "If you're going back in for my daughter, I'm going with you."

"We can't go in guns blazing. We can't—"

"I was a cop before you were born. I know a thing or two about what needs to be done, and I know what I'd do to keep my daughter safe."

At the end of his rope with indecision, Tucker snapped. "Like when a man tried to kidnap her and blinded her in the process?"

"He would have killed her," Duke said flatly. "But she's alive, because of me. She was hurt because of me, I get it. I don't know how to go back and change my life. I did what I thought was right, always. You perfect?"

No, he couldn't pretend to be that.

"Now, you got another one of those?" Duke asked, nodding at the gun in his hand.

"No." Tucker considered giving it to Duke. Tucker could fight better with his hands than Duke would be able to. It would—

The muffled echo of a *crack* interrupted the picturesque quiet. *Gunshot.* Tucker was off running before he'd even thought it through. He looked back at Duke once. He was running, too, but at a much slower pace.

"Go!" Duke shouted.

Which was all the encouragement Tucker needed to run at full speed back to the house. He'd break down the front door if he had to. He'd—

The explosion was so loud and powerful, it knocked

Tucker back. He managed to stay on his feet, but for a horrible second he watched the entire house go up in flames as the sound of glass shattering and debris thundering surrounded him.

Then, after that split second, he ran toward it. What other option was there? People were inside. Rachel. Shay. But as he headed for the door, flames and smoke already enshrouding it, people came pouring out.

Tucker didn't see Shay. He didn't know if that was good or bad. The people were bloody, burned, coughing. He tried to find someone who looked remotely communicative, but they were all in various shapes of injury and couldn't answer his demands as the fire roared around them.

Two figures emerged then, one dragging the other. It was Shay. He couldn't tell whom she was dragging, but it wasn't Rachel. It was a large man. Tucker ran to her.

"Sorry," she rasped. She let go of the man she'd been hauling as people rushed forward to help him.

"He'd been shot," Shay rasped. "I went to the questioning room and he'd been shot. I couldn't find Rachel or the new guy. The Dymon guy. He had to have taken her out the back." She swayed but Tucker managed to catch her before she fell in a heap. "The explosion went off before I managed to do anything. Got emergency services coming," she continued as Tucker helped her into a sitting position on the ground. "But I don't think I'm going to be much help with Rachel."

"Give me your gun," Tucker managed, though terror pounded through him. When she did, he handed it to Duke who huffed up to them. "Shay thinks Rachel got out—or was taken out with someone. I'm going to find the trail. You do the same," he instructed to Duke.

Much as it pained him to leave this misery in his wake, he had to find Rachel before she met a worse fate. He had to make a wide circle around the flames to get to the back. He didn't worry about how close Duke was. He only worried about getting to Rachel.

Debris had flown more back here, which made Tucker think the explosives had been detonated from the back. If whoever had Rachel had detonated the explosives by hand rather than remotely, it made sense. He'd have dragged Rachel out, then set off the bomb before he dragged her away.

Why drag her away and keep her alive, though? Why not let her die in the explosion?

But the guy hadn't. He'd taken her away, and regardless of the reason, Tucker had to believe that's what happened. Believe it and save her from this.

The yard was wooded. Tucker ruthlessly tamped down the panic gripping him. He had to think like a cop. Like the person he'd trained to be. Like his brothers. Calm in the face of crisis. In the face of someone he loved being taken.

He moved to the trees, looking for signs of tracks or struggle. There was nothing, but this was the only way the man could have gone. Tucker scoured the ground. He heard Duke's approach, though they didn't speak. They moved and they looked.

Tucker couldn't let himself think of Rachel being dragged out of that house by some Vianni thug. He couldn't think about the very real possibility that a Sons member was waiting to help—

"Wait." Tucker stopped. The rational thing to do was head for the trees and cover. Unless there was help waiting somewhere else. He tried to orient himself—the house—where it would be in relation to the Sons. The Sons current headquarters was a few hours away, *but* if they were meeting someone with a car, they'd need a road. It wouldn't have been the road Shay had instructed him to use, because that was the main thoroughfare and would be too obvious.

"Go back to the house. Get a car. Anyone you can find," Tucker instructed, already moving north instead of his original west. "Once you've got a car, start driving for Flynn via Route 5. But be careful. The Sons might be involved."

With no time to spare, Tucker took off for Route 5. It meant running through open land, and that was dangerous, but if he could get to Rachel before they got her into a car, he didn't care what they did to him.

Chapter Twenty

Rachel slowly came to. Someone was dragging her, swearing. She could feel the ground beneath her, tell it was still daylight as the sun beat down on her face.

"Stupid plan," the man muttered.

It was like her dream. The fear and his muttering, but she was bigger. She was a woman now. She'd tried to fight him back in that room, but then everything had gone black.

Now, everything hurt, and her head pounded with excruciating pain. He must have knocked her out. She tried to kick out, but her ankles were tied together. So were her hands. She wanted to sob, but she knew instinctively if he didn't know she was awake, she was better off.

She wasn't going to be able to escape him with her hands and feet tied, and she couldn't use the button Shay had sewn into her sleeve. But she was alive. She supposed that was the silver lining. She wasn't dead.

At three years old, she'd survived being cut in the face and losing her sight. She could survive this. She *would* survive this.

The dragging stopped and he dropped her without warning. She couldn't hold back the sharp groan of pain.

"You awake?"

Dymon nudged her with his foot, and she kept her eyes closed. She let her head loll as she made another soft groaning noise, trying to pretend she was still unconscious. Or just coming to.

He muttered something. There was shuffling, the methodical plodding of feet like he was pacing the hard ground beneath them. "I need help. You can't expect me to make it all the way to the road. Yeah, yeah, yeah. Had to shoot McMillan. No, I didn't check. I had to get her out. Yeah, I know no casualties but things went sideways."

Rachel realized he was on the phone, talking to someone about getting her to the road. And if he got her to the road, she'd be put into a car. There'd be more people.

How would anyone find her if she was in a car? Wasn't there something about not ever letting anyone take you to a second location? Better to be killed than make it to that second location.

She swallowed down the fear. Somehow, someway, she had to fight. There was no waiting for Tucker or Shay to find her if there was a car waiting. Once she got in that car, she was as good as dead.

Dymon continued to grumble, and she slowly realized he was done with his phone conversation and was instead just talking to himself. Nothing important or telling, just complaints about being the only one with the balls to do the dirty work.

Rachel continued to pretend as though she were unconscious as she tried to figure out how on earth she was going to get out of this. She couldn't get out of the bonds on her wrists and ankles—they were too tight—but there had to be *something* she could do.

Back in the room, this man had wanted to know about her dream. About the knife. So...maybe she had to give that to him to keep him occupied, to buy herself time.

Hopefully enough time for Tucker to intercept her before the man got her to the car waiting for him.

She groaned some more, started to move, thrashed a bit against her bonds for effect. She blinked her eyes open.

Dymon grunted. "Thought I knocked you out better than that." He sighed heavily. "Guess I'll have to do a better job this time. Maybe just fix the problem altogether."

He was going to kill her. Here and now. No getting to the road. No second location, just death.

"No. No. Please—please don't." She swallowed at the fear and the bile rising in her throat. She had to be braver than this. "I know where it is," she blurted out. He'd mentioned the knife. She knew which one he was referring to. "I know who you are. I know what you did. And most importantly, I know where the knife you want is."

"So does your father."

"But you have me. Not him."

Dymon made a dismissive noise, and Rachel didn't know if it was agreement or refusal. She had no idea what he planned to do. He was simply a shadowy figure above her and she had no means to fight.

But no matter what was against her, she did not have to die without *trying* to survive. She knew what side of her the man was standing on, and she knew she was on a little bit of an incline. She could roll. And scream. Maybe someone would be able to save her.

If not? At least she'd tried.

She tested the incline, the placement of her own body and rocked back and forth a little. If he noticed, he didn't say anything. She counted inwardly and then did her best to use momentum to move into a roll—screaming as loud as she could while she started to gain speed down the incline.

Dymon swore at her viciously, and there was the sound of hard footsteps and a stumble and more swearing. Then her rolling was stopped as she knocked into what she was assuming was him.

"You idiot," he yelled.

She had the impression of him getting ready to strike. She could only brace for impact, but instead of pain— a new voice yelled.

"Don't move."

Rachel almost cried out at the sound of Tucker's voice, but the sound caught in her throat as cold steel was pressed to her forehead.

She didn't know where he was, or if he could see her. She only knew there was a gun pressed to her head. She tried to see. Willed her eyes to work.

She could make out Dymon crouched above her, the gun pressed to her forehead. If she kicked out... He might shoot, but he might fall instead. They *were* on a hill. She just needed to place the kick in the right spot. Somehow.

"Rachel," Tucker's voice was very calm, and closer than it had been. "Do you remember what I told you about fighting?"

"She can't fight," the man said disgustedly. "I'm going to put a bullet through her brain. Then yours. Drop the gun."

"She's the only one who knows where it is," Tucker said, his voice so calm and...lethal. She might have shivered in fear if he weren't the only one who could help her survive this. "The evidence you're after. She's the only one."

Rachel thought about what Tucker had said about fighting. He'd told her to always go for the crotch. She just needed to kick the man in the crotch. She could figure out that general area, as long as she could position her body accordingly, she could do it.

"Curtis knows where it's at. I could kill her and—"

"I'm sorry, Rach. I know I promised never to lie to you again. So I won't. Duke died in the explosion."

Rachel jerked. It was a physical pain, even as she worked through what he'd *actually* said. He'd never promised not to lie to her. In fact, he had promised the opposite. So, Tuck was lying now? He had to be. He was supposed to get Dad out. There was no way Dad was dead. No way.

Please, God.

She didn't focus on the words. On what Dymon and Tucker continued to argue about. She focused on the shadowy outline of the man. Where best to kick. Her aim just had to be right.

Or she was dead. And so was Tucker.

TUCKER COULD SEE Rachel trying to figure out the angle. Slowly, he began to crouch, acting as if he were going to put his gun down. He held one hand up in mock surrender, slowly inching his gun closer and closer to the ground.

He needed Rachel to kick, just one kick even if it wasn't in line would push the guy back. The hill would help with momentum, the gun would go up and Tucker could get a shot off.

All as long as the other guy didn't pull that trigger first.

"That explosion shouldn't have killed anyone," the man finally said after a long tense silence.

Tucker had seen enough of the wreckage to understand where the explosives had detonated. So he had to lie and hope for the best. "Only if everyone was in the front of the house. The basement is another story, and I had a man in there getting Duke out. They're both dead."

He hoped the lies would give Rachel some comfort that Duke wasn't actually dead. That no one was.

Unless McMillan had died of his gunshot wound.

"What's the point of an explosion that doesn't kill anyone, anyway? And you clearly had an in with North Star. Why not take Duke and get what you're after?"

"I could have," the man agreed with a sickening sneer. "But that doesn't finish the job from twenty years ago, does it?"

"This does, though."

All three of them jerked at the sound of Duke's voice, but it didn't last long, since Duke immediately fired a shot that had the man falling to the ground. Lifeless.

"Dad?" Rachel asked tremulously.

Tucker was already halfway to her, but since Duke had come up from the direction of the road, he was closer. He was murmuring to Rachel and untying the bonds on her hands so Tucker took the ones on her feet.

"Dad." They wrapped their arms around each other, so Tucker gave them a moment by making sure the other man was dead.

Tucker couldn't find a pulse, but he still pulled the gun out of his hand and the knife out of his boot. They weren't out of the woods yet, even if they'd managed to end one threat.

"We have to get out of here," Tucker said reluctantly, since Rachel was still clinging to Duke. "I can't imagine he was working alone."

"He's not. He was talking to someone about dragging me to the car. Is everyone at North Star all right? He shot McMillan. I…" Her hands were shaking, but Duke took them in his. Rachel kept talking. "When Shay took me in, they had this guy. Dymon is his name. He… I recognized his voice, from my dream."

"*He's* the guy?" Tucker looked at Duke for confirmation, and got a slight nod.

Tucker swore. She'd been kidnapped twice by the same man.

"I had to tell McMillan. I didn't think he understood how dangerous he was. So I tapped Morse code into his palm. Then he…this Dymon guy, he shot McMillan. It was so close and McMillan has to be dead, doesn't he?" Rachel asked, trying to wipe at her face, wet with tears. Tucker crouched next to her and used the hem of his shirt to wipe the rest of them away and clean her up a bit. She gave him a small smile.

Tucker could feel Duke's disapproving gaze, but they didn't have time for *that*.

"Shay dragged him out. They were getting him medical attention. He might make it." Probably a bit overly optimistic, but Tucker was willing to give her that in this moment. She'd used Morse code and... God, she was a wonder, but they had to get out of here. "Is there a car down at the road?"

"Yes. Not too far. I didn't see anyone else." Duke helped Rachel to her feet. Tucker flanked her on the other side. The ground was hilly, uneven, and helping Rachel toward the road was no easy task. She stumbled a few times, but they both held her up.

Through the trees, Tucker could begin to make out the road, but it wasn't as deserted as it should have been.

"Get down," Tucker hissed, pulling Rachel to the ground as he ducked for cover behind a swell of earth.

"What is it?" Rachel asked.

"Three men and another car aside from the one Duke drove." Tucker moved so he could get another glimpse. Two men were circling the car Duke had parked in the ditch, and one of them was on his phone. "I need a better look."

Rachel's grip on his arm tightened. "No. You're not going anywhere. Let's just head back to North Star. I know I was unconscious, but it can't be that far."

Tucker didn't want to tell her there wasn't much of North Star left, but more importantly he wanted the opportunity to capture these men who were clearly in on the explosion and kidnapping attempt. The last thing anyone needed was them roaming free—to come after Duke or Rachel again, or whatever else was in their plans.

"Just give me five minutes. Stay put right here." He tugged his arm out of Rachel's grasp and had to trust Duke to keep her there and quiet.

He moved in silence, using trees and rocks and swells of land as cover, until he was close enough to see the three men. Tuck could hear them talking, but couldn't make out what they were saying. He considered getting closer, but with Duke and Rachel not that far away, it wasn't worth the risk.

Knowing he had to get them out of harm's way first, he carefully climbed his way back toward Duke and Rachel.

"Just the three men, but definitely waiting for their guy here to show up with Rachel."

"Vianni," Duke said disgustedly.

"No, they aren't Vianni men. Those are Sons men."

"You recognize them?" Duke asked.

"Got files on all three. The one on the right got off on a rape case because of a technicality. The one in the middle is my suspect on a murder case, but I don't have anything beyond circumstantial evidence and the prosecutor won't issue a warrant. The third has been in and out of jail for dealing drugs, armed robbery, you name it."

"Gotta love the legal system," Duke muttered. "What do we do, then? Pick them off?"

Tucker shook his head. "Too risky. They've got three guys, and three more high-powered weapons than we've got. Even if I use that guy's gun." Tucker glanced at Rachel. She wouldn't agree to this plan, but he didn't feel right trying to make it behind her back either. "Take her back."

"I will not—"

Duke spoke right over her. "What are you going to do?"

"They're accessory to kidnapping, possibly that explosion. I can arrest them."

"On your own, boy? Three against one isn't the best odds."

Tucker pulled out his phone. "I'll even the odds, then."

Duke's expression went even more granite. "And which of your brothers' lives are you willing to risk?"

It was a jab, but somewhere between that explosion and here he'd figured out what he hadn't fully understood until this moment. Yeah, four of his brothers were in love with Duke's foster daughters. Three of them had kids or babies on the way to support and protect. They had lives, and they shouldn't be taking unnecessary risks.

But they had. Over and over again this summer. Why?

Because nothing was ever going to be truly *good* until the Sons were gone. Truly taken out. The more of them they arrested, the more they had a chance of someone giving that last piece of evidence that brought the entire group to its knees.

"All of them, Duke. All of them."

Chapter Twenty-One

"I will not be carted off while you do something dangerous," Rachel said. She was careful to keep her voice quiet like they were doing, but what she really wanted to do was yell.

Her father's grip was tight on her arm and she wanted to shake it off and rage at him for even *considering* the fact they would go off and leave Tucker to do this, other Wyatt boys or no.

"Give me a second," Tucker said, and then she was being passed off and it was so *infuriating* because she couldn't exactly walk away, could she? Not in this foreign territory she didn't know.

"Listen. I'm not going to do anything stupid. My brothers, law enforcement agents who can also arrest these guys, are going to come and be backup. Maybe get some information that helps us land an even bigger blow to the Sons. I have to do this, and I'm sorry, I can't do it with you here."

Emotion clogged her throat. To get this far and then be relegated to...dead weight. Swept off by her father.

"It isn't right. I didn't *do* anything," she said, feeling

raw and cracked open. She *couldn't* do anything. She understood she was a liability in the here and now and it was an awful, awful feeling.

Tucker's hands cupped her cheeks. "Yeah, figuring out where the evidence was, punching Shay in the face, using *Morse* code to tell McMillan his double agent was really a double agent, getting abducted and dragged through the woods but being smart enough to stay alive—nothing at all."

It should have been patronizing, but instead it was soothing. Because Tucker sounded...awestruck. Not in an *oh-poor-little-Rachel-managed-to-do-something* way, but like she was strong and all that stuff had mattered.

And it had. What might have happened if she hadn't gotten the message to McMillan? Yes, he might not have been shot, but Dymon could have gotten away with a lot more, and done a lot more damage.

"The Vianni part of this is over. Now, it's the Sons part. Let your father take you back to North Star. You've contributed, and probably have the concussion to prove it. Now, it's my turn. Okay?"

It wasn't *okay*, but she understood he had to do this. For himself. For his brothers. She moved her hands to his on her face, then slid her palms down the length of his arms, over his shoulders and up to his face.

"Okay," she said, and then pressed her mouth to his. He stiffened, likely because her father was around, but she didn't care. Not when he was going off into danger, and she was letting him.

But he relaxed into it, kissing her back in a way that

felt like some kind of promise. He pulled back, taking her hands off his face.

"Be safe, and don't do a thing until your brothers are here." The kiss had felt like a promise, but she needed the words. "Promise me."

There was a pause, and he squeezed her hands in his. "I promise. Now, let your Dad take you back to North Star. You've got a hell of a bump on your head. I'm completely unscathed."

But he wouldn't stay that way necessarily. Still, there was nothing she could do about that. She'd only be in his way if she tried to convince him to take her along. Rachel knew she'd achieved some important things throughout this whole mess. Now her role was to step back and let him take the next step.

Hadn't she been harping at him to take help from his brothers—no matter what they'd been through and what he wanted to protect them from? Now, she had to take her own advice. Let him get the help he needed.

It didn't make it easy, but it also didn't make her a failure.

"Be safe," she repeated, giving his hands another squeeze before letting him pass her back to her father.

It was hard walking away, but as her father led her, the adrenaline began to fade into something heavier. Her head ached. Her body hurt. She felt nauseous.

"I don't know what you think you're doing kissing that boy," Dad grumbled, once they'd put some distance between them and Tucker. "I hope it doesn't mean what I think it means."

If she'd had any energy, she might have smiled. She was still so relieved he was alive, she couldn't muster any anger toward him. "If all of your daughters end up with a Wyatt, is that really so bad?"

"It is when they have to be dragged through pain and danger to arrive at that conclusion."

She frowned. *Dragged?* "It's your fault I'm even here. That Tucker is even here. This all begins with you."

"If this is all my fault, then the Sons are all those boys' faults."

She opened her mouth to argue, because of course that wasn't true. So, maybe it was true it wasn't her father's fault the Viannis were after him. But... "You had that knife. The one that hurt me. You lied to me, and made me doubt myself."

He was quiet for a few seconds as they walked. She could smell the acrid tinge of smoke on the air and knew they were close to getting to North Star.

"I did what I thought was right at the time. I'm sorry it hurt you, baby. You'll never know... I wanted you all safe. I'd been at the ranch in WITSEC for almost eight years when they found me again. I'd built a life. A better life than the one I'd grown up in, a better life than I'd had on the force. I had your mother, and I had you and the other girls. I could have run, but I wasn't going to give up this life I loved for some lowlife crime group. I needed something stronger than WITSEC, and evidence seemed the best way to keep them gone. An insurance policy."

"So, you let him go?"

"I didn't have him. I had to get you to the hospital. I couldn't go after him. But I could collect what he left behind. I could use it as my own threat. And it worked."

"Until now. Why now?"

"That's why I went to Granger McMillan. When I got a few veiled threats earlier this month, I went to his father. He'd been in charge of WITSEC when they moved me and we'd become friends. He recommended his son's organization to help get to the bottom of it. Because as far as I knew, the Viannis were all dead or in prison. Granger started looking into it, and when he found some connections between the Vianni group and the Sons, he brought me in."

"Of your own volition," she said.

"More or less. I wanted to protect you girls. Getting out of the way seemed the only option. Besides, I had the evidence. I knew I could use it if I needed to, and I thought McMillan could help me get it into the right hands, but I had to be sure I could trust him. I wasn't sure. I'm still not sure."

"He got shot. By this Dymon man. I told him he was the man from my dreams, more or less. He was going to help, but Dymon shot him first."

"Not Dymon. Vianni. The man who blinded you was Vianni's son," Duke explained. "McMillan told me he'd hired a Vianni underling in the hopes he'd be a double agent. He named some low level thug I hadn't ever had contact with, and I didn't recognize him. He must have had plastic surgery, taken on this new identity, because he was supposed to be dead. I was told a hit had taken him out right after your attack. I figured it was because he'd failed. You recognizing his voice is the only reason I put two and two together."

"So, you killed the man who was after you?"

"Appears so. I'm not saying that will end the Vianni

group, but the family I put behind bars is mostly dead. It should be over."

"Except Tucker is still out there, trying to take down the Sons."

"He's a Wyatt, Rachel. They can put on a good show, but they can't let it go. Not while the Sons still exist, not while Ace lives, even if he's in prison. You get wrapped up in a Wyatt, that's what you're getting wrapped up in."

He didn't say it like it was some failing, only like it was fact. Which, no doubt, it was.

"You couldn't let injustice go when you saw it. You wouldn't run away when that came back to haunt you." She inhaled. "I know you love them like sons, and I understand why you'd be protective of your daughters. But you gave us the example. Doesn't it make sense that we'd all see that in you, even if we didn't know the details, and admire it in others?"

Duke was quiet for a long while, though instead of holding her arm he slid his arm around her shoulders and led her that way.

"I want that head of yours checked out," he said, planting a gentle kiss near the place her head hurt the worst.

"Because of Tucker or just in general?"

Duke chuckled. "Both."

Something inside of her eased. She was still scared, worried for Tucker and all the Wyatts. Worried for McMillan and if he'd survived the gunshot wound. But her father was safe and here with her. One arm of this whole complicated thing had been taken care of.

Now Tucker needed to take care of his, and come back to her in one piece.

Tucker was intent on keeping his promise. There was just one little problem. The three men on the road weren't staying there. Apparently, they'd grown tired of waiting for the dead man.

Jamison and Cody were close enough that they'd be here in the next ten to twenty minutes, if they rushed, which they likely would. The other three were much farther away, and Brady and Dev were physically compromised in that group.

But Cody had messaged them all.

Tucker wouldn't hide from the men walking up the side of the hill. He'd promised Rachel he wouldn't do anything until his brothers were here, but he could hardly help it when two of the three men were coming for him—one staying behind and poking through the car Duke had left.

Still, Tucker remained still. He kept his gun ready, and he listened.

"These Vianni morons. Soft city idiots. I'm already tired of cleaning up their messes."

"You can't say no to that kind of cash, though. Not with everything falling apart. I've been thinking of heading to Chicago myself."

The other man offered an anatomically impossible alternative and they both chuckled good-naturedly.

Tucker might have been swayed by the fact they sounded like any two men shooting the breeze. But he had files on these guys and he knew what they were capable of. Monsters could walk and talk and laugh, but what they were willing to *do* was what made them monsters.

They were coming up on him. Whatever happened, his brothers were on their way.

"What a lazy SOB. Couldn't even drag her this far?"

"Oh, he got this far," Tucker said companionably.

They whirled on him, one with a gun and the other with a knife. The one Tucker knew from his files as Justin Hollie sneered.

"A Wyatt." He flipped the knife in his hand. "Your free pass is over. We don't have to worry about hurting Ace's kids anymore."

Which wasn't what Tucker had expected anyone to say, let alone so gleefully. "Oh, yeah? Why's that?"

The man snorted. "Guess you're the last to hear. Ace is dead. No need to come after us anymore. He can't do crap." He spread his arms wide. "Now, I'm a reasonable guy. I let you go, you leave us alone."

"Jail isn't dead."

"He died in jail. Crossed the wrong guy." Hollie snapped his fingers. "Boom. Gone. I heard it was even on the news."

Tucker couldn't process that. It couldn't possibly be true. "I don't believe you."

He shrugged. "No skin off my nose. Just telling you there's no beef here anymore."

"Of course, if you want one, we can give you one," the other man said. Travis Clyne, Tucker was pretty sure. The rapist who'd gotten off because the prosecutor hadn't thought the case was tight enough.

Tucker pushed away the thought of his father being dead. It just wasn't possible Ace Wyatt, the black cloud over his entire life, had just been…killed in jail like a common criminal, instead of the evil incarnate that he was.

Because there were two men who'd done plenty of evil right in front of him. "It turns out I've got a beef with kidnapping, explosions, killing people." He turned his gaze from Hollie to Clyne. "Rape."

"Your funeral." Clyne lifted his gun, but before he'd even gotten close to aiming, a shot rang out. It didn't appear to hit anyone, but Cody and Jamison appeared on either side of the Sons members.

The one with the knife whirled out toward Jamison, but Tucker shot, causing Hollie to stumble with a scream of pain. Cody punched Clyne before he could get a shot off at Tucker.

The third man came charging up, likely hearing the commotion. He stopped abruptly when all three Wyatts pointed guns at him. Looking at his friends writhing on the ground, then the guns, the man dropped his own.

"On your knees," Tucker ordered.

"Here. Tie him up." Cody tossed him some zip ties.

"Jeez. Do you always have these on you?" Tucker asked, quickly putting them to use.

"Never leave home without them," Cody returned, using more to tie up the man he'd punched. Jamison was doing the same.

They all stood at the same time.

"Unscathed again," Cody said with the shake of a head. "You've got the touch, Tuck."

Tuck let out a breath, almost a laugh. "Yeah, I felt bad about that for a while. I don't think I do so much anymore."

"I'll call county to pick these guys up. They've al-

ready got some guys collecting evidence on the explosives," Jamison said.

"There's also the car down on the road."

Jamison nodded. He quickly called all the information in. When he hung up, Tucker knew he had to broach
the topic he didn't really want to understand.

"They said Ace is dead."

Jamison and Cody exchanged a glance. "We heard
that too. Gage was getting everything confirmed when
you messaged. We told him to stay put, we had this."

"Do you think he actually listened?"

Jamison smiled wryly. "The county guys will pass
it along if he started heading this way."

"Do you think it's true?"

Both brothers sobered. Cody shrugged helplessly,
and Jamison ran a hand over his neck.

"I don't know what to think," Jamison said. "So,
let's focus on the here and now. Waiting for some guys
to cart these morons away. Making sure Duke and Rachel are really safe."

Tucker turned to Cody. "North Star is beat up pretty
good."

He nodded grimly. "They're all getting transported
to the hospital. Liza's got the girls so Nina could drive
over and pick up Duke and Rachel."

"She needs a doctor."

"I'm sure Nina will see to it."

Tucker nodded, but the possibility that Ace was dead
overshadowed everything. "If he's dead, that means...
it's over."

"We're law enforcement, Tuck," Jamison said, ever

the cop. "As long as they're out there hurting people, it isn't over."

"No... But he is. Ace existing, linking us to it. The emotional aspect. It's over." He rubbed at his chest. "He can't be the boogeyman if he's dead."

Cody nodded. "So, we'll hope he is. Dead just the way he deserved. Broken and in jail with absolutely no fanfare."

Tucker let that settle through him. It seemed impossible, but it *would* be fitting. No standoff. No showy end. Nothing that could be described as godlike or awe-inspiring to the wrong kind. Ace's worst nightmare. To have a boring death no one remembered.

Tucker smiled at his brothers. Yeah, that's what he'd hope for.

Epilogue

There was fanfare.

No one said they were celebrating Ace Wyatt's death. They were celebrating Duke being okay. They were celebrating Brady healing and Felicity finding out she was having a girl. They were celebrating life and joy.

But Rachel knew that at least some of that joy was in knowing the man who'd caused them such pain and fear was well and truly gone.

Grandma Pauline had made a feast fit for royalty. They'd shoved everyone around the table as they always did. Even Dev was smiling. It was the best dinner in Rachel's memory.

Dad was safe. Everyone was safe. The men Tucker and his brothers had arrested had even agreed to talk, which had led to more arrests and a complete federal raid on the Sons compound. They hadn't been eradicated, but they had been taken down quite a few pegs.

And Ace Wyatt was dead. All the Wyatt men seemed…lighter. A little out of sorts, but lighter. After dinner, no one was quick to leave. Even Dad and Sarah who had ranch chores to see to lingered.

"Why don't you go on out to the porch," Grandma Pauline said quietly into her ear.

Rachel frowned. "Why?"

"Just go on now."

Confused, Rachel did as she was told, stepping out into the quickly cooling off night.

"Rach? You're not headed back on your own are you?"

Tucker. She should have known. He must have snuck out, and Grandma Pauline had sent her to find out why.

"No." She moved toward his voice. "What are you doing out here all by yourself?"

He was quiet for a moment. "I'm not sure. Everyone's so happy. I'm happy. But... It's weird. I don't know how to feel about... I'm happy for all of them. Happy Ace isn't a shadow on our lives anymore, but I always assumed there'd be some big standoff. And now he's just gone. I'm happy, but it's...complicated."

"I think that's fair. I think you get to have whatever feelings on the matter you need to."

"Yeah, I guess so."

His arm came around her shoulders, so she wrapped hers around his waist. She sighed and relaxed into him. A good man, with a good heart. "I'm glad you weren't hurt."

"It seems we all managed to make it through okay. McMillan's going to be released from the hospital tomorrow."

"And Shay didn't lose her job, according to Nina."

"So, all's well that ends well, I guess."

Rachel thought on that. "It's not an ending, though.

It's just life. We endured some bad parts. Now, we get to enjoy some good parts."

"Good parts," he echoed. He wound a strand of her hair around her finger. "You know one good part we seemed to have missed? I've never taken you out."

"Taken me out. Like…a date?"

"Yeah, like a date."

She grinned. There hadn't been time to talk much about the things that had transpired between them on a personal level. She'd been nervous to bring it up. Unsure. But he was asking her on a date. "I guess you should probably do that."

"Tomorrow night?"

"I'll see if I can clear my schedule."

They stood in the quiet for a long while. It was a nice moment. A settling moment. He was an honorable man, who'd take her out on a date, and take things slow. But he'd take them seriously, too. She liked to think it was what they both needed after this horrible year.

She turned in his arms, wrapping hers around his neck. "You're a good man, Tucker Wyatt. You're all good men. Whether Ace is dead or alive. That's always been true. Whether you got hurt fighting him or managed to escape unscathed. Who you are doesn't change. I hope you know that."

"I'm getting there. It helps to hear."

"I think you'll find the Knight women are very good at telling you all that."

"I guess it's good I found me one, then."

"Yeah, it is." She moved onto her toes and kissed him. Without fear, without stress. Just the two of them.

His grip tightened, but the kiss remained gentle. Explorative. Because that's exactly what they had ahead of them.

They'd found each other, and somehow ended years of fear. Of worry. Of dark shadows.

Now, they didn't have to worry anymore. They could get to know each other as something more than friends, find a way to have a life together. With their family.

Happily-ever-after.

* * * * *